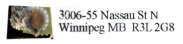
MANIFEST DESTINY

THE LOVES AND ADVENTURES OF PETER FARLEY
A CANADIAN IN THE KOREAN WAR

by Michael Czuboka

TO: RAY CRABBE

NOV. 2015

BEST REGARDS!

Mike

◆ FriesenPress

Suite 300 - 990 Fort St

Victoria, BC, Canada, V8V 3K2

www.friesenpress.com

ISBN

978-1-4602-7008-0 (Hardcover)

978-1-4602-7009-7 (Paperback)

978-1-4602-7010-3 (eBook)

1. Fiction, War & Military

Distributed to the trade by The Ingram Book Company

Foreword by Dan Bjarnason:

The Korean conflict six decades ago was a real meat grinder of a war. Canada suffered over 500 combat deaths in only two and a half years of fighting. By comparison, in Afghanistan, we suffered 115 deaths, spread over a much longer, nine years. Mike Czuboka's novel is a coming-of-age tale with Korea as the backdrop. Anyone familiar with Canada's role in this war will recognize thinly-disguised real-life events and people: the crusty but brilliant commander, Jim Stone; the unsung hero, young Mike Levy; the dashing 2nd Battalion Princess Patricia's Canadian Light Infantry, and the surrounded and outnumbered unit's unbelievable stand against the Chinese at a nowhere place called Kapyong. Czuboka tosses into the plot a (presumably fictitious) Soviet agent among the Canadian troops. Czuboka's own combat experience in Korea is particularly evident in describing the sheer terror of night patrols being ambushed behind enemy lines. Incidentally, Czuboka himself fought at Kapyong, a member of a machine-gun/mortar unit that prevented his headquarters from being overrun.

Dan Bjarnason was a television news and documentary reporter for The National at the Canadian Broadcasting Corporation for over 35 years. His worldwide assignments, including time as a foreign correspondent, allowed him to indulge his passion for military history and to visit dozens of battlefields from the Little Bighorn to the Falklands. He is the author of Triumph at Kapyong, Canada's Pivotal Battle in Korea. He lives in Toronto.

"Manifest Destiny is a fascinating, well-constructed novel that offers a unique glimpse into what it must have been like to be a Canadian soldier serving in the Korean War. The level of detail involved makes it clear that the author has done his homework. For the most part, he includes just enough detail to bring the past alive but not so much that we feel like we're getting a thinly veiled history lesson. The author has done a skilful job of combining action, adventure, espionage, fully realized characters, some surprising plot twists, and just the right touch of romance to make this novel appeal to a wide variety of readers. I was thoroughly engaged in the story, and I found the battle scenes particularly poignant."

-Editor

See more about the author on page 412.

DEDICATION

I dedicate this book to my late Ukrainian immigrant parents, Anthony and Rozalia Czuboka, both of whom had very little formal schooling, but who encouraged my journey and progress as a student and as a Canadian. They gave birth to me in Brandon, Manitoba, Canada, and I am grateful to them and to Canada for my good life.

I also dedicate this book to my family: Helena, Jill, Brad, Jane, Jeff, Gina, Laura, Bill, Carl, Daniel, Sandra, Nancy, Frank, Susan, Shirley, and Michael; to my friends; to my Korean War and other military comrades; to the 2nd Battalion Princess Patricia's Canadian Light Infantry, and all other Patricias, my regimental family; to my fellow alumni and colleagues at Brandon University and the University of Manitoba, and especially those who attended Brandon College with me in the distant but memorable past; to J.M.H., the first love of my life many years ago; to all of my former students and teaching partners; to my friends and colleagues at the Canadian Corps of Commissionaires; to the people of Rivers, Brandon, Beausejour and Winnipeg, my Manitoba home towns.

And I especially dedicate this book to Baby Kitty, alias Picasso (2004 - 2015), the feline love of my life. He followed me everywhere, slept with me and gave me massages on a daily basis. I miss him dearly, and also all of the other many cats and dogs that I have had over the years. Shortly after Baby Kitty's passing, I suddenly decided that I would finish writing *Manifest Destiny*, a book I had started several years earlier. For some reason, Baby Kitty was my sudden and powerful inspiration. He could not read, but he could certainly listen. He was very intelligent and affectionate. Thanks, Baby Kitty, for sharing your life and for inspiring me. Billie and Freddie, your feline companions, also miss you.

ACKNOWLEDGEMENTS

The author extends thanks and acknowledges:

Code Workun and the editors and administrative staff at FriesenPress.

Ray Serwylo of Winnipeg, Manitoba for reviewing an early manuscript of *Manifest Destiny.*

Kyle Will of Winnipeg for his assistance with the manuscript material and format.

Daughter Jane Czuboka for her photo enhancement services.

Helena Czuboka, my wife and passionate critic and strong supporter of my literary endeavours.

Marc Freve and Yanick Lacroix of Archives Canada for their help in obtaining the front cover photo.

Dahlia Kurtz of CJOB radio in Winnipeg for her supportive interview.

Bill Campbell, an RCR Korean War veteran, for finding and recommending the front cover photo.

Wonjae Song and Olivia Do Song of the Korea Times, strong supporters of my literary endeavours, as well as all of my other friends in the Korean Canadian community.

McNally Robinson Booksellers in Winnipeg for their promotional support.

Grandnephew Mike Czuboka, the Principal and Creative Director of Ignite Design for the design of the front and back covers.

ABOUT THE FRONT COVER PHOTO:

The front cover is a Korean War combat scene with three soldiers from the Royal 22nd Regiment under fire from enemy machine guns. One is carrying a .303 Lee Enfield rifle with a spiked bayonet. Another is holding a Bren .303 light machine gun. These are the weapons that Canadians typically employed in the Korean War. Some American weapons such as the 81 mm mortar and .50 caliber machine gun were also used. The soldiers in this photo are dressed in typical Canadian Korean War fashion. The soldier with the rifle is wearing a beret. The soldier with the Bren is wearing a peaked hat. The soldier on the ground is wearing a toque.

Thanks to my Korean War comrades from the Royal 22nd Regiment! *Veuillez croire, mes amis, a mes sentiments les meilleurs! Merci!*

Photo credit for the front cover: Paul E. Tomelin/Canada. Department of National Defence/Library and Archives Canada/PA-128848. Reproduced with the permission of Library and Archives Canada (2015). Source Library and Archives Canada/Credit Paul E. Tomelin/Department of National Defence fonds/SF-2982.

PROLOGUE

Peter Farley, in future years, often wondered about his sexual conduct. Had he committed a sin by sleeping with this woman? Would he commit additional sins if he slept with others? His reading of the Bible and history of marriage left him with a feeling of uncertainty. The messages in the Bible were often contradictory and unclear. Even distinguished theological historians often disagreed with each other. Many religious practices, including marriage ceremonies, were created long after the lives of the prophets and Jesus Christ. The prophets David and Solomon, he noted, each had hundreds of wives. Some of the Catholic popes had mistresses. Monogamy in the Christian church did not take hold until about the 9th century after Christ. It would be quite impossible, he concluded, to love hundreds of women at the same time. He loved Michelle Brown deeply, and his sexual liaison with her, even without the benefit of a formal marriage, he decided, was more morally acceptable than that of the Biblical polygamists.

-Excerpt from Chapter 2: Peter Farley's Early Introduction to Manhood.

CHAPTER 1
PETER FARLEY'S WORLD IN 1947

Peter Farley began Grade 12 at Sweet Grass High School at Sweet Grass, Manitoba on September 3rd, 1947. He celebrated his 16th birthday on September 17th, of that year, but he was more than six feet tall and looked to be at least 20. He was a gifted student with a photographic memory.

His birth in 1931 had been, in many ways, a miraculous one. Because of the once-in-a-million fortuitous way his father's sperm and mother's ovum had combined during his conception, he entered the world with exceptional intelligence, a sensitive, generous personality, and an extremely attractive physical appearance that made him very appealing to women. His red hair, green eyes, friendly smile, tall, muscular figure, and strong, athletic, masculine presence made him irresistible to every female that came into his life. The very best genes had combined to produce Peter Farley. He was unique.

Of even greater significance was an apparently inborn

characteristic that attracted Peter Farley with great intensity to beautiful women. His definition of beauty was generous and he was often enamored even with women who others considered to be ordinary. He loved women passionately and they loved him with an even greater enthusiasm. He was intellectually and emotionally, and not just sexually, addicted to women and this addiction would lead to intimate relationships with several willing females, all of whom initiated his sexual encounters. He did not know how to say no.

Farley knew that beauty and handsomeness provides many advantages. He had read summaries of scientific studies which concluded that physically attractive men and women are better liked, find good jobs with greater ease, are promoted more frequently, are paid more money, and that they have more successful romantic experiences. There are exceptions, the studies noted, but beautiful woman are attracted to handsome men, and handsome men are attracted to beautiful women.

Michelle Brown, the teacher who was assigned to teach mathematics to Peter and his Grade 12 classmates was, like Peter Farley, physically attractive and highly intelligent. Most mathematics teachers were men, but Miss Brown was very feminine. She had auburn hair, gray eyes, and a slim, well-rounded figure. Her pale, pronounced breasts were partially revealed whenever she wore low cut dresses, which was often. She frequently played classical music during her classes.

Peter was especially appreciative of her exceptionally white, shapely legs, which she provocatively exposed whenever she sat down or bent over.

The school's principal, Jeremy Stewart, spoke to Michelle Brown privately on two occasions early in the school year in regard to her questionable apparel. She smiled, graciously acknowledged his concern, but continued to dress in the same way. Jeremy Stewart was intimidated by the force of her personality and said nothing more.

One Friday afternoon in late September, at the end of one of her classes, Miss Brown called Peter Farley to her desk. It was the beginning of a weekend and the other students rushed excitedly and noisily towards the exit.

Peter was also anxious to leave, but he welcomed the opportunity to be in close proximity with the most beautiful teacher in the school. "She could easily be a model in the Eaton's catalogue or even in New York and Paris fashion salons," he told his friends, and they all agreed.

"Peter," she said, after all of the other students were gone, "I have noticed that you have a very strong aptitude for mathematics, and I am wondering if you would like to advance to a higher level, and ahead of the rest of the class."

"A higher level?" Peter asked. "What does that mean?"

"It means a higher level of senior high school algebra, geometry, trigonometry and especially university level calculus," she replied. "Sit here, Peter," she continued. She pointed to a chair next to her desk. "I have a bachelor's degree in mathematics so I think I can help."

Peter sat in the chair and waited for a more detailed answer. She moved the chair from behind her desk and sat cross-legged in front of him. Her short red skirt was now riding well above her knees. She did not wear stockings and her beautifully curved legs were now more exposed than he had ever seen them. She was, as usual, wearing a low cut blouse and the tops of her breasts were invitingly evident. Her auburn hair looked clean and beautiful. Her eyes were wide and friendly. She looked fresh and energetic even after a full day of teaching.

Peter felt a powerful surge of sexual excitement. *What was there about the legs and breasts of women that attracted him so strongly?* he wondered. He clasped his hands in front of him in an attempt to cover up his exceptionally well-endowed, enlarged manhood. His pants bulged and made him feel extremely embarrassed, which, when added to his sexual arousal, caused him to blush deeply.

Miss Brown smiled. She was very aware of the reason for his discomfort, but was secretly pleased and said nothing. She knew that she was a beautiful woman and she was grateful for her good fortune. She was quite willing to take advantage of her physical assets. Was this one of those occasions? Not yet. She was strongly attracted to Farley but realized that she would have to be careful. She was 27 and he was only 16. She was a mathematician but she was also aware of the law, which stated that the age of majority was 18. Any sexual activity with boys and girls under the age of 18 would likely result in a severe penalty, including, in all probability, time in a penitentiary. Men who exploited children sexually were treated more harshly than women who broke the same law, but she knew that she still had to be very careful.

"If you are interested, Peter, talk to your parents to get their permission. They will need to say that they are willing to have me provide you with additional, advanced instruction in mathematics."

"I'm very interested," Peter replied excitedly. "I'm sure that my father will approve. My mother is no longer here. She died when I was three years old."

"Oh! I'm sorry!" she exclaimed. She was genuinely sympathetic, but also encouraged because she believed that Peter would be more readily accessible since he no longer had a mother.

"When and where shall we meet for these extra classes?" Peter asked.

"I live by myself at the west end of 6th Street on the edge of town," she replied. "Actually, I am not alone! I have a cat. I hope you like cats. I notice that you ride a bike. It should be easy for you to get to my place on your bike."

"When should we begin? I love cats and in fact all animals. And yes, I can get to your place by bike."

"I suggest a Saturday as soon as you have received your father's permission."

"My father is interested in me but he does not pay much attention to what I do. I am often away all day on Saturdays and he says nothing to me. He will not have any objections if I visit with you. I'm really looking forward to it, Miss Brown! You are a great teacher! Forgive me for saying so, but you are also very beautiful!"

"Thank you, Peter. Please call me Michelle, but only when we are together and not when others are present. You are an appealing young man. I want to be honest. You arouse strong feelings in me."

"Michelle? It will take me a while to get used to calling you that. Thanks, Michelle. I have to practice saying that!"

"I have a suggestion in regard to what you should say to your father and anyone else who asks. Tell them that I am living with my mother. That should reassure them. Otherwise, they may think that we have some kind of an inappropriate, intimate relationship. That sounds dishonest, I know, but my mother actually does come to stay with me from time to time."

"How long does she stay?"

"She usually only stays for a few days because she has a home of her own in Brandon. My father died a few years ago and left her well off. She is financially comfortable and travels a lot. I've introduced her to several people in town, including Principal Stewart, and she is quite well known in Sweet Grass. They probably think she lives with me."

"I'll speak to my father as soon as I get home."

"Very good, Peter," she said while rising from her chair. "Thank you for meeting with me." She extended both hands to him and he immediately responded by holding her hands with both of his own. He had never touched her before and a strong sense of intimacy surged throughout his body. He wanted to get closer but resisted the temptation. They departed, but in their minds the stage had been set for them to experience, in the near future, an exciting adventure.

CHAPTER 2
PETER FARLEY'S EARLY
INTRODUCTION TO MANHOOD

Michelle Brown's mother arrived at her home unexpectedly the day after Michelle's meeting with Peter Farley and as a result their clandestine student-teacher meeting had to be delayed. A week passed and Peter became concerned. Had Michelle changed her mind? Had she decided not to meet with him after all?

Then, finally, on the second Friday following their first meeting, Michelle called Peter to her desk once again. After all of the other students were gone she smiled and said: "Are you ready for our session? I am sorry for the delay. My mother has been visiting, but she left this morning to spend a month with my sister in Vancouver. I am free all of this weekend. Can you come to my place tomorrow afternoon?"

Peter was relieved. She was still interested. Excitement ran through his mind and body. "Yes I can!" he responded enthusiastically. "My father is going to be away for the next several days working as a section man at Knox on the CN Railway, 50 miles from here, so I will not have to explain my absence to him. What time should I come?"

"What about 5:00 in the afternoon, or a bit earlier? We can have dinner at about 6:00. What would you like to eat?"

"Anything!" he said. Food was the last thing on his mind. "Whatever you have I will eat!"

"Very good!" she replied. "Do you like spaghetti? I'm a fan of Italian food. My mother and I visited Rome last summer. She comes from an Italian family. I make great spaghetti."

"I've had spaghetti at my friend Frank's house. I like it. His parents are Italian and his mother is a great cook. She also makes very good lasagna."

A short, dark haired girl suddenly entered the room. "Oh! Miss Brown! May I speak with you? I have a question," she said.

"Of course, Rhonda. Come in."

"Good afternoon, Peter," Miss Brown said with a smile. "We will speak more about calculus the next time we meet."

"Yes, Miss Brown. Calculus is an interesting topic. Thanks for telling me about it." He also smiled and quickly left the room.

He woke up the next morning, had a bath in a large four legged tub in the wash room next to his room and spent some time with the beloved animals in his life: Billie the cat, Fido the dog and Charlie the horse. His father had left for Knox on the railway line the previous afternoon and would not return for several days.

At 4:00 in the afternoon he packed a small handbag, climbed onto his bicycle and pedaled to the edge of town. Michelle's house, a green bungalow, was hidden in a cluster of trees. It was not visible from the road.

He parked his bicycle against the porch at the front of the house, climbed a short set of stairs and knocked on the front door.

She opened the door and greeted him with a burst of warm laughter. He stood motionless. She was stunningly beautiful. She was dressed in a short, light blue chemise dress tied tightly at her narrow waist and cut deeply to expose the tops of her prominent breasts. A ray of bright sunshine broke through the trees and made her auburn hair look lighter than usual. She stepped towards him and threw her arms around him.

He quickly responded. He held her tightly with both arms and rested his head on her shoulder. She was 27 but she looked to be no more than 18 or 19. He was 16 but looked to be at least 20 or 21. They were physically, intellectually and emotionally compatible but in an arbitrary, inflexible legal danger zone. They remained closely together for almost a minute. Then she laughed again and gently pushed him away.

"That's enough, Peter!" she said with a smile. "I'm sorry! I did not mean to greet you in this way. I just could not help myself. I hope that you understand, even though we have never talked directly about our relationship."

"I understand completely," he replied, "and I feel the same way. I knew, from the very beginning, that this was much more than just calculus." Sexual excitement surged though his body but he felt, at the same time, some intimidation in her presence.

His mind briefly flashed to the extramarital sexual teachings of his Ukrainian Catholic priest, but his brief feeling of guilt disappeared quickly in the passion of the moment.

A white cat appeared and approached Peter with a friendly look on its face.

"That's Bennie," she said. "He obviously likes you." Peter patted him. Bennie rolled over on his back and started to purr.

"Come inside Peter," she said. "Please sit in that comfortable chair over there. I can offer you cold lemonade, or if you prefer, red wine. But you are still a minor. Maybe I should not be offering you an alcoholic drink!"

"Red wine sounds good, Michelle. I have been to Ukrainian weddings and a lot of heavy drinking takes place at these weddings. Hoorewka is a powerful home made whiskey that Ukrainians consume in large quantities."

"When did you have your first drink?" she asked with a smile.

"I think that I had my first drink at the age of 13. My father and others did not seem to mind as long as I behaved myself. I am not a heavy drinker. It's cultural. Ukrainians are cultural drinkers."

She went to the adjoining kitchen and returned with a large bottle of red wine. She poured wine into two large glasses and gave one glass to Peter. "This is powerful, Florentine 17% wine from Italy," she warned.

He stood up and they raised their glasses simultaneously. "Cheers!" she said. Their wine glasses tinkled.

"Yes, cheers," he responded, "and here's to our friendship and good health!"

She sat down in a large chair directly in front of him, smiled, and remained silent for a minute. He looked serious and also said nothing. They both sipped at their wine.

Then she broke the silence. "So let's get on with it, Peter Farley. We are here to study advanced mathematics. What do you know about algebra, geometry, trigonometry and calculus?" she asked with mock seriousness.

"I have been taking algebra, geometry and trigonometry and I am quite familiar with these subjects. Calculus? I don't know much about calculus."

"There are two major kinds of calculus," she said. "Differential calculus concerns itself with rates of change and the slopes of curves. Integral calculus concerns itself with the accumulation of quantities and the areas under curves.

Calculus is used in science, economics and engineering to solve many problems."

"Curves? I'm certainly interested in curves, and especially yours if you don't mind me saying so. You are very curvaceous. You have perfect curves, but I don't know much about the areas under the curves," he said with a mischievous laugh. "I'm planning to go into medicine as soon as I can save up enough money. Will a knowledge of calculus be helpful when I study medicine?"

"You are a fast learner, but be patient and careful when you are dealing with the areas under curves. Don't rush. Be attentive, generous and thoughtful," she said with a suggestive smile.

"You ask about medicine," she continued. "Most medical schools ask students to take one or two semesters of calculus. I know because I have seriously considered going into medicine."

"So why didn't you?"

"I have tried and I have my application in at several Canadian and American universities. I plan to teach at Sweet Grass for only one year. I want to make some money for my future studies and I took the first teaching job that came along. I don't want to depend entirely on my mother even though she is willing to help me financially. I would prefer to study medicine and stay in Canada if I can."

"What about the University of Manitoba? Did you try Brandon College? Some of my friends have gone to Brandon. It's a good place to start. I don't think they discriminate."

"I applied to the Faculty of Medicine at the University of Manitoba and they turned me down. All medical schools in Canada have an unwritten rule. They impose strict quotas on Jews, Ukrainians, Poles, Italians, on all so-called 'foreigners' even if born in Canada, and also on women. Only a few in these categories are accepted. "

"Does that mean that they will turn me down because I am a Ukrainian?"

"Are you a Ukrainian? I did not know until you mentioned your attendance at Ukrainian weddings. And the university people will not be aware of the fact that you are Ukrainian if you do not tell them. Farley sounds like an English name. You do not have a foreign accent and you are very Caucasian in appearance."

"Actually, I am only a partial Ukrainian. In mathematical terms, less than 50%!" he said with a smile." My ancestors came mostly from other countries in Europe. The original Farley family began life in Ukraine when two red-headed Irish brothers came to Galicia, Ukraine in the 1750's to build a flour mill. O'Farrell, their name, eventually evolved into Farley."

"So you are at least partly Irish! My father was English, my mother is Italian, but I also had Irish and Icelandic grandparents," she said.

"Am I Irish? Yes. A long time ago. One of my great grandfathers, according to our family history, was very tall, at about two meters, or 6 feet and 6 inches. He was an exceptionally handsome, wealthy red-headed Ukrainian Jew, who produced an illegitimate son, my grandfather Anthony. Women loved him and it was rumored that he had many mistresses."

"Then you are at least to some extent, Jewish!"

"Yes, but included in my family, as well, is a Polish grandmother and a German grandmother. My mother was English and Scottish, but she also had some Metis, French, Cree Indian ancestry. There have been a number of red-headed people in my family over the generations. My Jewish grandfather was not the only one."

She paused for a moment. "You are an interesting mixture. You are tall, about 6 feet, 3 inches I am guessing, but not quite as tall as your Jewish grandfather. And you do, like him, have red hair. Have you ever been with a woman? "

He was startled by her question. "No," he said quietly. "You

14

are the first."

"I am an educator and I will teach you everything you need to know about women generally, and me in particular," she said in a seductive, enticing tone.

"You are great teacher, and the most beautiful one I have ever known. I'm looking forward to my first lesson. I confess to being a little afraid. I hope that I will not disappoint you."

"You make me happy, Peter, just by being with me. I think we are soul mates. I am attracted to you emotionally as well as intellectually and physically."

"I feel the same way, Michelle. I just don't know how to tell you. I dream about you every night, and think about you every day. You are the most important person in my life."

"Thank you, Peter. But let's change the subject," she said cheerfully. "Do you like music? Would you like me to play some music?"

"What kind of music?"

"It's classical. I love classical music, and especially the romantic composers."

"Who are the romantic composers?"

"They mostly lived in the 1800's. Rossini, Chopin, Strauss, Mendelssohn, Tchaikovsky, Bizet, Elgar, Wagner and others."

She walked over to a small table on which a record player was sitting. "I have long playing records that contain popular highlights of the music of several of the composers I have mentioned. I hope you like their music," she said.

She selected and placed several records and turned the record player on. The music began and played softly in the background as they continued to talk. They spoke about their lives in the past and present and their hopes for the future. They continued to drink the red wine. After about an hour both were considerably inebriated.

The spaghetti she had made earlier sat forgotten in a pot in the kitchen. They were not hungry. Bennie the cat slept peacefully on a rug near the front door.

An excerpt from Tchaikovsky's *1812 Overture* was followed by Bizet's *Toreador.*

"I love this music!" Peter said enthusiastically. "You played some of it in our mathematics classes. It's great!"

Strauss's *Blue Danube* was followed by the most popular part of Beethoven's *Symphony #5.*

"Peter," she suddenly said. "I want you to sleep with me but I am afraid. If people learn that we have been in bed together they may have me, an adult woman, arrested and charged with taking advantage of you, one of my students. You are still legally a child. I am 27 and you are only 16."

"Please don't worry, Michelle. I will never tell anyone about us. I would never do anything to hurt you. I am also afraid, but only because I have never slept with a woman before. I hope I will be able to satisfy you."

"I was married when I was 19 but my marriage lasted only a few months. You have nothing to be afraid of. I have noticed that you are actually very mature and well developed."

"Well developed? I remember the occasion. I was aroused and could not control myself. My pants bulged. I was embarrassed. They are bulging again right now. I'm sorry!"

Rossini's *William Tell Overture* played in the background.

"You have nothing to be sorry for or to be embarrassed about. I am impressed!" she said. She then got out of her chair and kneeled on the floor in front of him. She put her head on his knees and held both of his hands. He stood up and laid her gently onto the floor. He stretched out beside her and applied his lips gently to hers. The kiss lasted for almost a minute. Their hands roamed all over each other's bodies. Both of them were now deeply aroused. They stood up. She picked up her half glass of wine and downed it with a single swallow. His glass was almost full and it took him several swallows to finish it.

"It is time to go to bed," she said. "Take off your clothes, Peter," she said in a strong authoritarian manner. She began taking her own clothes off.

He quickly complied with her order. "Yes Miss Brown," he said. "I will do whatever you say. You are very, very beautiful, Michelle. This is like a dream."

She took his hand and led him into the adjoining bedroom. Their perfect bodies were both naked.

"Kiss me everywhere," she commanded, and he did.

Wagner's *Ride of the Valkyries* played in the background as they made love.

They would remember the ecstatic intimacy, climaxes and Wagner's accompanying music for the rest of their lives.

They slept together until the following morning. He woke up and started to dress.

He had to go home to feed his dog, cat and horse. She continued to sleep.

He found a notebook and pencil on the bedside table. "Dear Michelle," he wrote, "I love you. I will remember our time together for the rest of my life. I have to go home now to feed Billie, Fido and Charlie. When will I see you again? Love, Peter." He put the note on the table. He kissed her gently and then left.

Michelle's mother arrived suddenly and unexpectedly on the following afternoon. She had planned to stay in Vancouver longer but had a disagreement with her daughter's husband and decided to leave and return to Michelle's home.

On Monday Michelle received a letter from Florida Orange State International University in the United States. Due to a sudden withdrawal, a student vacancy in the School of Medicine at this institution was now available. She accepted and immediately submitted a letter of resignation with regard to her teaching position.

The school board accepted her resignation reluctantly because of the short notice. She regretted leaving her students without a mathematics teacher but this was a chance of a lifetime and she had to take it. She wanted to stay in Canada, like many other talented Canadians, seemed to be destined to becoming an American.

She started to write a letter to Peter to tell him how much she would miss him but she worried about the possibility of the letter accidentally getting into the wrong hands. She tore up her unfinished letter and tears came to her eyes.

Peter and Michelle met briefly in her classroom on the following Friday afternoon. It was her last day at the school. They said goodbye and shook hands but were unable to say or do anything more. The other teachers were holding a farewell tea for Michelle, and it was mostly for staff members. Michelle's mother was also present. Peter felt very sad and depressed. "Will I ever see her again?" he asked himself. "I hope so," he answered himself, "but I may need to get on without her."

But he did see her again when he began pre-medical studies at the University of Manitoba. During the next two years she visited him in Winnipeg on five occasions. She always rented a room in a hotel where they met. During each meeting their sexual adventures continued. She always brought a portable record player and they always listened to excerpts of classical music during their intimate encounters. She would come more often, she told him, but she lived a long way away and her medical studies left her with very little free time. After their fifth meeting in Winnipeg their contacts ended until many years later.

Farley's classical musical experiences with Michelle Brown, in her classroom as well as in her bed, encouraged him to read about the great composers and to listen to their musical productions. He became familiar with and especially enthusiastic about Wagner, Beethoven, Mozart, Brahms and Rachmaninov. He started listening to the opera music of Tchaikovsky, Verdi, and Puccini on CBC Radio. He bought a portable record player and began to collect classical music and opera recordings. His photographic memory was able to capture and remember, not only the histories of the classical music that he read, but also the music itself. He occasionally listened with moderate enthusiasm to the popular songs of Frank Sinatra, Chuck Berry, Jerry Lee Lewis and Elvis Presley, but classical music became a part of his heart and soul. The early Rock and Roll music did not appeal to him.

Farley, in future years, often wondered about his sexual conduct. Had he committed a sin by sleeping with this woman? Would he commit additional sins if he slept with others? His reading of the Bible and the history of marriage left him with a feeling of uncertainty. The messages in the Bible were often contradictory and unclear. Even distinguished theological historians often disagreed with each other. Many religious practices, including marriage ceremonies, were created long after the prophets and Jesus Christ. The prophets David and Solomon, he noted, each had hundreds of wives. Some of the Catholic popes had mistresses. Monogamy in the Christian church did not take hold until about the 9th century after Christ. It would be quite impossible, he concluded, to love hundreds of women at the same time. He loved Michelle Brown deeply, and his sexual liaison with her, even without the benefit of a formal marriage, he decided, was more morally acceptable than that of the Biblical polygamists.

CHAPTER 3
CANADA ENTERS THE KOREAN WAR

What were the political circumstances that caused Peter Farley and thousands of other Canadians to fight, and in some cases to be wounded, or even die, in the Korean War? Farley wanted to become a medical doctor but the Korean War interrupted his plans and appeared like a dark cloud on his horizon. What impact would this distant conflict in Korea have on his existence and future? Farley's life and the lives of thousands of other Canadian would depend upon the response of the Canadian Federal Government. Would the Government make the right decision for the right reasons? Would Canada be able to help save the people of Korea from authoritarian communism? What was Farley's destiny? What was Canada's destiny? Was the future preordained by some great power? These questions often came to Farley's contemplative mind.

The 10th Prime Minister of Canada, MacKenzie King, retired in 1948 and died on July 22, 1950. His successor, Prime

Minister Louis St. Laurent and members of his Cabinet went by train from Ottawa to Toronto for his funeral. It was during their return to Ottawa that a decision was made about Canada's participation in the Korean War.

"Uncle Louis" St. Laurent was a fluently bilingual French Canadian with great deal of personal charm. He projected a pleasant, grandfatherly image, and was in fact a man of genuine kindness. At the same time, St. Laurent was more practical, more innovative, more aggressive and more willing to take chances than the eccentric MacKenzie King, who had been mainly known for his cautious behaviour, and in later years, for his belief in supernatural forces and attempts to communicate with his deceased mother.

"Well, gentlemen, what shall we do about the Korean War?" St. Laurent asked his Ministers as their luxurious coach rumbled northeastward towards Ottawa. "As you know, the North Koreans, under the auspices of the Soviet Union, invaded South Korea on June 25th. Under pressure from the United States, the United Nations condemned the invasion and agreed to come to the assistance of the South Koreans. The Americans and British have had troops in South Korea since early July, but they are being pushed southward very rapidly. It is a very critical situation".

"I believe that we should assist the Americans," Defence Minister Brooke Claxton replied. "We need to support them for political as well as military reasons. And let's keep in mind that we are members of the United Nations and that we have been asked to help in Korea."

"But what about the cost?" Douglas Abbott, the Finance Minister asked. "Can we afford to send a force half-way around the world, and if so, how large should it be? Must we always cater to the Americans?"

External Affairs Minister Lester Pearson offered his advice.

"I believe," he said, "that the Russian bear must be stopped somewhere, and it might as well be in Korea. We can't let the United Nations become ineffective like the old League of Nations. We should be prepared to make a substantial contribution. Let's not repeat the same mistakes that we made in the 1930's with Hitler."

The Finance Minister looked agitated. "Gentlemen", he said impatiently. "We have just returned from Mr. King's funeral. It is somewhat ironic that we should be expressing approval for involvement in Korea. Mr. King, as you know, was opposed to any kind of action that would provoke the Soviets. But let me ask again. What kind of force are we talking about?"

"What about 10,000 men, or two brigades? It should be more than a token force," Claxton replied.

"Have we got 10,000 men to send?" St. Laurent asked.

"No, but the Chief of the Defence Staff tells me that we can raise 5,000 or more fairly quickly," Claxton answered.

"Let's compromise," St. Laurent said smoothly, a kindly expression coming over his face. "Perhaps 5,000 soldiers, along with some naval and air elements, should suffice. Can we afford that much?"

"Well, in my opinion, 5,000 is more reasonable than 10,000," Abbott allowed grudgingly. "We do have a lot of unemployed men at this time. Wars do stimulate economies. A lot of veterans from the last war may be willing to re-join the army. I just hope that this is not another step on the road to Manifest Destiny, the inevitable political and cultural assimilation of Canada by the United States as predicted and promoted by many Americans in the last century, and which is still current among many even today".

"You have been reading Canadian history again!" St. Laurent said with a chuckle.

"Yes", Mr. Abbott replied. "As a matter of fact, I was going through a book about Manifest Destiny on the day that Mr. King died. Included as an appendix was a fascinating letter from John O'Sullivan, the American journalist who first used the term. All of you should read it. Maybe it is an omen that we should not ignore."

"Manifest Destiny is a ghost from the past," Mr. Pearson observed. "We still need to be vigilant, but it is no longer an important issue. Let's talk in modern and practical terms. The Americans are not going to give us many orders for military supplies if we sit on the sidelines. There are three good reasons for participation in Korea. In the first place, our friends, the Americans, need our help. Secondly, the United Nations will certainly weaken and may collapse if its members, including Canada, don't uphold its principles. And thirdly, it's in our economic and democratic interests to support the Korean people and the American effort against totalitarian communism".

"Manifest Destiny, my dear Pearson, is not a ghost from the past!" Abbott exclaimed sarcastically. "The Americans, in fact, are always recruiting and stealing away many of our most talented citizens. How many medical doctors, scientists, hockey players, nurses, and teachers, for instance, do we lose each year to the United States? We may be politically independent, but our culture and economy is heavily Americanized. Manifest Destiny takes place, on an individual basis, whenever one of our highly trained citizens, such as a physician, leaves Canada and is absorbed into the United States."

"That's very eloquent!" the Prime Minister said. "I agree with your observation."

"Thank you. Transporting 5,000 soldiers to Korea will be expensive," Abbott continued. "How will this be managed?"

"I am away ahead of you!" the Defence Minister said with a chuckle. "I had a discussion last week with the Chief of the Defence Staff and with railway officials. The CN and CP railways both have an extensive supply of old wooden railway passenger coaches. They were built about 50 or 60 years ago and are rather primitive, but ideal for transporting rambunctious young soldiers to war. These conveyances were employed to deliver immigrants to the Prairies in the early 1900's. The railways have modern steel passenger coaches but are reluctant to have them used, and perhaps abused, by our soldiers."

"I am a bit uncomfortable about using old wooden coaches, but if the Chief of the Defence Staff is agreeable, let's give it our approval," the Prime Minister said. "The railways will transport our soldiers to the West Coast, but how do they get to Korea from there?"

"They will be taken across the Pacific on U.S. liberty ships," the Defence Minister replied. "These vessels are crudely built and with rather primitive dining and accommodation facilities. But the Americans use them frequently to transport their own soldiers to the Far East and Korea."

"Then it's agreed? We are going to go into the Korean War?" St. Laurent asked, his eyes moving from face to face across the line of chairs where his Ministers sat.

A chorus of "ayes" greeted the Prime Minister's question, although the Finance Minister merely nodded his head.

"Good," said Mr. Claxton. "I'll speak to the Chief of the Defence Staff in the morning. We will call for an army brigade of about 5,000 men, together with some air and naval support. It is the least we can do under the circumstances."

"Dinner is served," said a handsome, elegant-looking Negro waiter. The Cabinet Ministers then sat down at the dining table.

"There is nothing as delicious as C.N.R. dinners," said Mr. Claxton.

"Yes," said the Prime Minister, "and also C.P.R. dinners. Canadians should be proud of their railways and the excellent services that they provide. We live in a marvelous country."

CHAPTER 4
MANIFEST DESTINY

Douglas Abbott, the Minister of Finance, remained in a state of agitation for some time following the decision of the Prime Minister and Cabinet to send a brigade of about 5,000 men to Korea. His recommendation to proceed with caution, he felt, had been summarily rejected in favor of that provided by Lester Pearson. As a former devoted follower of the late Prime Minister MacKenzie King, Abbott had some serious reservations about entering the Korean conflict, primarily because it might result in a strong response from dictator Joseph Stalin and the Soviet Union. A second concern for Abbott was the additional military burden that would be placed on the Federal budget. He was also concerned about bowing to the pressure being exerted by American President Harry Truman. The Americans wanted Canada to provide a substantial combat force for service in Korea on an immediate basis.

Abbott finally decided that he would speak up again. He

would not try to change the decision to go to Korea. He simply wanted the Prime Minister and the members of the Cabinet to be aware of the danger of excessive American influence.

He called his secretary into his office. "Alice," he said. "I want you to take a letter. Copies are to be sent to the Prime Minister and to each Cabinet minister. I also want you to type and send a copy of a letter that was written by John O'Sullivan, an American journalist." He reached into his desk and handed Alice a book. "The letter is in the preface," he explained.

"Gentleman", he dictated. *"The recent correspondence from Washington is worrisome. President Truman is apparently not satisfied with our military contribution to the war in Korea. I believe that we must be firm and resist Truman's pressure. General Douglas MacArthur, his commander-in-chief in Japan and Korea, is an unrepentant war hawk and has even threatened to bomb the Communists into submission with a nuclear bomb. Although Mr. Pearson stated in our recent meeting that Manifest Destiny is a thing of the past, our Ambassador in Washington has pointed out that this expression is still sometimes used in the Senate and House of Representatives. Mr. King had good reason to believe that we should be cautious when dealing with the Americans. Please read the letter from John O'Sullivan that I am sending you. Although it is one hundred years old, it accurately describes Manifest Destiny as viewed by many Americans."* Sincerely, Douglas.

"Attached: Letter from John O'Sullivan."
The New York Journal:
November 13, 1850.
Henry Morgan, Esq..
Minnesota Legislature, Minneapolis, Minnesota.

Dear Mr. Morgan:

I have your letter of October 8th, 1850, in which you inquire about the origin and definition of the term "Manifest Destiny," which I understand that you need as background material for an introduction of a bill into the Minnesota Legislature for the "annexation, by consent, of all of the British provinces of North America."

Although I am pleased to take journalistic credit for the coining of "Manifest Destiny," I must confess that the concept itself was developed by numerous American patriots over a period of many years. It refers, of course, to the idea that all of North America should belong to a single political unit, inasmuch as the existing boundaries in the north are artificial and contrary to the principles of economics, geography and basic common sense.

As you know, the Presidential Campaign of 1844 featured the battle cry "54, 40 or fight." I certainly agreed with that proposal, except that I preferred going beyond the 54th parallel, and indeed right up to and including the North Pole. The following year, in 1845, I wrote an article on the annexation of Texas, in which I first used the expression "Manifest Destiny."

General Herman Cass of Michigan once said that "Americans have an awful swaller for territory." That may be true, but the territories that we have swallered are certainly much better off under the Stars and Stripes. Moreover, in the case of British

North America, we would be incorporating people of essentially the same language, culture and race into the Union, unlike those of the Mexican and California territories whose characteristics are much more foreign.

It is my understanding that a steamboat service was established between Minneapolis-St. Paul and the British Red River Colony during this past summer. This development will surely enhance your cause because the good people of that oppressed settlement suffer under the autocratic rule of the Hudson's Bay Company, and will not be able to resist the advantages of our Union much longer. Indeed, Manifest Destiny seems to be on the brink of fulfillment everywhere, and not just in your part of the country. I hope that these observations will be of some assistance to you in your presentation to the Minnesota Legislature.

I am, Sir, your Obedient Servant,
John O'Sullivan.

CHAPTER 5
THE NEGOTIATOR

On the same hot August day in 1950 that Peter Farley enrolled in the Fusiliers his future commanding officer, General Manager James "Big Jim" Strange, sat at the end of a large rectangular table in the ornate Victorian Room of Vancouver's Captain Cook Hotel. He was acting as the chief negotiator for the Great Pacific Bus Lines Company. He was a tall man of English origin but did not look English. He had black hair, a swarthy complexion, a long, thin nose and dark brown eyes. Strange had been hired into this position shortly after graduating from the University of Toronto with an honours B.A. in 1948. He was exceptionally intelligent and perceptive. An outstanding soldier, he had risen through the ranks to become a Lieutenant-Colonel and the Commanding Officer of the 2nd Battalion, Canadian Fusiliers in World War II.

Although he appreciated being a manager with important responsibilities and a decent wage, he hated the politics involved. He was used to giving commands and having them obeyed, and disliked having to report to the President of the Company and its Board of Directors. Strange, as a reserve army officer, had recently been interviewed by the Chief of Staff of the Canadian Army about re-enlisting as a battalion commander with the Special Force being recruited for the Korean War, and he looked forward to this possibility with a great deal of enthusiasm. He missed the army and wanted to return to its highly structured and disciplined environment.

Strange was flanked by two serious looking, sweating and bald-headed assistants. His task, and that of his assistants, was to negotiate a new contract with the International Bus Drivers' and Ticket Agents' Union of America, led by Henry "Buzz" Grabowski, the abrasive, heavy-set, muscular, blond-haired and icy blue- eyed President of the Union's British Columbia division. Grabowski sat directly across from Strange and appeared to be in a relaxed and confident mood.

One of Grabowski's aides was a tall, thin man with thick glasses and a subdued scholarly look. He sat with a pad of paper and a pencil and seemed to be recording all aspects of the negotiating meeting in great detail.

On Grabowski's other side was Maggie Marek, a voluptuous natural blonde in her mid-twenties. She also sat with a pad and pencil, but seldom wrote anything. She had an air of detachment and empty-headed arrogance on her face.

"I wonder if she can type or file," Strange thought sarcastically. He felt annoyed with himself because he could not resist the temptation of glancing into the top of her deeply cut blouse and at her sharply defined figure. He resented Grabowski's good fortune at being able to attract such a sexually attractive woman, someone who was obviously there for the Polack's satisfaction rather than legitimate business.

"We don't think that 95 cents an hour is too much to ask,"

Grabowski suddenly said with a snarl. "Shit, our people in Seattle recently settled for a dollar and five cents. How much are they paying you, Colonel? Probably a lot more than 95 cents. But knowing those cheap and greedy sons of bitches you work for, its probably not much more. I happen to know that the Company made a lot of money last year. Didn't they tell you? What do you say, Big Jim? Let's have it straight, and no more bullshit. What's your final offer? Or, are you just a flunky, with no real power to negotiate a contract?"

Strange stared upwards and fixed his piercing brown eyes onto the large glass chandelier that hung from the high ceiling at the opposite side of the room. He could feel the nostrils of his nose throbbing, one of his usual manifestations of suppressed anger. He was especially furious because Grabowski had touched upon the truth: the Company President, Malcolm Rogers, had ordered Strange to act "diplomatically, with tact, and with no outward display of impatience." It was, in fact, a stalling tactic, because Rogers needed more time to prepare his Company's case for an arbitration hearing.

"My dear Grabowski," Strange finally replied, "you must know that Seattle is not Vancouver, and that Washington is not British Columbia."

"Yeah? Is that right?" Grabowski shouted. "Who gives a damn. We are an international union, like several others in this country. Boundaries mean bugger all as far as we are concerned. Maybe Canada will one day be part of the United States. What have we got to lose? Look at Maggie here beside me, a Polish-American girl from Chicago, but she looks, acts and talks like a typical Canadian broad. Right Maggie?" He let out a loud and hoarse guffaw and did not wait for an answer. "The United States and Canada are one country, as far as I am concerned," he concluded emphatically with a serious look on his face.

"According to my notes," Strange replied calmly, "you chaps are asking for new uniforms every January, a defined benefits pension plan after 35 years of service, with one-half of the contributions to be made by the Company, and a wage of 95 cents an hour. I've also written down several points about your proposed grievance procedures. I need time to consult with my President. May we take a 30 minute break?"

"Yeah," Grabowski said with a sneering smile. "Consult with the big boy. We don't have to consult, but I could use a couple of cold beers. We will be back at 1:30. Let's go Maggie," he concluded, giving her a sharp slap on her shapely posterior after she rose from her chair.

Strange dismissed his assistants and remained sitting in the room alone. A telephone sat on the table in front of him and he dialed the number of President Malcolm Rogers. A secretary informed him that Rogers was occupied but that he would call back as soon as he was free. Strange hung up and waited. His dark eyes blazed and the skin on his face turned into a deep red. "*I can't tolerate this*," he thought. "*Why do I have to sit here and get pushed around by a crude Polack who never got past the rank of corporal in the last war?*" Strange had never known Grabowski before, but he reluctantly accepted Grabowski's claim that he had been a corporal in the Canadian Army during World War II. Grabowski's two years of service as a lineman in the Canadian Football League, on the other hand, was a well-known fact that had been documented in the newspapers. Grabowski was big and strong.

Strange's mind began to wander from the task and situation at hand. He had been preoccupied for the past several days with his recent visit to Ottawa, where he had been interviewed by the Canadian Army Chief of Staff for the possibility of assuming the command of the 2nd Canadian Fusiliers, one of the new infantry units that was being formed for the Korean War.

Four years had elapsed since his demobilization in 1946, and he found himself desperately wanting to return to a military life. Grabowski was a slob, but only one of many that he had to deal with.

Even President Rogers was intolerable, with his condescending attitude towards the Union on one hand, and his authoritarian, inflexible way of dealing with his employees on the other hand. Indeed, Rogers did not seem to have any kind of definable leadership style. He was inconsistent, indecisive and unpredictable. He had assumed the presidency of the company not as a result of demonstrated leadership qualities, but because he had married the daughter of the owner.

Strange felt trapped. He needed a job. He disliked his contacts with Rogers, Grabowski and the Union and although a manager, had difficult in remaining loyal to the confused management of the Great Pacific Bus Lines Company.

CHAPTER 6
A CANADIAN SOLDIER AGAIN

Strange closed his eyes and reviewed the events of his life. *"If the Canadian Army does not accept me where shall I go and what shall I do? Am I an Englishman or a Canadian? Is it true, as Grabowski says, that Canada will soon become a part of the United States?"* Grabowski, although a foreigner in Canadian eyes, was born in Canada.

Strange reviewed his early years, before the age of 13, when he had lived with his lower class English parents in East London, England, and again during 1946, when he had been stationed in London for the last year of his Canadian Army service. The Canadian Army had promoted him to the rank of Lieutenant-Colonel without any consideration of his class. If he had served in the British Army his chances of becoming a commissioned officer would have been was very slim indeed. His reading of history told him that the frequent blunders of the British Army in France during WWI were perpetuated by weak-minded officers from the upper classes.

Why was he so intolerant of the Polack Grabowski when there was so much in the cosmopolitan East London of his childhood that he admired? He fondly remembered the endless activity, colour and noise of the Cockneys, the Jews, the Chinese, the Poles and a multitude of other nationalities. He could almost smell the odours of Limehouse, Rotherhitke, and Pickle Herring Wharf with their, cheese, spices, tea, damp straw and human sweat.

These were the places where he had spent the happiest days of his life. At the same time, as a highly intelligent, sensitive human being, he felt a deep and bitter resentment towards the class-ridden structure of English society, and particularly as it was practiced in the city of his birth. Lord this. Lord that. What nonsense!

As a high school student in Toronto he had consciously tried to overcome his East London speech, but it was still present to a degree, although now grammatically correct and blended considerably with the inflexions of southern Ontario. In the years following the war Toronto was rapidly becoming a mixed ethnic society which in some ways was beginning to resemble East London. Canadians did not seem to pay much attention to his accent, except to occasionally note that it was "English". His swarthiness sometimes made people think that he must have some Spanish, perhaps Armada, blood in his veins.

The 30 minutes went by very quickly and Grabowski and his two assistants burst back into the room while Strange was still deep in thought. He was still waiting for President Malcolm Rogers to call. He was surprised at how quickly the time had passed. Strange's two assistants also returned and sat beside him again.

"Oh, you are back already!" Strange said in a friendly tone. "How was the beer?"

"Warm as piss," Grabowski complained. "Something wrong with the cooler." He wiped his brow with his handkerchief. "Maggie," he ordered, "bring us a big pitcher of lemonade with lots of ice. This room is as hot as hell and I'm parched." He took a large cigar out of his pocket, stripped away the cellophane, and lit it with a wooden match.

Maggie got up from the table and straightened her white blouse. Small beads of sweat covered her pale and pretty face. She reached up under her short blue skirt and tugged at her transparent nylon stockings. "I feel sticky all over," she said with an innocent smile. "What about you, Mr. Strange? Will you have some lemonade?"

"No, thank you," Strange replied. He was acutely aware of her exposed and shapely legs, but felt strangely serene and without any of the sexual tension that he had experienced during their first encounter earlier that morning.

"Well, what did the boss say?" Grabowski demanded in a loud and belligerent voice. "Do we get our reasonable requests, or do our people have to walk out and stop the buses from running during the peak of the tourist season?"

"Now, Mr. Grabowski, be reasonable," Strange replied in a firm voice. "You know that a strike will hurt your people as much as the company. Walkouts cause permanent damage. Some travelers will never return to the buses. They will switch to the railways, to private automobiles and even to the expanding airlines. That will mean fewer jobs for the members of your union."

At that moment the telephone rang on the table beside Strange. "*Rogers is finally calling*," he thought. "Excuse me for a moment," he said as he picked up the receiver.

"Mr. Strange, please," an operator said. "Long distance is calling."

"Strange speaking," he responded.

36

"Mr. Strange," another female voice interjected, "the Chief of Staff in Ottawa is calling. One moment please."

"Hello, Jim," said a deep male voice. "Did I get you at a bad time?"

"No, indeed, sir, you got me at a perfect time."

"Well, I won't keep you very long. I suppose that you are anxious to hear about the results of your interview last week."

"Yes, General, I certainly am."

"Then I am pleased to tell you that we are prepared to offer you the command of the 2nd Battalion of the Fusiliers together with a re-appointment to the rank of Lieutenant-Colonel. Do you accept?"

"Yes, sir, of course I accept, and with a great deal of gratitude, I might add."

"Excellent," said the General. "I'm delighted. May I suggest that you give immediate notice to your employer and report to Calgary as soon as possible? A letter of confirmation will follow shortly."

"Thank you again, sir. You have made me a very happy man." He hung up the phone and looked at the other negotiators with a wide smile on his face.

"General?" Grabowski asked incredulously. "Is the company now run by a general?"

At that moment Maggie came into the room carrying a tray with a large pitcher of iced lemonade and several glasses. Her high heels clicked provocatively on the hardwood floor and her body swayed gracefully. She deposited the tray in front on Grabowski who merely grunted as he looked quizzically at Strange.

"Well, Big Jim," Grabowski demanded. "What's the word? Do we settle or strike?" He puffed furiously on his cigar, waiting impatiently for an answer.

Strange stood up to his full height of 6 feet, 2 inches. His nostrils throbbed and his dark eyes blazed with fiery intensity. "My deal Grabowski," he said in clear and measured tones, "in my opinion you are nothing more than a crude and ignorant Polack, a disgrace to the Polish people. As far as I am concerned, you and the rest of your bloody union can go and jump in the Strait of Juan de Fuca. My final offer is 65 cents an hour, and even that is overly generous."

"You bastard! Have you gone nuts?" Grabowski shouted, his white face suddenly turning a deep red.

Strange did not reply. He jammed his file into his brief case, pushed his chair against the table with an air of finality, and marched quickly around to where Grabowski was sitting. Then he picked up the pitcher of lemonade, held it high over Grabowski's head, and poured its icy contents over Grabowski's face, shirt and pants. "Have some lemonade, Grabowski" Strange said savagely. "You deserve every drop."

Grabowski sat in stunned silence, his damp cigar now smoldering and hanging precariously from the corner of his mouth. His blond hair had turned into a medium brown. He blinked in disbelief, his body and mind immobile because of the shocking suddenness of Strange's bizarre action. In spite of his verbal bravado in dealing with Strange, Grabowski was intimidated because he was subconsciously aware of Strange's previous military rank. Strange was a Lieutenant-Colonel, and Grabowski was only a corporal.

Strange calmly returned the pitcher to the table and walked out of the room. He proceeded to the lobby of the hotel, found another telephone, and called President Malcolm Rogers.

"Yes, Jim, what is it?" Rogers responded impatiently. "Is your session over already? I'm counting on you to keep them talking as a long as possible. You know that I will be very angry if you have done anything to annoy them."

"I've made them an offer," Strange responded. "It's 65 cents an hour."

"What? Jim, have you gone out of your mind? Did you say 65 cents an hour? That's what they are getting now!"

"That's my final offer," Strange said triumphantly. "I refuse to meet with Grabowski again. In any event, he has probably contacted the union and advised them of our decision. They are likely preparing for a strike, so get ready. And by the way, I'm resigning my position effective immediately."

"Resigning? Where are you going?"

"To Korea."

"Korea? Where in hell is that?"

"Somewhere in the Far East. I'm not absolutely sure. I'm going to read a book about it."

"And what are you going to do in Korea?"

"I am going to defend democracy against communism. The world is in danger, my dear President. Hitler is gone, but some of us are being called upon to defend our country and civilization from a new and equally evil ideology. May I suggest, in leaving, that you change your attitudes towards your subordinates and operate on a more consultative basis?"

"What do you mean?"

"I am telling you that sitting at home during the war as a zombie, non-combatant obviously did not allow you to learn very much about leadership. To put it more succinctly, you are a confused and inconsistent weak leader. You pander too much to Grabowski and his union, and if you do not show more backbone in future, your company will collapse into bankruptcy. Do I make myself clear?"

A long silence followed. Strange waited patiently, a sly smile and look of satisfaction on his face. Rogers finally replied. "You may pick up your two weeks of severance pay this afternoon. There is no need for you to report for any further duties."

Strange hung up the telephone, walked across the lobby and

sank into one of the luxurious leather chairs that were located in the middle. He reached into his brief case and pulled out a book. *Korea: Land of the Morning Calm* was printed across its cover in mock oriental letters. *"Korea? What is it all about?"* he muttered to himself. A wide smile crossed his face.

CHAPTER 7
OTTAWA'S SOVIET EMBASSY:
THE SPY WITHIN

It was the 31st day of August, 1950, and on this hot, sunny summer day an important conversation about the Korean War was taking place at the Embassy of the Soviet Union in Ottawa. Peter Farley had arrived in Calgary from Sweet Grass earlier that week and was now training at Currie Barracks to serve in Korea as a Fusilier. The war in Korea, in which Farley would soon be involved, was destined to include an element of espionage.

First Secretary Nicholai Rykov, an N.K.V.D. secret police agent, sat in a large stuffed chair in the staff lounge of the Soviet Embassy in Ottawa, his right hand holding a cigarette in the traditional inverted European manner. He had been drinking whiskey since early that morning and had a bottle and glass on the table at his side. He was quite inebriated. He felt relaxed and expansive as he chatted with Ilya Zinoviev, an assistant press secretary who was also a Soviet undercover agent. Rykov began talking about things that were supposed to remain secret, even among his colleagues.

"Ah, to be in Moscow in August," Rykov said with a sigh. "Summer in all of its glory. I could be strolling in Gorky Square, watching soccer in the Luzhniki Sports Palace, or perhaps attending a concert at the Tchaikovsky Hall. My heart still aches for home, even after two years in Ottawa."

"Yes, I know what you mean, comrade," Zinoviev replied. "I've been here for only six months, but I'm already longing for the day that I will be able to return. Our old school, the Frunze Military Academy, had a reunion last month, and naturally I could not go."

"Things are more difficult now that our Korean Peoples' Republic is on the offensive," Rykov continued. "I've noticed a very pronounced coolness coming from Canadian politicians and diplomats. I was in Ottawa when that despicable Little Russian, the Ukrainian traitor Igor Gouzenko defected, and the atmosphere now is very similar. The communications of the Canadians are now suddenly very limited, abrupt and formal. Why, I have not been invited to a social event for almost a month, nor has the Ambassador!"

"Cheer up, Nikolai," Zinoviev said with a smile. "As you know, two or three years is usually the amount of time that we need to spend in any place. Eventually, we will be called back to Moscow."

"I long to return to Moscow," Rykov responded, "but I am happy. I made an important intelligence contact a few days ago. I had a meeting with a Canadian in a restaurant and an espionage deal was forged."

"An espionage deal? Who is he, and what can he do for us?"

"He is enlisting in the Canadian Army and he is going to Korea where he will be privy to military secrets."

"What kind of military secrets?"

"That will depend on how far he is able to penetrate. He is joining the Fusiliers, one of the regiments being sent to Korea. His rank has not been established, but it appears that he will be offered a commission. He has had previous military training and experience. If he can get into battalion headquarters, or even into a company command position, all kinds of important information may be available."

"Like what?"

"Like the names of units in the front line, their locations, strengths and weaknesses."

"How will he be able to pass on this information?"

"We are going to train him. Radio contacts may be possible. There are substantial numbers of Koreans with communist sympathies acting as our agents among American and South Korean forces. Some will offer their services to the Canadians as soon as they arrive. He should be able to establish contacts with these agents. To some extent, the conflict in Korea is a civil war. Koreans from two sides of the political spectrum are fighting each other, in some cases brother against brother. It is a brutal conflict."

"Who are these agents? Where do they come from?"

"They are simply Koreans who work as porters or servants. The Americans, I believe, call them houseboys. Our Koreans, naturally, are indistinguishable from their Koreans, and they are able to pass back and forth through the front lines rather easily. The most valuable ones speak English, but facility in that language is not essential. They can pass on written messages for someone else to translate."

"Forgive me, comrade," said Zinoviev, "but I am not very familiar with this kind of espionage. Is this a standard tactic? Has anyone done it before?"

"Frequently!" Rykov responded emphatically. "We often

talked about it at the Frunze Military Academy. Don't you remember? For instance, our own corrupt Czarist army was infested with German spies during the Great War of 1914 to 1918. Many historians believe that our heavy losses in that conflict were a direct result of enemy espionage."

"Is the Canadian politically motivated? Why is he willing to do this? Does he understand the dangers that are involved?"

"His motivation, comrade, is money. I have already given him $5,000, along with a promise of a lot more once he performs. $5,000 is equivalent to about three years of salary for the average Canadian. Naturally, we would like to think that he has communist sympathies, but it really does not matter. He is already trapped. We can ruin his whole life by tipping off the Canadian authorities, and he knows it."

"I hope that you are right, comrade," Zinoviev said with a sigh. "We need all the help we can get. The Americans are rushing large numbers of troops, planes and warships to Korea. They have intimidated a lot of other countries such as Britain, Australia, New Zealand, Greece and Turkey into joining under the so-called United Nations. Their Canadian lackeys are also going to help them. Canada is not a real country. It is an American colony. I don't think that our Soviet forces will be directly involved, but who knows? We may be back in Moscow sooner than we think!"

CHAPTER 8
ORDERS FROM THE CHIEF OF STAFF

Lieutenant-Colonel James Strange marched into the Ottawa office of the Canadian Army's Chief of the General Staff. He saluted and smiled. "Strange reporting once more as requested!" he exclaimed somewhat awkwardly. He was an outstanding officer, but was not known for his social graces.

General Charles Foulkes, a distinguished looking officer, rose from behind his desk and held out his hand. After shaking hands with Strange, Foulkes sat down again. Foulkes, like Strange, was an English immigrant to Canada. He was born at Stockton-on-Tees in northeastern England. He joined the Canadian Army in 1926, and was a major in the Royal Canadian Regiment when WWII started in 1939. He rose rapidly through the ranks, became a general and was appointed the Chief of the General Staff in 1946.

"Sit down, Jim," the General said. "Relax and make yourself comfortable. How was the trip? I'm sorry that I had to call you to Ottawa again."

"To tell the truth, our C-47 Dakota ran into some stormy weather over Lake Superior. It was very rough indeed. I almost became ill. That wouldn't do, would it? We have to set an example for those under our command, don't we?"

Strange felt very comfortable with Foulkes. Unlike many Englishmen, Foulkes was without affectations. He judged men on the basis of ability, merit and achievements rather than inherited social class.

"I've got a very busy schedule, Jim. I hope that you don't mind if we get right down to business. As you know, you and your Fusiliers are heading to Korea very soon. However, before you go, I've got to give you some very important information. It's something that you are going to have to keep to yourself. You can't even share it with your closest colleagues. This is top secret. That's why I decided not to phone or write. I did not want to take any chances."

"It sounds intriguing. I hope that I can handle it," Strange responded. A smile crossed his face.

"Essentially, my information is that you may have a spy in your midst. In other words, an enemy agent may have infiltrated your ranks. It is possible that one of your officers or men is working for the Soviet Union."

"That's absolutely shocking!" Strange exclaimed. "How do you know? And if there is a spy, why don't you arrest him?"

"Because we don't know who he is," the General replied matter-of-factly.

"Then why do you believe that a spy actually exists? Perhaps it's only a figment of someone's imagination."

"No, it's more than that. Ilya Zinoviev, an NKVD agent working as an assistant press secretary in the Soviet Embassy, defected to us a short while ago. He was very cooperative and gave us a lot of information about Russian operations in Canada."

"Then he must have told you about the spy," Strange interjected excitedly. "But didn't he give you a name? How do you know his information is reliable?"

"We cross-examined him thoroughly," the Chief of Staff replied. "We are convinced that he is telling the truth. He does not know the name of the spy. Another NKVD agent, Nicholai Rykov, told him that someone was joining the Fusiliers, but no name was mentioned. It was apparently just a casual conversation between two friends, both of whom had attended the same military academy in Moscow."

"Where is Rykov now? Is he still in Ottawa?"

"No. He is gone. Within hours after the defection of Zinoviev, Moscow cleaned out their nasty nest in Ottawa. Several officials, including Rykov, were promptly flown back to Russia. However, there is still some uncertainty."

"Uncertainty?"

"Yes. We don't know if this alleged spy has actually joined the Fusiliers. It may be that this is a planted distraction. Maybe Rykov was purposely feeding Zinoviev a false message. Perhaps he was just boasting or exaggerating while under the influence of alcohol."

"So we have a serious situation," Strange said quietly. "I may or may not have an enemy agent in my ranks, but I don't even know where to begin looking."

"Exactly," the General responded, "and you can't confide in a single soul. All of your officers and senior NCOs are suspects. Don't trust anyone. You will have to carry on an ongoing investigation on your own. Moreover, you can't be too obvious. If the enemy agent finds out that you are suspicious, or on to something, he will lay very low and be doubly careful."

"Do you know anything about him?" Strange asked. He looked perplexed and angry.

"We know that he is a Canadian," the General replied calmly. "He has apparently received an initial payment of $5,000 for his services, but he may have some political motivation as well. He has had some military experience and is probably a captain or major. If a spy with the rank of major exists he will likely have access to communications, to data on troop strengths, reserves, the names of units, their commanding officers and their positions in the front line."

"How do you know that I'm not the one?" Strange suddenly blurted out. "Maybe you are also suspicious of me!"

The General smiled and placed his hand gently on Strange's shoulder. "Jim," he said, "I don't blame you for being angry. This situation is frustrating for everyone. As a matter of fact, we did check you out. We had to be absolutely certain."

"In that case, how do you know that I am not the spy?" Strange asked.

"Because you have not been spending or depositing unusual amounts of money, and especially because you have been stationary in Vancouver for more than a year. The RCMP were suspicious of Rykov for a long time. They trailed him to several Canadian cities, but Vancouver was one city that he did not visit."

"I'm very relieved to hear that I am not under suspicion as a spy!" Strange exclaimed with a chortle.

"Rykov traveled as far west as Calgary, and as far east as Halifax. He was supposed to be doing research on Canadian agriculture and the fishing industry."

"Some research!" Strange said.

"Yes, research indeed. Naturally, I was very distressed over this situation," he continued. "We even thought of having you and your Fusiliers replaced by another unit. But it was just a momentary thought. Obviously, we can't keep our best infantry battalion out of action. The others are not ready and need a lot more training. And besides, we have to find this spy, if he exists, and bring him to justice. That won't happen if he remains in Canada. Korea is the only place he can be discovered."

"I understand, sir," Strange replied. "I don't think that you have any other alternative."

"I'm going to send you over to our intelligence headquarters right away," said the General. "They will spend the rest of the day and maybe tomorrow with you. Some RCMP espionage experts will also be present to give advice. I want them to give you a thorough briefing on all of the basic elements of espionage so that you will be prepared for any eventuality, and so that you will know how to set traps."

"I'm pleased to hear that," Strange said. "I've certainly never been involved in anything like this before."

"One final thing before you go, Jim. If you do find this traitor, and if you are absolutely sure of his guilt, you should consider the possibility of putting him away immediately. In my personal and unquotable opinion, an execution in the field is preferable to a messy court martial. You know, of course, that commanding officers have the legal authority to shoot deserters, and especially traitors, in the field. This conversation is off the record. Just do what you need to do."

"I understand and agree completely," Strange responded. "Perhaps I should not say so, but I do not have much faith in military justice. I am reminded of the case of Kurt Meyer, the German general who sanctioned the execution of 18 Canadian soldiers near Caen, France, in June, 1944."

"We all remember him. He is now free and living somewhere in Germany."

"That's outrageous. After the war he was sentenced to be shot by firing squad, but his sentence was commuted to life imprisonment. I will never forget this travesty of justice. Someone should have shot him after he was captured. I would have happily pulled the trigger on that bastard if I had been given the opportunity."

The General did not respond except to say "good luck, Jim." An intelligence corps corporal entered the room and said "this way, sir. My major is expecting you."

Strange saluted the General, turned, and marched out of the room.

CHAPTER 9
MORGAN'S COVE

Many of the Canadian Army volunteers for the Korean War Special Force came from the maritime and prairie provinces, areas of high unemployment. Jim Doherty in Newfoundland, like Peter Farley in Manitoba, was adventurous, curious about the distant places of the world, and without a job.

It was a cloudy morning in August, 1950 when Doherty walked along the rocky shore towards his home, a weather-beaten unpainted shanty near the south end of Morgan's Cove in Newfoundland. The familiar smell of cod and tarred fishing nets penetrated his nostrils. His mother, a sturdy, muscular woman with graying blonde hair, waited near the door. His two brothers and three sisters, all younger, all fair-haired, stood nearby with open mouths and misty eyes.

"Well, Jim, me b'y, what's they say? Is there any word on yer father?" his mother Martha asked with a shaking voice.

"Ma, it don' look too good," Jim replied in a husky voice.

"There ain't no sign of the schooner. She's been gone for four days. Kennedy says it's not likely she'll return. 'Tis not what you want to hear, I knows."

His sisters began wailing. His brothers let out sobs and desperately tried not to cry. Tears began running down his mother's face, but she showed no other signs of emotion. "Come inside, me children," she said, "it's time t' eat."

They all filed into a tiny green coloured kitchen where a kerosene lamp was burning in the semi-darkness. The smell of frying bologna filled the air. Beets and potatoes boiled in pots on a small wood-burning stove. A white porcelain water jug and basin stood on a small table on one corner. They took turns washing hands, with the youngest washing first.

They sat on the two long sides of a wooden table, except Martha, their mother, who began serving the beets, potatoes and bologna. Before they began eating they bowed their heads and she uttered a brief and impromptu prayer. "Lord Jesus," she said, "bless this food and help me husband and their father. My Jesus, we needs him. Tis getting late and I s'pose they may all be gone now. We ain't ungrateful, though dear Lord, 'cause we knows that he may be in a better place."

The girls began sobbing again, and the second oldest male of the family, Jack, a handsome boy of twelve, covered his face with his hands.

A large brown dog sat beside Jim and happily wagged his tail. "I am going to miss you," Jim said. He loved his dog. He felt tears coming to his eyes but resisted the urge to let them flow. Men in the Doherty family, and indeed in all of Newfoundland, were not allowed to show emotion, a sign of weakness. Only girls and women were permitted to cry. "Don't worry, I will be back," he said in a forced strong voice. He looked at Jack, who sat next to him. "Jack, look after Rover for me while I am away."

"I will," Jack said. He covered his face with his hands once again.

"Let's get goin' and eat," Jim continued. "There ain't nothin' to cry about. The good Lord has a plan for all of us, including our father. "Tis the way it is. Right, Ma?" He smiled, suddenly realizing that he was now the man of the family, the oldest male Doherty in Morgan's Cove.

"Ma," Jim continued. "I have to tell you that I have joined the army. The Canadian Army, 'tis. I did it when I went to see Uncle Arnold in Ottawa last week."

"My God! The army!" his mother exclaimed with shock. "The Canadian Army? Why we have only been in Canada for about a year and they are already takin' my son. I tells you, I can't weep no more. I'm losin' everythin'."

"You ain't lost me," Jim replied softly. "Ma, I'll be gettin' a 100 dollars a month clear, and I'll be sendin' you half of that. I don't want to be a fisherman like me father and me grandfather."

"But yer uncle Arnold is a radical trouble-maker and a communist. How did he get you into the army?"

"Uncle Arnold never helped me when I joined the army. He sent me fer a job, but there ain't any in Ottawa. Not for Newfies, there ain't. I joined to get a job."

"Where will ye live"? his mother asked.

"There's no army in St. John's," he replied. I'm goin' to Calgary in the West. I will go to Korea later after I'm trained."

"Korea? Where's that?"

"Tis a country, Ma. 'Tis a country close to Japan and China."

"Korea? Why Korea?"

"The Koreans want our help. We needs the money to live, Ma. You and me brothers and sisters. Our Pa is gone. I'm leavin' in the morning." He handed her five 10 dollar bills.

She took the money reluctantly. "Jim, me b'y, this is a lot of money. Where did you get it?"

"Never mind, Ma. I've got to get packed to leave in the morning'"

"All right, me son. I'll trust ye to God. 'Tis time fer a change in our lives. Children, finish yer eatin'. Kiss yer brother. He's leavin' in the morning' fer Calgary and Korea. My b'y is goin' to be a man."

CHAPTER 10
THE TOWN OF SWEET GRASS

Peter Farley returned home to Sweet Grass in late August, 1950 on a two week embarkation leave. Before leaving for Korea he was able to briefly visit the Sweet Grass Ukrainian Summer School, and more importantly, to serve as best man at the wedding of his cousin and namesake, Peter Farley.

When the Government of Canada decided to send armed forces to fight in Korea in 1950, its officials realized that many recruits like Peter Farley would come from small towns in various parts of Canada, and especially from the prairie and maritime provinces where jobs were scarce. Small town Canadians, at mid-century, was still living marginal lives without the benefits that would come in later decades. Television was in its early stages and did not appear in most homes until the mid-1950's. People listened to their radios. Running water and indoor toilets existed only in the homes of the relatively wealthy. Homes were heated by wood and coal burning stoves. Streets were unpaved. Incomes were low. Young men and women, even if academically talented, often left school in the eighth, ninth or tenth grades to work on the railways, farms or factories if they lived in central and western Canada, or on fishing boats and in fish plants if they lived in the Maritime provinces.

Sweet Grass was a typical in many ways, not only of the prairies, but of Canadian towns in all parts of Canada. In August it sat serenely in its full green and flowery mid-summer glory, its gravel streets lined with large Manitoba maples. It was located on a large plateau adjoining the nearby Little Saskatoon River and in the middle of a grain-growing area. Most of the people were of English or Scottish origin and had arrived from southern Ontario early in the century to work on the Canadian National Railway, and especially after Sweet Grass became an important railway divisional point with maintenance facilities. There were also significant numbers of Ukrainian, Polish and Irish newcomers, most of whom worked as section labourers on the railway.

Farley arrived from the west on the daily "Transcontinental" passenger train. He was happily greeted by his father Orest, his dog Fido, and his horse Charlie, who was hitched to the Orest Farley's two seated buggy.

Trains usually stopped for 15 minutes at the station on the main track, and many of its passengers strolled along the long, oiled wooden platform that adjoined the station and track. The delicious aroma of fresh coffee wafted from the station restaurant. A conductor and a trainman, both Anglo-Saxon in appearance, moved back and forth between the train and the station, their neat and clean uniforms contrasting sharply with the grimy and humble attire of the large Ukrainians in the nearby cinder pit. Many of the town's children walked with curiosity among the strolling passengers. When they saw Peter many rushed over and greeted him.

"Welcome home!" several yelled.

"I like your uniform," a young boy exclaimed. "I wish I could join the army and go to Korea."

Peter smiled and waved. "Thanks everyone! It's good to be home," he said.

School was out for the summer. "Meeting the train" was the most exciting daily event in town because it enabled the locals to catch glimpses of the exotic and prosperous-looking strangers as they passed through on their way to other parts of Canada and the world, places that most of the town's children had never seen. All the passengers seemed to smoke and they dropped cigarette butts, empty packages and match covers without any concern for tidiness or the environment. Collecting match covers from exotic locales from the railway platform was an interesting hobby for the town's young people, and even for some adults.

Peter looked wistfully as the three tall, white grain elevators rose majestically along the main railway track on the east side of town. A flock of pigeons circled overhead, waiting impatiently for the arrival of farmers' wagons and the inevitable small spillages of grain on the ground. They were hungry and he wished that he could stop and feed them.

Flowing swiftly along the eastern edge of the town, and in a deep valley, was the Little Saskatoon River, where a horde of teen-agers splashed happily. It had rained a lot during the spring and summer of 1950, and the river was unusually high. The young swimmers, however, were completely at ease, for they had spent every summer paddling in the river beginning at early ages. They had learned to swim without adult supervision or training of any kind. Peter Farley had spent many happy hours at this place.

Sweet Grass consisted of five streets running north and south and six avenues running east and west, with none more than a mile in length. Most houses were small bungalows with three or four rooms, although several larger, turn-of-the-century brick and stone structures similar to those found in southern Ontario were randomly situated in various parts of the town. These relatively affluent homes were mostly owned by prosperous businessmen with English or Scottish backgrounds.

Main Street accommodated most of the town's business establishments, and included three general stores, a telephone office, a movie theatre, a butcher shop, a building containing the office and printing presses of the Sweet Grass Gazette, a post office, a pool room, three service stations, a hockey arena, a curling rink, a bank, and a Ukrainian Hall.

Sitting next to post office was a white statue of a soldier in the uniform of the First World War, with names of 30 soldiers who had perished from 1914 to 1918 and a further 20 from the Second World War engraved on the base. The Korean War was next. Would any additional names be added at the end of this distant conflict? The members of the Canadian Legion and Anavets often asked this question.

As they passed Sweet Grass High School Peter experienced many fond memories. He especially recalled the exciting weekend he had spent with his mathematics teacher, Michelle Brown, three years earlier. She was his first love. As they passed the green bungalow at the west end of 6th Street where she had lived he wondered who resided there now. *"Where does she live? Somewhere in the United States? Is she happy and healthy? Does she miss me?"* he asked himself.

CHAPTER 11
THE SWEET GRASS UKRAINIAN
SUMMER SCHOOL

Father John Boleschuk was giving his final standard anti-Communist lecture at the Sweet Grass Ukrainian Catholic Summer School. He was a short, stocky, middle-aged man with balding sandy hair and large brown eyes. His 25 pupils, ranging in age from 10 years to 17 years, sat sweltering in the oppressive heat of the Ukrainian Hall, anxiously awaiting the conclusion of the annual summer session. Boleschuk's lecture was too advanced for many of them, but they sat quietly and listened. As usual, it had been a long and exhausting month, with the Father making extraordinary academic demands of his young charges.

"I want you to always remember," Boleschuk said in Ukrainian, *"that it was the Muscovite Communists that orchestrated the Great Famine in Ukraine in the 1930's in which about six million of our people died. These same atheists abolished our Ukrainian Catholic Church in western Ukraine, sent our priests*

and bishops to Siberia, and in some cases even executed them. Fortunately, I was able to escape to Austria, and then to Canada shortly after the war ended in 1945. We should all consider our-selves to be fortunate to live in Canada where we can live in peace and freedom, and where we can practice our religion without per-secution. But although the Russian and Ukrainian Communists are evil and anti-religious, we should not hate them. Our savior, the Lord Jesus Christ, told us to love our enemies and to pray for those who persecute us. After all, we learn certain things as children, including social attitudes, religious beliefs and philoso-phies of life. If some Ukrainians in the Soviet Union, and a few in Canada, are atheistic communists, we should forgive them. Conditions were harsh in Canada and the United States during the 1930's, and as a result, some academics and workers, includ-ing some Ukrainians turned to communism or socialism. They were wrong, but it not for us to pass judgment on them. One day they will answer to God. Nevertheless, as Christian Catholics, we must maintain the right of all people to express themselves politi-cally and economically in free societies. The highly-structured, inflexible system of the Soviet Union produces poor economic performance as well as hostility to our Catholic religion and indeed all religions. "

Sitting at the back of the room were two former summer school students, Peter Farley and Sonia Kereliuk, both of whom had attended these summer sessions in previous years. They had been invited as special guests for this final lesson in the summer of 1950, mainly because Father Boleschuk wanted them to serve as inspirations for his current students.

Peter Farley, with his light red hair, green eyes and freckles did not look like a typical Ukrainian. His companion, also of Ukrainian ancestry, was a strikingly beautiful girl with dark hair and brown eyes. Both were 19 years old.

Farley hated Father's repetitive and boring lectures even

though, unlike many of the others, he understood and remembered them completely. He had a photographic memory. He was an outstanding student in his regular high school classes as well as the Ukrainian summer school. He was proud of the fact that he was able to express himself with considerable fluency in the language of his Ukrainian ancestors. Although he sometimes complained to his Baba, his father's mother, about having to attend summer schools, he realized that his attendance meant a great deal to his father as well as Baba.

"Now, children," Father Boleschuk said with a clap of his hands, "you are almost free to go! Remember all of the things that you have been taught over the past four weeks, and don't forget to keep up with your Ukrainian reading. You have been a good class. Tell your parents how much you have enjoyed yourselves, and about how much you now know about our Ukrainian language, culture and Catholic faith. Jesus loves you, and wants you to come back next summer. We also have a winter school and I hope to see you then. God bless all of you! Goodbye! You are dismissed!"

Boleschuk made the sign of the cross and turned to Peter Farley and Sonia Kereliuk. "My children!" he exclaimed affectionately. "How good it is to have you back again!"

"Thank you, Father," Sonia replied. "I can see that your classes are as lively as usual!" She smiled sheepishly, hoping that he would not be offended by her teasing remark.

Boleschuk also smiled. "Of course," he said, "some of them are a bit exuberant at times, but no more so than the two of you. Do you remember Peter, when you were about 10 years old, that I had to switch your behind for talking too much in class?"

"Yes," Peter said. "I admit to being a rascal. But I did learn a lot of Ukrainian. I also got the strap several times when I was in the early grades in our English school." The wooden switch and leather strap were painful memories, but he felt curiously detached, without any kind of resentment towards his stern mentors. "You told me, Father, that I was probably bad because of my red hair."

"Ah, yes, your red hair," Father said with a sigh. "I wasn't serious. I was simply expressing an old Ukrainian superstition about red-headed people. Ukrainians, in the old days at least, believed that redness was a sign of wickedness. My youngest sister, for instance, had red hair, and our mother shaved it off several times, hoping that it would grow back into a different colour. Of course, it never did."

"That reminds me of something," Peter said seriously. "Now that I am an adult and have attended some pre-medical classes at the University of Manitoba, I would like to ask you a question that has been on my mind for a long time. I have been wondering, for some time now, as to whether or not we dwell too much on the things of the past, on events that happened in Ukraine, rather than those that occurred in Canada. Should we not forget about the superstitions, evils and wounds of our mother country? Are we not living in a new world and under different circumstances?"

Father Boleschuk frowned sternly. His eyes glistened with emotion as he collected his thoughts. He had never considered Peter's question before, and was at a temporary loss for words. "What did I tell you about red hair?" he finally responded with mock seriousness. "Where is my switch? That's not a proper question!"

"But Father," Sonia interjected I have asked myself the same thing, and my hair is quite dark, as you can see!" She laughed nervously, once again hoping that Boleschuk would not be offended.

Rather than respond directly to Farley's question Boleschuk gave another speech.

"*Of course, you were both born in Canada and will never be able to understand the feelings and emotions of those, like me, who grew up in the old country. In fact, those of us that came to Canada after the Second World War even think much differently than those who arrived at the turn of the century. The original Ukrainian pioneers, with some exceptions, were uneducated peasants with no knowledge of communism, and no strong feelings towards the Soviet Union which didn't even exist until after 1917. The famine of the 1930's in Ukraine was covered up by the Soviets and the rest of the world did not know about it until many years later. On the other hand, the Ukrainians who came to Canada after 1945 tended to be well-educated and proud tradesmen and professionals with very powerful anti-communist sentiments as well as intense loyalty towards their enslaved Ukraine. Don't forget that all national groups that come to Canada act in much the same way. English, Irish, Scottish, Italian and Greek people also retain bonds with their homelands. But perhaps you are right! It is possible that we should concentrate on being good Canadians rather than disgruntled and bitter immigrants from England, Ireland, Scotland, Italy, Greece and Ukraine. On the other hand, won't we be better Canadians if we remember where we came from, where we have been, and especially if we retain all of the unique things that we have to offer Canada?"*

"Father," Peter said with a warm chuckle, "you've never made that speech before! "

"No," Father replied, "but it's a good one! As a matter of fact, I like it so much that I will probably use it in next year's summer school. Won't you both come again?"

Although Farley had expressed some reservations about Father Boleschuk's preoccupation with Ukraine, he strongly agreed that communism was an evil ideology. His decision to join the army and go to Korea was made, to a considerable extent, because of Father Boleschuk's lectures as well as his extensive reading of history.

CHAPTER 12
THE WEDDING

The Holy Ghost Ukrainian Catholic Church stood in a grove of tall poplars at the western edge of the town of Sweet Grass, its golden, onion-shaped dome shining in the bright August sun. In a clearing at the rear of the church irregular rows of large and small crosses and tombstones protruded awkwardly out of the ground, marking the resting places of the parish's faithful deceased. The smaller crosses designated the graves of children or of the less affluent departed, or in some cases, simply those who had been given more modest markers. Large crosses and tombstones appeared only occasionally, their graves containing the remains of the community's leaders, or at least those who had been honoured with more expensive memorials.

A gravel road ran past the front of the church, its sides marked by deep ditches filled with water, bulrushes, saskatoon and chokecherry bushes. Parked on the right side of the road was a row of automobiles, most of them of 1930's vintage. A few newer models built in the 1940's were also present, their shiny chromium bumpers and streamlined bodies gleaming in sharp contrast to the older Model A's and T's. Several horses attached to buggies were tethered to fence posts.

It was hot and humid inside the church, where a large crowd of sweating and bronzed men, women and children witnessed the wedding of Peter Farley and Rosalie Prokopchuk. The air reeked of burning incense, its sweet, spicy smell penetrating the nostrils of those present. Icons of Jesus, Mary and traditional religious scenes covered the front of the church and the iconostas, a beautiful wooden screen that separated the altar from the pews and people. Two altar boys served the priest, their flaxen hair and white, embroidered robes contrasting sharply with their deep summer tans. The congregation was on its knees, making the sign of the cross.

"Let us be attentive! Holy things to the holy," Father John Boleschuk, the Ukrainian Catholic priest intoned.

"One is holy; one is Lord, Jesus Christ, for the glory of God, the Father, amen. O Lord, I believe and profess that you are truly Christ, the son of the living God, who came into the world to save sinners, of whom I am the first. Accept me as a partaker of your mystical supper, O Son of God, for I will not reveal your mystery to your enemies, nor will I give you a kiss as did Judas, but like the thief I say to you: Remember me Lord when you come into your Kingdom; remember me O Master when you come into your Kingdom; remember me O Holy One when you come into your Kingdom. May the partaking of your holy mysteries, O Lord, be not for my judgment or condemnation, but for the healing of my soul and body. O God, be merciful to me a sinner. O God, cleanse me of my sins and have mercy on me. I have sinned very often; forgive me, O Lord."

The bride and groom rose and came forward to receive communion, the bread and wine of the Eucharist. They were followed in a single file by the wedding party, their relatives and the rest of the congregation. The communicants made the sign of the cross after they received the bread and the wine in their mouths, and then returned to their seats. Many of the older people kissed a glass-covered icon near the iconostas.

The three-day Ukrainian wedding had started on Saturday, the previous day, when Rosalie Prokopchuk's wreath was made from myrtle and ribbon by her two bridesmaids. Musicians played, and there was dancing and singing by the young people of the town and district. On Sunday morning, Rosalie was dressed for church. In keeping with Ukrainian custom, before leaving for the religious ceremony her parents were seated in their home, a loaf of bread on the lap of each. Rosalie bowed three times to each of her parents, kissing the loaves held by her father and mother, who gave her their blessings. Then she and the members of her wedding party got into horse-drawn buggies and drove to church. Now, at last, the long religious ceremony was over, and they were married.

The wedding celebration continued at the nearby parish hall. The bride, groom, their parents, best man and bridesmaids stood in a reception line near the entrance. An accordion player, fiddler and drummer played the *Ukrainian Wedding March* as each group of guests entered. Coins were tossed into one of the musician's hats. Tears were shed copiously as the members of the wedding party embraced the incoming guests.

The dinner began with Father Boleschuk's blessing. Huge quantities of borsch, garlic sausage, perogies, potatoes, corn, peas, cabbage buns and dark rye bread crowded several large tables. The conversations became increasingly loud and excited, the celebrants steadily consuming large quantities of "hooree-wka" a powerful homemade whiskey contained in large milk cans. Outside, at a number of strategic locations, several men were posted to warn against the possible arrival of the Royal

Canadian Mounted Police, who occasionally raided Ukrainian wedding parties to enforce the liquor laws. A number of small children amused themselves by running around the hall.

Sitting at the head table was the other Peter Farley, the best man, cousin and namesake of the groom. Next to him was Sonia Kereliuk, one of the bridesmaids, the strikingly beautiful young woman who a few days earlier had visited with Peter at the Ukrainian Summer School. Unlike the groom, who was dressed in a blue suit, the best man wore the khaki battledress of the Canadian Army.

A series of speeches commenced, with most of the speakers reminiscing about the early lives of the bride and groom. After Peter Farley, the best man, had spoken, his father Orest rose to speak. He was a huge man with red hair, hazel eyes and with solid muscle packed onto his 6 feet, 6 inches.

"I want to speak about my nephew Peter," Orest said. He had a slight Ukrainian accent and a booming baritone voice. "Peter, the one just married, was born a year before my Peter. His father and me both wanted to call our sons Peter. His Peter came first, but I said what the hell, I'll call mine Peter also. There is a difference. My Peter's second name is Orest, and his cousin's second name is Dmetro. I am proud of my son. He going to Korea to fight evil communism. That's what Father Boleschuk calls it, and I feel the same." He raised his glass of hooreewka and said: "Everyone stand up. We now going to toast the two Peters." Everyone rose. "To our two Peters," Orest said after which he threw back and swallowed his full glass.

"Why are you wearing that uniform?" Sonia quietly asked Peter. There was a trace of annoyance in her voice.

"My father insisted that I wear it," he responded. "He is proud of the fact that I am going to provide a service to Canada. Actually, he has mixed feelings. He is worried and wonders why I have joined, but he is also proud."

"Why are you going to Korea? I love you, Peter, " Sonia continued, her voice betraying deep disappointment and betrayal. "I thought that you were going to be a medical doctor, and that I was going to help you through school by becoming a teacher. You said that we would probably marry."

"Yes, but I am worried about marriage. You probably remember that my father spent about a year in the mental hospital several years ago. They told him that he had schizophrenia. He seems to have recovered completely, but a relapse is always possible. I know that I am mentally healthy, but I am worried that I may be carrying genes for this illness. I don't want to pass it on to any children that I may have."

"I am willing to take a chance, Peter. I love you. We can adopt children if you do not want to have any of your own."

"I love you too, Sonia, but we are still very young. I am not ready to settle down. I did not realize how expensive things are in Winnipeg and at the University of Manitoba. I've run out of money. I actually found the first two years of pre- medicine to be relatively easy. One of my professors told me that I seem to have a photographic memory. That's an accurate observation. "

"Yes, I know it's true!" she interjected. "You do remember everything!"

"After I read a page once or twice I can recall and understand its contents completely even a week or two or a month later," he continued. "I even remember and can recite Father Boleschuk's lectures almost word for word! But money is a problem. You know that my father's crop was hailed out in June. He has been working on the railway extra gang fixing tracks, but he certainly can't help me financially at this time."

"What about your father's store? Isn't he making any money there?"

"All of the other farmers also have had crop losses. They just don't have as much money to spend this year."

"But you have helped a lot."

"I did while I was home. But remember that I was in Winnipeg for the best part of two years."

"Where are your brothers now? I don't hear much about them."

"They are in Vancouver now. They could not stand the cold, the dust and the flatness of the prairies, or so they said. They have gone to Lotus Land. They have made a lot of money in the construction business and real estate. They loaned my father the money he needed to buy the store, but my father is disappointed with them. He says they are English now. I could have asked them to lend me money, but I decided against it. I am too proud, I guess."

"I could have helped you go to the university. I'm going to be teaching at a one room school in Minnewawa at the beginning of September. I got my teaching permit in the mail on Friday. I'll be getting $800 for the year."

"Thanks, Sonia, but it's too late now. I can't get out of the army. They will find me and put me in jail if I don't show up. I'm in the Special Force for 18 months."

Tears began running down Sonia's cheeks. "You are a fool," she said angrily. "I have been reading about the war in Korea. The Americans are dying by the thousands. Why are you going there? No one understands what this war is all about."

"We are going there to help the people of Korea from being conquered and oppressed by a communist dictatorship. Actually, Sonia, I also have a hidden, selfish motive. You may recall that the veterans who returned from the last war in the years after 1945 were able to use their war credits to attend courses at the universities."

"Who paid for their educations?"

The Department of Veterans' Affairs very generously paid for their educations. It seems highly likely, I think, that they will do the same thing for me after I return from Korea."

"If you return from Korea," she sobbed.

"We are going to fight communism," he continued. "Haven't you been listening to Father Boleschuk's sermons? The communists are evil and have to be stopped."

"I guess I should have married your cousin, the other Peter Farley, when I had the chance."

"Why didn't you?"

"He asked me, but I did not love him."

"Do you still love me?"

"What does it matter? I'd probably be a widow within a few months!" she burst out resentfully. Then a feeling of regret for her words overcame her, and she ran from the table crying.

An old woman with graying red hair came up to Peter and sat in Sonia's seat. She wore a flowered print dress and a green shawl. It was Maria Farley, his father's mother, the woman who had helped to raise him. "My son," she said in Ukrainian, "you should not make Sonia cry. She loves you. She is a lovely Ukrainian girl and would make you a fine wife."

"Yes, Baba," Peter replied in Ukrainian. "I know. Maybe I will marry her one day. But right now I'm in the army and I can't afford a wife."

"I'm worried," Baba said with a frown. "Stay away from those English girls when you are in the army. They are all spoiled, and certainly don't know anything about our religion, language and customs."

"But my father married an English girl. Actually my mother's father was Scottish and her mother was English. Doesn't that make me partly English and Scottish as well as Ukrainian?"

"Yes, your mother was English and Scottish and so are you, at least partly. Your mother was different. I loved her as I would my own daughter. She tried to be Ukrainian and even learned a lot of our language."

"But my mother's parents did not like Ukrainians."

"Her parents did not want her to marry your father because, in their eyes, he was a foreigner with a funny accent. She married your father, in spite of her parents, because she had an independent spirit and she loved him. Your mother was very intelligent and a good Catholic."

"Don't worry, Baba", he said with a laugh. "There are no English girls in Korea. Only Koreans!"

"Well, stay away from them too."

"I will Baba", he said, but he felt guilty in making this promise. He found it difficult to remain faithful to one woman. He had always felt a very strong attraction to beautiful women, and in his earlier years he sometimes believed that he was in love with more than one woman at a time. At the age of six he fell in love with Rhonda Smith, his vivacious Grade 1 teacher. He wrote beautiful Martha Young, his Grade 3 teacher, a poem about his love and she liked it so much that she cried. That experience made him think that he might like to be a poet one day. Over the years he fell in love with several pretty young girls, his classmates, at the Sweet Grass School. He fell in love quickly and easily. He had been sexually aroused on many occasions, and still vividly remembered his first sexual experience with his teacher, Michele Brown, at the age of 16.

The wedding reception continued after the dinner, with the three musicians playing traditional Ukrainian music, including *Our Kolymayka*, the *Bride and Groom Waltz* and the *Natalka Polka*. Dancing continued until midnight, when the "presentation" began. The wedding party stood at the head table while the guests came forward to present envelopes containing money for the newly-weds. Men and women, the young and the old, the guests and members of the wedding party all hugged and kissed, and many cried with deep emotion. In the meantime, the band played traditional Ukrainian presentation music. After all the guests had given their gifts of money, the men in the wedding party grabbed the groom by the ankles and held him high in the air, ostensibly to relieve him of all the money in his pockets. It was a symbolic gesture. He would soon be poor, with a wife and children to support. Following this pocket-emptying ceremony, the groom was tossed into the air several times.

As all of these high-spirited activities were going on, the crowd formed a semi-circle around the participants. Peter Farley, the cousin of the groom, stood away from the others. He felt depressed, with his mind alternating between the recent words of Sonia and Baba. Sonia saw him at a distance and moved towards him. She took his hand firmly, but with tenderness.

"I'm sorry, Peter", she said softly, "I hope that I did not embarrass you."

"I'm sorry too," he replied with a sudden smile.

"Are you staying for the rest of the wedding celebration on Monday?"

"I can't. My train leaves for Alberta tomorrow at noon. We will probably be there for a while before we leave for Fort Lewis in Washington, and then Korea."

"I'll write to you if you like," Sonia said hopefully.

"Yes, please do. I'm going to miss you. I hope that you like teaching. I don't ever remember having a pretty teacher like you. They were mostly ugly English girls, as my Baba would say. Be careful. Don't let the big boys walk over you." He suddenly remembered his love for his beautiful teachers, and especially Michelle Brown. He thought briefly about correcting himself, but decided against it.

"I will miss you too, Sonia. I am also going to miss Billie, Fido, and Charlie."

"I don't know if I should laugh or cry, Peter," Sonia said with a sigh. "Will you miss them more than me? They are only animals. You know that I hate cats, and that I am not enthusiastic about dogs and horses either. I'm sorry. That's just the way I am."

Peter did not reply. Sonia was very beautiful and intelligent, but her lack of affection for animals was a serious fault, at least in his mind.

The music started again. Peter and Sonia danced closely together until midnight. Then they slipped away unnoticed from the crowded and noisy hall. They walked to heavily wooded banks of the nearby Little Saskatoon River. They removed most of their clothes, swam briefly in the warm summer water.

"Peter," she said quietly as they sat on the river bank. "I want you to make love to me."

He waited for almost a minute before he answered her. "Sonia," he said. "I want to make love to you but I am afraid. What if you have a child and I am somewhere in Korea. Who will look after you? Who will look after our child?"

"Peter," she repeated. "I want you to make love to me."

He said nothing more and took her into his arms. He caressed and kissed her in all the most intimate parts of her beautiful body for several minutes, and then made love, in her case for the first time. It was a miraculous event that they would always remember.

Both suddenly realized and regretted that Peter would soon be gone and that they would not be together again for a long time, if ever. The guilt and fear would come later. They were Catholics and they knew that they had committed a sin, at least in the eyes of Father Boleschuk.

In the morning, before leaving for the railway station, Peter went home to say good bye to Billie, Fido, and Charlie. Billie rolled over on his back and began to purr loudly. Fido wagged his tail continuously and rubbed against Peter's legs. Charlie neighed happily as Peter approached and offered him several handfuls of clover, which he quickly devoured. Peter climbed on Charlie's back and rode around the farm yard for several minutes. Billie and Fido sat together and watched. He climbed off and gave Charlie a farewell hug. Charlie let out a snort of contentment.

"Billie, Fido and Charlie are all leading good lives," Peter told himself. *"Tato also loves them, and he will look after them if I don't return from Korea."* Tato was the Ukrainian name for father that he always used.

"But Tato is getting older. He is not in good health and will not always be here," his inner voice continued. *"Baba is even older and is indifferent to animals, and Sonia told me that she does not like cats. I don't know why Sonia does not like cats. Will we be able to compromise if we marry? I will always have a cat, and also probably a dog and a horse."*

Peter's father had purchased Charlie, a brown and white horse of a mixed breed, from a neighbouring farmer. Charlie's only duty was to pull a buggy from time to time, although Peter also rode him bareback occasionally. His father Orest was a very large and heavy man, and as a result, he never tried to ride Charlie. Charlie lived in a warm barn and was well fed and much loved.

Billie and Fido had both arrived at the Farley farm, of their own accord, in emaciated conditions from places unknown. They were quickly adopted and allowed to stay in the farm house.

Orest Farley, like his son Peter, was a lover of animals. He kept two cows for their milk, and several chickens for their eggs, but refused to kill any animals for their meat. Meat was available in the Farley household, but it was purchased from neighbours.

Peter Farley ate meat reluctantly, and in later years became a vegetarian. But he knew that cats and dogs were carnivores, and that they could not survive without meat. Life on this earth, he noted, had mysterious and contradictory qualities. He could, in keeping with his love of intelligent animals, stop eating their meat, but his cat and dog could not.

Billie, Fido and Charlie all loved Peter and Peter loved them. How would they manage without him? Peter asked himself. He felt guilty. Maybe going to the army and Korea was not such a good idea. These were his friends who needed his attention and human contact. Sonia, his father and Baba also loved and needed him, but they would be able to manage without him. Billie, Fido and Charlie would miss him the most.

Peter and Sonia returned to their homes and met again at the railway station later that morning. Their farewell kisses were much more passionate than those of the past. Her tears flowed again as the train pulled way, its mournful whistle howling over the loud chugging of its steam engine. He was on his way to Korea, the land of the morning calm.

CHAPTER 13
DISASTER AT THUNDER RIVER

After spending the months of September, October and most of
November 1950 training at Wainwright in Alberta, and Camp
Borden in Ontario, more than 5,000 newly recruited soldiers
of the Canadian Special Force were moved to Fort Lewis,
Washington, where arrangements had been made to train them
for the Korean War. A total of 22 trains eventually made their
way through the Canadian Rockies, but the last of them was
involved in a disastrous accident in which 21men died. Because
of a missed or incomplete communication, an express train col-
lided head on with the last of the troop trains. The last troop
train contained some of the officers and men of the Canadian
Fusiliers, a battalion that was scheduled to go to Korea in
late November.

One of the soldiers on the last train was Peter Farley. He
had been claustrophobic since early childhood and found the
cramped, cigarette smoke and body odour filled quarters of the

train's coaches to be very stressful. Fortunately, the last coach of the train to which he was assigned was a modern steel observation car, which had a rear exit and a small open-air platform with a railing. It reminded him of a similar observation car with an open air rear end enclosure that he had witnessed as a child in 1939 when King George VI had passed through Sweet Grass. The King, he remembered, traveled on a modern steel train and waved to the people from the rear of his observation coach. Peter escaped to this similar rear area often during the trip to Fort Lewis, and he happened to be standing there when the collision took place. He was hurled into the air for several feet and landed uninjured in a bank of deep snow. He watched with surreal shock and disbelief as the wooden coaches at the front of the train loudly disintegrated into thousands of splinters before his eyes.

The next several hours were filled with horror. Peter and other uninjured soldiers helped to remove the dead, dying and injured from the smashed coaches. Bodies of the living and the dead were laid out on top of snow banks. The injured were covered with blankets, but it was very cold and shock seriously affected many. It took several hours for rescuers to arrive, but eventually Peter and the other survivors were loaded onto another train. Those who were alive and uninjured continued their railway journey to Fort Lewis in modern steel coaches.

The collision of the two trains and the horrible aftermath affected Peter deeply. In the days that followed he often relived the experience, and in the nights that followed he had very disturbing dreams. He had survived and felt guilty and depressed. But he kept everything to himself. Soldiers were expected to be strong. Talking about his feelings would be a sign of weakness and he remained silent.

The coaches of all of the troop trains going to Fort Lewis had been constructed mainly in the 1890's and early 1900's. They had served as passenger conveyances prior to the 1930's, and had also been used to transport tens of thousands of European immigrants to the Canadian prairies. They were primitive, creaking hulks, constructed mainly of wood, unlike the steel cars used for passenger trains during the 1940's and 1950's. They had been sitting unused and in storage in railway yards since the 1930's.

The troop train disaster at Thunder River, British Columbia, was therefore made much worse by the flimsy nature of the vehicles used for transporting the soldiers to Fort Lewis. It was obvious that fewer men would have died, and perhaps none at all, if the coaches had been made of steel.

The decision to transport the Special Force in old colonial cars was made by the Department of National Defence in consultation with government and railway officials. October and November were not months in which tourists traveled extensively, and sufficient modern steel coaches could have been assembled for the Army. However, the Canadian soldiers of the period had a reputation of being rough and occasionally destructive, and as a result the authorities had some reservations about exposing their first class facilities to the vagaries of 5,000 boisterous and unpredictable young men on their way to war.

Following this disastrous event, a manslaughter trial took place in Prince George, British Columbia, with John Klemper acting as defence counsel for the C.N.R. telegrapher charged with causing the wreck because he had allegedly sent an incomplete message to the crews of the two trains involved. The Crown Attorney, a former Army colonel, supported the position taken by the Canadian National Railways, in effect saying that the accident had been caused by negligence on the part of the telegrapher.

It was rumored, during these proceedings, that the accused

telegrapher, a pleasant young man with typical Anglo-Saxon facial features and an English surname, had changed his name and was actually of Ukrainian origin.

When a senior executive from the C.N.R. took the stand, John Klemper was able to use all of his considerable dramatic powers in defending his client.

"Is it not true," Klemper asked the executive, "that it was snowing heavily during the period of the accident?"

"Yes. That is true," came the hesitant reply.

"And is it not also true that a part of the transmitted message may never have reached the train crews because of the weather?"

"Theoretically, I suppose, but not very likely."

"Sir, I am not asking you to speculate on the extent of likelihood. Do you admit that the inclement weather could have caused an incomplete message"?

"Yes, but..."

"I suppose that putting these soldiers into wooden cars rather than steel cars was so that no matter what they might subsequently find in Korea, they would always be able to say, well, we had worse than that in Canada!"

Chaos erupted in the courtroom. The Crown Attorney objected loudly to Klemper's last remark. In a legal sense, the telegrapher was being charged with the deaths of employees and not soldiers. In this respect, the former Colonel, a veteran of World War I, tried to clarify the issue before the court. "I want to make it clear," he said, "that in this case we are not concerned with the deaths of a few privates going to Korea."

The Crown Attorney's indiscrete remark gave Klemper precisely the kind of opportunity that he needed. "You're not concerned about the killing of a few privates? Oh, Colonel!" he intoned with distain and contempt.

"Fucking kraut," the angry Crown Attorney mumbled to

his assistant. He was referring to Klemper's German origin. "Krauts are our enemies and should not be allowed into Canada. I fought them in France in 1917 and 1918 and I can't forget. Klemper loves and sticks up for Ukrainians and other foreigners. We should have kept them in concentration camps after the Great War. They are not Canadians and don't deserve to be in this country."

This dramatic exchange was a major factor in the case, and the telegrapher was later acquitted of the charge of manslaughter. After the trial the telegrapher shook Klemper's hand. "Thank you, sir," he said with emotion, "for helping me through this very difficult period of my life."

"I knew that you were innocent from the beginning," Klemper replied. "Moreover, I believe that the railway officials were at least partly responsible for using those ancient wooden coaches. I've heard that the Federal Cabinet made the decision to send troops to Korea while riding in a lavish railway car from Toronto to Ottawa."

"I did not know that," the telegrapher said. "You have obviously done a lot of research."

"Isn't that ironic?" Klemper replied. "They travel in style while the troops they send to war ride in coaches that are scarcely fit for cattle. Besides, I will never understand why the Government decided to send 5,000 of our soldiers to Fort Lewis, an American base. I suspect that we were pressured by the Americans who want to have control over our armed forces, and in fact our whole country. It's what the Americans call Manifest Destiny. Someday, if I have my way, things will change."

CHAPTER 14
THE PALLADIUM

When Peter Farley arrived at Fort Lewis, Washington in late November, 1950, a letter from his father Orest was waiting for him. Although he was disappointed that the letter was not from Sonia, he opened it eagerly hoping that it would contain something about her. Their love-making at his cousin's wedding remained vividly in his memory. It was something he would never forget.

"*Dear Peter,*" his father began. "*I hope that you liked the wedding. Why in hell have you not written to me? I sure miss you here.*

Believe me, you should get out of the damned army and marry Sonia pretty quick. She won't wait for a long time. Watch yourself with those English and other foreign girls. Lots of them are ugly and have got diseases like you can't imagine even in doctor books. Remember what I told you about being responsible and pregnant. We sure don't need no trouble in this family. Be a good Catholic

Christian. Your mother was not a normal English girl. She was beautiful, smart, English, Scottish and Catholic.

I know that you are probably worried about Billie, Fido and Charlie. Don't worry. I love them just like you do. Billie and Fido still sleep on that red blanket at the foot of your bed. They sometimes look at the bed and sniff it. Their eyes are sad. They must be wondering why you don't come home.

I have been feeding peanuts to your squirrels and wheat to your pigeons. The squirrels see me and come running, but they will not eat peanuts out of my hand like they do for you. The pigeons also get excited when I come. The raccoons came to eat after it is dark. All of these God's creatures have got lots of brains.

I hitch Charlie up to the buggy every Sunday and we go to church together. Father Boleschuk always asks about you and says that he prays for you.

I'm not too happy about you not finishing your doctor training. Those Englishmen at the university at Manitoba might think you are a Ukrainian failure. You told me that they don't even know that you are Ukrainian, but I don't believe that. They won't say anything, but they know who you are. Like I told you many times, my parents came from Ukraine and got a farm of 160 acres for 10 dollars. I was born on that farm and spoke no English until I started school. I only finished Grade 7. I had brains and wanted to go to school but we had no money. I had to work on the farm. That's why I want you to be a doctor. I want you to have a life that I did not have. You should be proud to be Ukrainian, but mostly you are a Canadian. Don't forget that.

Next year maybe I will have a good crop and give you money for your school. I worked lots of days on the railway extra gang this summer.

I still don't know why you went into the dangerous army. But I am proud of you. I never had a chance to serve Canada. I was too young for the First World War and too old for the second. I am also proud of Nick and Harry who were in the Fusiliers in the last war. Nick got wounded in Italy, but he is healthy now. Like I said before, they think they are English because they have lots of money and live in big, fancy houses in Vancouver. You know better than that. Can you think of any reason why anyone would like to be English?

I'm waiting for you to get out of the army, marry Sonia and finish your doctor's school. Sometimes I hear strange voices and I don't feel so good and I think maybe after Peter is a doctor he will be able to make the voices go away. I don't tell anyone about these voices because I am afraid that they will lock me up at the mental hospital again.

I talked tough to you when you were a boy but it was for your own good to make you a better man. Believe me that I love you as my son even when I am mean. I am proud that you are a Canadian soldier. Be brave but also careful. Canada is our country and don't you forget it."

Peter folded the letter and put it into the locker at the end of his bed. He sat at the edge of his bed staring into space and thinking about the events of the past several weeks. His train had narrowly escaped the disaster at Thunder River. He considered himself to be very fortunate to be alive and hoped that this was a significant portent for Korea.

A large blond Fusilier in the bed next to him rose from his prone position and looked at Peter quizzically. "I'm Jim Doherty," he said while holding out his right hand. "Wadda ya at b'y? I mean, what are you doin'?"

"I'm Peter Farley," Peter responded as they shook hands. "I was just thinking about my father, grandmother, girl friend, cat, dog and horse back home."

"I'm from Morgan's Cove in Newfoundland, b'y," Jim continued. "It's a small fishin' village on the southern coast. I hope you don' think I talks funny. You knows yourself that we are different and have only been in Canada about one year. I'm tryin' to lose my accent. I've been listening to CBC radio. I'm proud to be from Newfoundland, but I also likes to be a Canadian."

"Were you a fisherman?"

"Yeah. I worked wit me fadder. We caught mostly cod. I did not go sealing."

"Why did you not go sealing?"

"I went once and I be sick. Da sealers clubbed baby seals. Der red blood ran onto the white ice. Dey cried. Der mudders cried. I also cried."

"I understand completely. I would feel the same. I love animals. I have nothing but contempt for the Japanese, Norwegians and Icelanders for hunting whales."

"We don't hunt whales in Newfie. Seals and whales be mammals just like us. They think and suffer pain."

"I have a low opinion for the Spanish who have bloody bull fights. The English who hunt foxes with dogs are sub-humans from another planet. Dog fighting in the United States is illegal, but still takes place. Cockfighting is ancient, has existed in many places, and is also repulsive. " Farley's eyes flashed angrily as he spoke.

"Da world is a cruel place," Doherty responded quietly.

" Let's change the subject. Animal abuse is a painful subject for me. Maybe I can learn to speak English with your interesting dialect," Farley said with a smile.

"Ain't possible, b'y! All of our out ports are different. They be isolated and not the same. People in Morgan's Cove don' talk like the ones in Humber, another fishin' village I once visited. They all be different. And St. John's, she be not the same."

"I saw you win the Canadian Army heavyweight boxing championship at Wainwright last October. It was great watching you. I don't know how you managed to knock out four guys in two days. Were you not tired?"

"Yeah, I be tired, but so were t'others. Bein' left-handed gives me a big advantage. Right-handed boxers have a hard time wit big punches comin' from the left side. They ain't used to fightin' with left-handers. I also often get strong surges of power when I box. Major Karpinski, our medical officer, tol' me that I have unusually powerful adrenaline rushes. He calls it a flight or fight response. It seems me strength increases a lot at such times, much more than is normal."

"That's interesting. I also get strong surges of power caused by adrenaline, according to what I have read. My father is a big and strong man like you, and he even talks funnier than you do," Peter said with another smile.

"Funnier than me?"

"He was born in Canada but grew up in a small Ukrainian town in Manitoba where everyone spoke English with an accent. Instead of saying lunch he says 'launch'. He says 'Addmonton' instead of Edmonton. He calls a threshing machine a 'trashing' machine."

"So you be a Ukrainian?"

"I'm a Canadian, I hope. Yes, I'm a Ukrainian, but my mother was English and Scottish. My family was also Irish a long time ago. I'm actually a European mixture with even some aboriginal blood. If people get angry with me, and want to insult me, they call me a bohunk. That's a nasty name for Ukrainians. Isn't Doherty an Irish name?"

"Yeah, it's Irish, I guess. But my family has been in Newfie for many generations. We be fishermen. My fadder was lost a storm off the Grand Banks a few weeks ago."

"I'm sorry," Peter said. "I lost my mother when I was three years old. I was raised by Baba, my father's mother. Baba spoke only Ukrainian to me so I learned the language".

"So wadda ya at before ya joined the army?" Doherty asked.

"What did I do? I attended university for two years. I want to be a medical doctor."

"That sounds like havin' a time. I mean a lot of fun. I was a very good student and my teachers tol' me to keep goin'. One of them said that I have a very high IQ. But my fadder bought a fishing schooner and needed my help. I dropped out of school after I finished Grade 10. But that's history. Today is today. Are you goin' to Seattle?" Jim asked.

"Yes, I guess I will. Do you want to come with me? I may need your muscles if I get into trouble!"

"Why not. Let's get on the go. Going together is a good idea," Jim said. "We are in a foreign country. We gotta be careful. You looks pretty strong to me, so maybe you'll be able to help me."

"I'd like to go dancing," Peter said. "Most Canadian and American cities have dance halls where people meet. There are several dance halls in Calgary and I went to them a lot when I was stationed there in the army. Soldiers go a lot."

"Yeah, I went a few times."

"Maybe we will find some nice girls in Seattle, or maybe some not so nice girls. I feel guilty. I have a beautiful girl friend at home and I don't want to be unfaithful. But I am obsessed with beautiful women. I want to meet as many as possible while I am young. I'm not ready to settle down."

"I think I knows what you mean. I'm not much of a dancer," Jim replied, "but let's give it a try. There's nothin' to lose."

It was with considerable reluctance that Lieutenant-Colonel Jim Strange gave his Fusiliers a 24 hour pass on the last weekend before they were due to leave Fort Lewis for Korea. Company commanders were instructed to warn their men that they were to be back in their barracks by Monday morning or else suffer serious consequences. In actual fact, they were not scheduled to leave for their ship until Wednesday, but previous experience had shown that about three days of lead time was necessary to ensure that all or most would return from short leaves.

On their last Saturday night at Fort Lewis, Peter and Jim went to Seattle, Washington, where they discovered a dance hall called the Palladium. It was a large and impressive building and filled with several hundred young people by the time they arrived. The men present wore mostly drapes, or strides, the baggy-kneed, narrow-cuffed trousers that had become popular, along with zoot suits, in the late 1940's. Some of the girls also had strides, but most of them wore pleaded skirts, white bobby socks and loafers. A lot of American and Canadian soldiers were also present.

As they looked around the dimly-lighted hall, Peter's eyes fell upon a beautiful fair-haired girl who was standing alone at the edge of the dance floor.

"Jim," Peter said to Jim. "I'm going over to ask that blonde to dance."

"Yeah. She's right pretty. But don't hold your breath 'cause she may turn you down."

"It's worth a try, don't you think?"

"Anythin' is worth a try. I'll get on the go for that dark-haired one standin' next to her."

The two Canadians walked across the floor, smiled simultaneously, and asked the young ladies to dance. Much to their surprise, both invitations were accepted without hesitation.

"You must be one of the Canadians at Fort Lewis," the blonde said to Peter as they moved onto the dance floor."

"Yes," Peter replied. "I'm Peter Farley. What's your name?"

"Jean."

"Jean? That's a nice name, but is that all?"

"Isn't that enough?" she teasingly asked with a bright smile.

"I guess so. It's enough for the time being!"

Peter was a very good dancer, and his beautiful blonde partner fitted into his rhythm very quickly and smoothly. She clung closely to him almost immediately, without any kind of encouragement on his part. She was mysterious and desirable.

He felt confident and completely at ease. They continued dancing and talking for several dance numbers, without any indication from her that she wanted to leave. In the meantime, Jim and his dark-haired companion had disappeared.

"Can I buy you a drink?" Peter asked after the band stopped for a break.

She immediately agreed and they sat down at a nearby bar. Alcoholic drinks were available, but only surreptitiously because the bar did not have a legal status.

"Where are you from?" she asked.

I come from a small town in Manitoba called Sweet Grass. I'm famous. Everyone in Sweet Grass knows me," he joked.

"So if I want to write to you I will address my letter to Peter Farley, Sweet Grass, Manitoba?"

"That will work. But I suggest that you use my full name, Peter O. Farley. That's because I have a cousin whose name is also Peter Farley. My second name is Orest."

"Are you going to be in Fort Lewis for long?" she asked.

"No. I'm leaving for Korea next week."

"Korea? Isn't there a war going on there? You are much too attractive and young to be in a war. It seems like such a waste. I mean, you could be hurt or even worse."

"Not likely. I'm a very careful person. I don't take unnecessary chances. And what do you do for a living? You look like you could be a model."

"You asked me that before."

"But you didn't answer."

"I do various things. I need money because I am going to university."

They sat together for close to half an hour and each had several drinks of whiskey mixed with soda. Both were starting to feel the relaxing effects of the alcohol.

Although she was obviously intelligent, and had a warm, cheerful and engaging personality, Peter was perplexed by her vague answers. She seemed to have a genuine liking for him, but had not even been willing to reveal her full name.

"You are a mysterious lady," Peter said with a laugh. "I like you very much, but I can't get much out of you."

"Well, what do you want?" she said in a suddenly husky voice, her eyes flashing. The alcohol she had consumed was starting to have an impact on her speech.

"I'm not sure. You are very charming and beautiful. I guess that I would like to know you better."

"All right, then you can come home with me if you like. I live not far from here," she replied.

Her sudden invitation came as a surprise, and he was speechless for several seconds. "Yes, I'd like to go home with you," he said.

"Good. It will cost you 25 dollars."

"25 dollars?" he asked in confusion. "What are you saying?"

"It's very simple. If you want me, all of me, it will cost you 25 dollars."

"I get about 25 dollars in pay each week. You must be kidding," he said angrily. "If this is a joke, I don't like it."

"Listen, soldier," she said hoarsely while getting up. "I've already spent an hour with you. My time is valuable. You wanted to know what I do for a living, and now you know. I also dance at a strip club. Take it or leave it."

"I still can't believe that all of this is real. You are much too smart and beautiful to be involved in this kind of thing," Peter said in a shaky voice. He remained seated even though she was standing and waiting for him.

"Are you coming or not?" she asked with her hands on her hips.

"No, I'm not."

Her demeanor suddenly changed again. "I'm sorry, Peter," she said, sounding like a little girl. "I really do like you a lot. Please forget what I said about the money." Tears glistened in her eyes.

"How can I forget? I really thought there was something special between us."

"Maybe there is. Peter, believe me, I don't like what I have been doing. In fact, I hate it. I was making 25 dollars in a week in a restaurant. I now make as much money in an hour. It's just a temporary thing. Don't you understand?"

Peter did not reply.

She took a small notepad and pen from her purse, tore out a sheet and quickly scribbled on it. "Here," she said, "is my full name, Jean Haines, my address and phone number. Call me if you ever change your mind."

"Why should I change my mind?"

"Please forgive me, Peter, and forget about the money. I would just like to be an important part of your life. Money has nothing to do with it."

He stared past her towards the dance floor where the band was playing *Good Night Irene*. She waited for a few more moments, the tears running down her face. Then she turned and walked away. At that moment he was convinced that she was one of the most beautiful and desirable women that he had ever met, but he could not bring himself to follow her. His mind was blurred with anger and disillusionment. He got up and walked around the dance floor until he finally found Jim.

"How was your ducky? The blonde, I mean. How did you make out?" Jim asked.

Peter then described his encounter with the beautiful blonde, including her offer to take him home for 25 dollars.

"She's just another whore, Red. You done the right thing."

"But she later changed her mind. I think that she really liked me. Maybe I could have altered her life".

"Red, you can't change a woman like that. Once a whore, always a whore. She woulda made your life miserable."

"Do you really believe that, Jim? Are you saying that people can't change?"

"Yeah, that's what I believes. Our lives be all laid out. God is all powerful, so he knows what is goin' to happen to us tomorrow, next week and years from now. It's what me minister calls predestination."

"But what about your girl, the brunette you danced with?"

"Forget her too. She be friendly, but I couldn't even get her to dance close. She's probably the kinda nice girl you wanted the blonde to be."

"Actually, I'm not surprised" Farley concluded bitterly. "I have two brothers who served in the Fusiliers in the last war. They told me that the women who hang around army camps are often easy-come-easy-go types. I think I now know what that means."

They took a bus and returned to their barracks at Fort Lewis. It was 12:10 a.m. They drank some whiskey from a bottle that Doherty had hidden in his locker. Doherty quickly fell asleep but Farley lay awake and remained fully-clothed.

Farley could not get the very beautiful blonde out of his mind. He had a deep, passionate and unrelenting desire to be with her. He reached into his pocket and took out the notebook page that she had given him. He noted the address, which appeared to be only a short distance from the camp. He glanced at Doherty who was now snoring loudly. He rose quietly from his bed, headed to the camp gate, and showed his pass to the guard corporal.

"I hope you know what you are doing," the corporal said. "This leave expires at 0800 hours. That's only seven hours from now. You will be in deep shit if you don't get back in time."

"Thanks, corporal," Peter replied. "I do know what I am doing."

He went out the gate and headed in the direction of Wyoming Street, the name that Jean Haines had written on the sheet of notepad paper. He remembered that the street was located next to the bus stop at the edge of the camp. When he reached the bus stop he opened the paper again. "218 - 319 Wyoming Street," he read aloud. He began walking down the dimly lighted street and after about three blocks he came to 319. It was a large red brick apartment building. He tried the front door but it was locked. A pay phone was located next to the building. He deposited a nickel coin and dialed the number that she had given him.

The phone rang several times, and just before he was ready to give up, a sleepy, soft female voice answered. "Yes," the voice said. "Who is calling?"

"Jean, it's me, Peter. Remember from earlier this evening? I'm outside and calling from the phone booth next to your apartment building. Can I see you?"

A long silence followed. "I'll come down and get you. Wait there," she answered.

She met him at the door and let him in. She wore a dark blue housecoat. He followed her up a flight of stairs to apartment 218. It consisted of a bathroom and a combined, single room kitchen and bedroom. A black cat sat on a queen-sized bed and looked with friendly interest at Peter.

"You have a cat!" Peter exclaimed. "I do too. I have one at home in Canada. Mine is red. I call him Billie. I also have a dog and a horse".

Jean smiled. "My cat is called Minnie. She seems to like you. I'm glad you came," she said. "I have been thinking of you constantly since we met earlier this evening. As you know, I cried when you left. I hope that you have forgiven me for my behaviour, for how I have been making money so that I can go to university." She removed her housecoat. She wore sheer pajamas that clung to her body and revealed firm breasts, a thin waist and long, slender legs.

"I have been thinking of you too," Peter replied. He was deeply aroused. "You are a very beautiful woman. I am also impressed by your intelligence."

"Intelligence? That's a different tactic! Thank you! I'm flattered. Would you like to celebrate our reunion?" she asked mischievously. "I hope that you like apricot brandy. It's all that I have." She went to her kitchen and returned with a bottle. She poured brandy into two large glasses and gave one to Peter. "Here's to our friendship," she exclaimed happily.

"To our friendship," Peter replied as he raised his glass and drank quickly until the glass was empty. She followed his example and filled both of their glasses again.

"I'm glad that you love cats," she said with a smile. "I once had a boyfriend. I cared for him a lot. But one day he told me that he hated cats and asked me to get rid of mine. I decided, at that moment, that he was not for me. I kept my cat and got rid of him."

Peter laughed. "I understand completely! I would do the same!" he exclaimed. "If someone tells me that he or she does not like cats, I am repelled and I back away. Cat haters are from another planet. I can't maintain a close friendship with cat haters, or even those who are simply indifferent. I consider them to be insensitive and lacking in character. Does that sound strange and eccentric to you?" He suddenly remembered Sonia and her dislike of cats.

"No, I feel the same way," she replied.

"It is warm in here," he continued. "I think I will take my tunic off." He stood up, removed his tunic, and sat down again.

"Yes, you look hot!" she exclaimed. "Let me help you take

your shirt off." She stood next to him and began slowly unbuttoning his shirt. He felt very aroused.

They both finished their glasses of brandy quickly and Jean filled their glasses again.

"Oh! I can see that you are very well endowed!" she said with a giggle as she glanced at the front of his pants. "I hope that you do not mind me saying so. I don't want to sound crude, but I want you to know that I am very attracted to you, and it isn't just a physical thing. Maybe I should not be doing this, but you are going to Korea, to a war, and I may never see you again. This may be our one and only time together. I want you to make love to me. "

He was embarrassed but the swelling was uncontrollable. "I feel the same way about you, Jean," he said. "Now it is my turn to help you," he said with mock seriousness. He stood up, clutched the bottom of her pajama top with both hands, and pulled it over her head. "You are spectacular," he said in a hoarse whisper.

She removed the bottom of her pajamas by herself and sat provocatively at the edge of her bed. She now wore nothing but very brief black panties.

He removed the rest of his clothing, except his khaki army shorts, and lay down on the bed beside her. She took off her panties, rolled on her side, and kissed him on his lips very tenderly. "You have become the most important person in my life," she said gently. She turned off the light at the side of the bed.

He wanted to be sure that her sexual experience with him would be meaningful, complete and climactic, and he spend several minutes caressing her with his tongue in all of the most sensitive parts of her body before he finally entered her. The consummation took place, a few minutes later, with a simultaneous blur of ecstasy. Both fell asleep shortly afterwards. The brandy was a powerful sedative and they had consumed a lot.

Bright sunlight from the apartment's single large window woke him up in the morning. He glanced at his watch. It was 0730. He had 30 minutes to get back the base before his leave expired. He dressed quickly and gazed at the beautiful naked woman who remained sleeping on the bed. For a moment he wondered if he should stay in spite of the rapidly expiring time on his pass. He decided against it. He opened and closed the apartment door quietly, walked out onto the street, and began running to the base.

He arrived at the camp gate at 0750. The same corporal was still on duty. "So, you managed to get back in time with just 10 minutes left," the corporal said with a smile. "I hope it was worth it."

"Yes, it was worth it, corporal," Farley said. He returned the smile and ran quickly towards his barracks. "*Will I ever see her again?* he asked himself. "*Should I call her when I get back from Korea? Can she be saved? Does she really care about me as much as she claims? Is this affair realistic? We have been together for only a very short time.*"

Shortly after returning to his barracks he developed a severe headache. He sat on his bed and held his head. "*Too much brandy,*" he said to himself.

Jim Doherty arrived at that moment. He had been spending some time in the barracks common washroom. "Where ya been?" he asked. " I been worryin' about you. In Newfie we have a funny saying. Oh! the billy goat chased the nanny goat and tore her petticoat. Is that your story?"

"Maybe, Jim," Farley quietly replied. "I went to see her again. I just got back a couple of minutes ago."

"We got weapons lectures all day today. You better get cleaned up and ready. 'Tis almost time to go."

"I have a bad headache. I am going to the MIR to ask for some kind of medication. If anyone finds that I am missing, tell them that I have gone to the MIR." He was referring to the base Medical Inspection Room.

"Yeah, Red. I will. Be careful."

Farley went to the MIR and was given aspirin tablets by a medical orderly. He washed them down with a few sips of water and left the premises.

Although he still had a headache, he suddenly decided to contact Jean Haines again. He walked to the nearby Other Ranks Canteen, took the paper with her phone number from his wallet, put a nickel in a pay phone slot, and waited as the phone rang.

"Yes?" she answered. "Who is calling?"

"It's Peter!" he said excitedly.

"Peter! I woke up this morning and you were gone. Why didn't you say goodbye?"

"I didn't want to wake you. You look very beautiful when you are without clothes. I confess that I spent a lot of time just looking at you!"

"I'm flattered, but you should have said goodbye."

"Jean, I am at the Other Ranks Canteen at the base. It is open to the general public. They will let you in as long as you identify yourself at the gate. Please come to see me for at least an hour or two. I can't leave because they will stop me at the gate and ask for identification. I don't have a pass."

She remained silent for several seconds before she responded. "Alright. I have classes scheduled all day today but I will come. This may be my last chance to see you for a long time. I will be there in a little while."

They had an emotional reunion in the Canteen about an hour later. He held her very closely in his arms. Happy tears came to her eyes. "Peter, I love you very much," she said.

"And I love you, Jean," he replied. "I can't get you out of my mind. Let's get out of here. I'll buy some sandwiches and drinks and we'll go to the small park across from the Canteen. We will have a picnic. No one will bother us there."

The next three hours in the park went by very quickly. They told each other about their lives and their plans for the future. Their conversation was often playful, light-hearted and not always serious. They felt very comfortable and happy together. They laughed often.

She told him that she came from a small town in Oregon. She said that she was training to be a teacher. He elaborated on his plans to be a medical doctor.

She revealed that she had experienced some difficulties with her parents during her high school years. "I had an eating disorder," she said. "I lost a lot of weight. I became very depressed and seriously considered suicide. I recovered, and with the financial assistance of my father, began my university studies. But my father was oppressive. I quarreled with him and he withdrew his support. I left home and began working as a waitress. I could not manage and began earning money in other ways. I am so sorry."

Farley's knowledge about the personalities of human beings, obtained by reading many psychiatric books in the University of Manitoba, swirled through his head. He knew that he was not a psychiatrist and that he had to be careful. *"She seems to have a borderline personality,"* he told himself. *"She has abused herself. She feels rejected, and especially by her father. What will happen if I leave her and never return. Is she now going to depend entirely on me?"*

"Peter," she said, "after meeting you at the Palladium, and after our night together, I have decided that I am no longer going to behave like I did in the past. I can manage very nicely on the money I have. I will be graduating this year, and there are lots of teaching jobs available. I hope that you will understand and accept me in spite of my questionable previous behaviour."

"I am very happy to hear that," he said. "I can't promise you anything, because as you know, I will be leaving for Korea shortly. I will write to you. I have your address. Please write to me. You mean a great deal to me. I will not forget you."

Two military policemen suddenly appeared and interrupted their conversation. One of them was a sergeant and the other a corporal.

"Are you Private Peter Farley?" the sergeant asked.

"Yes, I am," Farley quietly admitted.

"Come with us. You are under arrest for being absent without leave."

"I'm sorry, Jean!" Farley exclaimed as they led him away. "Goodbye! I will write to you."

She stood in silence and tears ran down her cheeks. "*Will I ever see him again?*" she wondered.

Farley was deposited in the Base Detention Barracks overnight. In the morning he was marched in front of the Commanding Officer. "Farley," Lieutenant-Colonel Strange said. "You are lucky. We are going to Korea tomorrow and I am going to let you off easy with a $25 fine. That is about one week of pay. But don't worry. We are still going to feed you on the boat and you will have a place to sleep. Under normal circumstances I would put you in the piss can for a week. Don't ever let this happen again."

"Yes, sir, thank you sir. It will not happen again!" Farley said. He was truly ashamed and repentant. "25 dollars?" he said to himself. "I hope that I will never hear this number again."

CHAPTER 15
THE OCEAN VOYAGE

The Private J.P. Villanova, a WWII United States liberty ship, sailed out of Port Angeles, Washington, bound on a three week voyage to Pearl Harbor, Yokohama and Pusan, Korea. Aboard were Peter Farley and more than 800 officers and men of the Canadian Fusiliers, one of the Special Force units recruited in Canada for the Korean War. About 500 American soldiers were also on board. It was late November, 1950, and General Douglas MacArthur's United States and UN forces seemed to be bringing the war to a rapid conclusion.

On June 25, 1950, the Communist North Koreans, with Soviet logistical support, had achieved almost complete tactical surprise when they invaded the American-backed Republic of Korea in the South. The R.O.K. forces, lacking tanks, anti-tank weapons and proper training, had been pushed rapidly south-wards even after being reinforced by two U.S. divisions from Japan. By early August, 1950, the U.S., R.O.K.s and recently arrived British forces had been contained within a small area around the southeastern South Korean port of Pusan. Defeat for the United Nations had seemed to be inevitable.

However, on September 15, 1950 General Douglas MacArthur launched a daring amphibious attack at Inchon, on the Korean peninsula immediately west of Seoul, the South Korean capital city. The United Nations forces quickly recaptured Seoul, pushed eastward and southward, and in the process cut off virtually the entire North Korean army in the south. More than one-half of the original North Korean invaders were taken prisoner.

Meanwhile, from their Manchurian border in the north, the newly victorious Chinese Communist regime watched developments with jaundiced eyes. They had recently overwhelmed the pro-American Nationalist forces of Chiang Kai-shek in China itself, and were in no mood to allow the capitalist U.S. to establish a puppet Korean state on their border. As MacArthur's U.N. forces rushed northwards towards the Yalu River and Manchurian border, signs of a Chinese intervention became more and more apparent. By early November elements of numerous Chinese divisions were identified in forward U.N. areas. Then, with devastating swiftness, massive Chinese attacks drove the United Nations forces southwards, and in early January, 1951, Seoul fell to the Communists once again.

When the Fusiliers began their Pacific voyage in late November, 1950, it appeared that the war would soon be over. However, by the time they reached Pearl Harbor the fighting had escalated into a major conflict. More than one million Chinese and North Korean soldiers eventually confronted an army of approximately one-half of that number, with troops from the U.S., South Korea, Greece, Turkey, the United Kingdom, Australia, New Zealand, Canada and several other nations being included within the United Nations forces.

Shortly after leaving Hawaii the Pacific calmed considerably, the seasickness experienced by many abated and life aboard the ship returned to its normal routine. Several poker games had started shortly after the ship had left Port Angeles, but all were stopped because of the widespread seasickness. Poker games now began again in various parts of the ship. Farley entered into these games.

Farley had learned how to play poker during his two years at the University of Manitoba. Several students at the Faculty of Medicine gathered in a room in the men's residence every Saturday evening, Farley among them. The stakes were not high, with only pennies being bet, won and lost. After losing at the beginning, Farley decided to do some research on the game. He borrowed several poker books from the Winnipeg Public Library. He learned about how to keep a poker face, when to fold, how to bluff, how to interpret the telling signs on his opponents' faces, and that he should avoid alcohol when playing poker. He then began winning consistently. He loved the game and played whenever he could.

The poker stakes on the ship were much higher. In total, about $10,000 was involved from the pockets of about 500 players. Many of them lost all of their money quickly and dropped out. Farley always moved to the games with the most "action", meaning those with highest betting.

Eventually, only 10 players, including Farley, remained with any money. At one point his earnings reached close to $2,000, but he then started to lose and was left with only about $1,500. That was a lot of money, slightly more than the amount that he was earning annually as a Canadian soldier. Farley decided to quit. He was very pleased with his success and concluded that he should not take any more risks, and especially because the remaining players were the most skilled survivors. The weak players had run out of money and had folded. He had purchased a money belt at Fort Lewis and now used it to store his new wealth in Canadian and American dollars. The ship, unfortunately, did not have a bank.

In the meantime, Lieutenant-Colonel Strange decided that it would be a good time to evaluate his senior officers, and in particular to search for clues into the identity of a spy that might be present. He opened his RCMP produced "Fusiliers Korean Security" file and once again read the top secret information contained in its pages.

"In keeping with the request of the Canadian Army Chief of Staff, the intelligence service of the Royal Canadian Mounted Police is pleased to provide you with information about the officers in your battalion who hold the rank of major.

As an important part of our investigation we secured access, via the courts, into the records of banks in the various places where the subjects lived. We were not able to find any instances of unusually large deposits of money. Spending patterns were also unchanged. If in fact reward money was received by one of these individuals, he has hidden or deposited in some unknown location. It is virtually impossible, at this time, to locate funds that are deposited in so-called offshore banks, as in the case of Switzerland.

At various times during the past several weeks we have interviewed these officers and during these interviews we have also administered the Minnesota Multiphasic Personality Inventory (MMPI). A "communist factor" was incorporated into the inventory. We specifically tried to discover any socialist or communist tendencies or sympathies that might be present. Research was conducted in the places where these officers had lived in earlier years. In order to avoid suspicion of our motives we explained that these interviews and tests were being administered on an experimental basis to selected members of the Special Force. The purpose of the MMPI is to detect and measure the personalities of those being tested. In extreme cases certain pathologies are identified. Our testing showed that all of these officers appear to be relatively "normal" in most respects, although some noticeable deviations were present in some cases. The following are summaries of the results of our research, interviews and testing.

Major Charles Smith, the Commanding Officer of Able Company, is from Toronto, Ontario. He was born on April 11, 1919 in Toronto. Completed Grade 13 education. Joined the army as private in 1939. Promoted through the ranks. Ended up as a company commander with the Prince Edward Regiment in Italy and northwestern Europe. Competent and courageous. Mentioned in dispatches. Admired by all ranks. Worked as a real estate agent in Toronto after the war. Gained a reputation as a racist because he refused to sell homes to non-white immigrants. Reserve army after the war. Joined the Special Force in August, 1950. Claims to have no strong political opinions. His MMPI score shows a fairly strong "lie" factor, which means that his answers are not entirely reliable.

Major Henry Henderson, the Commanding Officer of Baker Company is from Calgary. He was born on January 23, 1920 in Shanghai, China, where his father was a Baptist missionary. He went to the International English school in Shanghai until the age of 15 and then returned to Canada with his parents in 1935 because of the conflict between the Japanese and Chinese forces in and around the city. He has stated that his knowledge of the Chinese Mandarin language is limited. One of his classmates from the International English School was located in Ottawa and he confirmed the details of Henderson's education in China. Henderson joined the army in 1939, was promoted quickly, and was a sergeant in the Dieppe Raid in 1942. He was one of the few to escape and return to England. He landed in Normandy on June 6, 1944 as a lieutenant with the Canadian Scottish Highlanders. He was later promoted to captain and then major with the same regiment. He was wounded in Holland, and returned to Canada in 1945. He obtained a B.Sc. degree from the University of Alberta in 1949. Worked in the oil industry. Volunteered for the Special Force in October, 1950. Says that he always votes for the CCF even though this socialist party has pacifist tendencies and often does not support the military. His MMPI scores were normal in most cases but the lie factor was quite high and there was some response inconsistency.

Major Michael Medwick, the Commanding Officer of Charlie Company, was born in Oxford, England on July 27, 1918 and came with his parents to Canada at the age of 13. His father, a strong socialist, was a medical doctor. The Medwick family in England can be classified as upper class and is apparently quite wealthy and owns several parcels of land. He attended the University of Toronto for two years. While attending university, he enrolled in the Canadian Officers Training Corps and graduated as a 2nd lieutenant. He went overseas with the Northshore Light Infantry in 1941. Discharged in 1945 as a major. Entered medical school at U. of T. but left after two years because of low grades and failed courses. Worked at Eaton's in Toronto. Joined the Special Force in August, 1950. All of his MMPI scores are within the normal range.

Major Patrick O'Brien, the Commanding Officer of Dog Company was born on June 25, 1912 in Halifax, Nova Scotia. Fought with the pro-communist MacKenzie Papineau Battalion in Spain in 1935-36, but strongly denies that he has any communist sympathies. He claims that he simply wanted a military adventure and had no political motives. After returning to Canada from Spain he completed a reserve army officer training course at Camp Borden. He apparently did not disclose his illegal Spanish experience and as a result was accepted into the Canadian officer training program. He would have been rejected if the authorities had known about his communist-affiliated military service in Spain. He served as a lieutenant in Italy and was promoted to captain in France. He was discharged as a major in 1946, worked as a life insurance agent, and then joined the Special Force in August, 1950. His MMPI scores revealed a number of possible problem areas. Some faking, denial and evasiveness was present. These scores were discussed with Chief of the Defence Staff, but it was decided that there was not sufficient evidence to remove him from his command. It should be noted that MMPI scores are only indicators, and that no conclusions should be made on the sole basis of these scores. More evidence is needed. However, the behaviour of this officer should be closely monitored.

The commanding officer for Support Company, Major Stanley Grimes, is already in Korea. He is working with the 24th American Infantry Division in order to familiarize himself with U.S. support weapons such as the 81 mm. mortar. He can be ruled out as a communist spy because he was previously stationed in the United Kingdom for two years in a liaison role. He was not present in Canada during the time of the alleged contact by the Soviet Embassy in Ottawa. He will be joining the Fusiliers as soon as they arrive in Korea.

Major Paul Karpinski, the Battalion's medical officer, was born on a farm near Melfort, Saskatchewan on March 18, 1923. He graduated as a medical doctor from the University of Alberta in 1948. He must have been an outstanding student because Ukrainians, like him, as well as women, Jews and other foreigners, have a difficult time getting into medical schools. He has an uncle who is a prominent member of the Communist Party of Canada but he denies having any kind of communist or socialist sympathies. He was relaxed during the interview and displayed a good send of humour. His MMPI scores were all within normal ranges, although he may have scored well because of his medical knowledge and intelligence."

Strange stopped reading, returned the report to its envelope and reviewed its contents in his mind. *"This information is helpful,"* he thought, *"but only to a limited extent. I now know something more about the backgrounds of my senior officers, but the so-called MMPI does not identify a spy or even confirm that one exists."*

Strange went back re-read the report on Medwick. This officer had distinguished himself in the last war, but there was something about him that made Strange uncomfortable. He had had several discussions with Medwick during the past several weeks and now the reason for his discomfort became evident. Medwick was from the English upper class and still retained some of his class accent. Strange, on the other hand, was lower class and when he spoke he betrayed the language of his forebears in East London. *"So that's it,"* Strange said to himself. *"That's why he speaks to me in a condescending manner. I have more education and a higher rank, but in his mind I am lower class."*

CHAPTER 16
COMMUNISM DEFINED

After reading the RCMP report Strange ordered all of his senior officers to attend a mess dinner at 6:00 p.m. He sat with his majors in a small dining room. The junior officers, the lieutenants and captains, sat at other tables in another room.

An exception was Intelligence Officer Captain Mike Levinson, who was also serving as the Battalion Adjutant. Strange decided to include Levinson with his senior officers because Levinson was privy to the same kinds of critical information as the majors who commanded the Battalion's companies.

After they had finished eating, Strange produced several bottles of scotch, whisky and vodka for those at his table. "Gentlemen," Strange said, "this evening we are going to continue our series of discussions about various topics of interest. You will recall that we previously talked about warfare in mountainous regions such as Italy and Korea, discipline in front line circumstances, the history, culture and language of Korea, and the traditions of the Fusiliers. This evening we are going to discuss communism, including its origins, beliefs and presence in the Soviet Union, China, Korea and Canada. But first of all, a toast. All rise and drink to the health of King George VI!"

The five majors, Levinson and Strange all stood, raised their glasses, and drank to the health of the King. Strange glanced at all of their glasses to ensure that they were all well-filled. Alcohol, he believed, would lower their defences and cause them to talk more freely about their attitudes and political beliefs. If there was a spy in their midst, he reasoned, it seemed likely that he would reveal some sympathy towards communism.

During his RCMP espionage detection training session in Ottawa the previous fall Strange had learned about a "fake real estate strategy" that could be employed as a way of identifying the spy in his midst. He would tell his officers about a very profitable property sale, but one which required a substantial amount of money on an immediate basis. The spy had apparently received $5,000 and this money was likely sitting somewhere. Only those with large sums of money would show interest in this transaction. The $5,000 was the equivalent of about two years of salary for a major in the Canadian Army in 1950.

Strange had a liking for scotch, but he wanted to be fully alert and drank moderately on this occasion. For the first half hour he allowed his companions to engage in casual conversation on various topics. During this period he encouraged everyone to drink and fill their glasses frequently. "Don't worry, gentlemen," he said from time to time, "you are not going anywhere except to bed. Drink up. Lots of scotch, vodka and whisky here."

After the half hour had passed and it appeared that everyone was in a relaxed mood, Strange then introduced the subjects he wanted to discuss. "Gentlemen, before we begin our assessment of communism, I would like to provide you with some personal information that may be of value."

Everyone was suddenly silent. All eyes turned towards Strange.

"My Uncle Harry," Strange continued, has a beautiful cottage on five acres of land at Wasaga Beach, which as you know is near Camp Borden in Ontario. He is now into his 90's and no longer able to maintain it. He plans to sell it at some time during the next several months. He told me that he would sell it to me, his favourite nephew, for $$6,000, but it is probably worth at least $12,000. I have only $3,000 in my bank account which means that the cottage will go to an outsider unless I can raise more money. You are my friends and I am giving you this opportunity. Are any of you interested? Maybe we can be partners and joint owners. I can provide $3,000 but I need another $3,000 on an immediate cash basis."

The right hands of Medwick, Henderson and Levinson were all raised as expressions of interest. Smith, O'Brien and Karpinsky did not raise theirs.

Strange's agile mind immediately began to assess the results of this fake real estate strategy. Medwick's family, he believed, was wealthy and held parcels of land in England. The Levinson family was Jewish, business-oriented and probably with lots of money. Henderson had worked in the oil industry in Alberta and was well-paid during his tenure there. Was his spy one of these three? He decided that he would need to interpret these results more carefully in future.

"Thank you gentlemen," Strange said after a considerable pause. "I have noted that Mike, Henry and Michael are all interested, and that the rest of you are not. I will keep you informed about this matter. It may take several months before I have any further information."

"I am interested," O'Brien said with a smile, "but $3,000 I do not have. That's a lot of money. Banks in my experience are tight-fisted. No immediate money there. Getting money from banks takes a long time and is complicated. "

"Thanks, Patrick" Strange continued, "now let's begin by each of us briefly explaining the meaning of communism. We will start with Major Karpinski. What do you know about communism, Doc? Did you study anything about it at medical school?"

"There was a chapter on communism in my first year history class," Karpinski replied. "That was about all. But I do a lot of reading and am familiar with the concept of communism."

"I understand that you are of Ukrainian origin," Strange interjected. "Is that correct? Some Ukrainians in Canada are communists, I think. Do you know any communists?" Strange did not believe that Karpinski was the spy he was looking for. In any case, his medical officer would not have ready access to military information such as troop deployments and the locations of particular units and formations. Doctors were well paid and would be less likely accept large sums of money from the Soviets. His purpose in confronting his medical officer was to confirm, in his own mind, that Karpinski was not the spy he was looking for and to eliminate him from his list of suspects.

"I'm a bit embarrassed to admit this," Karpinski replied," but I have an uncle in Canada who is an ardent communist. However, Uncle Nick is the black sheep in our family. No one takes him seriously. Our family ignores him. He lives in the North End of Winnipeg and runs unsuccessfully as a communist candidate in every provincial and federal election that takes place. And incidentally, most of his communist friends and colleagues are extreme English socialists, and not Ukrainians. It is sometimes hard to tell the difference between communism and socialism."

Strange laughed. He felt reassured by Karpinski's openness and honesty. This officer is not the spy we are looking for he told himself. As Karpinski spoke Strange glanced furtively at the expressions of the others in the room. He wanted to see if any would betray any strong emotions about the topic at hand.

"Levinson," Strange said with mock seriousness. "You are next. Tell us something about your background, and how you define communism."

"I guess I am also, like Major Karpinski, a Ukrainian, except that I come from a Jewish family. My grandparents came from Ukraine and settled in Montreal. They spoke Russian and Ukrainian. I was born in Montreal but spent my childhood years, from ages five to 17, in Peking, where my father, an engineer, worked for an American company. I went to an English language international school, but I had many Chinese friends. I went to a Saturday school and to evening classes where I studied and became quite fluent in Mandarin, the principal Chinese language. I attended McGill University and obtained a B.Sc. degree and took officer training after I returned to Canada. I worked as a researcher in a medical laboratory before I enrolled in the Fusiliers to go to Korea."

"We are pleased to have you as our Intelligence Officer," Strange said. "Your knowledge of Mandarin will be very useful. But what are your views about communism? How do you describe it?"

"I took several courses in economics while taking my Bachelor of Science degree. In my opinion, communism will never be successful in economic terms. It is contrary to human nature. Eventually, it will collapse. I strongly believe in the free market economic system. I also believe in human freedom, which is denied in the Soviet Union and other communist states such as China."

Strange was not sure about Levinson. His Intelligence Officer was obviously very bright, well-informed and apparently unsympathetic to communism. He did not appear to be a strong suspect, but could not be ruled out entirely.

"What about you, Henry?" Strange suddenly said to Henry Henderson. He faked a laugh to give the impression that he was joking. "Are you a communist?"

Henderson had been drinking quite heavily. His pale face suddenly turned a deep shade of red. "Of course not, sir," Henderson seriously replied. "Karl Marx wrote Das Kapital in 1867. That's 83 years ago. Times have changed. Labour is no longer exploited by capitalists to the same extent. Unions have provided a lot of protection for workers. I don't believe in communism or very much socialism either, for that matter."

"I'm impressed, Henry," Strange said. "You seem to know a lot about communism. And you don't believe in socialism? How does socialism differ from communism?"

"Fuck you, Henry, you lying bastard," Smith suddenly blurted out. He had consumed large amounts of vodka and was clearly inebriated. His speech was slurred. "You once told me in Calgary, after several drinks, that you always vote for the socialist CCF party, and that you would even vote communist except that they never elect anyone and so votes for them are wasted."

"If I said that I was only joking," Henderson angrily retorted. "In fact, I don't remember ever saying that. I am opposed to communism. I believe in moderate socialism, and that's it. You are still mad at me because I took all of your money in our poker game that evening. Don't tell me to fuck off, you son of a bitch!"

"Gentlemen!" Strange shouted. He stood up and pointed his forefinger at Smith.

"Mr. Smith, you are drunk. Off to bed with you. We are all gentlemen here. I will discuss this with you more in the morning. Good night."

Smith staggered to his feet. "Sorry, sir," he said meekly as he left the room. The apology was to Strange and not to Henderson.

Strange was secretly pleased with Smith's outburst because it provided him with some food for thought. His mind went back to the RCMP report. Although Smith had obtained a high lie factor in his MMPI test, his outburst against Henderson seemed to show that he had strong anti-communist feelings. Henderson appeared to have a lot of knowledge about communism, but his strong rebuttal to Smith indicated that he also did not have any sympathy for this political philosophy. But Henderson had lied about his voting for the CCF, and that had created some suspicion in Strange's mind. Perhaps both were faking. Maybe one or both were fellow travelers.

"Major Medwick," Strange said after Smith had gone. "What do you know about communism? Have you had any personal experience with it?"

"My father was a strong socialist for many years, and at one time even expressed some favorable comments about the Soviet Union. But his enthusiasm cooled after the war and especially after horror stories began to emerge from behind the Iron Curtain."

"What do you mean by socialism?" Strange asked. "How does it differ from communism?"

"It is in some ways difficult to distinguish between the two. Socialism is close to communism in some ways. My father was a medical doctor," Medwick replied. "He was an intellectual and read a lot. You should keep in mind that a lot of British intellectuals during the 1930's and the war years, including a number at professors at Oxford and Cambridge Universities, were very impressed by what was happening in the Soviet Union. The atrocities of Stalin were still largely unknown at that time."

"So how does your father feel about your expedition to Korea?" Strange asked. He was trying to hide his hostility towards Medwick and his upper class pretensions.

"He died two years ago," Medwick quietly replied. "I don't

think that he would have objected. He never tried to convert me in any way. He always said that I should march in step with my own drummer."

Major O'Brien had been sitting quietly for the whole evening. He had consumed several ounces of scotch but it did not seem to affect him very much. "Gentlemen," he suddenly blurted out in a deep voice. "I think we are getting too personal with this discussion. We should be thinking about communism in Korea, and not what our fathers, uncles or anyone else thinks, or what we think. My understanding is that we are intervening in a civil war in Korea. We have a strong leader in the north, Kim Il Sung, and another strong leader in the south, Syngman Rhee, both of whom have recruited followers, and frequently by means of coercion and intimidation. The average Korean does not know much about communism or democracy or capitalism."

"I'm impressed," Strange said. "It's obvious that you have been doing lot of reading and thinking about the war in Korea. But in your opinion, is our intervention justified? Should Canada be involved in this war?"

"Justified? Yes, Canada is justified," O'Brien replied. "The Soviet Union has to be stopped somewhere, and it is clear that the Soviets are using the North Koreans as puppets to help expand their empire."

Strange had suddenly developed a severe headache. "Thank you gentlemen, for giving us your thoughts about communism. I'm off to bed. But feel free to stay and finish off these bottles if you wish. I want to see all of you at 0800 hours. We are going to discuss, in more detail, attack and defence strategies in mountainous countries like Korea. Good night, gentlemen."

CHAPTER 17
ACROSS THE PACIFIC

Conditions for the other ranks sailing on the Private J.P. Villanova were much different than those for the lieutenants, captains, majors and Lieutenant-Colonel Strange. The Canadian Army, in keeping with British tradition, was very class conscious, except that one's Canadian rank and class was established mainly on the basis of merit and education rather than hereditary privilege. The officers on board lived in relative luxury, with semi-private rooms, fresh fruit, well-cooked meals, liquor, a well-stocked library and motion pictures in a private theatre.

Peter Farley had been meaning to write to Sonia Kereliuk, but he delayed doing so because he knew that his letter would not be posted until after their arrival in Japan or Korea. One day the sun arrived after several days of heavy rain, the Pacific became calm and he decided that it was an ideal time to write.

"Dear Sonia," he wrote. *"I'm writing this letter as our ship*

prepares to enter Yokohama harbor after about 20 days of sailing from Port Angeles, Washington, via Pearl Harbor. Our boat is called the Private J.P. Villanova. It's a so-called 'liberty ship' from W.W.II, welded together, cheaply-constructed and not very fancy.

There are several hundred Canadians and Americans on board. Our bunks are piled four deep, and so closely together that it is hard to turn sideways when lying down, or to walk in the very narrow aisles. One of our men, Jim Higgins, an obnoxious and disagreeable ex-convict, says that it is worse than being 'in stir', meaning a jail. I won't even try to describe the odour of hundreds of unwashed bodies living together in such cramped quarters! We only get to shower about every second day. I have been playing poker almost every day since we left Pearl Harbor.

There were no poker games from Port Angeles to Pearl Harbor because everyone, including yours truly, was seasick. There were probably 500 players when the poker started, but only about five us are now left with any money. People play until all of their money is gone and then they drop out. I have won about $1,500. Don't worry, though. I plan to use my savings carefully. In fact, $1,500 will get me through another year or maybe even two at the university very comfortably. Our Special Force enlistment is for 18 months so I should be home and out of the army in the spring of 1952.

I am having a hard time eating on this boat. We are given two meals a day, but because of the limited kitchen and dining facilities, feeding takes place in a continuous line up 24 hours a day. My turn comes when a funny Yankee voice on the P.A. system blares 'yellow cards will chow now, will chow now!' The cooks and servers in the mess hall are all very heavy Negro Americans, who sweat a lot into the soup and other food they prepare. As a result, I have trouble working up an appetite.

Our officers have much better food and superior dining facilities. They even have apples, oranges and other fresh fruit and vegetables. Joe Wilson, a private like me, sleeps in a nearby bunk. He is Major Medwick's batman. A batman is a kind of servant to an officer. He shines his officer's shoes, presses his clothes, and makes him coffee.

Major Medwick, the commander of Charlie Company, is a mean officer. He constantly yells at Joe and never seems to be satisfied with Joe's services. Medwick has an English accent, has upper class pretensions, and tries to impress everyone. One day I asked Joe how he manages to put up with this kind of abuse. 'It's easy,' Joe said. 'I often take an apple or an orange from his supply when he is not looking. And on days when he is particularly nasty, I secretly put piss in his coffee. Not much piss. Only a few dribbles. He seems to like the slightly salty taste, never complains, and I feel a lot better'.

As you can see, my fellow soldiers have ingenious ways of dealing with problems. Joe puts up with Major Medwick because, unlike the rest of us, Joe gets to eat fresh fruit. He is also rewarded whenever he sees Medwick drinking his urine-laced coffee. This has bothered me and I have cautioned Joe about his behaviour, but he just laughs. There is not much that I can do. If I squeal on Joe I will be severely punished by the whole Battalion. Everyone hates Medwick. I just shut up and mind my own business. As Joe says, a little bit of piss won't hurt. I'm not so sure.

The Americans on our ship are all conscripts. They did not sign up to go to Korea. When we tell them that we are all volunteers, they shake their heads in disbelief. 'You Canadians are all crazy!' they say. Maybe they are right. Do you agree with them?

Sonia, I'm sorry that I can't be more definite about our relationship. It's just that I need more time to think about my life, my future, and where I am going. I hope that you will understand and bear with me.

Please write to tell me about Billie, Fido and Charlie. Do you see them very often? Has Tato been feeding my pigeons, squirrels and raccoons? I still remember the mother raccoon who came to visit me with her five cute little babies. All of them miss me, I am sure, and I certainly miss them, almost as much as I miss you, and that's a lot."

The following morning Farley woke up and encountered an unusual smell. Unpleasant body odours were still strong in the bowels of the ship, but something much more agreeable was also present. Farley rubbed his eyes and looked around. Scattered on the floor under the bunks in his compartment were numerous apple cores as well as banana and orange peelings.

"What has happened?" he asked the man in the bunk across from him. "Apples, bananas and oranges? Where did they come from and where did they go?"

"Some guys broke into the officer's mess food storage area last night," his companion answered. "Everything was then carried to the bunk areas of the Canadians and Americans. The fruit was shared with everyone and eaten in a short period of time. You must have been asleep and missed everything. It was great! They were the first bananas, oranges and apples that I have had since leaving Fort Lewis. The bananas were a bit soggy but I loved mine. "

Farley sat in stunned silence. He regretted missing the bananas, oranges and apples, but felt relieved at not being involved in a clearly illegal activity. "So, it's breakfast time, but I have to wait for the announcement over the loudspeaker. It's probably porridge again," he said with a sigh.

In the meantime the senior officers of the Fusiliers gathered in Lieutenant-Colonel Strange's dining room for breakfast of their own. A waiter put bowls of porridge in front of each officer.

"I have some bad news," Strange announced. "A gang of men broke into our food storage area early this morning and took all of the fresh fruit stored there. It's all gone, gentlemen. No more fruit. From now on we have to eat like the other ranks."

"So who did it?" Major Karpinski asked.

"We don't know," Strange answered. "Three men wearing improvised cloth masks overpowered the guard. The orderly officer found the guard tied up in the morning. The door to the storage area was smashed in with a fire axe. Orange and banana peelings and apple cores were found all over the ship, including in the quarters of the Americans. The fruit was shared with everyone except the officers and senior N.C.O.s. The Americans have no senior officers on this ship. They are conscripts and replacements and don't belong to a specific unit like ours. There is not much leadership there."

"I'm not surprised," Major Medwick said. "It's our Special Force recruiting system that has caused the problem. Our government has enrolled the dregs of humanity into our ranks. Some have criminal records and have served time in prisons. They should have been more selective."

"I hate to say this, gentlemen," Major Henderson blurted out after swallowing a spoonful of the bland, tasteless porridge in front of him, "but I admire the initiative taken by this gang of Robin Hoods. Why haven't the other ranks been getting fresh fruit like us? If I was a private I probably would have done the same thing. We are all soldiers together and should be treated equally."

"That sounds like something Marx or Lenin would say," Major O'Sullivan observed. "From each according to his ability to each according to his needs. But regardless of whether or not the policy of providing fresh fruit to officers only is fair or not, the fact remains that a criminal act has taken place. Those responsible should be discovered and punished according to military law."

"My dear Mr. Henderson," Medwick said sarcastically. "Didn't you enthusiastically eat the oranges, apples and bananas when they were available? Stalin and Mao preach equality through communism, but they live in personal luxury. Are you not behaving in a similar manner, although on a smaller scale?"

"You are putting words in my mouth!" Henderson protested angrily. "I was not endorsing Marx, Lenin, Stalin or Lenin. I was talking about fairness. We are all soldiers, regardless of rank, and we should be treated equally. You all remember, of course, the train wreck at Thunder River where many of our men died. Why were they forced to ride in those ancient and dangerous wooden coaches?"

"I have a suggestion, gentlemen," Major Smith said. "I believe that we currently have about 100 dollars in our mess fund. I suggest that we offer a reward of 75 dollars to anyone who steps forward and reveals the names of those responsible for the raid."

"Gentlemen," Major Karpinski said, "let's keep in mind that every soldier who ate an apple or orange last night is technically guilty of possessing stolen goods. That means that a large part of the battalion needs to be punished. I don't think that this can be done in any practical or just way."

Strange also had some serious doubts about the strategy being recommended by Smith. On the other hand, he realized that theft in his battalion, if not punished, could seriously undermine morale. What would they steal next time?

"Gentlemen," Strange announced. "Thank you for your opinions. I have made a decision. I want each company commander to assemble his men tomorrow morning for the purpose of presenting an anti-theft lecture. Keep them standing at attention for at least an hour. Tell them why theft of any kind is harmful to everyone and that they need to be able to trust each other. The next time it may be their own food, beer or boots that disappear. I will personally speak to each company for a few minutes. You and your junior officers will fill in the rest of the time. The weather forecast for tomorrow is for strong winds and big waves. Making them stand on a swaying deck for an hour should be sufficient punishment."

At that moment Captain Levinson, the Intelligence Officer, unexpectedly burst into the room. "Excuse me, sir!" Levinson said to Strange. "Excuse me, gentlemen!" he said to the others. "I have some important information that I need to share with you."

"What is it?" Strange asked. "You are the Duty Officer today and are supposed to be patrolling on the main deck."

"That is exactly where I have been, sir," Levinson responded. "I was walking along the deck on the port side and stopped for a moment. Then I heard some voices from a hidden alcove in front of me. Some of our men were talking about the theft of the fruit last night. They were not aware of my presence. One of them said that the guard had been overpowered and that the fruit was taken by Privates Jim Higgins, John Busby and Albert Perkins."

"Good work, Levinson!" Strange exclaimed. "Round up this riff raff. Bring them to my office at 0900 hours. We have had disciplinary problems with these characters in the past. They are petty thieves."

At 0900 hours Captain Levinson, as directed, marched the three alleged offenders, accompanied by three military policemen, into the waiting room next to Strange's office. Strange interviewed each of them individually. Higgins and Busby denied any involvement in the theft of the fruit. But Perkins, after a lengthy cross examination by Strange, finally admitted that all three of them were guilty as charged. Higgins and Busby were then interviewed individually again. After being confronted with the information provided by Perkins, Higgins and Busby admitted their guilt.

All three of the offenders then stood at attention in front

of Strange. "We do not have a detention facility on this ship," Strange declared. "We do not have a piss can, but from now and until we get to Korea all three of you will be responsible for cleaning the toilets and urinals on this vessel. All of them. And that's three times each day. And I will personally check to make sure they are clean."

Later that day Levinson checked the personnel records of the three convicted thieves. He noted that all three had criminal records, mostly for assault and robbery. All three had spent time in various penitentiaries. *"Why were these characters allowed to join the Canadian Army?"* Levinson asked himself.

Higgins, Busby and Perkins were close friends and had all grown up in the notorious St. John's slum ward in Toronto. They did not believe in following the rules of society. They felt no guilt or empathy. Their home lives were chaotic. They had alcoholic, frequently absent fathers, and un-attentive mothers who toiled in marginal jobs to provide income for their dys-functional families. They did not want any sympathy and did not receive any.

The following morning the four rifle companies and the support company stood in formation on different parts of the ship's deck. Although the boring and lengthy lectures given were not identified as a measure of punishment, this purpose was evident to all. The three soldiers who had done the steal-ing were no longer looked upon as heroes. Most on board had received only a single banana, apple or orange, and having to stand to attention on a rocking ship for an hour was not worth it. Many were seasick again for the first time since leaving Hawaii. It was a lesson that they would not forget.

CHAPTER 18
WAH CHING REPORTS

During the time that Peter Farley and his comrades in the 2nd Battalion Fusiliers were crossing the Pacific the Chinese communists were making preparations for a major offensive against the United Nations forces in Korea. An informational meeting with regard to Chinese plans took place in Peking in early 1951.

The large room in the Tse Tung Building at the north end of Tin A Ming square in Peking was crowded with officers of the Peoples' Liberation Army as well as civilian officials from the Defence Ministry. They chatted, drank tea, smoked cigarettes and exchanged greetings among themselves. Before long a thin young man in a padded jacket, glasses and military cloth cap arrived at the podium at the front of the room. A large map of Korea hung on the wall behind the podium. The young man appeared to be a soldier but in reality was a political commissar who had recently returned from the war zone in Korea. His name was Wah Ching and he began speaking after a brief introduction.

"Comrades, I am honoured to be able to report to you today about my work with the Peoples' Liberation Army in Korea. Allow me to introduce myself to those who do not already know me. I am a member of the Communist Party and have been since the days of my youth. My father participated in the Long March and died in January, 1949 during a battle with the reactionary forces of Chiang Kai-shek. I was appointed as a political commissar in November, 1950 at about the time that our peoples' volunteers crossed the Yalu and attacked the Americans. And what, some of you may ask, do commissars do? In brief, our function is to provide political guidance and support to the units in our army. Commissars were first used by our comrades in the Soviet Union during their recent war with Germany. We do not, like our military officers, give direct orders, but we watch carefully to ensure that the socialist principles as advocated by Mao Tse Tung are carried out. If I see that one of our officers is neglecting his duty by not acting in a heroic and selfless socialist manner, or in some other questionable way, I speak to him to remind him of his duties to our nation."

"I have a question," a young officer interjected. "What happens if a military commander and a commissar disagree on strategy or tactics? How is the dispute resolved?"

"I am glad you asked," Wah Ching responded. "The military commander has the final say in matters of strategy and tactics. However, he must always keep in mind that his actions will be reported by the commissar, and that he may eventually be disciplined if higher authority decides that he acted in an inappropriate manner." He then continued with the rest of his speech.

"Let me now provide you with a brief summary of our war of liberation in Korea. In mid November, after Mao Tse Tung decided that we must come to the aid of our Korean brothers, five armies of the PLA began crossing the Yalu River in North Korea. Our

forces marched only at night and we moved along the hills rather than the valleys. The Americans, on the other hand, with their large numbers of monstrous vehicles, stayed in the valleys. Their soldiers are badly conditioned and can't march very far without getting exhausted. They rely on their trucks, half-tracks, jeeps and tanks for most of their movements. Although we managed to drive the Americans and their puppet forces south, and although we captured Seoul, we suffered many casualties from November, 1950 and into the winter. We were not prepared for the intense cold and many of our soldiers were disabled because of frozen hands and feet. The American Air Force bombed and machine gunned us on a continuous basis. We were also subjected to napalm."

"What is a napalm?" a civilian official asked. "I know that it is dropped from airplanes, and that it burns. Can you give us more details?

"Napalm," Wah Ching responded, "is a jellied gasoline. It is contained in large metal barrels. When these barrels hit the ground the jellied gasoline spreads over a large area. According to American manuals that we have found, the temperature at the point of impact can be as high as 1,200C. Water, as you know, boils at 100C, so you can imagine how devastating this substance is on human flesh. We have learned how to make underground bunkers that protect us from napalm, but a lot of work is involved."

"Are our forces well-armed?" a gray-haired senior officer asked.

"I serve with the 13th Infantry Battalion of the 27th Army. We rely heavily on the Soviet PPSH41 submachine gun. The Americans call it a 'burp gun' because of the noise it makes. This weapon contains 72 rounds in its magazine and produces many rounds per minute. We agree with the Soviet belief that single shot, accurate rifles are not as effective as relatively inaccurate high volume submachine guns."

Wah Ching paused, took a drink of water, and then concluded his observations.

"We also use a lot of captured American weapons and equipment. During the first three months of the war, our North Korean comrades captured enough material from the puppet South Koreans and Americans to equip about 10 divisions, or about 100,000 men. Some American equipment was also captured from the reactionary and defeated forces of Chiang Kai-shek's Nationalist forces. We are dedicated and well-prepared, comrades! We will be victorious!"

CHAPTER 19
ADVANCE TO CONTACT

The Private J.P. Villanova, after its long Pacific voyage, finally arrived in Yokohama. It stayed only briefly and three days later landed at Pusan on the southeastern Korean coast. A U.S. military band greeted them with: *"If I knew you were coming I'd have baked a cake."* They were also greeted with a powerful, sickening blended odour of fish, charcoal and human feces.

The Fusiliers spent the next three weeks training in the mountains south of the front line. Their immediate task was to learn how to use American weapons and equipment, as well as how to function as a self-contained unit in formation. Finally, by the end of January, 1951, they were ready for action. The Communists, although very numerous, were hampered by a lack of airpower and heavy weapons. At the same time, U.S. planes were inflicting heavy losses upon them. They gradually withdrew northwards under the pressure of the United Nations forces.

Early one morning in late January rifle companies Able, Baker, Charlie and Dog were loaded onto U.S. trucks and moved northwards along the valley of the Chojung River. They were followed by the half-tracks of Support Company, which carried the Battalion's 81 mm. mortars, medium machine guns, anti-tank guns and their crews. It was a wet, cold day, with periods of icy rain interspersed with slushy snow. Thick fog obscured the surrounding white snow-covered mountains as they drove northwards along winding, narrow and muddy roads to their objective near the base of a prominent mountain known as "Big Smokey," or Hill 857.

Finally, after about five hours driving, the convoy reached its destination. The Fusiliers scrambled out of their trucks with their rifles and equipment and began to form up in platoons and companies at the shouted commands of their officers and N.C.O.s. The now empty U.S. trucks and American drivers quickly turned and drove away.

On this first day of action the Canadians were exposed to a frightening scene that they would remember for the rest of their lives. Scattered on both sides of the road were the frozen and naked bodies of many African American soldiers.

Farley and Doherty, members of Baker Company's #5 Platoon and the Fusiliers from the other companies looked on the horrific scene.

"My God!" Doherty exclaimed. "There must be at least a 100 bodies scattered all over this field. They be all black 'cept that older man with the bald head."

Farley was in a state of shock but he responded calmly. "I think the pink, naked body belongs to their white commander. Negro Americans are rarely in command. They always have white leaders."

No. 5 Platoon Sergeant Herbie Jones joined Farley and Doherty as they viewed the ghastly field of death.

"What has happened to these people?" Farley asked. "Their arms and legs are frozen at grotesque angles. There is blood everywhere. They have no weapons and their clothing is gone."

"They fucked up badly," Jones responded. "Captain Levinson, our Intelligence Officer, told me a while ago that they had been shot and bayoneted early this morning while in their sleeping bags. They must have been all asleep with no one on guard duty. Their clothing and weapons have been removed by the Chinese. Ring fingers had been cut off and the rings removed. The Chinese love American military clothing. Many Chinese are equipped with captured U.S. weapons."

It was a grim and important lesson for the Canadians. Thereafter they would take their guard duties much more seriously. Sleeping bags were prohibited in front line positions. Only blankets would be allowed by Lieutenant-Colonel Strange.

Farley had seen a lot of dead and mangled bodies at the Thunder River train wreck two months earlier, but the horrible scene that he witnessed on his first day in the front line affected him deeply. He wondered about the lives of the Negro Americans who had been slaughtered at this place. He said nothing to his companions because he did not want them to think that he was a weakling. He was a proud Canadian Fusilier and would never do anything to dishonour his regiment and country. He said nothing and ate almost nothing for the next three days.

Strange called his company commanders together for a briefing session before the Fusiliers began their attack. Majors Charles Smith of Able Company, Henry Henderson of Baker Company, Michael Medwick of Charlie Company, and Patrick O'Brien of Dog Company all gathered at his headquarters bunker. Adjutant Captain Mike Levy, the temporary C.O. of Support Company, was also present. The regular C.O. of Support Company, Major Stanley Grimes, had arrived a week earlier, but after a sudden outbreak of malaria, had been sent to an American M.A.S.H. for treatment.

The possible presence of a spy in his battalion was still uppermost in Strange's mind. Perhaps this spy was a diversionary tactic. Maybe the secret agent in the Soviet Embassy in Ottawa had created this spy in his imagination. Strange was not sure, and he had to act carefully and on the assumption that the spy was actually in existence and in the upper ranks of the Fusiliers.

"Our objective," Strange told the gathering, "is to advance up Hill 857 and secure its peak. We have two alternatives. We can do a direct frontal attack or an assault on one or both flanks. Any suggestions, gentlemen?" Strange's request for input was unusual. He almost always made decisions like this on his own. But on this occasion he wanted to search the minds of his senior officers, once again, to see if any kind of espionage symptoms could be detected.

"Let's get philosophical for a moment," Strange continued. "What is the Chinese communist commanding officer on that hill thinking? Is he willing to take a lot of losses? Will he retreat only if he is subjected to a strong attack? The Chinese are gradually retreating northwards at this time. Maybe a minor push by us will send them running. Should we probe lightly or send a strong force?"

"I am sure that he is just as concerned as we are with regard to losses," Henderson quickly responded. "The Chinese are human beings just like we are. They suffer and grieve just like we do."

"I do not agree," Smith blurted out in a loud voice. He sounded angry. "They attack in waves and seem to totally disregard their losses. Their commanding officers obviously do not give a shit."

"I agree with Charlie. Henry is wrong. The Chinese and their Soviet sponsors are insensitive and without any kind of compassionate feelings," O'Brien forcefully interjected. "Stalin and Mao are cruel brutes who have killed millions of their own people."

"I think that Henry is probably closest to the truth," Medwick said. "A frontal attack will likely cost us a significant number of casualties. In any case, should we not have a mortar and artillery bombardment first? Air strikes would also be helpful."

"We are not even sure if there are any Chinese on this hill," Henderson noted. "It may just be a proverbial walk in the park. I volunteer Baker Company."

Strange was puzzled by conflicting responses of O'Brien, Medwick and Smith. "Why was Henderson more positive than the others?" he wondered. It did not matter. He pounced on Henderson's offer to serve.

"We can't wait," Strange announced after a brief pause. "Our orders say we must go now. Henry's Baker Company will be in the centre and lead the advance up the hill. Able Company will be on Baker's left, Charlie Company on Baker's right, and Dog Company will be in reserve at the rear. We don't know if the hill is occupied or not. We have to walk up and find out. There is no other way. But before we climb the hill, there is a village at its base that we need to secure. We have been getting sniper fire from some of the houses. We are going to pulverize the village with mortar fire and then move in."

Lieutenant Richard Harvey, the commanding officer of Baker Company's #5 Platoon, returned to his position to relay the orders he had been given by Major Henderson, his C.O. A tall, thin man with a pock-marked face and deep-set brown eyes, Harvey spoke nervously in a squeaky voice and did not project confidence. "Leave your kits at Dog Company headquarters," he ordered. "Bring your water bottles, four bandoleers of ammunition and six grenades each, four boxes of ammunition for the Bren, and fix your bayonets."

Peter Farley and Jim Doherty had been members of #5 Platoon since September of the previous year. They looked questionably at each other but said nothing.

"Who is carrying the Bren?" a small soldier called Ron Smith asked. "I'm number two on the Bren, but Dickson, the number one, broke his leg and has gone to a M.A.S.H., an American field hospital."

"Thanks for reminding me, soldier," Harvey said. He looked around and his eyes fell on big and muscular Jim Doherty. "We need someone that's strong. The Bren and ammunition are a big load. You fit the bill, Doherty. You will carry the Bren and Smith will remain as number two. Each platoon in a Canadian infantry battalion carries one Bren, a very effective light machine of Czech and British WWII vintage. I wish we had one or two more."

Doherty had some doubts about being a Bren gunner. He had heard that machine gunners attract a lot of enemy fire and that the life expectancy of machine gunners was lower than that of riflemen. But he knew that complaining would not produce any results and said nothing.

"This is it," Farley said to Doherty as he fixed his spike-like bayonet onto his .303 Lee-Enfield rifle. "It's the real thing!"

"Yeah," Doherty replied. "I gotta funny feeling in me stomach and all over. To tell the truth, I'm scared as hell."

"Everyone is scared, Jim. It's natural. My guts are churning too."

"But this is different. I've been scared before, but I ain't never had this kinda sensation. I've been on the Grand Banks in fishin' boats in violent storms and I was scared then. But it was nothin' like this fear."

"Okay, move out," Platoon Sergeant Herbie Jones yelled. "Stay about five yards apart and don't fucking lag behind. Follow me. I'll be leading you. Lieutenant Harvey has decided to follow in the rear to make sure there are no stragglers." Jones was highly experienced in combat. He had won a Military Medal as a Canadian infantryman in Italy in WWII.

"Stragglers, my ass," one of the soldiers in #5 Platoon said in a low voice. "Harvey is a fucking chicken. He should be in front doing the leading, and not Jones." The soldiers on his left and right nodded in agreement. "You are fucking right," one of them said.

#5 Platoon, led by Sergeant Jones, advanced to within a 100 yards of the village, took cover in a shallow ravine, and waited for the mortar barrage to start. They did not have to wait long. Before long a series of thumping sounds began echoing from their rear. Long whistling sounds were followed by more, much louder thumping as the mortar shells dropped into the village. Some of the shells were of the phosphorous variety and fires broke out in many of the houses. Shortly afterwards a small group of women, children and old men in white clothing came running out of the village. The children cried and the women screamed as they ran past the Canadians.

"Ignore them!" Jones ordered. "Into the village. Let's fucking go".

The mortar barrage had apparently wiped out the snipers. Or perhaps they had fled. No further rifle shots were heard as #5 Platoon moved into the village.

Farley and the other riflemen moved from house to house in order to be sure that all of the snipers were gone. Suddenly, as Farley approached a house with a collapsed roof, he heard the cries of children. He kicked the door in and entered the house with his rifle cocked and ready to fire. The scene that greeted him filled him with anxiety and dismay. Laying on the floor was a woman covered in blood. Her head was almost decapitated. A mortar bomb had plunged through the roof and killed her. Two small children, a boy and a girl were bleeding from slight shrapnel wounds and cried hysterically at her side. A small black dog and orange cat sat huddled beside the children. The children and animals all looked suspiciously and fearfully at the stranger who had entered their home.

Farley was overwhelmed with grief, horror, intense sympathy and guilt. This woman had been killed by Canadian mortar bomb and he, a Canadian, was partly to blame. "How can I help?" he asked himself. He desperately wanted to help in some way. "Are you hungry?" he asked the children. He pointed a finger to his mouth because he knew they would not understand his words. He reached into his knap sack, pulled out two cans of beef and opened them. "Here," he said. "Please eat."

The children continued crying and did not move. The dog and the cat, however, smelled the beef and came running to Farley's side. He put the cans on the floor and the two animals began eating with famished intensity. He reached into his knap sack once again and put four cans of ham and lima beans on the floor next to the children. He had nothing more to give them. At that moment Corporal Ronato Fontano, a medical orderly attached to the battalion, entered the room.

"I will look after the kids," Fontano said. "There is a refugee camp a couple of miles away. I will take them there. You had better get going. Your platoon is forming up at the north side of the village."

"What about the dog and the cat?" Farley asked as he picked up his rifle and started to leave.

Fontano smiled. "I have a dog and two cats at home," he said. "I know how you feel. The dog and cat will go with the kids. That's all I can promise."

Farley took one more anguished look at the children, dog and cat before he left the house and joined his platoon on the northern edge of the village. He remembered his cat Billie, his dog Fido and his horse Charlie at home and wondered how they were doing. He arrived just in time to join the attack on Hill 857.

The long, extended line of soldiers from Baker Company climbed slowly up the steep slope of Hill 857, their U.S. issue combat boots crunching in loose gravel and stones. Patches of fog swirled ahead of them.

"There must be an easier way of doin' this" Doherty said to Farley. "We are kinda like sittin' ducks."

"There is no other way, Jim," Farley replied absently. His mind was still on the dreadful scene that he had just witnessed. "The infantry always has to march in to take places. The air force and navy, and even the armoured corps, can't do it." He wanted to tell Jim and those around him about his anguish, but decided to keep it to himself.

Baker Company moved up the slope for about half an hour without seeing or hearing any sign of the enemy. Finally, Major Henderson ordered his men to sit down and rest. It was now snowing heavily, with wet large white flakes gradually soaking the perspiring Canadians.

"Shit!" Doherty exclaimed as he lay down beside his Bren and boxes of ammunition. What do we need this God-forsaken hill for anyway? It's like thousands of others in this country. All rocks and bushes. It's useless."

"The Chinese," Farley answered, "are probably asking the same thing. They likely think that they should be at home planting rice, or whatever it is that they do."

"They've got laundries and restaurants, b'uy," Doherty observed with a sarcastic laugh. "There's an awful lot of laundries and restaurants in China."

"We have a Chinese restaurant in Sweet Grass," Peter said absentmindedly. "Every small town in Canada has a Chinese restaurant."

At that moment Platoon Sergeant Jones came forward.

"Okay, #5 Platoon, we're moving up again. Major Henderson thinks that we are not too far from the peak. We have been given the point position again. Keep on moving until we make contact, and then hit the fucking ground."

"I sure as hell will," Doherty said sarcastically. "I knows how to do that. No instructions are necessary."

The Fusiliers of #5 Platoon rose wearily to their feet and moved forward again, led by Sergeant Jones. The slope ahead was now much steeper, and a heavy fog obscured their objective.

Suddenly a loud burst of machine gun fire burst into their ranks, followed by a series of fiery grenade explosions. The Canadians fell to the ground and scrambled on their hands and knees to find cover behind the many large boulders that lay around them. They fired their rifles towards the peak but could not see the enemy.

Doherty balanced his Bren on top of a flat rock and fired a long burst. He removed the empty magazine, inserted another full one and fired again. "Smitty!" he yelled to his Number Two. "More magazines. Give me more mags!"

Ron Smith, the Number Two on the Bren lay face down on the ground beside Doherty, his hands covering his head. He did not look up or answer.

"Smitty, you silly ass! Doherty screamed angrily. "Get up! Ammo! I need ammo!" Smith, he thought, must be terrified by the firing and cowering on the ground behind the rock. He grabbed Smith by his left arm and gave him a violent shove. Smith, a small man, rolled over like a rag doll. His eyes and mouth were open but bright red blood gushed out of his forehead where a Chinese bullet had entered. He was dead.

"Oh, shit, Smitty, I'm sorry," Doherty said in a shaking voice. "I didn't know." He held Smith's head gently in his hands for a few moments before releasing it onto the ground. He found a full magazine under Smith's body, loaded it into his Bren and began firing wildly at the slope and unseen enemy above. "You filthy Chinese bastards," he screamed.

"Move back, move back," Sergeant Jones began yelling. "We are going to go back a couple of hundred yards to dig in. In the morning we'll hit them with artillery and an air strike. Move back, move fucking back!"

The men of #5 Platoon turned and ran back down the slope until they reached a slight elevation covered with bushes. Jones sent one section of 10 men back to pick up the shovels, pack sacks and the rest of the Platoon's equipment that had been left earlier with Dog Company in its reserve position in the rear. As soon as they returned, the whole Platoon began digging slit trenches into the frozen ground.

"Whose equipment is this?" Lieutenant Harvey asked. "I count six kits here that have not been picked up."

"You have not been paying attention, sir," Jones said sarcastically. "We lost six men during our advance to the peak. We will pick up the bodies in the morning. They will not need their kits."

"Yeah, lieutenant, you were too far back to know what was going on," a voice shouted from a distance.

"Who said that? Harvey snarled. "Who said that?" He was very angry and his pock-marked face turned a beet red.

There was no response. The only sounds were those of shovels clanging as they hit rocks in the frozen ground. Harvey waited for a moment and then turned to his batman. "Dig here," he ordered. "Behind this large rock. That will be my trench. Then dig one for yourself. There is always a chance that the Chinese will counter-attack. We need to be ready."

Farley walked over to the slit trench that Doherty was digging. "Let me help you with this hole," he said with a smile. "The lieutenant says that I can be your Number Two on the Bren."

"That's great, Red. Welcome. I was goin' to invite you anyway. But be careful. Machine guns attract a lot of attention."

At that moment shells from the Battalion's 81 mm. mortars began landing with loud crunching sounds into the Chinese positions at the peak of the hill. Farley and Doherty watched and listened briefly, and then began digging their trench deeper. They said nothing more for the rest of the night.

It became very dark soon afterwards as the weak winter sun sunk quickly behind the mountains to their west. The cold, wet and exhausted Canadians shivered in their blankets and settled in for their first miserable night in the front line.

Early the next morning Lieutenant-Colonel James Strange called for a heavy New Zealand artillery barrage and an air strike by the United States Air Force. Corsairs, with their gull-shaped wings, swooped down on Hill 857 and dropped many canisters of napalm. The jellied gasoline covered the Chinese trenches, exploded into fires that reached about 1,200 degrees centigrade, and burned hundreds of Chinese to death.

The men of Baker Company moved up the slope again shortly afterwards. There was no opposition. They found some of the blackened bodies of the Chinese still in their trenches, and others in the open on the reverse slope. Some had tried to escape but the napalm had reached them as well. It was a horrible way to die, much worse than even the poison gas used in WWI.

Major Henderson climbed to the peak of the hill. He wanted to see the results of the napalm attack. "Devastating,' he said. "Absolutely devastating." He seemed to be grieving even though the dead were his enemies.

"Hey, look at this, sir!" Sergeant Jones exclaimed. He was looking at the partially burned bodies on the reverse slope. "Some of these guys are wearing American nylon shirts under their padded jackets. Maybe it's the same bunch that wiped out the Negro Americans that we saw."

"That's possible, that's entirely possible," Henderson observed. "But maybe they got them from the South Koreans. They are issued American uniforms and many have been killed or captured by the Chinese and North Koreans."

The bodies of the six Fusiliers killed the previous evening were wrapped in blankets and carried on stretchers to Battalion Headquarters. Lieutenant-Colonel Strange conducted a brief ceremony of remembrance prior to their removal by an American graves registration unit. During WWI, WWII and during the Korean War, the bodies of Canadians who had died were not returned to Canada. They were buried in temporary graves not far from where they fell. All who died in Korea would eventually be laid to rest in the United Nations cemetery in Pusan.

Later that day Corporal Renato Fontano, the medical orderly who had earlier met Farley at the destroyed Korean hut with its dead woman, injured children, and terrified cat and dog, happened to pass through the area where Farley and Doherty were located in trenches. A small black dog walked by his side.

Farley recognized Fontano and the dog immediately. "Corporal," he shouted. "It's me, Peter Farley. Remember me? We met in that hut with the dead Korean woman. You promised to look after the children and animals. So what happened?"

"As you can see," Fontano replied with a smile. "The dog is still with me. I gave the cat to an American at a supply depot and he promised to look after it. The children were taken to a refugee camp at Kaesong."

"What are you goin' to do with the dog?" Doherty asked.

"I don't know. It is hard for me to keep him. I do a lot of traveling on foot and in a jeep. I don't stay in any one place for very long."

"Can I keep him, b'uy?" Doherty asked. "Our commanding officer wants us to train a few dogs for use in the front line. I'm hopin'. They be good companions, he says, and they can detect enemy activity much more easily than we can, and especially at night when they can smell intruders."

"I hate to give him up," Fontano said. "We are close friends. But maybe you can look after him better than I can." He attached a leash to the collar on the dog's neck and handed the leash to Doherty. "I call him Blackie".

"Blackie it is," Doherty replied enthusiastically. Fontano took one last sad look at the dog and walked away.

In the meantime, on Hill 589, a further 10 miles north, Commissar Wah Ching sat writing in candlelight in a deep underground bunker in a new and reinforced Chinese front-line position.

"Comrade General," he wrote. *"Greetings from the front line of your Chinese Peoples' Volunteers. I have recently returned from our position on what the enemy refers to, in their radio broadcasts, as Hill 857. I regret to inform you that the commander of the battalion on that hill, Wang Yalin, ignored my suggestion that proper fortifications be prepared, and that as a result, American planes delivered many napalm bombs and killed most members of his battalion. I fortunately was not present at the time or I also would have been eliminated. Wang Yalin was one of those who escaped, and he did so under questionable circumstances. He apparently left the hill shortly before the American aircraft strikes. He did not have deep, covered shelters built because his men complained that the work was too hard, and that they would, in any event, be retreating north in the near future. Wang listened to his men and the results were tragic. He is currently cowering in a nearby shelter and pondering his fate. His battalion no longer exists. I recommend that he be tried and punished severely in keeping with our code of military discipline."*

The recommendation for severe punishment for Wang Yalin was accepted and carried out two days later. Yalin was blindfolded, tied to a tree, and shot by a firing squad. The other Chinese battalion commanders paid close attention. They concluded that the recommendations of political commissars should be classified as direct orders, and that these orders should be carried out immediately and without questions of any kind.

CHAPTER 20
AT REST

The bright May sun rose above the eastern mountains bordering the Kapsang Valley. The Canadian Fusiliers Battalion, in reserve and at rest, was located the centre of the valley next to Kapsang village where their officers occupied a number of empty Korean houses. Further south, near the banks of the Kapsang River, were a number of large, cottage-shaped khaki-coloured tents belonging to a U.S. Army Mobile Army Surgical Hospital, otherwise known as a "M.A.S.H.".

On the eastern edge of the Valley a dozen New Zealand 25 pounder artillery pieces pointed ominously northward. Encamped behind them, in small pup tents, were the soldiers of the 1st Royal Australian Battalion, easily recognizable by the floppy fedora style hats folded on one side. 10 U.S. medium M26 Pershing tanks sat in a semi-circle near the Australians. Several shirtless Americans lay motionless on top of the tanks in an effort to tan their white winter skins.

The Canadians were very distinctive in their appearance. They were dressed in baggy, wind-resistant pants, Canadian Army arctic parkas, and U.S. Army combat boots. Now that a warm spring had arrived, only the outer detachable parts of the parkas were being worn. Some wore brown berets at various angles while others covered their heads with balaclavas; knitted toques that could be pulled down to cover the whole face except the eyes. The Fusiliers did not wear helmets, even under battle conditions. The uncomfortable dish-shaped WWII helmets that had been issued in Canada had been either discarded, or kept to be used as wash basins.

Peter Farley felt very happy and reflective. Korea was in fact the "land of the morning calm" on this occasion. After a period of fighting, the Fusiliers were having a well-deserved rest, with nothing to do but clean their weapons, wash their clothes, swim in a nearby reservoir, and go on occasional parades.

Sitting next to Farley was Kim, the platoon's teen-aged houseboy. It appeared that everyone in Korea was called Kim. Houseboy Kim had arrived a month earlier from parts unknown and had been adopted by the Canadians. He cleaned boots, prepared food and carried ammunition. He learned English quickly, and on this occasion was engaged in an informal English lesson given by Farley.

Farley's conversation with Kim was suddenly interrupted by the appearance of three Canadian Fusiliers carrying rifles, one of whom Farley immediately recognized. It was Jim Higgins, the short, blond private with a weasel face and beady dark brown eyes. Higgins was leading a young cow on a tether. Trailing immediately behind them was a sobbing young Korean girl of about 10 years of age. Farley then recognized the two other Canadians as John Busby and Albert Perkins. They were the ones, Farley remembered, who broke into the officers' food storage facility during the Pacific crossing. They were thieves.

Stolen boots, money and other items were found in their possession. All were notorious for their disruptive behaviour and disobedience. They had spent time in the battalion's detention barracks and were being prepared for expulsion to Canada.

"What are you doing with that cow?" Farley asked.

"None of your fucking business, Farley," Higgins snarled. "You want to know? We are sick of ham and lima beans and are going to cook some nice beef. Veal actually."

The young Korean girl stood in the background and continued sobbing.

"Kim," Farley said to the houseboy, "ask this girl what happened and why she is crying."

After speaking briefly with the girl Kim told Farley that the young cow was being raised by her family as a milk producer and not for meat. The three Canadians, Kim said, "steal cow from mother and father. They cry but Canadians have rifles. They said shut up or we shoot."

"So what else did the Gook girl say?" Higgins asked. "Did she tell you that we all fucked her mother? It was the best fuck we have had for quite a while. We would have fucked the girl but she was too small." He raised his rifle and pointed it at the cow. "Might as well get it over with right now. Stand back. I am going to shoot. Veal is on its way!"

The adrenalin rushed into Farley's bloodstream and, as in the case of similar previous critical occasions, his body was charged with extraordinary strength. He walked up to Higgins and delivered two violent blows to his face. Higgins collapsed and lay unconscious on the ground with blood pouring out of his mouth. Busby and Perkins were paralyzed with fear and both ran into a nearby forested area.

"Kim, tell the girl to take her cow home," Farley said to the houseboy. Farley then sank to the ground and held his head. All of his energy had been drained and he felt totally exhausted.

The girl, now with a smile on her face, grabbed the cow's tether and began walking away. "Ahn-yung-hah-sim-ni-kah," she said in Korean. "Thank you."

Farley was relieved by the successful conclusion of this ugly episode. Higgins, Busby and Perkins were all marched in front of the Commanding Officer the following day. In addition to theft, they were charged with the rape of the young Korean girl's mother.

They all denied raping the Korean woman. "We left her several cans of food," Higgins explained. "She liked it. She thanked us for the food."

"According to the Korean girl," Farley interjected, "they threatened the woman with their rifles. There was no consent."

"Where is this woman? I would like to speak with her," Strange said.

"I questioned her yesterday," Farley said. "Our houseboy translated for me. She is terrified and will not say anything about her encounter with Higgins, Busby and Perkins."

"Alright," Strange concluded. "That will be 90 days detention for all three of you, and after that expulsion to Canada and dishonourable discharges."

Peter was contented by the decision of Strange with regard to Higgins, Busby and Perkins, but also troubled because earlier that morning he had received a letter from Jean Haines, the beautiful blonde that he had met at the Palladium Dance Hall in Seattle. Their encounter remained vivid in his mind and he frequently thought of her. He was, at the same time, anxious about his disloyalty to Sonia Kereliuk, another woman who meant a great deal to him. Did he love Sonia? Yes, in many ways, but at times she seemed to fade from his memory, and especially when he saw other beautiful women. He was angered by his disloyalty and wondered why he behaved in this way.

The letter was addressed to *"Peter O. Farley, c/o Canadian*

Army, Sweet Grass, Manitoba" and had been re-addressed and forwarded to him in Korea.

"*Dear Peter,*" Jean Haines wrote. "*I think of you every day and I hope and pray that you are still safe and in good health. I know that you are somewhere in Korea. I follow the news and read about the war, and your unit, the Fusiliers, is sometimes mentioned. About a week ago I went to see the movie 'Gone with the Wind' and the Movie Tone News, at the beginning, showed your unit in action. I am sure that I saw you!*

I hope that you will be pleased to know that I have vacated my apartment and returned home to live with my mother. I plan to begin studies for a Bachelor of Science degree next September at the University of Washington.

My aunt Mary died recently and left me a large legacy. This money will allow me to attend university for as long as I wish. I am very grateful to Aunt Mary. She remained single and left a lot of money to her family and charities when she died.

But I am mainly writing to tell you, Peter, that I am pregnant. Please believe me when I tell you that I am absolutely certain that you are the father. Yes, regretfully, I have had encounters with other men, but I have always been careful with the others. You were an exception. I will always remember our time together as one of the most beautiful events in my life. I will never forget you.

I have delayed going to the university until after I have had the baby. That's why I said next September rather than this September. My mother, who recently retired as a nurse, has agreed to look after the baby until he or she is ready to go to school. I can also afford to hire a nanny, which I plan to do, and this will greatly relieve my mother's responsibilities and the amount of time that she will need to spend with the baby.

I hope that this information does not trouble you too much, because I know that you have many other things to worry about at this time. You are in a war and must try to survive.

I have hesitated to write this letter, but finally decided that I should tell you about our baby. I would like to see you again when you return from Korea, but I want you to know that returning or not returning will be your decision and that I will not press the matter if you decide to stay away. Are you obligated to anyone else? You never did tell me.

Are you interested in seeing me again? Please write. My new address is on the envelope that comes with this letter. I love you very much. Love, Jean."

"*Yes, I love this woman,*" he said to himself. "*But this love does not make a lot of sense. I knew her for only a few hours. I seem to fall deeply in love with every beautiful woman I meet. What should I do?* " It was a troubling question that he could not answer.

This was also the day of the "big fight" between Jim Doherty, the Canadian Army heavyweight boxing champion, and Miles Lewis, the champion of the 23rd U.S. Regimental Combat Team.

According to reports, Lewis was a large African American with an impressive semi-professional boxing record. Although the 23rd R.C.T. was a white formation, Lewis had been commandeered by its commanding officer for the sole purpose of bringing athletic prestige to his unit and himself.

The fight was not scheduled to begin until 1:00 p.m., but truckloads of Americans began arriving about an hour earlier. A boxing area was roped off on the ground next to a steep slope on the southern edge of the valley, and the U.S. soldiers moved in quickly to take up their allotted positions. They were joined soon afterwards by the Fusiliers as well as large numbers of Scots from the Glasgow Highlanders, the Australian Battalion, and New Zealanders from their artillery regiment.

"The Yanks are fuckin' poor fighters," one Scot said loudly. "It's sure tough oot here. They only get ice cream once a week!"

The Americans in Korea were often teased by the fact that

ice cream was served regularly to their forces. Ice cream was considered by many, including the senior officers of the British Commonwealth Division, to be an expensive and unnecessary addition to a military battlefield diet.

Four American nurses from the M.A.S.H. arrived in two jeeps and were seated in a separate area by themselves. A lot of friendly whistling took place. The nurses smiled but looked embarrassed. They were, after all, officers and most of those in the crowd were other ranks.

Farley noticed that one of the nurses had bright red hair and a beautiful, pale, freckled face. *"What is a spectacular woman like that doing in this God-forsaken place?"* he asked himself. He wanted to walk over and speak with her but noticed that two large and menacing military policemen stood near her and the other nurses. Meeting the redhead would be impossible he decided, and he turned his attention to the fight.

Many bottles of Japanese Asahi beer appeared, as well as prohibited bottles of hard liquor. Before long many in the crowd were inebriated.

"Hear Hear! Let's have a jeer for the boxing Fusilier," a self-appointed American cheerleader shouted. The other Americans began laughing, clapping and yelling.

"Combat team?" a loud Canadian shouted. "Hell, you bastards are only famous for shagging ass, bugging out, in other words, panic retreating. You can't even fight your own battles. Your champ is a bloody import!"

"Excuses, excuses," the American cheerleader yelled. "Listen to the Canucks make excuses. Go back to your igloos, you frozen northern turds!"

Then other soldiers from the two opposing sides began insulting each other. Many Australians and New Zealanders joined with the Canadians and began fighting the Americans. Some empty beer bottles flew through the air. Fights broke out in several places, as well as wrestling and shoving matches. Several American and Canadian officers and military policemen moved in to break up the antagonists, but only with moderate success.

The arrival of the two boxers in the ring stopped the fighting and the surly, drunken crowd turned its attention to the main event. Sergeant Jones accompanied Doherty. The American's second was a short, bald U.S. lieutenant. The referee was a large Australian corporal.

Miles Lewis, the American boxer, was a tall, rangy man with light chocolate coloured skin, a handsome face and very long arms. Doherty's face, hands and forearms were deeply tanned, but the rest of his muscular body was a pale white, almost the same colour as his blond, curly hair.

The Australian referee moved into the centre of the ring and called the two fighters to his side. They touched gloves, backed away, and began circling each other cautiously.

"Fight, you bastards!" one of the Americans shouted.

It was apparent, even before any punching began, that the American was a superior boxer. He danced gracefully from side to side and feinted punches with obvious skill and experience. He had fought many fights and knew what he was doing.

Doherty, on the other hand, was flat-footed and awkward looking. He was more muscular, and appeared to be stronger, but his arms were considerably shorter than those of Lewis.

Suddenly Lewis lunged forward and caught Doherty squarely in the jaw with a powerful right. The Canadian seemed to freeze in his tracks, and then sank to his knees in apparent bewilderment. The Americans cheered wildly. Blood poured out of Doherty's nose and down his chin. The referee counted to eight before Doherty was able to stagger to his feet. Lewis took another long and fast swing, but missed. Doherty began moving quickly around the ring to avoid the aroused and confident American. Finally the Australian referee waved his arm to signal the end of the first round.

As the two fighters were attended to by their seconds the Canadians, Australians, Scots and New Zealanders sat in relative silence, while the Americans cheered and danced around excitedly.

"Hear! Hear! Let's have another jeer for the wounded Fusilier!" the American cheerleader shouted.

Meanwhile, Sergeant Jones barked anxious commands to his bloodied fighter. "Your left, Doherty, your fucking left. He's right-handed and isn't used to southpaws. It's your natural advantage. And move in close, because he's got a longer reach."

"Yeah, yeah," Doherty replied sarcastically. "You make it sound easy."

As the boxers rested momentarily, Peter Farley moved among the Canadians in the crowd. "I'm taking bets on Doherty," he announced. "I've got a 100 bucks saying he will win." Farley had made an agreement with Doherty prior to the fight. He promised to place a 100 dollar bet and to share the proceeds equally with Doherty. He hoped that the money would stimulate Doherty towards a win. A victory seemed highly unlikely now, but Farley had made a promise and could not back out.

Several Canadians rushed forward to take up Farley's offer. Most placed 10 dollar bets. They obviously wanted Doherty to win, but thought that they would at least be able to salvage a monetary reward as compensation for his disappointing performance.

"You are crazy, Red," one of the Canadians said as Farley wrote their names and bets onto a sheet of paper. "Doherty is a dead duck."

The second round began slowly once again, with both fighters circling each other cautiously. Then the American unleashed another powerful right, catching Doherty squarely above the left eye. Doherty's blood began pouring again, from above his eye as well as his nose.

But at the moment of impact a feeling of overpowering fury swept through the Canadian. It caused a sudden and very powerful adrenaline rush. He had had this feeling before, and whenever it came over him, strength seemed to surge through him in a superhuman manner.

Doherty began jabbing furiously at Lewis, and the surprised American retreated backwards into a corner. Doherty then moved in until he was very close to Lewis. The long arms of the American were no longer an advantage. Doherty planted his feet firmly and suddenly delivered a powerful left-handed blow to the American's stomach. Lewis doubled over, clutching instinctively to his middle as Doherty moved his left hand back as far as he could reach. Then the Canadian threw a circling punch with all of his greatly enhanced strength and landed it squarely in the face of the American. Lewis seemed to smile for an instant, as though the blow was inconsequential, but then his arms dropped to his sides, his knees buckled, and he fell face forward onto the ground with a heavy thud. He remained on the ground as the referee counted to 10, and even then did not move.

The Canadians, Scots, Australians and New Zealanders burst into loud cheers and began jumping up and down and shouting insults at the stunned American spectators. Several fist fights broke out once again. Canadian and American military policemen began herding the two groups away into opposite directions.

"Frozen northern turds!" the American cheerleader yelled. An Australian rushed over and punched the cheerleader in the face. The cheerleader was suddenly silenced and he, along with the other Americans, climbed onto their waiting trucks and were driven away. The American nurses boarded their two jeeps and left for their quarters at the nearby M.A.S.H.

Farley shoved his way through the cheering Canadians until he finally reached Doherty, who sat on an empty ammunition can in his corner of the ring. Doherty's face was cut in several places. Both eyes were swollen and blackened and two of his front teeth were missing.

"We won, Jim, we won!" Farley shouted excitedly to Doherty who sat passively with a stunned look on his face.

"Are you kidding, b'uy?" Look at me bloody face."

"Don't worry, Jim, it will heal. As promised I bet a 100 bucks on you and I am going to give you half of it."

"Thanks, Red. That's 25 bucks for each tooth. Where did I hear that before? 25 dollars, I mean."

"Don't remind me," Farley said with a sad look on his face. "It still hurts to think about her. She was a very beautiful American girl. Did you see those lovely American nurses today? I love American women."

"Forget it, Red. The blonde broad in Seattle was a whore. You done the right thing."

At that moment Miles Lewis suddenly appeared in front of them. His face was unmarked and he looked fresh and rested as though nothing had happened to him. He held out his right hand to Doherty. "Great fight," he said. He had been ordered by his commanding officer to demonstrate good sportsmanship.

Doherty stood up and shook hands with Lewis. "Thanks," he said. "It looks like you actually won the fight. You be in great shape and I'm goin' to take a month to recover."

Farley then introduced himself to Lewis. "I'm sorry about all of the nastiness that happened among the spectators. I am surprised. Canadians are usually very close to Americans," Farley said.

"I am too," Lewis said. "I blame it on the beer, liquor, and a few hotheads."

"It was that cheerleader who started it all. One of your guys. He got everyone stirred up. I hope that we will meet again. Maybe we can schedule a re-match," Farley said with a smile.

"Not bloody likely," Doherty said. "I've had enough for a while."

"The next time you are in our area give us a shout and we will find you a beer," Farley said.

"Thanks. The same here. Let me know if you are ever around my unit."

They all shook hands again and left.

The men of the nearby battery of the Royal Canadian Mounted Artillery were also at rest at this time, and most of them had attended the fight between the Canadian and American. A few, however, had slipped away and had traveled to nearby Seoul, the devastated capital of South Korea.

One of those who had not been at the fight was a blond sergeant with the Artillery. He had "rented" a jeep from a Royal Canadian Service Corps corporal who was in charge of a Canadian vehicle compound. The "rent" consisted of two bottles of Canadian whiskey and two cases of Asahi Japanese beer.

"Be sure to bring this jeep back after four days sergeant," the corporal said, "or else both of us will be in deep shit."

"Yeah, I understand," the sergeant said. "Don't worry. I'll be back."

The artillery sergeant drove to Kimpo Airport on the outskirts of Seoul and waited impatiently at the passenger arrival centre. Several planes arrived but they carried supplies and no passengers.

Finally, after several hours had passed, a United States army transport plane rolled to a noisy and windy stop near the arrival centre. The pilots gave their engines a final burst of power before shutting them down. A line of passengers, mostly American soldiers, disembarked down a precarious metal ladder.

After the soldiers and other passengers had left the plane, a beautiful blonde appeared in the plane's door. She hesitated for a moment and then carefully climbed down the ladder. Her short green dress revealed long and shapely legs. She also had a well-developed upper body, a beautiful smile and an exceptionally pretty face.

"Maggie!" the Canadian sergeant yelled. "It, me, Buzz! Over here!" It was Henry "Buzz" Grabowski, the former chief negotiator for the International Bus Drivers' and Ticket Agents' Union of America.

Maggie Marek, Grabowski's former assistant and union employee, came running as fast as she could. Her high heels pounded an erotic tattoo on the concrete runway. She fell into Grabowski's arms and shrieked with delight.

"How did you manage to get me a ticket to Seoul?" she asked. "I was told that civilians are not allowed into the war zone."

"It took a lot of intelligence and money, baby," he boasted. "Have you heard of Maggie Higgins? She is a famous war correspondent who has been living and working in Korea. So I figured, if Maggie Higgins can come to Korea why not Maggie Marek? You are both beautiful American women, so why not? You can stay in Korea as a correspondent as long as you like. I will be able to visit you from time to time whenever my unit is in reserve and at rest. And if you need money, I can always help. The Rockwood Gazette does not pay much, I know."

"You are very smart, Buzz," Maggie replied. "I did everything you told me to do. I took the train from Vancouver to Rockwood, that small town in the interior of British Columbia. I met with Ed Bailey, the editor of the Rockwood Gazette."

"Yeah, I remember that cheap, sneaky son of a bitch."

"He said that he knew you because you were both in the union at one time. He had press credentials for me but said that they were not quite ready. He said I was beautiful. I needed to speed him up. I had to please him, I'm afraid."

"That bastard! I had to pay him big money to get your press credentials!" Grabowski said with an angry scowl. "Okay, Maggie, I don't want to hear anything more about it. The important thing is that you're here now. I have been going nuts waiting for you."

"Where did you get all of this money, Buzz?" she asked. "All of this must have cost you a fortune."

"Never mind, baby," he said with a smile. "All you need to know is that I had a big payday!"

In the meantime a group of American servicemen gathered around to stare at Maggie as she stood talking with Grabowski. They gaped at her blonde hair, pale skin, large blue eyes, prominent breasts, slim waist and shapely legs with a mixture of envy, admiration and lust. Why was this beautiful but unattainable American woman in their midst? Korean women could also be very beautiful, but only if they lived and worked in cities and dressed in modern, western-style clothing. The half-starved rural Korean women that these men had encountered worked in filthy rice paddies, were dressed in shapeless and strange clothing and were without attractive features of any kind.

Grabowski stared at the intruders with obvious displeasure, but they seemed to be totally oblivious to his presence. "Fuck off, bloody American pigs!" he yelled.

"Buzz!" Maggie protested. "Remember that I'm an American, too!"

"Yeah, I forgot, baby," he said. "There's my jeep over there." He pointed to where several vehicles were parked and they walked over.

"A jeep!" she squealed as they climbed in. "Money will buy everything!"

"You are so right. You don't know how right you are," Grabowski said with a smile.

The jeep rumbled along through a series of rubble-strewn streets lined with mostly lifeless and shattered buildings. After about 15 minutes Grabowski pulled over to a dingy but still intact structure that carried the name "Oriental Hotel" over a false Roman portal. He pulled the jeep into a nearby parking lot. They got out, walked to the front of the building, and climbed up the dozen steps that led to the entrance. But as they were about to enter, they were confronted by an American Army captain and three large U.S. military policemen.

"Do you have a pass, sergeant?" the captain asked. He was short, had small dark eyes and a round face. He was sweating profusely.

"Of course, sir," Grabowski replied. He reached into his pocket and produced a rumpled piece of paper.

"This does not appear to be in order," the captain announced belligerently after only a very brief glance at the document. "And who is the lady you are with?"

"Maggie's a reporter, a war correspondent. So what's wrong with my pass? It's perfectly legitimate."

"A war correspondent?" the captain asked with a sigh. "That's too bad. I'm afraid that you are contravening regulations of the U.S. Army. Other ranks are not allowed to fraternize with correspondents. You'll have to return to your unit. Go quickly now, or we will have to arrest you."

"But sir," Grabowski protested loudly. "You can't do this. I'm a Canadian. I don't have to follow American army regulations. You are just making this up. I'm with the forces of the United Nations. What in hell is going on here? Maggie and I are good friends. She has come all the way from Canada to see me. I had to pay a fortune to get her here. You can't…"

Two of the military policemen grabbed Grabowski by his arms and tried to lead him away. Anger surged through Grabowski's powerful body. He was desperate. He cocked his right fist and drove it with a loud thud into the face of the closest policemen holding him. As the policeman fell to the ground in a semi-conscious heap the second policeman hit Grabowski over the head with his baton. Grabowski sank slowly to the ground in a stunned daze, and as he did so the second policeman snapped handcuffs onto his wrists. Shortly afterwards the policeman that Grabowski had punched rose up. The policemen then led Grabowski away to their waiting vehicle. Grabowski shouted and cursed but it was to no avail. He had struck an MP and was guilty of a serious offence. He would spend the next week in an American military detention centre.

In the meantime the American captain took Maggie by the arm and led her towards the door of the hotel. "You must be very tired after such a long trip," he said smoothly and reassuringly.

"But what about Henry?" she asked. "Please let him go."

"Don't worry, my dear. They are just sending him back to his unit. He'll only get into trouble if he stays in Seoul."

"I'm also worried about myself," she said with a sob. "What am I going to do? Henry made all the arrangements. How will I get home?"

"I will look after everything. I have connections."

"Gee, you seem to be a very nice guy," she said with a nervous giggle.

"I'll look after you. Here. Give me your bag. I'll help you get a room and unpack. Seoul is a dangerous place. We wouldn't want you to fall into the hands of the enemy, would we? Maggie? That's a lovely name. Let's go, Maggie. Hold my hand. Those high heels are beautiful but also dangerous. Watch you don't fall!"

CHAPTER 21
THE FEVER

Shortly after the advent of the big fight Peter Farley was sent to take a non-commissioned officers course at Taegu. Captain Levinson, the Battalion Adjutant, noted that Farley had some university education and that he would be a good candidate for promotion. A corporal or sergeant forward observer was needed by the 81 mm. Platoon because one had recently been killed by a Chinese artillery shell. Farley was reluctant to leave Doherty and #5 Platoon, but went to Taegu quietly because he realized that a protest would not change anything.

Jim Doherty had also been considered because an IQ score of 147 was recorded on his personnel document. A score of 100 was supposed to designate average intelligence and Doherty's score was deemed to be superior. For some reason Farley did not have an IQ score on his file. Farley was chosen because he had two years of university education as compared to Doherty's Grade 10. Farley and Doherty were both unaware of these considerations. In fact, Doherty did not even know that he was being considered. The Canadian Army of the 1950's did not consult with private soldiers or follow human relations guidelines of any kind. Orders were given and obedience without questions was expected and demanded.

Farley spent two weeks at Taegu. He studied leadership, map reading, radio handling and communications, tactics and weapons, and especially the operation and function of the 81 mm. mortar. He had an advantage over his classmates, most of whom had not completed high school studies. He stood first in his class. After the course was finished he was promoted to the rank of corporal and sent back to the Fusiliers.

Shortly after his return Farley experienced chills, muscle pain and a high fever. He began to sweat profusely. He dreamed about the death and destruction that he had witnessed at the Thunder River train wreck, and especially about the dead Korean woman and wounded children in the village that had been destroyed by his Battalion's mortars. Bad dreams and disturbing flashbacks were becoming increasingly frequent. *"The fever is probably caused by the flu,"* he thought, summoning up knowledge from his limited medical training. He tossed and turned during the first night of his illness, sleeping fitfully. However, the next morning the fever, pain and chills stopped and he said nothing. He did not want to gain a reputation as a "lead-swinger", a label that was given to men who pretended sickness, lied, or who even ran away to escape the dangers and rigors of front-line duty.

The method of getting out of the war was not difficult. It consisted of pretending to have stomach pains, or back problems, or even hallucinations, anything that a medical doctor could not accurately diagnose. It depended upon the characters of those exposed to the dangers and terror of front line combat. Men with strong feelings of loyalty, self-respect and revulsion at the thought of being labeled as failures or cowards would endure any kind of pain, participate willingly in hazardous missions, and sometimes even take very dangerous chances in battle situations. The Fusiliers, as a Canadian regiment with a glorious history of engagements in WWI and WWII, was a semi-mystical brotherhood that provided an additional support for its members to be heroic and stoic in battle. Fusiliers were expected to fight and die if necessary. The members of this brotherhood would never surrender or retreat unless ordered to do so.

The American Army in the years following WWII was quite different. "Bug outs" or unordered retreats in Korea were fairly common. At the insistence of the U.S. Congress, the American Army after WWII had been forced to become democratic and sensitive to the rights of its soldiers. According Col. T.R. Fehrenbach, a U.S. Korean War veteran, the young men in the American army "found that they could get away with plenty. A soldier could tell his sergeant to blow it. In the old Army he might have been bashed, and found immediately what the rules are going to be. In the Canadian Army he would have been marched in front of his company commander, had his pay reduced, perhaps even been confined for 30 days. He would have learned instantly that orders are to be obeyed."

The U.S. Marines, on the other hand, largely escaped this democratic weakness. The Marines, like the Canadians, were all volunteers, and they lived with a strict code of military discipline. Marines did not "bug out" when attacked by the enemy. Most American soldiers didn't bug out either, especially if they had strong officers. A lack of discipline, however, sometimes caused problems in some U.S. Army units.

A total of 25 Canadians in WWI had been executed by firing squads because they had deserted from the front lines, allegedly for cowardice. "Battle fatigue" was not an acceptable excuse.

Executions of deserters did not take place in WWII or Korea, but men who left their front line positions, or who feigned illness, were held in contempt. Even self-inflicted wounds were used occasionally by those who could not cope. A shot in the foot might bring a trip to Japan, 30 days detention and a dishonourable discharge, but these results were better, in some fragile minds, than being shot dead by a blazing Chinese burp gun, or being blown into bloody shreds by a mortar or artillery shell.

Lieutenant Colonel Strange had a simple remedy for lead-swingers. "Send these chicken bastards home," he told Major Karpinski, his medical officer. "I don't want riff raff in my battalion. Get rid of them."

Karpinski was glad to oblige. He was tired of seeing the same people day after day at his medical tent. After the battalion's first contact with the enemy, he labeled 15 Fusiliers as "unfit for combat" because of various "psychological and physical problems". Karpinski and most other military medical doctors were not trained to recognize, diagnose and treat war neurosis. Canadians in Korea suffering from the stresses of combat were promptly sent back to Canada and released from the army.

Farley was an intelligent romantic with visions of glory for himself and his comrades. He had voluntarily read a great deal of military history while in school. He had listened attentively to the war stories told by his two older brothers, both of whom had served with the Fusiliers in WWII. He had accepted, although with some reservations, the "we're the best regiment" lectures given during his basic and advanced infantry training, as well as similar talks given by Lieutenant-Colonel Strange. He would rather run the risk of dying than be called a coward. Canadians, he believed, were among the best soldiers in the world, and he was proud to be one of them.

On his second day back to the Battalion his fever returned with even greater intensity. As his temperature soared he felt strangely uninhibited and emotionally high, as though he had been drinking heavily. He could not sleep well.

Farley decided to discuss his problems with Jim Doherty, rather than with Major Karpinski. Farley walked to the small tent where Doherty was sleeping alone and gave him a shake.

"What is it, Red?" Doherty asked. "You woke me up from a very pleasant dream."

"How can you sleep and have pleasant dreams?" Farley asked plaintively. "You have experienced the same horrible things as I have, but they don't seem to bother you."

"I ain't a psychologist, Red, but I got an idea. Some people, like you, they be born extremely sensitive. I feels sympathetic when I sees people and animals wounded and dyin', but I don' allow my emotions to overpower me. Your extreme sensitivity seems to be a serious handicap. I knows you suffers a lot."

At that moment Sergeant Herbie Jones came walking up to Farley and Doherty. He immediately noticed that something was wrong with Farley.

"Corporal," he demanded. "Are you sick? Your face is red and you seem to be shaking."

"Yeah, I guess I am sick," Farley replied.

"Then get down to Major Karpinski right away" Jones ordered. "We need another mortar forward observer and we want you to be healthy and available."

It took Major Karpinski about 30 seconds to make a diagnosis. "I think you have malaria, young man," he said. "We have had several cases recently. Have you been taking your anti-malarial pills?"

"Yes, sir, I have" Farley replied. "But to be honest, sometimes I forget. It's easy to forget, especially if we are busy."

"I don't have facilities to test you for malaria here, so I am going to send you to the American M.A.S.H." He looked at the medical orderly standing next to him. "Anderson," he said, "take my jeep and drive this man to the M.A.S.H." He quickly scribbled on a note pad, tore off a page, and gave it to Anderson. "And take this note to the medical reception area. They know me and will help the corporal with his problem."

Anderson and Farley climbed into Major Karpinski's jeep and in about 10 minutes arrived at a cluster of large M.A.S.H. tents.

"Admitting" read a large black and white sign in front of one of the tents. Further down, in letters of slightly smaller size, was printed: "12th Mobile Army Surgical Hospital, United States Army Medical Corps."

The two Canadians entered the admitting tent and were greeted by a lanky U.S. sergeant sitting at a makeshift table piled with papers, files and a cup of instant "C ration" coffee.

"Hey, corporal," the American said with a cocky smile, "you've got your stripes on upside down." He pointed to his own stripes, with the tips of the V's pointing upwards rather than downwards as in the case of the Canadian.

"My stripes are V for victory," Farley retorted. "Yours looks like an A, and you know what that means." His fever was making him aggressive.

The American frowned and looked annoyed but did not pursue the matter. "What can I do for you?" he asked.

"Corporal Farley is sick," Anderson, Farley's driver volunteered. "Can one of your doctors have a look at him?" He handed Major Karpinski's note to the sergeant.

"I'll get someone," the American replied.

"Good luck, corporal," Anderson said. He then climbed into his jeep and drove away, leaving Farley alone with the American.

Farley was feeling the effects of a very high fever. He suddenly felt ebullient, friendly, confident and on top of the world. It was as though he had been drinking heavily and was drunk.

All of his normal inhibitions seemed to have disappeared.

The American took Farley to one of the nearby M.A.S.H. tents, told him to lie down on one of the empty beds, and left him alone. Several wounded men lay beside him, and one of them groaned continuously, frequently calling for his mother. Farley felt guilty. "I'm just another lead-swinger," he thought. "I don't belong in this tent with these wounded people."

Soon afterwards a short, middle-aged, pleasant looking American officer with U.S. Medical Corps insignia on his uniform came up to Farley's bed. "I'm Major Powers," he said with a slight southern American accent.

The Major questioned Farley thoroughly about his symptoms, took his temperature, and peered into his throat, eyes and ears. "Lieutenant Morgan," he called loudly, "come in here please."

A very attractive, slim, tall, red-headed young woman in a U.S. Army Medical Corps uniform came into the tent and up to the bed where Farley was laying. She looked curiously at Farley, realizing by his uniform that he was not an American.

"Yes, sir, who do we have here? I don't think that he is an American. Then again, he's obviously not a Korean. I see red hair sticking out of that funny hat!" she said. Farley was still wearing his balaclava.

"He's one of the Canadians camped in the valley to the north of us," the Major explained. "He has a temperature of 106 F degrees, and according to what he's told me, he had a fever two days ago, skipped a day, and then got it again. Some delirium is evident, probably caused by his high fever. Take a blood smear and sponge him with alcohol. We have got to get his fever down. It's highly likely that he has malaria." Then he turned and left, leaving Morgan alone with Farley.

"Aren't you the beautiful nurse I saw at the boxing match?" Farley asked.

"Yes, I was at the boxing match," she responded with a smile. "There were other beautiful nurses there as well, and not just me."

"Yes," he said, "but I only had eyes for you."

She looked at Farley with a faint look of embarrassment. "Strip down to your shorts, and take that silly hat off," she ordered. She grasped his right hand, quickly punctured his forefinger, and smeared blood onto a glass plate.

In the meantime, Farley was not paying attention to what was happening. He stared in complete fascination at the beautiful young woman in his presence. *"Is she real, or am I just dreaming?"* he wondered half-seriously.

Hyong, a male South Korean orderly, entered the tent. "Lieutenant? I here to help," he said with a thick Korean accent. The anxious look on his face revealed that he took his work seriously.

"Help this man take his boots off while I get some alcohol". She left the tent briefly and returned carrying two bottles of rubbing alcohol. She gave one to Hyong. "Turn over on your stomach," she said to Farley.

"But I don't like alcohol," Farley said with a laugh. "It does nothing for me except give me a headache!" He felt strangely happy, bold, aggressive and confident. His eyes were glassy and sweat poured down his flushed face and burning body. He felt like he had been drinking a lot of alcohol.

Morgan poured some alcohol into a cupped palm. She splashed it on Farley's back and swished it all over, rubbing vigorously. Hyong did the same on Farley's legs.

"You like that, don't you Morgan?" Farley asked, his voice quivering with mock seriousness.

"Don't get impertinent, young man. Remember that I am an American officer."

"Okay, Lieutenant Morgan. I did not mean to offend you.

I just feel silly and happy. The whole world has gone crazy. I can't believe that this is actually happening to me."

"I understand, Farley," she said.

"Peter is my first name. Why don't you call me Peter?"

"Alright, Peter. Your name is not very important right now. Turn over on your back."

Farley turned over but at the same time threw his arms upwards in a gesture of mock surrender. "I'm yours!" he said with a howl of laughter.

"Peter! I mean Corporal Farley! Behave yourself!"

"I'll try. But what's your first name, Morgan? Where are you from?"

It's Laura and I'm from Minneapolis."

"I think that I like Morgan even better than Laura. They are both lovely names and they suit you. Morgan sounds more distinguished and mysterious. Do you mind if I call you Morgan?"

"It's acceptable for the time being."

"After you cure me, will I ever see you again, or are we just two ships passing in the night?"

"I'm impressed, Corporal Farley. That's from Longfellow. I memorized that passage when I was going to school in Minneapolis. 'Ships that pass in the night, and speak to each other in passing. So on the ocean of life we pass and speak to one another. Only a look and a voice; then darkness again and a silence'."

Hyong, the Korean orderly, remained quiet and impassive during this verbal exchange. Farley suddenly eyed him suspiciously. "Who is this guy? Does he speak much English? Is he on our side?" he asked Morgan.

"Hyong is one our very best orderlies," Morgan replied. "Be thankful he is here."

"Thanks, Hyong. I did not mean to hurt your feelings," Farley said seriously. Hyong smiled but said nothing. Farley liked Koreans, but remembered being told that a few of them were probably communist sympathizers.

Morgan produced a thermometer and inserted it into Farley's mouth. "Hold this under your tongue," she ordered. He complied and continued to look at her with deep fascination.

She read the thermometer and looked at Hyong. "Get more alcohol, Hyong. And please hurry."

"Yeah, Hyong, don't leave me too long with this beautiful woman!" Farley exclaimed.

Shortly after Hyong left the tent a series of loud explosions suddenly filled the air and several holes appeared in the roof of their tent.

"We are being shelled!" Farley shouted. "Get down! He rose from his bed, grabbed Morgan and threw her to the ground. They lay motionless for a few seconds. Then Farley took Morgan by the hand and ran out of the tent. "Let's get out of here," he ordered. There was a lot of shouting as the wounded soldiers in the tent ran, and in some cases limped, to nearby foxholes.

Morgan and Farley ran outside and jumped over the edge of a nearby rice paddy. He pushed her into a small corner where two paddies adjoined, and instinctively covered her body with his. Shells continued landing and exploding all around them in loud crunching sounds.

Morgan began sobbing. She had been in Korea for six months and had seen much bloodshed as a member of the 12th M.A.S.H., but had never been exposed to shellfire before. She held on to Peter closely, her body shaking with fright.

"It's going to be okay, Morgan," Farley said reassuringly. They will run out of shells eventually."

A powerful feeling of warmth and attachment came over Morgan. She felt calm, assured and relaxed, with her sense of military propriety almost completely dissipated.

The shelling stopped as suddenly as it had started. It was

almost as though a sinister magic spell was broken. Farley sat up, his body and shorts covered in mud.

Morgan's uniform and face were also splattered. They both began to laugh.

"I'm ashamed of myself," Morgan said sheepishly. "I'm afraid that I did not show much courage."

"Don't worry about it. I was shaking just as badly," Farley replied. "I think I should lay down again. My fever seems to be gone but I feel very weak and dizzy."

"Let's go back to our tent," she replied. "Except for a few holes it seems to be intact."

As they walked towards the tent they came across a body sprawled on the ground. It was Hyong, the Korean orderly who had helped to sponge Farley down. He lay on his stomach, with a bottle of rubbing alcohol still in his right hand. The whole top of his head had been sliced away by shrapnel and the ground around him was soaked in bright red blood.

"Oh, Hyong, I'm so sorry!" Morgan said as she paused in front of his body.

"I'm sorry too," Farley said awkwardly. He bent down and pulled the bottle of alcohol from Hyong's grasp. "I guess this was meant for me," he said sadly while looking at the bottle. "You asked him to get it." He handed the bottle to Morgan.

Morgan took the bottle from Farley and looked into his face. Tears were running down her cheeks. "I should tell you that I wasn't just afraid for myself. I thought that I was going to lose you. That thought was very distressing for me."

They walked back to the tent together. She led him to his bed, ordered him to lie down, and covered him with two dark brown woolen blankets.

"It gets cold at night," she said.

"Yes, it does."

"Major Powers and I will see you again in the morning."

"Morgan, I don't know how to say this, but I feel very attracted to you. You are a beautiful woman. But it's more than that. My whole life has suddenly changed. You mean everything to me."

"I'm attracted to you too, Peter, but we don't know very much about each other. Besides, I'm an American, and you're a Canadian. I'm an officer and you are a corporal. Right now we are worlds apart. We have to be very careful."

"Yes, I guess we could get into a lot of trouble just by being together. Officers and other ranks are not allowed to be friends in both of our armies. Fraternization is illegal."

"Good night, corporal," she said with an air of authority and finality. "I'll see you in the morning."

"I love you, lieutenant," he responded with a smile. "You are the first lieutenant that I have ever loved." He was surprised at how easily these words came to him.

She smiled and started to reply but quickly turned away and left.

Major Powers and Lieutenant Morgan arrived at Farley's bed the following morning at 0800 hours. Peter was still asleep. Powers shook him gently by the shoulder. "Wake up, soldier," he ordered.

Farley opened his eyes and looked around him. "Good morning, sir, good morning ma'am," he said cheerfully. "What's the diagnosis?"

"It will take a while for the results of your blood smear are returned," Powers answered. "But I'm virtually certain that you have malaria. Lieutenant Morgan has some medicine to give you."

"What is it?" Farley asked.

"It's chloroquine," Morgan replied. "It should suppress your malaria."

"Does that mean that I can go back to my unit?"

"Not for a few days at least," Powers said. "I may send you back to a field hospital for a while. Your fever may return."

"Please, sir, let me stay here. I don't want to get too far away from my unit. As you know, they are only a few miles from here."

"Well, we will see how it goes," Powers replied. "You can stay here as long as we don't get a new flood of casualties. Right now it's fairly quiet."

"Thank you, sir," Farley said as he looked into Morgan's face. She remained silent, but he could tell that she was pleased with the prospect of having him stay longer.

Powers and Morgan then continued their rounds with other patients and eventually disappeared from Farley's tent. However, Morgan returned early in the afternoon to see him again.

"It's a beautiful sunny day," she said. "Why don't you come outside? I have to take your temperature, so I will sit with you for a while."

"That sounds like a marvelous idea!" he exclaimed. "Can we talk?"

"Not for very long. I have other patients that I also have to look after."

Several unoccupied folding chairs sat in an area behind the tent. Farley sat in one of them and waited for Morgan to arrive. He watched in fascination as she circled the tent and walked gracefully towards him.

"You are an absolutely stunning woman," he said with some hesitation. His fever and delirium were gone and he did not feel as confident as he had during his first meeting with Morgan the previous day.

"Thank you," she replied as she inserted a thermometer into his mouth. "But be careful. Remember that you haven't seen any American or Canadian women for a long time. Maybe I just look good for that reason."

"No. You would look good anywhere and at anytime. I feel as though I have known you for a long time. It is almost as though we were pre-destined to meet. Maybe it's our manifest destiny."

"Pre-destined? Are you a Calvinist?"

"No. I'm a Catholic. A Ukrainian Catholic, actually, but not a very good one. I don't go to church much. I believe that we are responsible for our own destinies. We have free will."

"And manifest destiny? Where have I heard that before?"

"Don't you know? I read about it in a history course. It's a term that Americans used in the 19th century. It meant that Canada was destined to become a part of the United States; that a union was pre-ordained; that nothing could prevent it from actually taking place."

"That sounds exciting! I have always been in favour of unions, and especially with attractive and wealthy countries like Canada. I have to confess that many Americans are uninformed about Canada. You sound exactly like someone from Minnesota. You accent is more American than that of Major Powers who is from the deep south."

"But both sides have to be in favor of a union," he noted. "Otherwise, it's a case of unrequited love. That's fascinating, but don't you think that we should be talking about ourselves? As you say, we don't have much time."

"Maybe we should. I have to confess that I'm going through all kinds of inner turmoil. Under other circumstances, I could go for you very quickly. You have suddenly become a very important person in my life. In fact, I could hardly sleep last night. I couldn't stop thinking about you."

"I'm very happy to hear you say that," he replied. "I feel exactly the same way except that I am not experiencing any kind of turmoil. I'm absolutely sure."

They continued talking together for several minutes, their

eyes in almost constant contact. They seemed to be oblivious to everything and everyone around them, including several soldiers sitting in the area nearby.

"Morgan," he said, "I'm scheduled to go on a five day rest and rehabilitation leave in Tokyo in early August. Do they give you leaves of this kind?"

"Yes, I'm also going to Tokyo on R and R for five days, but not until early September."

"Can you can switch and come in early August?" Farley asked hopefully. "Our schedules are very rigid. Changing mine would be impossible," he added.

"I'm not sure that I can change, but I can try. That sounds exciting! The two of us in Tokyo together!"

"Lieutenant Morgan!" a loud voice suddenly rang out. "Come over here, please". It was Major Powers who stood near the entrance of one of the tents.

Morgan jumped up and ran over to where Powers was standing. "Yes, sir," she said. "You were calling me?"

"Laura, do you realize that you have been sitting with that Canadian for at least an hour? It looks bad. The other soldiers are laughing and pointing fingers."

"I'm sorry, sir. I did not realize that I was there that long."

"Well, I don't blame you. He seems to be a very nice young man. I'm sure that it is not necessary for me to tell you the military facts of life."

"Yes, sir, I understand. I will stay away from him."

"Thank you, Laura."

Farley remained at the M.A.S.H. for five more days. He woke up each morning hoping to see Morgan again but she did not appear. Another nurse was assigned to his case. He sank into a state of anger, depression and frustration, his mind trying to find ways of overcoming the obstacles that prevented him from being with Morgan.

Finally, early in the morning of the fifth day, Morgan suddenly appeared beside him as he sat eating breakfast. "I'm not supposed to talk to you, Peter, she said in a low voice, but I wanted to say goodbye".

"Goodbye?"

"Yes, Major Powers is sending you back to your unit today. The results are back. You have malaria but the medication should keep it in check."

"Will I ever see you again?"

"I don't know. Probably not in Korea. But we can write to each other. Here are the addresses of my mother, brother and sister in Minneapolis. Any mail that you send to them there will eventually get to me." She handed him a slip of paper.

"Remember, Morgan." he reminded her, "that I live in Sweet Grass, a small town in Manitoba. Everyone there knows me. Send any letters that you write to me to Sweet Grass and the post office will find me!"

"All right, I will. Good bye, Peter."

"Good bye, Morgan."

"Lieutenant Morgan!" a voice with a southern accent suddenly shouted.

"Yes, sir, coming sir!" she shouted back. Her military and personal inhibitions seemed to have suddenly disappeared. Peter Farley was an important part of her life, and all of the military regulations in the world would not prevent her from seeing him again.

After returning to the Fusiliers Farley was advised that he was, in fact, scheduled to go on R and R leave to Tokyo on August 1st. Shortly afterwards he met with two friends from home, Corporal Jamie "Big Indian" Swampy and Private Luke "Little Indian" Fontaine. Swampy was a 6 foot, 4 inch Cree and Fontaine was a 5 foot, 5 inch Cree. Both were from the Red Lake Reservation in western Manitoba, and both had worked during the harvest season on Orest Farley's farm in the late 1940's.

Farley, a high school student at that time, also worked on his father's farm and he became good friends with Swampy and Fontaine. They had had an unexpected and happy reunion on the Private J.P. Villanova on the way to Korea and had kept in touch ever since then. Both had handsome, clean-cut, aboriginal features, although Fontaine's eyes, a dark blue colour, betrayed a white admixture of some kind. They were intelligent and courageous soldiers who joked and laughed frequently and who had no objections to their nicknames. They were aware and appreciated the fact that Farley, although a Ukrainian, also has a small stream of aboriginal blood in his veins.

"What's up, Red Ukie?" Fontaine asked. "Someone said you've been sick."

"Yeah, I had a fever. They tell me it is malaria. I have to take pills for while. I just came back from the M.A.S.H."

"We just came back from Tokyo from rape and rampage, otherwise known as rest and rehab, or R and R," Swampy said with a smile on his face."

"Tell me more," Farley said. "I'm scheduled to go in early August."

"They will give you $200 dollars to go on leave," Fontaine said. "A Canadian dollar brings about 400 yen in Japanese money. It's tough trying to spend 80,000 yen in five days."

"All the Canadians go to a leave centre called 'Shimya Barracks', but nobody stays there. Everybody shacks up in Japanese hotels," Swampy explained. "After we arrived at our hotel we went to the bar on the main floor and the girls were there waiting for us."

"Waiting for you?" Farley asked with an incredulous look on his face.

"Yeah," Swampy continued. "You pick the one you want, negotiate a price, and they are then all yours. Some of them are very pretty. You get what you pay for. They seem to like the Americans the best because they are generous and buy them gifts. They said that the Brits are polite, the Australians and New Zealanders are rough, and Canadians are cheap."

"Of course, we went to a museum," Fontaine said with a smile. "Big Indian, what was the name of that museum? I have forgotten."

"I don't remember what it was called. The Japanese girls had a rating system for their customers," Swampy continued. "If you were the best you were a number one boy-san. If you were the worst you were a number 10 boy-san. They were either very loyal, or maybe very jealous. If you dared even look at another girl they would burst into tears."

"All of this is very interesting," Farley told them. "I have other plans, but it's good to know that I will get $200 and be able to go wherever I want."

"As soon as I remember the name of the museum I will let you know," Fontaine said with a giggle.

"Okay, thanks," Farley said. "And by the way, a big patrol is being planned. Why don't you guys come along?"

"Thanks for telling us. We love patrols. I haven't scalped anyone recently," Swampy said with a laugh. "Put our names in for us and we'll go."

"Consider it done! I have influence!" Farley said as he turned and left. He knew that Swampy and Fontaine were experienced and courageous patrollers, and that their presence would provide him with an increased level of confidence.

CHAPTER 22
THE LANGUAGE CODE

A letter from Sonia Kereliuk was waiting for Farley when he returned to his unit. He carefully opened the envelope and began reading. *"Dear Peter,"* it began. *"I picked up your letter at the post office this morning but I did not get a chance to read it until noon when all of my pupils were having lunch and playing outside.*

I have 37 pupils all together, including some in all grades from one to eight. I'm living at the home of the local school board chairman, which is about a half a mile from Minnewawa School, and 30 miles from Sweet Grass. I walk to the school and back every day. I eat lunch at my desk. The children have to be supervised and the noon hour also gives me a chance to catch up on marking papers, as well as the many other chores around the building.

The older boys help me with carrying coal and removing ashes, but I have to be here by 8:00 a.m. each morning to start the fire and warm up the building. There is always a crust of ice in the inside water tank in the winter months, so you can see that it gets very cold overnight.

I am seriously thinking about saving my money and getting an arts or science degree at Brandon College in another year or two. I've heard that Brandon College is a great place to live and learn. My school inspector tells me that there is a very good future in education, and especially for people with university degrees, including even women. My marks in Grade 12 physics, chemistry, mathematics, history and English are all in the 90's and are probably good enough for medicine. Forgive me for boasting! I'm trying to impress you! But six or seven years at the University of Manitoba or elsewhere would be financially very difficult. No medicine for me.

Johnny Michaluk came home to Sweet Grass last weekend. As you may have heard, he played six games with the Toronto Maple Leafs at the end of this N.H.L. hockey season. He scored a couple of goals and thinks that he has a good chance to play for Toronto on their regular roster next year. If he plays for them, he thinks that he will get $7,000 a year! I'm making $800! That's approximately what most rural teachers make in 10 months.

You were always a better player than Johnnie, but I guess that he was simply more dedicated to hockey. You will remember that he went to the Brandon Elks junior A's last year, at about the same time that you were taking your pre-medical studies at the University of Manitoba. He went to Brandon College for a while but had to drop out because hockey was taking too much of his time.

Brandon, as you know, is the home of Leaf goalie Turk Broda, a Ukrainian. The Ukrainians in Brandon and here at Sweet Grass are proud of Broda. They also like Ukrainian stars Billy Mosienko and Bill Juzda. Johnnie was the Elks' highest scorer last year, which is why Toronto gave him a chance to play. The whole town is naturally very thrilled to hear Johnny's name on the radio on Foster Hewitt's Hockey Night in Canada.

I went to the dance at Sweet Grass last Saturday night, where I saw Johnnie. We danced together quite a bit, and he insisted on taking me home afterwards. I should tell you that he seems to be very interested in me, even though I told him that you and I are sort of half-engaged. Is that the right way to put it? We've never really talked about our relationship enough, Peter, so I hope that what I am saying and thinking is true. If it isn't, in fairness, please tell me.

I worry about you. We do not hear much about the Korean War. The Winnipeg Free Press and Winnipeg Tribune newspapers print casualty lists and occasional stories, but they usually appear on their back pages. Short film clips are sometimes shown on the Movie Tone News at our Rex theatre in Sweet Grass. I think that people are tired of war. After the last one ended in 1945 they wanted to forget about all of the violence, destruction and death that had occurred in the world. As a result, the war in Korea seems to be largely ignored. But I have not forgotten. I believe that the Korean people will thank you one day for saving them from communism. I pray for your safety."

Peter was touched by Sonia's concluding words, and for a few minutes he forgot about Laura Morgan, the other very important woman in his life. He remembered, in particular, his miraculous love-making with Sonia on the banks of the Little Saskatoon River on the evening before he left for Korea. He recalled that Sonia was an exceptionally pretty, interesting and intelligent woman, and especially that she was, as Baba said, "one of our own people". And then he suddenly remembered Jean, the gorgeous blonde in Seattle. *"Is it possible that I am in love with three beautiful women all at once?"* he asked himself. *"Is there something wrong with me? Is my behaviour unethical? Why can't I be loyal to just one woman?"*

His thoughts were suddenly interrupted by the voice of a runner who had appeared in front of his tent. "Corporal Farley," the runner said, "Captain Dale, the commander of the 81 mm. Mortar Platoon, is ready to see you. Please report immediately."

After completing the N.C.O. course, Farley had been assigned to the Battalion's 81 mm. Mortar Platoon as a forward observer. He had learned his lessons well at Taegu and he had especially impressed his instructors with his quick comprehension of map reading. Maps of Korea were difficult to read, with their endless hills, mountains, rivers and valleys. But Farley demonstrated an almost uncanny ability to immediately identify particular features.

The Fusiliers were in reserve and were quartered in tents. Farley arrived at Captain Jack Dale's tent and was warmly greeted with a smile. "Welcome to the 81 mm. Mortar Platoon," Dale said. "I have heard a lot of good things about you." Dale did not extend his hand. Officers very rarely shook hands with other ranks. He was an affable and competent WWII mortar veteran from Truro, Nova Scotia.

"Come with me," Dale ordered. "I think that you know a lot of this already, but I am going to go over it again just to be sure." He led Farley to an 81 mm. mortar and a three man crew that was waiting nearby. Dale carefully explained how the three man crews worked and the crew demonstrated. Mortar barrels had sights attached to measure elevations. Low angles were for long distances and high angles for short distances. "Our maximum range," Dale pointed out, "is about 5,000 yards, but we don't have much accuracy at that distance. Conversely, by pointing our barrels almost straight up, we can land shells about 100 yards in front of us. We can also increase or decrease the range by adding or removing charges that are attached to the ends of the shells. The mortar is considered to be a very effective infantry weapon," he concluded.

"Thank you, sir," Farley said with a smile. "It looks like I have an important and interesting job. I will do my very best."

Farley spent four days with the men of the 81 mm. Mortar Platoon. He participated, as a forward observer in a lot of practice firing . He then moved forward about 300 yards to where Baker Company was dug in. He had a happy reunion with Jim Doherty.

"Am I s'posed to call you corporal"? Doherty asked with a grin.

"Only if others are present". Farley responded. "I understand that we are going on a patrol together. I'm looking forward to it."

"Red, I've been waitin' to see you again about somethin'," Doherty said very seriously.

"Well, what it?"

"I have a confession to make. I've got an uncle in Ottawa. Uncle Arnold , he be a communist."

"So what Jim, you are not a communist."

"No, but when I been in Ottawa Uncle Arnold gave me a 100 dollars. In return for dis money, he asked me to send him letters from Korea. He said that he was interested in knowin' about how the Canadian Army was operatin' in Korea. I was suspicious but I yielded to temptation. I gave some of this money to me mudder in Morgan's Cove before I left. I've written to Uncle Arnold a couple of times, but he has complained about the fact that I have not said much information 'bout da army."

"I don't know what to say, Jim. I can loan you a 100 dollars. You can send it to your uncle when you get to Japan. That way you won't feel any obligation to him. Maybe he is trying to be a spy but it would be pretty difficult to prove anything."

"That's a good suggestion, b'uy. I still got money from the big fight and I can use that. I will give this more thought and, if you don't mind, discuss it with you again later."

"Alright. And by the way. You are starting to lose your Newfie accent. You are a fast learner!".

"Thanks, Red. I am tryin'. I want to be Canadian."

Farley, Doherty and the rest of Baker Company were located on a mountain numbered 577, otherwise known as Old Smoky, the scene of vicious earlier fighting between the Chinese and U.S. Marines. Since the arrival of the Fusiliers, however, the area had been quiet, with the Chinese apparently content to occupy another range of mountains somewhere on the other side of the Han River valley.

The following day Farley was ordered to attend a meeting with Baker Company commander Major Henry Henderson. Also present was Lieutenant Richard Harvey, the commander of #5 Platoon, Farley's former unit; Captain Dale; and Platoon Sergeant Herbie Jones. The five men gathered at the Major's bunker and within a few minutes were joined by Jim Strange, the Battalion commander.

"Gentlemen," Strange began. "We are going to send a patrol of 30 men, mostly from Baker Company, across the Han River to find out what's going on over there. The rest of Baker will act as a back-up. The Divisional commander, U.S. General Watkins, wants to obtain information about the strength of the Chinese at this location. If this patrol is successful he may launch a major offensive in this area. If the Chinese position proves to be too strong, he will delay further action and remain with a defensive strategy."

"I volunteered Baker Company," Henderson said with a smile, "because everyone knows that we are the best. Captain Harvey's #5 platoon was selected by means of a draw. He drew an ace of spades and won."

Sergeant Jones and Corporal Farley said nothing. Both felt intimidated by the presence of the officers, and especially

181

by that of Strange. They were also beginning to experience a peculiar tingling sensation, a churning in their stomachs and powerful spasms of apprehension of the kind experienced by those waiting to go on a dangerous battle mission.

"Are you going, Lieutenant Harvey, or are you leaving this patrol to Sergeant Jones?" Strange asked. He was aware that Jones was a courageous and competent veteran of WWII, and that Harvey, a younger man, had much less experience.

Harvey had been thinking about his possible participation ever since the idea had been mentioned by Major Henderson two days earlier. He wanted to go, feeling that this might be an opportunity to gain valuable experience, and perhaps even win an award. He planned to have a lifelong career in the army and a Military Cross, or some other decoration, would be a very valuable asset. And yet, the patrol seemed to be exceptionally dangerous, with only 30 men probing against much larger numbers of Chinese. He had decided to send Sergeant Jones instead.

"I'd like to go," Harvey finally replied, "but..."

"Good," Strange said quickly, cutting Harvey off before he could say anything more. "I think that it will be a damned good experience for you. I want Sergeant Jones to go as well. I'm told that Corporal Farley is a very good map reader, but your assistance may be helpful. Remember, we need to locate the exact location of the Chinese with precise coordinates. We would love to get some prisoners, but that is not our main objective."

Harvey lapsed into a stunned silence, with even stronger feelings of apprehension than those being experienced by Jones and Farley.

Strange opened his map case and pointed to the range of mountains that the Chinese were apparently occupying. "The General," he said, is sending out similar patrols across our whole front, beginning at 0100 hours. Our intelligence sources tells us that we are facing elements of the CCF 27th division, which is evidently an experienced, well-led formation. However, that remains to be seen."

Strange then pointed to the most prominent mountain immediately to the north of their position. "The distance from our position to this mountain, 657, is about 3,500 yards or about two miles. It is a very wide no-man's land. The main Chinese mountain seems to be located at 050 degrees from where we are standing. We are not sure and need to find out. Have a look, Farley, because you will be carrying a radio, and you may have to call for mortar fire once you contact the Chinese."

"Yes, sir," Farley said with some hesitation. "But won't they hear our transmissions? We were told at our N.C.O. school that the Chinese have radio operators who understand English, and that they monitor our radio calls on a regular basis."

"A good point, Corporal," Strange said. "The Americans had the same problem during WWII in the Pacific against the Japanese. They solved it in at least a few places by using Navaho Indians as radio operators. Almost no one except the Navahos themselves could speak Navaho, and so the Japanese were baffled by the transmissions. They didn't even know what language it was."

"I don't speak Navaho, sir," Farley said with a smile, suddenly feeling very confident, "but I can speak Ukrainian."

"Corporal," Strange exclaimed. "You have just hit upon a brilliant idea! We have someone else, a Private Metro Kabaluk, who probably speaks Ukrainian. There are other Ukrainians in the battalion as well, but I don't think any of them know much Ukrainian. Kabaluk has a Ukrainian accent, so I assume that Ukrainian is his first language. Unfortunately, he is currently in our detention camp serving 30 days."

"What did he do, sir?" Farley asked.

"While assigned to B Echelon, about 20 miles behind the

line, he set up a still and was selling home brew not only to our men, but to the Americans as well. He is a talented individual, but was carrying on an illegal activity. I had no choice. I had to give him 30 days."

"Is he reliable? Can we use him on this patrol?" Jones asked.

"I can arrange it. I'm sure he will cooperate," Strange replied. He scribbled a note on a pad of paper, and handed it to his batman. "Adams", he ordered, "take my jeep and drive to the detention centre. Give this message to the sergeant in charge and tell him that I want Kabaluk immediately. Then load Kabaluk up and bring him here. Carry on with your plans, the rest of you. I will make all necessary arrangements for the radio communications to be used by the patrol."

In about an hour Adams returned with the jeep and Kabaluk in the front seat beside him. Kabaluk had a black "P" painted on the back of his tunic. His head was shaved. He had large, expressive brown eyes. Because he was not wearing a hat, he did not salute. He stood to attention in front of Strange and looked straight ahead.

"Kabaluk," Strange said. "I am going to give you a break. You are currently serving 30 days detention and still have about 25 days to go. You have a choice. You can stay in the piss can, or you can agree to a special assignment."

"Anything is badder dan the piss can, sir," Kabaluk said with a thick Ukrainian accent.

"All right, then," Strange continued. "How is your Ukrainian? Do you speak it well?"

"Yes, sir, I was borned in a Ukrainian part of Poland in 1920. I came to Canada wit' mine parents in 1928. We lived on a farm in Alberta. I speaked only Ukrainian at home and I went to a Ukrainian summer school each July and August until I was about 16 years old."

"So how did you get into the home brew business?" Strange

asked. It was not a relevant question but he was curious and secretly impressed.

"My father teach me. Making white lightening is an old Ukrainian tradition. We bringed it to Canada from the old country. We believes dat Canadian liquor laws is not fair. We don't understand why we can't make our own. It's badder dan the government stuff."

"Okay. That's all in the past, soldier," Strange said. "I am going to introduce you to a corporal who also speaks Ukrainian. He is going on a patrol and will be sending back reports by radio. My headquarters radio operator will be there with you and assist you in the operation of the radio. You will be speaking with Corporal Farley in Ukrainian."

"But why Ukrainian, sir?" Kabaluk asked.

"So the Chinese will not understand. We don't think any of them speak Ukrainian."

Kabaluk nodded his head and said nothing.

Strange then summoned Peter Farley to where Strange's jeep was parked. Strange stood near the jeep with his arm folded.

"Kabaluk, this is Corporal Farley," Strange said. "Let's see if the two of you can communicate in Ukrainian."

Farley and Kabaluk shook hands. Farley began speaking in Ukrainian with some hesitation. "My Baba says that my Ukrainian is very good, but that I speak with an accent like a Russian or a Jew. What do you think? Is my Ukrainian understandable?"

"Not bad," Kabaluk replied in Ukrainian. "Not bad at all. You actually sound like a Hutsul. That's the mountain people who live in the Carpathians. My family and I came from Galicia, a Ukrainian province which was a part of Poland before WWII. It's now under the Soviet Union."

"I think that it is very important that we check our numbers," Farley said, "because I will likely be sending you coordinates and compass bearings." He then called out the numbers from one to ten in Ukrainian. "Ohdan, dwa, threh, shtereh, pyat, sheesh, sheem, wesheem, daweet, dasheet." He stopped briefly and then continued counting until he reached 50.

"Dobreh!" Kabaluk exclaimed. "Dooshe dobreh!", meaning "good" and "very good".

"I don't think that we should be afraid to use an English word once in a while" Farley suggested. "Ukrainians in Canada do that all the time. If we say 'shovelski' or 'mortarski' or 'rifleski', I don't think the Chinese will understand. The Ukrainian words will leave them in a state of confusion."

"I think it will work," Kabaluk agreed.

Farley turned to Strange. "We understand each other very well, sir" he announced. "I suggest that I continue speaking in Ukrainian with Private Kabaluk for another hour or two. I need the practice more than he does."

"Excellent!" Strange said as he climbed into his jeep beside his driver. "I will introduce Kabaluk to my headquarters radio operator later this afternoon. He will be helping Kabaluk with his radio transmissions."

Farley saluted. Strange returned the salute and drove away.

In the meantime, preparations for the patrol continued. The Han River was usually 10 feet deep and 300 yards wide at this time of the year, but a prolonged drought had reduced it to a third of its volume. A section from #6 Platoon had patrolled its shore the previous evening and had marked its shallowest point with prominent white painted boulders. This was the point at which the patrol from #5 Platoon was to cross on its way northward to the Chinese positions.

Shortly after their meeting with Strange, Lieutenant Harvey, Sergeant Jones and Corporal Farley met with the other men who had been picked for the patrol. Doherty with his Bren gun was among them and Farley was pleased. The Bren gun, .303

rifles, and .38 revolvers were cleaned, oiled and loaded. Faces were blackened with a carbon powder. Hand grenades were primed and attached to belts and webbing. Then they all lay on the ground and dozed fitfully, waiting for the warm spring sun to disappear behind the snow-covered peaks to the west.

Two of the men selected for the patrol were "Big Indian" Corporal Jamie Swampy and "Little Indian" Private Luke Fontaine, who had spoken to Farley earlier about the patrol. Farley had recommended that they be included because they had proven, on previous occasions, to be very talented and courageous patrollers.

"Here we are, Red Ukie," Big Indian said. "I don't think I will blacken my face," he joked as he cleaned his rifle. "It's dark enough."

"Me neither," Little Indian said. "Hey, Big Indian, are we getting any treaty money this month? I'm short of cash and want to get some firewater."

"No firewater allowed on patrol, Little Indian. Wait until we get back. They always give shots of rum after we return from patrols. Be patient."

"Okay, Big Indian. I can wait."

In the meantime, Lieutenant Harvey sat by himself, pretending to study his map. His mind was filled with apprehension. "*How in hell did I get into this mess?*" he asked himself. "*Why didn't I tell Strange that Jones is quite capable of leading this patrol by himself?*" Then he remembered some of the psychology he had learned at the University of British Columbia. He tried to force himself to think positively. "*Maybe things will work out,*" he told himself. "*After all, the Chinese don't know we are coming and the smallness of our numbers will probably help. We will be harder to detect, and once they start shooting we can get out fast.*"

Peter Farley lay on the ground a short distance from Harvey.

Although he was half-asleep, Farley's mind kept wandering back to the recent week had spent at the M.A.S.H. *"Will I ever see Morgan again? Does she really care about me? Or will she decide that we are living in two different worlds, with nothing in common except a temporary infatuation?"* he asked himself.

Farley's thoughts were suddenly interrupted by a voice coming out of his radio. It was Metro Kabaluk, calling him from the 81 mm. Mortar Platoon at Battalion headquarters.

"Kapusta," he heard Kabaluk saying, using the Ukrainian word for cabbage. "This is Hooreewka calling," meaning whiskey in Ukrainian. "How do you hear me? Over". They had chosen these identification codes during their earlier meeting.

"I hear you loud and clear, strength five," Farley responded. He then switched to Ukrainian. "The sun is almost ready to go. I'm amazed at how quickly it disappears in this mountainous country. It's not like the prairies, where we have long and glorious sunsets. Over."

"I'm from the prairies too," Kabaluk answered in Ukrainian. "But I lived in western Alberta, where the sun also goes down fast. It's a lot worse in the valleys of British Columbia, where I picked fruit for a couple of summers. Over."

"This is supposed to be a military conversation," Farley said while laughing, "but I guess it does not matter. No one understands us anyway! Over."

"You're right," Kabaluk replied. "They probably also miss the English words that we slip in once in a while. I guess I'll close down now. I'll be waiting for your report after you cross the river. The mortars are ready to go at your command. Remember your numbers. Take it easy and good luck. Over and out."

"Roger to you Hooreewka. Over and out."

Soon afterwards the hazy orange sun disappeared behind the snowy western mountains. An eerie darkness descended on the Han River Valley. The full moon was obscured by dark, low-lying clouds. The members of the patrol gathered in a small semi-circle while Lieutenant Harvey called the roll. His voice sounded strangely weak and muted. Each man replied "sir" after his name was called.

"Remember," Harvey said, "that we will be moving forward in a single file, with Sergeant Jones in the lead. I'll take up the rear, behind Corporal Farley and his radio. Stay at least five yards apart, but don't lose sight of the man in front of you. Once we get over the river we will be stopping for a minute or two about every hundred yards to listen for signs of the Chinese. There will be no unnecessary talking. Walk as quietly as possible. Any questions?"

"Yes, sir," Jim Doherty asked. "What happens if and when we make contact?"

"Farley will radio back to advise Battalion Headquarters," Sergeant Jones forcefully replied. "We will probably call for covering mortar fire. Remember our main goal. The Colonel wants to know the precise location of the Chinese. It's also possible that we will run into a Chinese patrol."

"Wait for orders from Sergeant Jones or me," Harvey added. "Remember that Farley, Jones and I are the only ones with compasses. It's very hard to find your way in the darkness. If you can, go back with someone who has a compass. Once you return to our lines, use the password 'Regina'. If you get lost, stay hidden until daylight. The sun rises in the east. Face the sun, make a right turn, and head south."

As the Canadians prepared to cross the Han River radio operator Fu-shun Kai of the 27th Chinese Division listened attentively for more radio transmissions on the usual Canadian band locations. Two radio sets sat next to him. He had lived and worked in Chinese laundries and restaurants in Winnipeg, Toronto and New York during the 1930's and prided himself on the understanding of the English language. Moreover, his familiarity with regional North American accents often enabled him to identify the units making the calls. He could distinguish Maritimers, central Canadians, French Canadians and western Canadians from each other and from Americans. "I can tell," he would often tell his superiors, "that the U.S. Marines are in our area by the expressions they use. The soldiers from the Canadians prairies have accents that are similar to those of the Dakotas and Minnesota, but there are differences."

A Mandarin language call suddenly began to emit from the second radio. The caller had a pronounced North American accent, but his message was clear and understandable. "Canada Fucius calling! Do you hear me?"

Fu-shun quickly responded in Mandarin. "I hear you Canada Fucius. Transmit your message." Canada Fucius was the agreed upon call name of the Canadian spy in the Fusiliers ranks. It was a purposeful play on the name of Confucius, the revered Chinese philosopher.

"I have important information to give you with regard to a Canadian patrol that is being prepared for incursion into your 27th CCF Division territory."

"Yes, comrade, what is it?"

"The Fusiliers are sending a patrol of about 30 men into your area. They will be crossing the Han River at its shallowest point right across from their front line. The coordinates are 945 086. They will be leaving, heading in a direction of 045 degrees, at 0100 hours tomorrow morning. Pass this on quickly. By destroying this patrol you will discourage a larger Canadian attack in the near future."

"Thank you, comrade. Your important message has been received and will be forwarded."

After receiving this information from Fu-shun, the Commanding Officer of the 27th Chinese Division quickly organized a larger counter patrol of about 200 men. "Move out, intercept and kill them all," he ordered.

Fu-shun was pleased with himself, but he had been baffled by an earlier transmission that had emanated from the Canadians. He had been turning the dial on his receiver and until he heard the familiar words of the English language. He had been poised with a pencil and paper ready to record important details.

"Hooreewka" a voice said. "This is Kapusta, how do you hear me? Over."

"Hooreewka here," a second voice replied. "I hear you loud and clear. Over."

Fu-shun quickly scribbled the two obvious code words onto his pad. *This may be something important*, he thought. Fu-shun smiled, waiting for more. Suddenly, however, the second speaker began emitting words from a language that Fu-shun had never heard before. The first speaker replied, apparently in the same mysterious language. Fu-shun felt confused and annoyed.

"The Canadians are using a strange language," Fu-shun told a nearby communications officer.

"What language?"

"I don't know. I've never heard it before."

"Did you get anything at all?"

"The two parties called themselves 'Hooreewka' and 'Kapusta'. That's all."

"As you know, Canada is a land of many nationalities," the officer observed. "People have gone there from all over the world. Even some of our own live in Canada. It will be hard to identify a particular language."

"So what should we do?" Fu-shun asked.

"The best idea would be to record their conversations, but we obviously do not have any equipment to do so. All you can do is copy down as many words as possible."

"I'll try, but it's a funny-sounding language. They speak

very quickly."

"All languages sound funny if you don't know them. Try your best."

"Yes, comrade, I will try."

CHAPTER 23
THE PATROL

Historians of the Korean War would in future often refer to the conflict as a "war of patrols," and in particular during 1951 when permanent front line trenches had still not been constructed. Large areas of unoccupied territory, often two or three miles wide, referred to as "no man's land", separated the two opposing armies. The generals on both sides insisted that frequent patrols be sent into the unoccupied territories so that enemy activity could be monitored.

The 30 man Canadian patrol ordered by Lieutenant-Colonel Strange moved out in a single file, gingerly picking its way through a marked opening through the mined, barbed wire area in front of Baker Company's trenches. Sergeant Jones led the way, with Corporal Farley and Lieutenant Harvey bringing up the rear. Within a few minutes they reached the southern shore of the Han River.

A full orange moon shone in the southeast. Ominous dark

clouds blown by a strong western wind gathered in the north and floated rapidly eastward. The wind rustled the fresh green spring leaves on the trees and advantageously covered the noise of the soldiers' boots as they occasionally crunched on gravel or stumbled on unseen small rocks. The stench of fermenting human manure from nearby rice paddies filled the air.

"Here we are," Jones whispered as he reached the large white painted rocks planted the previous evening. This is the shallowest part of the river where we are supposed to cross."

"Wait here," Jones quietly said to Doherty, who was about five yards behind him. Doherty carried a box of ammunition as well as his Bren light machine gun. Doherty raised his right arm and crouched to the ground and the others behind him did the same.

Jones unbuckled his ammunition belt and raised it and his American carbine sub-machine gun over his head. He waded into the dark, cool water, which became progressively deeper as he moved across. The water reached his armpits near the centre of the river and then gradually became shallower again. A fringe of low bushes came into view on the opposite shore. Jones darted forward to their edge, fell on his knees, and quickly re-attached his ammunition belt.

The men on the opposite shore waited for three minutes as previously planned. If there were any Chinese at the river, they would fire on Jones and the rest of the patrol would escape. If nothing happened after three minutes, they would know that Jones had safely reached the other shore without any kind of hostile contact.

The patrol moved across the river in single file, each man keeping about a five yard interval. These intervals were important because soldiers in close proximity were more vulnerable to enemy fire. Like Jones before them, they all held their ammunition belts and weapons over their heads.

As well as his large and heavy radio, Farley carried a .45 U.S. issue revolver that he had purchased from an American for a case of Japanese beer. Within a few minutes they all sat at the edge of the bushes on the opposite side.

"So far, so good," Jones said very quietly. "Okay, let's fucking go." The patrol moved in a single file through the shoreline bushes and began veering in a northeasterly direction towards the mountain where the Chinese main line was believed to be located. Jones stopped every 40 or 50 yards, crouched down, and listened attentively for any telltale noises coming from the enemy. At every second stop, he pulled out his compass and peered at its luminous dial. *"Zero, four, five,"* he kept mumbling to himself. He searched for reference points but found it difficult to find any because of the darkness. Rain fell intermittently, at some times heavily, as each dark cloud passed.

The patrol moved further and further northeastward on a course of 045 degrees. Tension mounted with each step. The Fusiliers sweated in spite of the cool early morning spring air. Stomachs churned, hearts thumped, and breathing became increasingly heavy. The mountain was getting steeper but the enemy was nowhere to be seen.

After an hour and five minutes had passed Jones suddenly came up against a very steep cliff. "Go back and get Lieutenant Harvey and Corporal Farley," he ordered Doherty.

Harvey and Farley came forward quickly. As they passed the others in the single file they were bombarded by whispered questions: "What's wrong? Why have we stopped? Has Jones seen something? When are we going back?" The questions were ignored.

Jones, Farley and Harvey crawled into a small cave at the face of the cliff. The air reeked with the odour of decaying human flesh.

"This place looks and smells like an old Chinese position,"

Jones observed. "I think they were subjected to a U.S. air attack with rockets and napalm. There are abandoned trenches, some burned bodies and lots of shrapnel laying around."

Harvey spread his map out and shone his flashlight on it. "Where are we?" he asked.

"We are here," Farley said. He pointed to a spot on the map. "We are in front of a very steep elevation, which is, in fact, a cliff. But it's not too wide. We can move left about a hundred yards, and then continue up the slope."

"You had better call headquarters," Harvey said weakly. "Maybe they want us to go back." His voice lacked authority and decisiveness. The smell of decaying flesh had moved him into a deeper state of panic and depression. He feared for his life.

"Yes, sir," Farley replied. He removed the radio from his back and spoke into the microphone. "Hooreewka, Hooreewka, Hooreewka this is Kapusta. How do you hear me? Over."

"Kapusta, Hooreewka here. I hear you strength four," came an almost immediate response in Ukrainian. Kabaluk was obviously awake and waiting.

"Hooreewka," Farley said in Ukrainian, "we have been moving on a course of 045 and are presently located at the face of a cliff. The map coordinates are 946820. We have had no hostile contacts. What are your instructions? Over."

"Wait, Kapusta. I'll relay your question. Hang on. Over."

A very long three minutes passed. "Proceed at least another thousand yards or until you make contact, over," Kabaluk's voice finally rasped.

"Okay, Hoorweeka, over and out."

Lieutenant Harvey sat motionless and speechless. Feelings of fear and panic had rendered him immobile.

"Well, sir," Jones said calmly. "I guess that we should move left to get past the face of this cliff and then proceed northeastward again at 045. Is that what you are suggesting, Farley?"

"Yes, sergeant. But what do you say, sir?" Farley said as he looked at Harvey.

Harvey hardly heard the suggestion and question. "Carry on," he mumbled. "I'll wait here and bring up the rear."

"If you don't mind, sir," Jones said, "I'd like Farley to fall in behind me. I may need him to call in 81 mm. mortar fire, or for more instructions from headquarters. Right now, he's too far back."

Harvey did not reply. He crawled into the back of the cave, pulled out his .38 revolver and placed it by his side. Jones and Farley stared at Harvey for a moment and then moved out together. Harvey remained in the cave.

Harvey was suffering from combat stress, which in the earlier wars of the century was called "shell shock" or "battle fatigue". He felt tired, indecisive and had a hard time connecting with his current circumstances. *Why am I here? What am I doing?"* he asked himself. He feared for his safety and his life.

The patrol, except for Harvey, moved in a westerly direction along the face of the cliff. As predicted by Farley, after they had walked about a hundred yards its sharp elevation gave way to a gently sloping hill. Jones then veered northeastward on a course of 045 degrees again, with Farley close behind him.

Farley was in excellent physical condition, but the radio was now beginning to feel very heavy. He looked upwards, where the bright full orange moon how shone in the southern sky. He looked at his watch. 0250. "*It seems like we have been here forever,*" he thought. Images of Laura Morgan came into his mind. "*Will I ever see her again?*" he wondered. In spite of his perilous circumstances, he felt strangely content, as though there was some overriding significance to what he was doing. Low bushes now appeared on both sides of their path, as well as scrubby evergreens of the kind frequently found on Korean mountains and hills.

The air smelled fresher at this higher elevation. Farley was relieved. The rice paddies, with their fermenting human excreta, were located at lower levels in the valleys. Farley remembered the words of one of his instructors at the N.C.O. school in Taegu, who had observed that "the Koreans have been fertilizing their rice paddies with their own shit for thousands of years. The shit stinks and carries diseases, but it is great fertilizer and has kept the Koreans from starving to death."

The moon suddenly disappeared behind a thick, black cloud and it became very dark. As Jones and Farley approached the peak of yet another hill, Jones suddenly fell to the ground. Jones motioned to Farley, the man behind him, and both quickly stopped and crouched. Low voices could be heard in front of them. Farley crawled into a dense bush on his right, cocked his .45 revolver and waited, with excitement and tension surging through his body. The voices became louder and louder. They were un-mistakenly oriental, with high-pitched, nasal sounds.

Jones came crawling back to the bush where Farley was located. "It looks like a patrol is heading south to the river," Jones whispered. "They are making a lot of noise, and that tells me that there are a lot of them. I think that the whole fucking Chinese army is coming. Let's get out of here."

"Okay, sergeant, but I had better call headquarters!" Farley exclaimed. But it was too late. Burp gun and rifle fire suddenly broke out behind them. At the same time, Canadian and Chinese voices began shouting on all sides. Farley looked up from the thick bush in which he was crouched and saw shadowy figures running past him. Then he heard the crunching of feet in gravel directly in front of him. He rose slowly, aiming his .45 in the direction of the sound. A very small Chinese soldier in a cloth cap, quilted jacket and a burp gun came into his sight.

Both men hesitated for several seconds, their minds frozen with shock. Time seemed to stand still. For at least one of them, the world was coming to an end. Their lives passed before their eyes in a blur of accelerated memory.

The Chinese fired first. His burp gun sprayed the bushes around Farley but missed their target. The Soviet weapon that he was using was capable of producing a high volume of bullets at great speed, but it was notoriously inaccurate.

Farley held his .45 with both hands and aimed it at the enemy's chest. He fired several times. It was an automatic response. His mind reeled in disbelief as the surrealistic drama unfolded. The Chinese soldier dropped his burp gun and fell backwards onto the ground. Farley heard a clicking sound and suddenly realized that he had fired all of the bullets in his revolver. He sat down in the bush and put in a fresh loaded clip. He crawled forward a few paces and the moon suddenly appeared again. He looked into the face of the dead Chinese soldier. The eyes of the Chinese were open and his mouth was frozen into a lopsided smile. He looked very young, with delicate facial features, and appeared to be only 15 or 16 years of age. Farley felt overwhelmed pity and guilt. He would never be able to forget this young soldier's face.

An eternity seemed to pass, but in fact it was only five minutes. The shooting had finally stopped, but he could still hear Chinese voices shouting at some distance behind him. The other members of his patrol had disappeared.

"I've got to think straight and keep calm or I am finished," he told himself. *"I can't stay here and I can't go south because they are all over down there. I'll go north for a while and then take a different route to get back to the river."*

Farley bent his body into a low crouch and moved ahead into the darkness. He breathed heavily and was forced to stop every few yards to regain his strength. Soon the oriental voices behind him faded away. The slope in front of him became increasingly steep.

Farley decided that he needed to rest. His climb up the steep mountain was exhausting him. His head ached. He began sweating profusely and felt very hot. *"Is my malarial fever returning? Did I miss taking any of the medication that was prescribed?"* he wondered. He felt delirious and began thinking about Morgan again. He removed the radio from his back and lay down behind a large rock.

"What should I do?" he asked himself. *"The objective of our patrol is to discover the exact location of the Chinese front line. Am I the only survivor? Nothing has changed. It is still our duty, my duty, to find the Chinese line and report it to headquarters."*

As he lay on the ground he suddenly noticed that his money belt with about $1,500 was still strapped to his waist. *"How stupid can I be!"* he angrily chastised himself. *"I was supposed to leave this hidden in my kit bag at battalion headquarters."*

After resting for about five minutes Farley slowly rose, loaded the radio onto his back and began climbing the mountain again. A black cloud obscured the moon. It began to rain heavily. A thick fog suddenly appeared and he could see only a few feet in front of him. As he picked his way slowly and laboriously around many large boulders strewn in front of him, he suddenly heard the sound of oriental voices. This time, however, they were subdued and calm, and apparently unaware of his presence because of the downpour and very limited visibility.

Farley pulled himself past a very large boulder just as the moon broke out again through a gap in the clouds. He realized that he had reached the peak of the mountain. The rain stopped as suddenly as it had started. He gasped. The valley on the northern side of the mountain was alive with movement. Hundreds of men and many horses were assembled into close formations and hundreds more were marching in a long column from the north. The horses had large containers on their backs, and were obviously being used to carry ammunition and supplies. They were about 300 yards away. The orange moonlight gave them an unearthly appearance.

Farley turned on his radio and spoke in a low voice. "Hooreeka, Hooreewka, Hooreewka, Kapusta calling. How do you hear me? Over."

Several seconds passes but there was no response. Farley was about to try again but Kabaluk's finally responded. "Kapusta, this is Hooreewka. I hear you loud and clear. Over."

"Hoorweeka, that's a relief. I thought for a moment that I had lost you. I'm on top of 637 overlooking a peanut shaped valley. It's crawling with hundreds of Chinese and many horses. It looks like a major staging area for an attack. I calculate my coordinates as 948 898. Ask headquarters to check their map. This is definitely a part of the Chinese main line. Get the Mortar Platoon ready. Ask them to try the range. We may be able to do a lot of damage down there. Over."

"Roger, Kapusta. Where is the rest of your patrol? Over."

"Good question. I don't know. We ran into a large Chinese patrol heading south to our lines. All hell broke loose. I lost track of everyone. Hurry, Hoorweewka. Get the Mortar Platoon ready. Over."

"Wait a bit, Kapusta. I need to translate your message. The commanding officer and Captain Dale from the Mortar Platoon are both standing by. Over."

Farley waited apprehensively for what seemed like a very long time before Kabaluk's voice finally returned. "Kapusta, watch for a ranging shot coming up. Call back corrections. Over."

"Roger, Hooreewka. Fire away. Over."

A puff of white smoke and flash of fire appeared at the northern edge of the valley. It was followed a few moments later by the familiar crunching sound of an exploding mortar shell.

"Hooreewka, Hooreewka, down 500!" Farley shouted excitedly into his microphone.

"Roger, Kapusta, coming up," Kabaluk replied.

The next shell landed in the valley, but was still long. Peter remembered that distances are deceptive at night, and especially at extended ranges. "Kapusta," he ordered, "down another 600 and right 100. Over."

The third shell landed in almost the exact centre of the valley. By now the Chinese soldiers were running in all directions, obviously aware that someone was ranging in on them. The horses had panicked and were neighing loudly.

"You're right on, Hooreewka! Rapid fire a hundred or more rounds. The valley is full of them. You can't miss! I'm getting out of here! Over and out."

Within a minute large numbers of mortar shells began crunching into the valley, their puffs of white smoke and fiery explosions landing among the screaming and fleeing Chinese and terrified horses.

Farley watched in fascination for a few moments, his mind sweeping wildly from one emotion to another. He was appalled at the destruction of human and animal life caused by his direct intervention. He loved animals as much, or sometimes perhaps more, than he did people, and their deaths, especially at his hands, caused him great anguish. On the other hand, he realized that the people in the valley were his enemies, and that they would kill him and his comrades if they had the opportunity. He was pleased with his competence as a forward observer and thankful that he had escaped injury and death. He shut off his radio, checked his compass and began moving in a southerly direction. It began to rain very heavily again. Some delirium had returned. He felt hot and cold at the same time.

Soon afterwards he once again heard Chinese voices. They

sounded more excited this time. They were probably wondering about all of the shelling in the valley. *"It must be their defensive line again"* he told himself. *"I have to try walking through. They won't expect anyone coming from their rear."*

He took off his beret and stuffed it under his belt. By now he was completely soaked, with his clothes clinging closely to him. He veered to the left a few yards, hoping to find a gap between the Chinese trenches.

One of the Chinese noticed Farley's partially obscured figure as it moved in the rain down the slope. "Who is that big fellow?" he asked his companion. "Is there another patrol moving out?"

"I don't know," the other soldier answered. "I don't see anyone going with him. He's got a radio but no hat."

"Hey, there!" the first Chinese soldier yelled in Mandarin. "What's going on? Is there another patrol going out?"

Farley heard the Chinese voice and instinctively knew that he was being challenged. He wanted to run but resisted the urge and plodded steadily forward. Soon the voices disappeared behind him. He then broke into a slow jog, feeling relieved at the relative ease of moving down the mountain. After a few minutes he stopped, looked at his compass and shot a bearing. *"I will move in a southeasterly direction,"* he told himself. *"If I walk at 135 degrees I will eventually hit the Han River, although probably in front of the U.S. Marines positions. I can't go back to our own lines. That large Chinese patrol is probably still in our area. In fact, maybe they have started a major attack."*

He moved down a series of slopes for about half an hour, pausing occasionally to listen for the possible presence of Chinese patrols. The sky remained black and it continued to rain. As he reached the top of a steep rise he suddenly stumbled and fell into a deep ravine, tumbling over and over until he was eventually stopped by a large rock in his path. Flashing lights came to his head. He lay in a semi-conscious state for several minutes, not knowing where he was or what had happened.

He finally sat up. He felt all parts of his body for possible fractures but none were evident. His head was very sore. He took the radio off from his back. It was badly smashed, so he decided to leave it against the rock. In any event, he was not sure that he could walk much further, let alone carry the heavy radio.

Six fully primed hand grenades remained attached to his belt. They were not heavy and he decided to keep them. His .45 revolver remained in its holster. He took out his compass, turned again to a heading of 135 degrees, and moved out.

A painful two hours passed before he finally reached the shore of the Han River. As he peered carefully through the bushes at the edge of the river, he noticed that the water had deepened considerably, its current surging with the kind of violent flood waters that frequently descend down Korean streams after torrential spring and summer rains.

A scene of desolation and death greeted him on the banks of the river. Scattered on both shores were pontoons of the kind used by U.S. military engineers in the construction of temporary bridges. Laying among them, in deathly silence, were the bodies of a large number of American engineers, their shattered remains still dressed in life jackets.

The sound of Chinese burp guns broke out at some distance to his right, and then to his left. "*Another damn patrol,*" he mumbled. "*They are all over. I have got to get out of here.*"

There appeared to be no way to escape except into the river. He rushed forwards to one of the American bodies. It was that of a young man who looked to be in his early twenties, or perhaps late teens. His blond hair and scalp were parted with a massive wound. "*Excuse me,*" Farley heard himself saying, "*but I need your life jacket.*" He struggled with the heavy and lifeless body until the life jacket was free. The odour of death filled his nostrils. He then slipped the jacket over his shoulders, fastened the front and quickly ran towards the water. He felt very weak. Flashes of light came to his head again.

At that moment a line of Chinese soldiers emerged out of the bushes, their burp guns blazing in his direction. He plunged into the water, hoping to disappear into its depths, but the life jacket kept his head and shoulders exposed. The Chinese were now no more than 50 yards away. He could hear the plunking sound of bullets as they sprayed the water around him, as well as the excited shouting of the Chinese soldiers on the shore. Before long, however, the swiftly moving current pulled him into the darkness and the shooting and shouting stopped. He lapsed into semi-consciousness.

CHAPTER 24
THE PATROL RETURNS

Following their sudden encounter with the large Chinese patrol, the Fusiliers were engaged in a brief but deadly battle. Bloody chaos reigned for several minutes in the darkness and a thick fog as the two sides ran around in wild disorder. They fired at each other at point-blank range and, in some instances, clubbed each other with their weapons. Several Chinese died when the spike-like bayonets of the Canadians penetrated them. The Chinese had burp guns but no bayonets. The Fusiliers quickly lost 21 of their lives. Jones, Farley and seven other Canadians escaped, but they were all badly dispersed, with each man having to find his own way back to the Canadian lines.

All of the Fusiliers had performed valiantly, and if their actions had been witnessed by officers they would all have been recommended for Military Medals, or perhaps more prestigious Distinguished Conduct Medals, or maybe even the highest of them all, a Victoria Cross. But as is often the case in spontaneous and sudden battles of this kind, their heroism went unseen and medals would not be given to some of those who deserved them.

Jim Doherty cursed as he ran southwards through the darkness and a heavy rain towards the Han River. He had managed to fire two magazines of ammunition into the Chinese ranks and had watched several Chinese fall, but he felt angry and humiliated at having to run for his life. He was alone and wounded. Bullets from a Chinese burp gun had entered his right shoulder and right arm and he had lost a lot of blood. Fortunately, he was left-handed and after escaping from the conflict, he managed to stop the flow of blood by applying bandages from his first aid kit. He was no longer bleeding, but he felt weak and disoriented.

The large Chinese patrol was from the 27th C.C.F. Division, located on a mountain about two miles north of the Fusiliers front line position. They were now reduced to about a hundred members, but they reorganized themselves quickly and began moving again towards the Han River, confident that they had effectively neutralized the small group of Canadians that they had encountered. The Chinese patrol had been ordered to locate and describe the main Canadian defensive line so that preparations could be made for a major assault.

Captain Lee Chiang was the aggressive and fearless leader of the Chinese patrol. "Don't stop, keep moving!" he kept shouting. "Our glorious general and comrades are counting us!"

As the Chinese approached the Han River three very bright flares suddenly soared high over the sky from the Canadian lines. The Chinese were spotted, and within a minute a devastating 81 mm. mortar and artillery barrage tore into their ranks. The machine guns of the Canadians added to the decimation of the Chinese patrol. Many died instantly, while the others broke ranks and began fleeing northwards in disarray.

Captain Chiang and six of his soldiers jumped into a deep

and large crater, a bowl-shaped depression in the ground, where they waited for the barrage to stop. By this time the sun began to rise above the eastern mountains. The rain had stopped and visibility was greatly improved.

Jim Doherty continued to stagger down into the valley. He still had his Bren gun and some ammunition, but felt very weak because of his wounds and loss of blood. As soon as the flares illuminated the sky, he realized that he was veering too far to the right. He corrected his direction and pressed forward even though he could see that a mortar barrage was taking place in that area. As he approached the shore of the river he suddenly came to the crest of the deep crater where Captain Chiang and his men lay hiding. He reared up, pointed his gun in their direction and shouted in a loud and delirious voice: "Okay! You bastards, throw down yer weapons or you be all dead ducks!".

Captain Chiang turned rapidly in Doherty's direction and raised his pistol. But before he could fire he was met with a hail of bullets from Doherty's Bren. Chiang collapsed into a bloody heap. The six remaining Chinese had been resting and had laid their burp guns on the ground. It was too late to pick them up now. They raised their hands into the air.

Doherty suddenly felt very weak. He sat down on the edge of the crater and tried to regain his strength. His Bren remained pointing menacingly at the Chinese below and they were completely cowed, with no desire to emulate the heroism of their dead leader. Doherty tried to get up but he could not move.

"It's a case of tits up in the rhubarb!" he said to himself, which meant, in Morgan Cove's Newfie parlance, that he was ready to fall down and pass out. He awaited his fate grimly and with great apprehension. Only his fear of the Chinese below him kept him marginally conscious.

In the meantime, at the cave located at the base of the cliff that the Fusilier patrol has discovered and passed earlier that morning, Lieutenant Richard Harvey woke from a deep and troubled sleep. He had escaped all of the later fighting with the Chinese patrol and in fact had never left the cave. He was immobilized with fear. On two occasions he tried to get up, but his body seemed heavy and unresponsive. *"I'm sick,"* he told himself. *"There is something terribly wrong with me."* Even if he did leave, where would he go? His patrol had left without him.

Shortly after the sun rose above the mountains in the east Harvey to feel better. The darkness and rain were gone. The sky was blue and clear. He crawled out of the cave and looked around him. Everything was calm and quiet, with no sign of his men or the enemy. He began walking southwards towards the river. As he approached shore he suddenly heard a familiar voice shouting from a distance.

"Lieutenant, It's me! Doherty!"

Harvey stopped and looked around him. About 50 yards to the right he saw the large and familiar figure of Doherty sitting on the ground, his Bren in his left hand.

Doherty had no hat and his blond hair was badly disheveled.

Harvey's fear suddenly dissipated; his mind cleared and a feeling of power surged through his body. "I'm coming, Doherty, I'm coming," he shouted. He began running in Doherty's direction.

When Harvey reached the edge of the crater he saw the six Chinese cowering below, their dead captain at their feet. He waved his .38 revolver furiously. "Get up!" he shouted.

By now Doherty was on the verge of passing out. He leaned to his left side, holding himself up with his elbow. "I don' think I can move, sir," he said with a weak smile.

Harvey ran to the bottom of the crater. He grabbed one of the Chinese soldiers by the arm and pointed in Doherty's direction. "Get up there!" he yelled. He jammed his .38 against the head of another Chinese and pulled him to his feet. The other four quickly jumped up on their own, their hands high over their heads.

"Do what he wants," one of the Chinese said, "or he'll probably shoot us all. He seems to be possessed of the devil!" They did not understand what Harvey was saying, but they knew that they had to move out of the crater.

In compliance with Harvey's wildly gesturing directions two of the Chinese soldiers approached Doherty and took him by the arms. Although they were about a foot shorter than the Canadian, their strong peasant bodies were able to support him quite easily. Doherty could not to walk very far on his own, but the support provided allowed him to move forward.

The group began walking towards the river's edge, with Doherty, his two supporters and four other Chinese at the front, and Harvey at the rear. Harvey carried Doherty's Bren. He continued to shout.

As they approached the water's edge Harvey scanned the opposite shore. He spotted the white rocks previously laid for the purpose of marking the shallowest part of the river about a 100 yards to his right and he directed the group to move in that direction.

The group began wading across the river, with Doherty, his two supporters and the other Chinese at the front and Harvey at the rear. The short Chinese soldiers were all barely able to keep their heads above water, but all of them managed to stagger ashore on the opposite bank.

"Regina! Regina," Harvey began yelling as they moved up the slope toward Baker Company's position. He hoped that the password had not changed and that they would be recognized.

"Okay, we see you!" a loud Canadian voice responded.

"I have Doherty, who is wounded, and six prisoners," Harvey shouted.

"Wait at the wire. Help is coming," the Canadian yelled.

Two stretcher bearers with a stretcher and five Fusiliers with rifles met them at the edge of the barbed wire protecting Baker Company's position. Doherty protested, but was loaded onto the stretcher and carried to the Medical Officer's Regiment Aid Post, a heavily fortified bunker at Battalion Headquarters.

The Chinese prisoners were led away to be interrogated by Captain Mike Levinson, the battalion's intelligence officer. Harvey was enthusiastically greeted by Lieutenant-Colonel Strange.

"Well done, Harvey!" Strange exclaimed jubilantly. "The general will be very pleased when he hears about the prisoners. Levinson is fluent in Mandarin Chinese and should be able to extract a lot of valuable information. Unfortunately, however, 20 of your men have still not returned from the patrol."

"Where are they, sir? Who is missing?" Harvey asked.

"We don't know," Strange replied, "but many are not back, including Corporal Farley. Sergeant Jones and seven riflemen made it back to Able Company's position about 30 minutes ago. They think the others are dead. We've sent out another patrol to find and recover the bodies."

A de-briefing session followed an hour later at the Regimental Aid Post bunker. Doherty was conscious and received a blood transfusion and Major Karpinski recommended that he not be moved. Doherty, Jones and Harvey all described their encounter with the Chinese patrol.

Soon after Doherty arrived at the RAP he was joined by his dog Blackie, who had been kept by Metro Kabaluk during Doherty's absence. Blackie wagged his tail excitedly and Doherty gave him a hug. "I missed you, Blackie!" he said.

"Metro," Doherty said plaintively, "I think that they are goin' to send me to Japan to recover. Willya look after Blackie while I be away? Red likes cats, but I be a dog lover!"

"Yeah, I look after him," Kabaluk said. "We great friends. I got two dogs at home and I know how to handle them."

"That's great, Metro. Just don't forget that he is my dog and that I want him back when I return from Korea."

"Don't be worry. He your dog and you get him back."

Although Doherty and Jones were suspicious of Harvey's behaviour at the cliff, they were not aware of the fact that Harvey had remained there for most of the night. Doherty was in a weakened condition and his doubts about Harvey's earlier questionable behaviour were suppressed by the fact that he had been rescued by Harvey. Without Harvey, Doherty knew that he would never have been able to escort his prisoners back to the Canadian lines and that even his own survival was highly unlikely.

"I'm recommending you for a Military Cross," Strange told Harvey. I am putting Farley in for a Distinguished Conduct Medal. "Doherty and Jones will have their names submitted for Military Medals. Unfortunately, it looks like Farley's award will be posthumous."

"Thank you, sir," Harvey replied with undisguised excitement. He was suddenly overcome with a powerful feeling of euphoria.

Harvey wanted to cry with joy, but instead gritted his teeth and stared straight ahead. His whole career as an officer in the Canadian Army had suddenly taken a giant leap forward. His mind projected him into the future, where he saw himself a major, a Lieutenant-Colonel, a brigadier and finally a lieutenant-general and the chief of the Defence Staff in Ottawa. He would be one of the few who wore the purple and white ribbon of the Military Cross in officers' messes, at social functions and on parades at various bases and outposts. He knew that he would always be promoted ahead of others; that soldiers, officers and civilians would be impressed by his citation for heroism; and that a Military Cross in the Army is like a Ph. D.

in civilian life.

While these thoughts were going through Harvey's head, the other members of the patrol sat in angry silence. They wanted to tell Strange that he was making a mistake, that in fact Harvey had shown cowardice in the face of the enemy, and that Harvey, if anything, deserved a court martial. At the same time, however, all of them were pleased with their own awards. They felt intimidated by the presence of Harvey and Strange and were reluctant to speak out.

A strong feeling of revulsion and anger finally overcame Jones. "Sir," Jones suddenly said to Strange, "I am only a sergeant and I'm not an expert on awards, but you should know that Lieutenant Harvey was not present during our main encounter with the Chinese patrol."

Strange looked startled. He looked at Doherty. "Is that true, Doherty?"

"Yes, sir," Doherty reluctantly replied.

Strange then looked at Harvey. "Is what Sergeant Jones saying true, Lieutenant Harvey?"

"Yes, sir," Harvey calmly replied. "I became very ill, so ill in fact, that I should have returned to our lines immediately. However, I decided to stay so that I could help my men once I recovered. Of course, as you know, that's exactly what happened. Once I was able to function again, I moved immediately to assist Doherty. If I had not arrived, Doherty would have passed out and the Chinese would have killed him and escaped."

"Is that true?" Strange asked Doherty. "Were you ready to pass out?"

"Yes, sir."

"And do you think that you could have brought back the prisoners on your own?

"No, sir."

"And you, Sergeant Jones, were you anywhere in the

vicinity? Could you have helped with the prisoners?"

"No, sir, I came back on Able Company's front," Jones reluctantly admitted. "I didn't see Doherty after our battle with the Chinese patrol." He hung his head and looked at the ground.

"That will be all, gentlemen. The awards will all stand," Strange announced abruptly. He was a very strong leader, but had an Achilles weakness that sometimes interfered with his decision-making. He refused to admit that he was ever wrong and once he made a decision it would stand regardless of new information that came to his attention. He now had some doubts about Harvey's behaviour, but felt that an award was justified, in any event, because of Harvey's very valuable procurement of the Chinese prisoners.

The patrol members then all dispersed and went to sleep in their respective bunkers. They were exhausted and could barely walk. The previous 24 hours had been a very difficult experience and one they would remember for the rest of their lives.

The following morning Strange called Harvey on the battalion's field telephone. "I've just had a conversation with the British general, the commanding officer of the Commonwealth Division," he told Harvey. "He has agreed to accept all of my recommendations concerning the awards we talked about last evening, except that Farley will be given a Military Medal rather than the higher DCM. I am angry, because Farley, in my opinion, does deserve a DCM. "

"That's wonderful, sir" Harvey replied. "I am very grateful."

"Corporal Farley is still missing," Strange continued, "and Doherty is on his way to a U.S. military hospital in Tokyo. One of our officers in Japan will present him with his Military Medal."

"What about Farley?" Harvey asked. "Should I write a letter to his next-of-kin, or is Jack Dale going to do it? Farley's no longer in my platoon, but I still feel responsible for him."

"No, don't send a letter yet, at least not about his probable death. Write to his family to tell them about how he won a Military Medal. Tell them that he directed the fire of our 81 mm. mortars into a heavy concentration of enemy troops. Besides that you can explain that he deserves the award because he continued to advance deeply into enemy territory at great personal risk. But don't say anything about his likely death. Our patrol picked up 20 bodies this morning, but Farley's was not among them. He is still missing. Ottawa will be sending a telegram."

"What about the men who did die? Apparently they fought valiantly against overwhelming numbers of Chinese. Are you going to recommend any decorations for them?"

"I can't," Strange replied. "Witnesses are always required for the awarding of decorations. You brought in the valuable prisoners under obviously difficult circumstances. The commendable actions of Doherty, Jones and Farley are also apparent and justifiable. I am sure that the men who died fought valiantly, but their actions were not seen by officers. The battle, I am told, was fought in darkness."

"I understand, sir," Harvey replied.

"I am concerned about your health," Strange continued. "What was your problem on the patrol? Perhaps you should see Major Karpinski."

"I'm sure that it was just a temporary thing. I'm feeling fine. I don't think that I will have any more problems."

"All right then," Strange said emphatically. "I want you to come to a special parade at my headquarters at 1400 hours tomorrow. Be there and I will present you with your Military Cross."

"So soon? Thank you, sir!"

"Well, we might as well get it over with, eh, Harvey?" Strange said with a chuckle. "Just make sure that you are on time and that your boots are shined!"

"Yes, sir. I'll be there. Everything will be spotless!"

Harvey woke up at 1000 hours the next morning. He shaved, polished his boots and put on his cleanest uniform. His head ached, but he was in high spirits. Major Henderson, his company commander, had agreed to let him use the company jeep the previous evening.

At 1230 hours Harvey climbed into the jeep and began driving down a narrow, winding dirt road towards Battalion Headquarters. It was only about 15 minutes away, but he did not want to be late for this very important event in his life.

However, also on the previous evening a group of North Korean guerrillas had planted a mine on the same road that Harvey now traveled. They had dug under the road in the cover of darkness and had buried a wooden mine, one of the most dangerous used in the Korean War because it could not be discovered by metal-seeking mine detectors.

As Harvey veered around a sharp curve his jeep's left front wheel ran over the mine. A thunderous explosion followed. The vehicle and Harvey were blown into a deep ravine. He tumbled over and over and finally stopped at the rocky bottom. The jeep landed on top of him and burst into flames. Lieutenant Richard Harvey, MC, was dead.

CHAPTER 25
FARLEY RETURNS

After diving into the Han River with the life jacket taken from the dead American Corporal Peter Farley was swept rapidly westwards for several miles by the swift current. His earlier fall against a rock in the valley had resulted in a concussion and he was only semi-conscious for most of his time in the water. A sudden stop in a clump of bushes on the southern shore of the river restored his senses. He felt extremely cold and shivered uncontrollably. The sun was beginning to rise over the eastern mountains as he pulled himself out of the water.

He took off his life jacket and threw it on the ground. "*We depend upon the Americans for everything,*" he said to himself. "*Even in death they have helped me. I am deeply in love with an American woman. We look like Americans and talk like Americans. We drink Coke and Pepsi and watch Hollywood movies. Some of the best American actors and actresses in the movies are actually Canadians. Americans are our best customers, friends, neighbors*

and even relatives, and yet some Canadians dislike them. Why?
Maybe we are just jealous of their power and prosperity." He was
surprised at his mind's sudden philosophical musing in spite
of his current very difficult circumstances. He stared at the life
jacket on the ground and suddenly remembered its original
youthful occupant. "*Thanks, American friend,*" he said in a soft
voice. "*I am going to dream about you for the rest of my life.*"

He noticed that his .45 was still in its holster and that his
money belt was still attached to his waste. The beautiful pen that
his Baba had given him for his 18th birthday was thankfully
in his pocket. His beret and radio was missing, but six primed
hand grenades were attached to his webbing. He checked his .45
and it was fully loaded with seven bullets. He also had an extra
clip of seven .45 bullets.

His shirt and pants were torn and his body was covered with
cuts and bruises. A large discoloured gash appeared through a
hole in his shirt on his left shoulder at the place where a Chinese
bullet had grazed him. He felt weak. "*I need food and medical*
help soon," he told himself, "*or I am not going to make it.*" It
was starting to get light but it was hard for him to see where he
was going.

As he walked slowly and painfully along the shore he suddenly heard some oriental voices and laughter coming out of a
cluster of trees immediately ahead of him. He also heard several
dogs barking. *What are these dogs doing here?*" he wondered.
"*Did the voices belong to the South Koreans, his allies, or to his*
North Korean and Chinese enemies? He believed that the South
Korean lst Division was located in this area and he decided that
he would try to establish a contact with this friendly unit.

He crawled slowly and carefully through the thick bushes
and towards the location of the oriental voices and barking
dogs. He had to be careful and confirm that they were friends
and not enemies. His .45 was drawn and his six hand grenades

were ready.

As he crawled forward on his hands and knees he suddenly came to an opening in the bushes. A startling scene confronted him. A log fire was burning in the middle of a clearing. He saw several Chinese soldiers, all of whom were all sitting in a circle around the fire. It was, Farley quickly concluded, a Chinese listening post located in the wide no man's land located next to the Han River. A unmanned medium machine gun sat in a sandbag shelter a short distance away from the fire. Farley counted 10 Chinese. They held bottles and cups and had obviously been drinking heavily. They were laughing boisterously. No guards were on duty. They were in a drunk and careless condition.

Chained to posts about 30 yards away from the fire were seven dogs of various colours, breeds and sizes. An unsteady, inebriated Chinese was beating the dogs with a large stick. Some barked continuously and others lay cowering on the ground. Three of them were bleeding from blows they had received. Farley noticed that they had collars and that they looked like animals who had recently been kept as pets. It appeared that they had they been stolen from their owners. The Chinese with the stick returned to the fire and sat with the rest of his comrades. He laughed, pretended to bark, and pointed at the dogs.

Farley quickly and accurately assumed that these Chinese soldiers had been drinking all night and that they had started a fire shortly after the sun had risen. The no man's land site in which they were located was about three miles wide and empty except for occasional patrols by both sides. Camp fires were easily spotted at night but were not very visible in the daytime. They had waited for daybreak. The dogs would be killed and cooked as soon as the fire was hot enough.

While in Grade 12 at Sweet Grass Farley had read a history of China and he remembered a disturbing chapter in this publication about a dog festival at a place in southern China called Falin where thousands of dogs were collected annually for meat dishes. According to this account, many were stolen or lost domesticated pets. They were caged, beaten, boiled and sometimes skinned while still alive.

Farley recalled this barbaric, inhumane Chinese custom and he was enraged. It appeared that these Chinese soldiers were preparing a dog eating festival of their own. They would pay a steep price for their cruelty.

Farley remained laying on the ground. He was hidden behind a large rock and in a copse of short bushes. The rock, he hoped, would protect him from shrapnel and gunfire. He pulled the six grenades from his belt, piled them on the ground in front of him, pulled their pins, and lobbed all of them rapidly into the direction of the fire. The resulting explosions tore into the bodies of all of the Chinese. They were sitting closely together, heavily intoxicated and almost asleep. Six were killed instantly. Four were badly wounded and pools of red blood poured onto the ground from their badly shattered bodies.

The Chinese were all dead or on the verge of death, but the one who had beaten the dogs with a stick picked up a revolver and pointed it in Farley's direction. Farley aimed his .45 and fired twice. One bullet hit the dog abuser in the head. Blood gushed from his forehead. He screamed, rolled over and died.

Farley felt no sympathy for the Chinese but he decided that he would not let them suffer. They were heartless creatures and would kill him if they could. It was kill or be killed. Some were still living but were badly wounded. Their deaths were inevitable. He walked calmly to the cluster of bodies and fired his .45 into the head of each survivor.

He found some cans of British Army beef, fed the dogs, and released them from their chains. The dogs ran away in all directions. He hoped that they would return to the homes from which they had been stolen. He could do nothing more to help them.

His heart was broken. He wished he could do more for them.

Suddenly a loud voice boomed out from a short distance away: "Don't move, buddy, until we find out who you are!" It sounded like a Canadian voice.

"Take it easy!" Farley yelled back. "I'm Corporal Peter Farley from the Canadian Fusiliers!"

A tall U.S. Marine sergeant carrying a carbine appeared from behind the top of the river bank. Several other Marines also came into view.

"A Canadian?" the sergeant asked. "What in hell are you doing in this fucking place? I thought your battalion was about 10 miles further east."

"I was on a patrol. We ran into some Chinese and I got separated. They chased me into the river." Several of the Marines laughed nervously.

"Yeah, that's what happened," Farley continued. "A lot of your people were dead and lying on the shore where I went in. I think that they must have been trying to build a pontoon bridge."

"Shit!" the sergeant exclaimed. "That must be the 18th Engineers. They were ambushed. Somebody was supposed to go in and recover the bodies and equipment, but the Chinese have been sending patrols all over the place."

"I know that," Farley replied. "We ran into a big one."

"Well, we're on a patrol too, Corporal," the sergeant said with a smile. "We're heading back to our lines, and you can come back with us if you want."

"I'm glad to hear that, sergeant. I sure as hell don't want to stay in this ugly place all by myself! I just had a fire fight with a bunch of Chinese! "

"Yeah, we heard that!" the sergeant said. "Lots of explosions."

"Hey, sarge!" one of the Marines exclaimed, "this guy sounds

like someone from North Dakota! Maybe even Minot, like me!"
he joked.

"I live just across the border in Manitoba," Farley said with
a loud laugh. "We taught you all the English that you know.
That's why you sound like us".

The Marines all grinned. One of them handed Farley a heavy
sweater. The shivering Canadian gratefully put it on. "Thanks,
pal," Farley said, "I'll dance at your wedding!"

"He's already married," the sergeant said with mock grim-
ness. "Let's move out."

They arrived at the Marine base and took him directly to
their field kitchen.

Do you have an ice cream making machine here?" he asked a
tall, slim, clean cut and well-dressed negro Marine cook. Farley
remembered the negro cooks on the ship coming to Korea and
was impressed by the difference. This one was classy and would
be at home even in the gourmet kitchens of the Waldorf Astoria.

"Of course. Don't you?"

"No. I haven't had any ice cream since I left Fort Lewis."

"We have chocolate or vanilla. Take your choice."

"What about some of each?"

"Coming up."

After eating, he was assigned to a sleeping bag in the depths
of a well-constructed bunker. Although he was very tired,
he began to question himself about his recent shooting of the
Chinese near the Han River. His mind was troubled. He knew
that the killing of prisoners of war was legally and morally questionable, but finally decided that he had performed an act of
mercy. They were not really prisoners. He also recalled that one
of the wounded had reached for his revolver, and that he had
simply carried out a necessary act of self defence. He reported
this episode to the Commanding Officer of the Marines.

The Marines sent a patrol into the area that Farley had

described. They found the bodies of the 10 Chinese and concluded that Farley had acted bravely. The Marine Commanding Officer recommended that Farley be given an American Silver Star for his heroic act. The recommendation was sent to the headquarters of the Canadian Infantry Brigade, but it languished there because the Canadian military authorities were reluctant to approve foreign awards for Canadian soldiers. Farley's Silver Star was not awarded to him until after he had returned to Canada.

Farley was uncomfortable in the Marine bunker because of his claustrophobia, but he soon fell into a deep sleep from which he did not awake until 12 hours later.

The Marine battalion commander sent a radio message to his headquarters informing his superiors that he had a Canadian temporarily in his care. However, the receiving operator, after writing the message down, threw it into a pile of other papers and forgot about it until two days later. Farley was safe, sound and recuperating with the Marines, but the Fusiliers further down the line did not know until three days had gone by and not until Farley was driven back to his unit in a Marine jeep.

While Peter Farley was in the M.A.S.H. recovering from malaria, and again while he was on patrol and then missing from his unit, letters from his friend Sonia and his father Orest arrived and were deposited at Battalion Headquarters waiting for his unexpected but possible return.

About a week after Peter Farley was reported missing his father Orest Farley was telephoned by the telegrapher in the railway station in Sweet Grass. The telegrapher told him that a telegram had arrived from Ottawa. He rushed to the station, tore open the envelope containing the telegram, and read as follows:

"Canadian National Telegraphs,
World Wide Communications,
WAH 69/82 Report Dely 5 Ex.
Army, Ottawa Ont. 16819B
29 June 51.

Priority Mr. Orest Farley,
Sweet Grass, Man.

Rec 506 CAS Sincerely regret to inform you
that your son SH800313 Corporal Peter Farley
Canadian Fusiliers has been reported missing
in action STOP Your son was on a patrol and
failed to return STOP Further information will
be forwarded immediately upon receipt from the
overseas authorities STOP."

Orest Farley stood in silence. Tears appeared in his eyes. "Oh God! Not Peter! Not my youngest son!" he muttered to himself.

Carl Schmidke, the telegrapher, looked sympathetically at the bewildered and shaken old man. "I'm sorry, Orest," he said. "I hope he comes back. He's a good boy."

"Thanks, Carl," Orest said numbly. He walked out of the station, stopped, and stared westward past the nearby grain elevators. A flock if pigeons landed nearby and began eating spilled grain. Orest remembered that Peter used to bring wheat to feed the pigeons. Peter was an animal lover, and also fed all the dogs, cats, squirrels, raccoons and birds in their neighborhood. As Orest stood in silence he heard footsteps behind him. It was Sonia Kereliuk. She had been running and tears poured down her cheeks.

"What's happened?" she asked anxiously. "People are saying that you got a telegram."

"Yes, Sonia," he replied quietly, "he's missing."

"Oh, no, God no!" she yelled. "Not Peter. I can't believe it!" She covered her face with her hands.

Farley put his hand on her shoulder. "Go and speak to Father Boleschuk," he suggested. "Ask him to pray for Peter. Let's all pray for him."

On the day that this telegram arrived in Sweet Grass, Peter Farley was already back and recuperating with the Marines, but Orest, Sonia and the people of Sweet Grass would not learn about his safe return until another telegram arrived a week later.

Shortly after returning to his unit a Postal Corps private delivered Farley's letters to him. "We were almost ready to send these back to Canada, Corporal" the private explained. "Thanks for saving us the trouble! Welcome back!"

The letters were from his father and Sonia. He hesitated for a few moments and then decided to read his father's letter first.

"*Dear Petro*", his father's letter began. "*Sonia has been reading your letters to me and I get some from you but you don't talk much about the fighting that makes me interested. I liked your letter back in March about the war. Didn't I always teach you to speak up? Don't worry, we know that you probably won't get killed. I told Father Boleschuk that he should pray for you at the church. This year I have been giving even more money.*

Ho at the Chinese restaurant said to say hello to you. That Ho sure got smart kids. They always do good in school. They are smarter than the white kids. Ho said his oldest son wants to be a doctor like you, but they won't let him into the university at Manitoba because he's a Chinaman. Hell, I said, at least he's better off than the Indians around here. Those poor buggers don't even go to no high school. Once in a while they round them up and put them in residential schools. Some of them can read now but they say that their teachers beat them up and are mean to them. I feel sorry for the Indians and as you remember I give them jobs on our farm at harvest time. Maybe you can get Ho's kid and one or two Indians into medicine after you are a doctor and get to know the Englishmen at the university at Manitoba. Don't forget that you have got a bit of Cree Indian blood in you.

Like I said before, write to tell me more about the war. Your brothers Nick and Harry were the same in the last war. They did not want to talk about it. Tell me why soldiers are like that. I was too old to be in the army. Nick and Harry are making lots of money in the construction and real estate business in Vancouver. They make me mad by living there. What's wrong with Manitoba? We need houses here too. Sometimes I think I should write to the Vancouver newspaper and tell them that Nick and Harry are Ukrainian and not English. Did you know that they go to the United Church now? The United Church is better than nothing but it's not Catholic and it's not Ukrainian. Don't ever do that to me. I'm counting on you. And don't forget to write again soon."

Farley smiled and quickly opened Sonia's letter. *"Thank you,"* she began, *"for your interesting but infrequent letters, including the one I received this morning. I must confess that I read each one of them several times, even though I am disappointed about how little you say about our relationship.*

One of the good things about teaching is that it makes provision for recuperation during July and August. Although I love working with children, I'm not sure that I could survive without two months of 'rest and rehabilitation', as you call it. I have become very envious of Peter, your cousin, and his wife Rosalie. They are very happily married and are expecting a child. Perhaps it is just the warm, sunny days of our prairie summer, with lots of time for contemplation that makes me feel this way. Whatever the reason, I want to tell you that I often pray for your safety, and that my love for you has not changed. In fact, it has become even stronger since you left for Korea. Won't you write to tell me about your plans for the future? Am I included in any way? As always, I shall look forward to hearing from you again. Love, Sonia."

Peter decided to reply to his father immediately. He also felt obligated to write to Sonia, but was having trouble deciding what he should say to her. Should he tell her about Morgan? Jean Haines was also in his mind. He loved Morgan very deeply, but he also loved Sonia and Jean. He wanted to keep all three of them. The prophets had hundreds of wives, so why could he not have three?

"Dear Tato", he wrote. He always used the familiar Ukrainian word for father, even when he was speaking to him in English, which was most of the time. *"My platoon commander told me about the telegram that was apparently sent to you by Army Headquarters in Ottawa. Actually, as you hopefully know by now, it was all a monstrous mix-up, because I am safe and sound and back with my unit. I hope that my temporary absence didn't cause you and Sonia and everyone else too much grief!*

What happened was that I went on a patrol and got separated from the others. I finally ended up with a U.S. Marine unit, where I stayed for a few days. They were all very friendly and helpful. I really like the U.S. Marines. Like us, they are all volunteers. They are very dependable and courageous. I even had a chance to eat some of their ice cream, something I had not tasted in several months.

Apparently the signalman that was supposed to advise my Battalion forgot to send a message and as a result our people thought that I was lost. Don't worry, Tato, I don't get lost that easily.

Thanks for sending me Ho's good wishes. I know his son Lee very well. Lee almost always scored 100 in Chemistry, Physics, and Mathematics. I was always slightly ahead of him, but only because I had better marks in History and English. I find it difficult to understand how the University of Manitoba Faculty of

Medicine can deny him a spot.

The days, weeks and months are passing by slowly, but passing nevertheless. If all goes well, I should be home for Christmas. Are we going to have our traditional Ukrainian dinner?

A letter from Sonia arrived here about two weeks ago. She told me about Baba's death and funeral. I felt very bad and was sorry that I was not home to say goodbye during her brief illness. I still have the beautiful pen she gave me for my 18th birthday. I will miss Baba very much. I am sure that you will as well.

I'm getting ready to go on a week long Rest and Rehabilitation Leave to Japan. We call it 'R and R'. We get one of these leaves about once every six months. I look forward to hearing from both of you. Love, Peter."

CHAPTER 26
REST AND REHABILITATION
IN JAPAN

A week after returning from the patrol Farley was advised that he would be going on five days Rest and Rehabilitation Leave (R & R) to Tokyo in Japan. He immediately sat down and wrote Laura Morgan a letter.

"*Dear Morgan,*" he wrote. "*I'm writing to tell you that I am going to Tokyo on five days R and R on August 1st. I'll be staying at a place called Shimya Barracks. Do you think that you could have your own leave scheduled for this time? You will recall that we discussed this possibility when we met at the M.A.S.H. It seems like ages since I last saw you. Please try. If you are able to come, I suggest that you leave a note with Corporal Jim Doherty at the Shimya gate. He is a big guy, about 6 ft., 1 in., with blond hair. He served with me in the Fusiliers until he got wounded and sent to a hospital in Japan. He is now temporarily posted and works at Shimya Barracks, a British Commonwealth R & R centre.*

He will probably eventually return to our unit in Korea once he completely recovers from his wounds. He is a good friend of mine and you can trust him with whatever information you may wish to pass on. I have heard that your American R and R base is located close to ours.

I'm 'Sergeant Farley' now, but in spite of my promotion, we will still run into some serious difficulties if both of us are seen together in uniform. Sergeants are higher than corporals, but sergeants and lieutenants are not supposed to fraternize in the Canadian army any more than in the American army, as you well know! Do you think that you can beg, borrow or steal some civilian clothing for yourself? I won about $1,500 playing poker on the boat coming over, and would be more than pleased to buy you a nice dress and shoes, or whatever else you need. Forgive me if I sound presumptuous.

That reminds me, by the way, that I need to find a bank in Tokyo where I can either deposit most of this money or send it home. I hate carrying it around and no banks are available in Korea, at least not for Canadian soldiers. Maybe I can deposit it with you. Do you have an account where I can leave it? About a half of it is in Canadian bills and the other half in U.S. bills.

I have many other important things to say to you, things like 'I miss you very much' and 'I think about you all the time', and especially 'I love you very much' but I would rather save them for our possible meeting in August. This may be our last chance to see each other for a long time. Please do everything in your power to try to come. Love, Peter."

Farley sealed the letter in an envelope and addressed it simply to "Lt. L. Morgan, 12th M.A.S.H." He then walked over to battalion headquarters to find Metro Kabaluk, the C.O.'s new driver and Ukrainian-speaking radio operator. He found Kabaluk asleep in a tent.

"Metro! Wake up!" Farley shouted. He grabbed Kabaluk by

the shoulder and shook him vigorously.

"Yeah! What is it, Kapusta, I mean, sergeant? What in hell do you want? I was havin' a beautiful dream."

"I need your help, Metro. Badly."

"What kinda help? I don't want no more troubles. The colonel tore a strip off me yesterday 'cause I got pissed. He threatened to send me to da piss can again, either dat or to a rifle company. If it wasn't for our Ukrainian radio caper, he probably would have done it. He knows he may need me again, but no more bullshit. I need to be careful."

"I hear that you are driving the colonel down to brigade headquarters," Farley said. "Do you think you can deliver this letter for me? It's for an officer in the American army."

"An officer? Why you write a letter to American officer? What's an American officer doing at Brigade Headquarters?"

"The officer I am sending a letter to is not at Brigade. The letter is going to a lieutenant at the 12th M.A.S.H. I am told that they are presently only about five miles from brigade."

"You mean dat I have to drive fucking five miles out of my way? That's impossible. The colonel is meeting with da brigadier. He could be with him for five minutes or five hours. I can't just fucking drive away and leave him."

"It's worth 50 bucks to you, Metro" Farley said with a sly smile. He pulled out a roll of bills and peeled off five 10's.

Kabaluk big brown eyes gleamed. "You must be nuts! " he exclaimed. "50 bucks to deliver a letter? That's two weeks pay!"

"It's only some of my poker money. I won't miss it."

Farley extended the money to Kabaluk who took it with some reluctance, an astonished look still on his face. "I try," he said, "but I not guarantee anyting."

Later that afternoon Kabaluk picked up Lieutenant-Colonel Strange and Captain Levinson, the Battalion Adjutant. As they drove to Brigade Headquarters Kabaluk worried. *"How am I going to deliver this letter?"* he asked himself. *"If the colonel's meeting ends early and I'm gone, I've had it. It either 30 days in the piss can or a rifle company, or both. Is the risk worth 50 bucks?"* He thought about his present advantages, a jeep to drive, a radio, a warm cot, a sleeping bag and hot meals. A rifle company was much less inviting. It meant climbing hills and mountains with heavy burdens, sleeping in freezing trenches with a single blanket, eating cold canned "C rations" and experiencing the terror of Chinese attacks with burp guns, mortars, artillery and hand grenades with all of their exploding furies.

The jeep was only on the road for 15 minutes, heading in a southerly direction when its occupants noticed a road block ahead of them. As they approached slowly they were flagged down by an American military policeman. The M.P. saluted the Canadian officers and walked up to the jeep. "We will be about another 10 minutes, sir. One of our trucks hit a mine on the road. We are removing the debris and the casualties."

"All right," Strange replied. "I guess we will have to wait."

The three Canadians got out of their jeep and walked forward to watch the road being cleared. Kabaluk noticed a jeep ambulance parked nearby. He walked up to the driver and extended his hand, his face beaming with a wide smile. "Hi, Yank, I'm Metro Kabaluk from da Canadian Fusiliers," he announced.

The surprised American shook Kabaluk's hand and returned the smile. "Sam Wilkins," he said. "It's good to have you guys here to give us a hand. I've been to Canada. Montreal. Know anybody in Montreal?"

"Oh, sure, lots of people. About a half a million people live there but I know lots of dem," Kabaluk said with a straight face. "Sam", he continued, "are you goin' to da 12th M.A.S.H. by any chance?"

"Yeah, I am. As soon as they patch up that guy in the ditch

and load him up, I'm going there. I live and work at the 12th."

"That's great! Then maybe you would not mind to take dis letter to an officer der called Lieutenant Morgan!" Kabaluk exclaimed.

The American took the envelope and looked at the name. "Lieutenant Morgan?" he asked with a look of surprise. "You mean the pretty, red-headed nurse? Do you know her?"

"No, it's from someone else, a friend," Kabaluk stammered, suddenly understanding the significance of the letter. *"Aha!"* he thought. *"A pretty nurse, eh? That Farley's a sneaky devil!"* All of his thoughts were in Ukrainian, his principal language.

"There's 10 bucks in it for you," Kabaluk said. He handed the American one of Farley's ten dollar bills.

The American took the money reluctantly. "Okay, I'll give her the letter. She is a good type. I don't really need the 10 bucks."

"Go ahead, keep it! Buy yourself some beer. It's on me. I be one of your Canadian friends and neighbors!" Kabaluk exclaimed happily, his mind suddenly relieved of the burden of having to deliver the letter. *"Wait until I see Farley,"* he chuckled to himself. *"He will have a hard time living this one down!"*

Farley's letter was delivered to Morgan later that afternoon. It made her very happy and excited. She read it several times. She had difficulty sleeping that night. *"He loves me,"* she kept telling herself. *"He loves me and I love him."*

Early the next morning Morgan walked into the M.A.S.H. headquarters tent. Major Powers sat at a table piled with files.

Powers looked up. "Yes, Laura, what can I do for you?"

"I'm wondering, sir, if I can change my R and R to Tokyo from September 1st to August 1st."

"I'm not sure, Laura. You know that it is hard to change leave schedules." He gave her a sympathetic look. She reminded him of his teen-aged daughter in Atlanta, with her red hair, freckles, dimpled cheeks, bright blue eyes, honesty and intelligence.

"I've already spoken with Lieutenant Courtney. She is due to go on August 1st and says that she will switch with me if you give us permission."

"Why can't you wait until September?"

She hesitated before answering. "To tell you the truth, sir," she finally said, "a friend of mine is going on leave at the same time. That's my reason. Please, sir. This is very important to me."

"She is indeed like Linda," his daughter, he told himself. *"Like Linda she knows how to turn on the charm and come out openly and honestly."*

Powers smiled. "If it's alright with Lieutenant Courtney, it's alright with me. I hope that he deserves you."

Morgan blushed. "Yes, sir, thank you sir." She saluted, turned and quickly left.

August 1st came quickly. On July 31st Farley traveled to Kimpo Airport near Seoul in the back of a two ton Canadian army truck. A total of 19 Fusiliers sat on folding wooden benches on both sides of the vehicle and on the floor. They talked excitedly in anticipation of their five days in Tokyo. Some of them let out shouts of joy as the truck rumbled southwards down a narrow, dusty and winding road.

The truck pulled up to a large, single story building next to one of the runways at the airport. The building's walls were pock-marked with bullet holes, some of its windows were shattered, and a gaping, jagged opening in the roof let in a bright beam of light into the interior. The capital city of Seoul had been lost and retaken twice by the United Nations forces, and much of the city and nearby airport had been devastated in the process. A crude, hand-painted sign was nailed above the front door, its message of "Thanks to the U.N. Forces" apparently sincere and not intentionally ironic.

The Canadians piled out of the truck and went into the damaged building where they sat or milled around impatiently, waiting for their aircraft to arrive.

Waiting nearby, in a separate area, was a small group of African American soldiers. Farley glanced over and saw one particularly tall sergeant who looked familiar. "That looks like Miles Lewis, the guy who fought Jim Doherty!" he said to himself. He walked over to the sergeant. "Miles," he said, "is that you, Miles Lewis?"

"Yeah, that's me," the sergeant responded with a look of surprise. He did not immediately recognize Farley.

"I'm Peter Farley. We met at the fight you had with Jim Doherty. You remember Jim and the fight, I'm sure!"

"Yeah, now I remember! Sorry about that. So what are you doing here?"

"I'm going on five days R and R to Tokyo. And you?"

"Same here. But I have a problem. Our truck was late and I missed my plane this morning. The loadmaster blames me and has put me on charge. He has ordered me to wait here. He says that he is going to ask that my leave be cancelled. We are waiting for word from my unit. I'm very disappointed and mad as hell. I'd like to kill the bastard but there is not much I can do."

"Maybe we can solve your problem," Farley said. "We have 20 places reserved on our plane but one of our guys didn't show up for some reason. So we have one vacant seat. Maybe you can take it."

"Thanks. That sounds great if it can be arranged," Lewis said.

At that moment an American sergeant, the loadmaster, came into the building. He was carrying a nominal roll on a clip board. He was obviously drunk, with watery eyes, slurred speech, wobbly legs, and whiskey reeking from his breath.

"Now hear this!" the loadmaster yelled above the loud din. "Listen for your names. Your C-47 will be here shortly." He then proceeded to call out the 20 Canadian names on his list.

"Sergeant", Farley said, "you will notice that one of our men is not present. He missed our truck this morning and will not be coming with us. That means we have one empty seat on the plane. I'd like this friend of mine to come with us. I understand that he missed an earlier flight because his vehicle was late."

"That won't be possible," the loadmaster said.

"Why not?" Farley asked.

"Bug out, sergeant, I have put this man on charge. He missed his plane to Japan and its his fault," the loadmaster replied sarcastically. "This is U.S. business. Negroes in our army have separate units. He can't go with you. Fraternization is not allowed."

"But we don't mind, do we guys?" Farley asked, his eyes quickly surveying the Canadians standing around him. Many nodded and grunted in agreement. "In fact, if Sergeant Lewis is not allowed to come with us we are going to be very unhappy. Maybe we will have to complain to your commanding officer," Farley said.

"Are you threatening me, sergeant?" the loadmaster yelled. "If you are not careful, all of you might just miss your plane. I'm in charge here, and not a bunch of yahoos from the north country." He rocked back on his heels and almost fell over.

"Sergeant, you're drunk," Farley said with authority. "I know damn well that the American army doesn't allow boozing on duty any more than ours does. Let this guy come with us or I'm calling the military police."

"You bastard," the loadmaster shouted, "I'll have you locked up!"

"Both of us in a cell together?" Farley said sarcastically.

At that moment the crowd of Canadians surged forward,

with several raising their fists in a menacing manner. "You are not going to leave this room alive, Yank," one of them shouted. "You haven't got room for 19 of us in your bloody piss can!"

The loadmaster backed against a wall with his face etched in fear. "Okay, okay," he said weakly, "get the hell out of here and take the black boy with you. That's your C-47 pulling up now."

The Canadians and Sergeant Lewis rushed out of the building and out to the edge of the runway where a twin-engine brown C-47 aircraft sat with its motors still running. They scrambled aboard past a surprised crewman who waited near the plane's door.

"Animals! These Canadians are all animals!" the crewman exclaimed.

"You're right," said the loadmaster as he staggered up and handed the crewman the passenger list. "You are absolutely right."

The C-47 took off quickly and droned southeastward through a clear blue sky, far above the mountains below. It crossed the Korean coastline 30 minutes later and continued over the Sea of Japan.

Sergeant Miles Lewis sat beside Farley on the starboard side of the aircraft. For a long time both of them remained silent. Finally, Lewis turned awkwardly in Farley's direction and spoke in a low, husky voice. "That took a lot of guts, sergeant, and I want you know that I appreciated it."

"You are welcome. Peter Farley's the name. Call me Peter, or Red if you like. Jim Doherty often calls me Red."

"And where is Jim Doherty? Has he been doing any more fighting? Is he still with your unit in Korea?"

"Jim was wounded on patrol and they sent him to one of your hospitals in Tokyo. He is stationed temporarily at Shimya Barracks, the place where I am going. He will be going back to our unit in Korea once he fully recovers."

"I think Canada is a great place. I don't think that I would have had that kind of help from white Americans," Lewis said.

"To tell you the truth, we don't have many Negro Americans in Canada, at least not in Manitoba, where I come from."

"I'm from Detroit, but I have an uncle who works as a porter on the Canadian National Railway".

"Yeah," Farley observed. "All of the porters on Canadian railways are Negroes. In fact, the C.N.R. and C.P.R. both have a kind of unwritten racial pecking order, with the Negroes as porters, Ukrainians and other foreigners as section laborers, and Anglo-Saxons at the top as conductors and engineers. That order has broken down a lot since the end of the last war, but not in the case of the Negroes. They are still hired only as porters."

Lewis smiled and looked at Farley. "What about the Indians? Where are the Indians in this pecking order?"

"They are mainly on reservations. I'm afraid that they are treated very badly, something like your people. Most of them don't have jobs, although my father hires a few at harvest time each year. But we do have a lot of them in the army."

"In separate units, like African Americans?"

"No. The Canadian Army is very fair in that way. Everyone is integrated. Our most decorated soldier is an Indian who won a lot of medals in WWII."

Their conversation continued as the C-47 droned across the Sea of Japan towards Tokyo. Lewis revealed that he had grown up in a Negro section of Detroit, and that his father worked as a janitor in an automobile plant. Like Farley, he had been forced to drop out of university after one year due to a lack of money. He was very athletic, 25 years old, single, and had held a variety of jobs, including two brief stints as a semi-professional boxer. He was familiar with the Canadian prairies, having played in the Manitoba-North Dakota Dakman Baseball league in the summer of 1948. Like most of the other Negroes his unit, he had been unable to avoid the American draft and had been sent into action in Korea after a short period of inadequate training.

As the C-47 began its descent towards Haneda Airport in Tokyo, Farley and Lewis realized that their brief friendship was probably coming to an end.

"Thanks again, Peter," Lewis said as he extended his hand. "I'll always remember how you helped me. And say hello to Jim when you see him."

Farley handed Lewis a pen and tore a page out of a notebook that he kept in his pocket. "Here," he said, "please write down your home address and phone number as well as your present unit. If I am ever in Detroit maybe I can give you a call."

"Beautiful pen. Probably very expensive," Lewis said as he wrote on the paper.

"My Baba, I mean by grandmother, gave it to me for my 18th birthday. She died recently. It has a lot of sentimental value for me," Farley sadly replied.

At that moment the C-47 entered some strong turbulence and lurched wildly.

"Call me if you can find the time," Farley replied when the plane stabilized again. "Shimya Barracks, I think, is not far from where Americans stay when they go on R and R leave." Farley's invitation was genuine, but he did not think that Lewis would accept his invitation. They lived in worlds apart.

"Okay," Lewis said as their aircraft touched down. "We'll see how it goes." They had landed and were in Tokyo for five days of R and R. Although Lewis was very impressed with Farley, and although he found him to be very likeable and interesting, he did not feel comfortable with him. Farley was, after all from another predominantly white culture and he found this circumstance to be very difficult.

In the summer of 1951 the city of Tokyo had almost seven million people, with a total of about 25 million living within a 30 mile radius of its centre. Unlike European and North American cities, with their largely stone and concrete construction materials, Tokyo had consisted mainly of wooden buildings prior to the war. The U.S. bombing raids of WWII had destroyed large sections of the fragile city and new buildings had been constructed with more durable materials. Modern Tokyo consisted of a blend of Japanese and western cultures, life styles, and architecture.

The Japanese people were outwardly very polite to the American and other personnel that poured into Japan during the period of the Korean War. The Japanese had been humiliated during WWII and were now forced to swallow their pride. On the other hand, there still existed hostile elements within the population consisting primarily of disbanded soldiers, sailors and airmen. These violent men had returned to a shattered Japan, a country where honour was deemed to be of supreme importance.

The Emperor and the Japanese government refused to acknowledge the fact that some Japanese soldiers and civilians had committed war crimes, for which some were tried and executed, or that prisoners of war and civilians had been kept in brutal and cruel prison camps. The Emperor and his government, however, were prepared to accept defeat quietly.

The militant gangs of former servicemen, on the other hand, bitterly resented the presence of the U.S. and other foreign troops and they secretly yearned to continue the struggle that had ended in 1945. Although the Japanese were a law-abiding people, with relatively little crime in their streets, these bands carried on criminal activities, including robbery, smuggling of stolen goods, and involvement in prostitution. One of these groups would soon touch the lives of Peter Farley and Laura Morgan.

Farley and Morgan both arrived in Tokyo on August 1st, but

Morgan left Kimpo Airport at Seoul about two hours earlier than Farley. After landing at Haneda Airport in Tokyo she proceeded directly to the American military leave centre, and after a brief stop, took a taxi to Shimya Barracks where Farley and the other Canadians were scheduled to stay. Jim Doherty was not immediately available, but one of the guards at the gate eventually found him.

"Jim?" she asked. "I remember you from the fight. You persevered and won over a strong opponent. I was impressed. I am one of the nurses who watched you." She hesitated for a moment and then continued. "I'm Laura Morgan, Peter Farley's friend. Can you give him this message?" She handed him a sealed envelope.

"Of course," Doherty replied with awe. "Red wrote to tell me that someone might be bringin' me a message, but..."

"But you did not expect to find an American officer, a woman" she said with a smile.

"Yeah, and a very attractive one, if you don't min' me saying so."

Doherty, after his time in the Canadian Army, and after a concerted effort, has lost some of his Newfoundland dialect and distinctive vocabulary.

"Thank you. Is he here yet?"

"No. Accordin' to our schedule his plane is expected to arrive in about another two hours. Do you want to wait for him?"

"No, I think I will leave. Tell him that I've taken a room at the Yamate Hotel. But give him my note as soon as he gets here. And Jim, please keep this to yourself, will you? My identity, I mean. I am going to change into civilian clothing, but we have to be careful. Peter and I could get into a lot of trouble".

"I know. He's a sergeant and you are a lieutenant."

"Thanks, Jim, "I've enjoyed meeting you. I am one of your fans!"

"I also enjoyed meeting you, lieutenant," Doherty concluded. He could not bring himself to call her Laura. "I hope that you and Red like Tokyo. It's a very beautiful, exciting and interesting city."

Several hours later, after receiving her note from Jim Doherty, Farley met Morgan in the lounge of the Yamate Hotel, a modern five story building on Ginza Avenue, the main thoroughfare for shopping in Tokyo. He had been sitting by himself for half an hour, wondering if she would ever come. Finally she appeared before him, stunningly beautiful in a bright red dress, matching hat and high-heeled red shoes.

Peter rose from his chair, his heart pounding furiously. He felt very inferior in his plain Canadian army summer khaki uniform. "Morgan," he said softly, "you're absolutely gorgeous!" He held out both hands and she slipped into his open arms. They held each other in a gentle embrace for a long minute. Then they sat together in two adjoining soft chairs.

"You look splendid too, Peter, or at least better than the last time I saw you!" she said in a sweet and teasing voice.

"You mean wearing only shorts and covered in mud. You didn't seem to mind."

"I was grateful that we escaped with our lives. That was a very frightening experience."

"It was unexpected," he said. "I was told afterwards that the Chinese had recently acquired some long range Soviet artillery. That's why they were able to reach the M.A.S.H."

"Yes, they have now moved us back several miles so that we will not be in range. But how was your trip from Korea? Did you get settled in to your leave centre?" Morgan asked.

"Yes, but Jim Doherty told me that you are staying here. The desk clerk speaks some broken English. I paid him a bribe. I asked him where you are staying and he gave me 512, your room number. I've registered in Room 513 across the hall from you on the fifth floor."

"Oh! That's sneaky!" Morgan exclaimed. "A bribe? I hope that you did not pay too much. But I guess that I'm secretly pleased. I've noticed that there are a lot of Americans and Europeans staying here, but I didn't feel very comfortable before. The Japanese here can see that I'm probably not in business or the diplomatic corps, like most the other foreigners here. They probably wonder who I am and what I am doing here by myself. Now that's all changed. I'm with you and that's all that matters. "

"Most Canadians, and Americans too, apparently don't stay in the R and R military leave centres. After registering they take off and shack up all over Tokyo. There is nothing unusual about our decision to stay here. And by the way, will I be able to visit you in your residence here?" Farley asked with a smile.

"As long as you behave yourself. Remember that we are still virtual strangers. I am not a shack up," Morgan said firmly with a smile of her own.

"But not just ships passing in the night, I hope," he answered. "Allow me to change the topic for a moment. That's a beautiful dress you are wearing. Where did you get it?"

"My mother bought it for me after I graduated with my degree in nursing. I kept it in one of my kit bags when I came to Korea just in case I needed it for some special occasion. This is a very special occasion. I'm glad I brought it."

"You would look good even in a potato sack!" Farley exclaimed.

"What about you?" Morgan asked. "How long are you staying in the army? You told me that you have finished two years of medicine and that you will probably go back after you get out."

"I do plan to go back. I have about another eight months to go in the army. I think that Veterans' Affairs will pay for my

243

tuition and expenses when I enroll again at the University of Manitoba. They very generously helped veterans after the last war and they will probably do the same for me." He reached into his pocket and pulled out a folded and worn piece of paper. "Read this," he said as he unfolded and handed it to her. "You may be interested."

Morgan took the paper and began reading. It was a typed letter on University of Manitoba letterhead, dated July 3rd, 1950 and addressed to Mr. Peter Farley at Sweet Grass, Manitoba.

"Dear Mr. Farley," the letter began, *"the Dean of the Faculty of Medicine has reminded me that you achieved very high honours marks in your studies at the Faculty during the 1949-50 academic year. He also noted that you failed to register for the following academic year in spite of the fact that you were awarded the prestigious Howard Menzies Scholarship.*

Please be advised that you must register again within the next two years or lose your present eligibility. In other words, it will be necessary for you to repeat your pre-medical studies unless you begin classes again no later than September, 1953.

On a more personal note, I would like to say that your service as the highest-scoring forward with the University Buffalo hockey team was also very much appreciated. They could certainly use you again in light of their present record.

Under the above circumstances, it is our sincere hope that you will give some thought to returning to the Faculty of Medicine in the near future. In the meantime, we extend to you our best wishes. Sincerely yours, J.B. Anderson, Ph.D., Vice-President, Academic."

"Very impressive!" Morgan exclaimed as she handed the letter back to Farley.

"Thanks," he said with a laugh. "That's why I gave it to you! I want to impress you!" He folded and stuffed the letter back into his pocket awkwardly.

"So why did you go into the army?" she asked.

"Mainly because I ran out of money. The scholarship was not enough. My two brothers, Nick and Harry were in the Fusiliers in the last war. I was too young and envious of their great adventure. The Special Force for Korea was recruiting for a period of 18 months only, a short period which appealed to me."

"It sounds like you acted impulsively!"

"Yes, I was impulsive and acted quickly without too much thought. I genuinely wanted to help the people in Korea even though I did not know much about them. I wanted to prove that I was a good Canadian, and that I was opposed to communism. I have to confess, also, that I hoped Veterans' Affairs would help me return to the university after I got out of the army."

They moved into the nearby hotel restaurant and sat at table. A waitress in traditional Japanese attire came to serve them. She had a fair complexion and had a bun of black hair piled at the back of her head. Her eyes were curiously round, unlike those of most Japanese. She bowed deeply. "May I bring you something to drink?" she asked in accented English.

"Saki, please. I think I'll try some saki," Morgan cheerfully replied.

"I'll have the same, thank you," said Farley.

A band walked onto a nearby stage, its five Japanese musicians carrying a guitar, trumpet, saxophone and drums. One of its members sat down at a piano located at the side of the stage and the others clustered in front of him. Soon afterwards American popular music began to fill the room. *Goodnight Irene, Blueberry Hill, Love Letters* and *Stardust* emerged in beautiful renditions.

Morgan and Farley danced very closely together, oblivious to the groups of people who were beginning to fill the room. They said very little and were contented and very happy in a euphoric world of their own. He stopped once to ask the band leader if they could play *Laura.* The band responded and played the music requested immediately afterwards.

Finally, after about a half hour had passed, Morgan and Farley sat down at their table again. Their silence broke as they told each other the stories of their lives.

Morgan had been born into a well-established upper middle class family in Minneapolis, where her late father had been very successful in the real estate and land development business. Her mother, one brother, one sister and Laura had been left a sub-stantial estate by their father, who had died when Laura was 11 years old. She had wanted to be a medical doctor, but had been discouraged by her mother, who felt that medicine was a man's profession. Nursing had been her second choice, but she had few regrets. Her mother had wanted her to meet and marry a medical doctor. The idea had been initially appealing to Laura as well, but a broken romance with a married medical doctor had left her hurt and suspicious. She had learned about the doctor's marriage only by accident and she had broken up with him immediately after her painful discovery.

"You aren't married, are you?" she suddenly blurted out in an unusually serious and forceful manner.

"No, I'm not!" he replied with a laugh. "I swear on the Bible and I give you my word as a gentleman and scholar. I'm a Catholic, but not a very good one. I rarely go to church. Catholics can only be married once. Divorce is not allowed."

"Yes, I remember the story of Henry VIII," she said. "I don't approve of Henry's behaviour, but I have to admit that I'm an Episcopalian, a protestant like Henry! However, I'm afraid that I have not being going to church regularly since leaving university. I should tell you, though, that my mother has anti-Catholic feelings."

"Does she have any strong anti-Ukrainian feelings?" Farley

asked half-seriously.

"I don't think so. In fact, I'm sure that we never thought about Ukrainians at all. There were probably Ukrainians in Minneapolis, but we never noticed them. I guess that they looked and acted just like everyone else."

"I know what you mean. It's called the Great American Melting Pot. Everyone gets melted except maybe the Negroes and Mexicans. All the people of North America, including Canada, are destined to become the same people, with one language, one government and a common culture."

"You make it sound so exciting!" she said with a laugh. She leaned over and kissed him on his cheek.

"Is that all?" he asked mischievously.

"I should tell you, Morgan," he said seriously, "that I have some concerns about my father's mental history."

"What is it?" she replied with a smile on her face. "I am interested in you. Your father's mental history is not very important."

"Several years ago my father spent some time in a mental hospital. Schizophrenia was the diagnosis. He recovered and now appears to be healthy. But I am worried about the possibility that I have inherited a predisposition for this illness. I am sure that I do not have schizophrenia, but what if I pass on this genetic weakness on to my children, if in fact I have children? Maybe I should not even marry."

"All human beings have genetic weaknesses of some kind," she replied emphatically. "My father and his two brothers were alcoholics, and I understand that alcoholism is at least partly hereditary. My mother and her mother both had breast cancer, also caused by bad genes. I am a nurse and have read a great deal about these things. We should live our own lives and not worry about our ancestors. Life must go on."

Morgan's positive response put his mind to rest. Speaking

openly about his father's circumstances was a wise decision. He would never again worry about his genetics or that of his father and the rest of his family. Life, as Morgan said, must go on.

They danced and talked until shortly after midnight. He told her about his small town life in Sweet Grass, and she told him about her urban life in Minneapolis. They had many of the same interests. Both had read widely, including many of the same books. Both were downhill skiers and enthusiastic swimmers. She told him about her love of classical music and opera. He said that he also liked classical music, but with some hesitation because he suddenly remembered his classical musical experiences with his eccentric mathematics teacher, Michelle Brown.

"I think it's time to go to my room and to bed," she suddenly announced.

"May I come with you?"

"Where? To my room or to my bed?"

"To your room, at least for the time being."

"It's very hard for me to say no to you. I feel as though we are soul mates and that we are already married."

They went to Morgan's room together with feelings of uncertainty. He felt a very powerful urge to be with her, but did not know how far he should try to go. She was equally passionate, but not sure if she should let him make love to her if and when he tried.

A tentative, parting good night kiss turned into more kisses and embraces that engendered even greater burning desire in both of them. He decided that he could not leave. She decided, at the same time, that she wanted him to stay.

They made prolonged and ecstatic love, in her case for only the second time, and in his case for the third time. His previous encounters were temporarily blocked from his memory. He was totally entranced in her presence. They did not fall asleep until early that morning.

Morgan and Farley awoke at 11:00 a.m. the next day and after eating they went on a tour of some of Tokyo's magnificent cultural centres: the Imperial Household Museum, the National Museum of Modern Art, the Metropolitan Fine Art Gallery, and the Okura Museum of Antiques. They were on a rushed, guided tour, intended only as an overview, and they decided to return in future to the places that interested them the most.

After the tour they walked down Ginza Avenue where many shops, restaurants and night clubs were located. "I'd like to buy you another dress and some shoes," he said.

"I thought you like this red dress," she replied with a smile.

"I do, but you can't wear it every day. We still have four days left."

They entered a large store with a sign in English reading "Regal Dresses and Shoes for Women." An adjacent sign in Japanese presumably said the same thing. As they entered they were immediately approached by three enthusiastic sales ladies, one of whom spoke broken but understandable English.

At 5 feet and 9 inches, Morgan was taller than most Japanese, and the selection for her was limited. She finally selected two dresses, one a pale blue and one a dark green, with shoes to match. "Which one do you prefer?" she asked Farley.

"You look very beautiful in both, and we'll take both," he insisted. She protested, but not for long.

"They also have rings here," he said. "I'd like to buy you one."

They looked at the selection of rings. She expressed her preferences, and he bought the ring that she wanted the most. Japanese merchants always expected some haggling to take place over the price, and after a brief exchange, he paid the sales lady $225 American dollars. That represented about two months of salary, but he still had most of the $1,500 that he had won in poker during his Pacific voyage to Korea.

"Does this mean that we are engaged and are going to live happily ever after?" she asked with a smile.

"Yes, that's what it means. Will you marry me?"

"Yes, I will marry you." She kissed him on his cheek, much to the delight of the Japanese sales ladies.

Shortly afterwards they found a branch of the Bank of Japan. Farley located a teller who could speak English and deposited a large part of the Canadian and American money he was carrying in his name as well as Morgan's.

"It's your money and I will never spend it," she said, "but I don't mind you putting it in my name if you think it is going to be safer."

"I'm planning to live a long time," he replied, "but if I don't I want you to have it rather than the Bank of Japan."

"The guys in my company would pronounce me insane," Farley observed wryly, "if they knew that I was spending my time with a beautiful woman visiting museums and going shopping."

"What's wrong with being with a beautiful woman?" she asked.

"That part is alright. It's the museums that they would question!"

In the evening they returned to the Yamate Hotel for dinner. The dining hall was full of people, mostly Japanese, unlike the previous evening when a lot of westerners had been present.

The Japanese waitress with round eyes and fair skin waited on them once again.

"What is your name?" Farley asked.

"I am called 'Baiu'. I was born during the gentle summer rains. These rains are called Baiu in Japan."

"It's a lovely name and you are a lovely Japanese lady," Farley continued.

Baiu blushed.

"I am getting jealous," Morgan said with a smile. "But you are absolutely right. Baiu is lovely."

"I'm only half-Japanese," Baiu said shyly. "My father was an official in the British Embassy before the last big war."

"Of course!" Farley exclaimed. "It all fits. The round eyes, the white skin and the good English."

"Where is our band?" Morgan asked. "Aren't they playing tonight?"

"No," Baiu answered. "They only come three times a week. Most of our patrons tonight are Japanese, as you can see."

Baiu left to serve at a nearby table. Peter looked over and noticed that four Japanese men were sitting there eating and drinking saki. They were all dressed in the uniforms of the disbanded Japanese armed forces, minus the insignias, badges and other military marks of identification. From time to time they glanced over at Morgan and Farley, their faces seeming to reveal a sinister hostility.

Shortly afterwards, two of the men got up, drew pistols from their jackets and walked to the table of Morgan and Farley. The other two walked away from their table and left through the door at the rear of the restaurant.

"Come with us!" The man closest to Farley said in English. "This is a patriotic exercise being carried out for the honour of the Japanese people. You are required to be our honourable hostages. Come quickly or you will die!"

Farley instinctively reached for the .45 he usually had strapped to his belt and then suddenly realized that he did not have it with him. One of the Japanese noticed his movement and held his revolver to Farley's head.

Morgan and Farley reluctantly rose from their table and were pushed and herded at gunpoint towards the rear exit. As they stepped out into the night, they noticed that two automobiles were parked and running. They hands were quickly bound with ropes, their eyes were covered with cloth blindfolds and they were gagged. Morgan was pushed into the back seat of the first car and Farley into the back seat of the second car. Both cars then sped off into the night.

The Osaka Gang, the kidnappers of Farley and Morgan, were actually members of Yazuka, a criminal organization that first appeared in Japan in the early 17th century. In some ways it resembled the Italian mafia. It had branches in all of the largest Japanese cities and, by paying bribes, enjoyed a semi-legal status. The Yazuka members were often involved in gambling, peddling stolen goods, loan sharking, prostitution and kidnapping. Young women in the Philippines, Korea and Europe were brought to Japan under false pretenses and forced to become the providers of sexual services.

CHAPTER 27
EDO STREET

Morgan and Farley remained gagged, blindfolded and bound by the wrists. The two cars roared away, their charcoal burning engines sending off clouds of rancid smoke. After about 30 minutes they came to screeching stops. The two prisoners were pushed out roughly into the humid evening air. They were taken into a small house and then into a small room, tied to two chairs and left sitting for several minutes while their captors sat on the floor conversing excitedly. Then one of the Japanese removed their blindfolds and gags.

"Do not shout or make any other noises," said Yasu, the only Japanese among the four who spoke English. "If you do, we will have to cover your eyes and mouths again."

"What do you want with us?" Farley asked angrily. "We have done nothing to you."

"You are our hostages," Yasu replied. "We are sending a message to the American military authorities in Tokyo. "We are demanding money. We are a secret brotherhood. We need funds to carry on our honourable struggle against you because you are unwelcome foreign invaders. We think the Americans will pay. They don't want to see any of their people getting hurt."

"Please let us go," Morgan pleaded. "We have not harmed you in any way." Her dress was torn, her hair was disheveled and a red welt marked her forehead where the blindfold had been tightly tied.

Farley decided to change his strategy. "You speak English very well," he said to Yasu in a friendly tone. "Where did you learn it?"

"In California, before the last war," Yasu answered. A wide smile crossed his round face. "I worked for an importing company. After I returned to Japan I became an intelligence officer in our army in the Philippines."

"Do your friends understand English?" Farley asked.

"No. They do not understand," Yasu replied. "Meiju knows a few words, but not many. Behave yourselves. After we get our money we will let you go."

Yasu then left the room, leaving Morgan and Farley with the three other Japanese men.

The leader of the gang was Sendai, a former captain in the Imperial Japanese Army. Another was Meiju, who had been convicted as a violent criminal in Japan prior to the war, who had subsequently served as a cruel and vicious guard in one of the notorious Japanese prisoner-of-war camps, and who was now in hiding from American military prosecutors. The fourth man was Tokugawa, a fanatical Japanese nationalist who had been training to become a suicide Kamikaze pilot when the war ended in 1945.

Meiju got up from the floor and walked over to Morgan. He ran his fingers across her bare shoulders and through her moist red hair. "Very interesting!" he exclaimed, an evil glint in his eyes. "I've never been with an American woman!"

"Keep your filthy hands off her, you bastard!" Farley shouted. "You son of a bitch! I'll kill you!" Intense anger, frustration and revulsion surged through him as he tore violently at the ropes binding him.

Meiju did not understand Farley's words but he could see that they were not friendly. He smiled calmly and then punched Farley in his face with all the force he could muster. Farley's head was smashed violently to the left, blood began pouring out of his nose, stars and flashes of light exploded in his head and he lapsed into unconsciousness.

Morgan began sobbing. "Peter!" she yelled. "Don't say anything more. He's crazy!"

Farley did not reply. His head was drooped onto his chest. Blood poured from his nose and trickled onto his shirt.

"That's enough, Meiju!" Sendai ordered. "You have made your point. I may just take the woman for myself, but not right now. The rest of you can have her after I am through. I will decide when the time is right."

On the morning after the kidnapping of Morgan and Farley a taxi carried Miles Lewis from his American leave centre to Shimya Barracks. He had discovered Farley's beautiful and expensive pen in his pocket and had suddenly realized that he had forgotten to return it to Farley. The plane had lurched violently, he recalled, and as a result he had shoved the pen into his pocket. Lewis remembered that this had been a birthday gift from Farley's grandmother and felt that he should return it. "*It is the least I can do,*" he said to himself, "*after all the help he has given me.*"

The taxi carried Lewis to the gate of Shimya Barracks where a guard greeted him. "Yeah, sergeant," the guard said. "Can I help you?"

"I'm looking for Sergeant Peter Farley."

"He's not here, but one of his friends, Corporal Jim Doherty came back an hour ago. Do you want to speak with Jim? He may be able to tell your where Farley is."

"Yes, I am acquainted with Corporal Doherty," Lewis said with a laugh. "We met on a special occasion in Korea a few weeks ago."

Lewis waited at the gate until Doherty arrived.

Doherty immediately recognized Lewis. "What's up?" He asked with a look of surprise. "What are you doin' here? How is she goin'? Not looking' for another fight, I hope!" Doherty smiled as they shook hands.

Lewis held Farley's pen up for Doherty to see. "This is Peter's pen," he said. "We met at Kimpo Airport in Seoul. We were both going on R and R. I had a serious problem and he solved it for me. I missed my plane and he got me a seat with his group of Canadians. On the way to Japan he loaned me this pen and I forgot to return it to him. It's a gift from his grandmother and very important to him."

"Peter is stayin' at the Yamate Hotel not far from here. We can go there together if you like. I ain't had a chance to talk to him since he checked in."

"Thanks, Jim," Lewis said. "Why don't I just leave you the pen and you give it to him whenever you see him."

"That's up to you. But I think he will be disappointed. I'm sure that he will want to thank you personally. I knows him very well. He's like that."

"Okay," Lewis said reluctantly. "But I can't stay long. I'm supposed to go out with some of my friends later this evening."

"We won't stay long. I also have to get back," Doherty said. He hailed a nearby taxi and they drove off towards the Yamate Hotel.

They arrived at the Yamate Hotel and spoke to the clerk at the hotel reception area. "Is there a Sergeant Peter Farley here?

Did he leave a message for anyone?" Doherty asked.

"Mr. Farley is registered here, but I not seen him lately," the clerk explained in heavily-accented English. "He not leave a message. I not know where he is." He spoke with hesitation and had a worried look on his face.

"Let's stop for a drink," Doherty said to Lewis. "Maybe he will show up. We won't stay long."

"Okay," Lewis said, once again reluctantly, "but no more than half an hour. I have to get back."

Doherty and Lewis went into the bar to order a drink. Baiu, the half-Caucasian, attractive waitress served them as they spoke about Farley and speculated about his whereabouts.

"It's funny Red did not leave a message at the reception desk," Doherty said.

"He said that he would."

"Excuse me sirs, but are you looking for two people with red hair?" Baiu suddenly interjected as she served them their drinks.

"Yeah!" Doherty said with a surprised look. "Have you seen them?"

"A handsome red-headed young man was here," Baiu continued. "He was with a beautiful woman with hair of the same colour."

"Where are they now?" Lewis asked.

"Please, sirs, I may get into great trouble for speaking with you about this matter." She suddenly regretted saying anything because she was afraid of getting involved in a serious situation. But it was too late. She had spoken spontaneously and now they knew her secret.

"Believe me, my very pretty lady, we won't tell a soul," Doherty said. "I give you my word. Where are they?"

"The two of them have been taken away by four evil men. They are members of the Osaka Gang. They took your friends away somewhere. They had guns and forced them to go."

"But where are the Japanese police?" Lewis asked. "Were they here? What have they done about it?"

"Yes, they were here, but they couldn't do very much," Baiu replied. "Everyone at the hotel is afraid to give any information. The Osaka Gang has many members in all parts of Tokyo. They have a lot of sympathizers and informers. They seem to hear everything and are very powerful. I've heard that even some police help them."

"Do you know any of these men?" Doherty asked very forcefully.

"Please, sir, I may get into very great trouble," Baiu replied. She had been very impressed by Morgan and Farley and wanted to help them, but she was very afraid of the Osaka Gang.

"Our friends lives are in great danger!" Lewis exclaimed. "You must tell us what you know!"

"One of the men," Haiu whispered with hesitation, "is called Meiju. He was here about two weeks ago by himself and became very drunk. He wanted me to go to his place, but I declined. People say that he is a war criminal and that the American military police are looking for him. After I said no he became angry, but he later wrote down his address on a piece of paper and told me to visit him. He said that he would pay me a lot of money. Soon afterwards he passed out. Two of his friends came later and took him away."

"Do you still have the address?" Doherty asked excitedly.

"I destroyed the paper but I could not forget the address. It has haunted me."

"What is it?" Doherty and Lewis asked in unison.

"1965 Edo Street."

Doherty dropped a 10 dollar bill on their table to pay for their drinks and to leave Baiu a large tip. The drinks were priced at 25 cents each. He was very impressed by Biau. She was a lovely woman.

Doherty and Lewis leaped from their chairs and ran out to the street to where several taxis were waiting.

"English!" Doherty yelled. "Who speaks English?"

A small man standing next to his taxi raided his hand. "Where to, soldiers?" he asked.

"1965 Edo Street!" Doherty yelled.

"Edo Street? Are you sure? There is nothing of interest to soldiers on Edo Street. No geishas there. "

"We are absolutely sure!" Lewis said with a fierce glare. "And make it fast. You know what I mean?" He moved towards the driver in a menacing manner.

"Yes, sir," the driver answered fearfully. "But please pay me in advance. We not supposed to take Americans into that area."

"I'm a Canadian and not an American," Doherty said as he handed the driver a five dollar bill.

"It's the same. Canadians are Americans as far as the Japanese are concerned," the driver said as they all climbed into the taxi.

The taxi sped off into the night, weaving its way through a maze of narrow and crooked streets. They were in a purely Japanese district of Tokyo where foreigners rarely ventured.

After several minutes passed the driver pulled his vehicle over to a curb."1965 Edo is the house on the next corner on the right side of this street," he said. "Please, I'll let you off here."

Doherty and Lewis climbed out of the taxi and began walking down the narrow and dimly-lit street. There were few people in the area and those that were present looked curiously and suspiciously at the two hulking strangers. One was a white man and the other a black man. They were creatures from another world whose only commonality seemed to be their giant sizes, and in all probability, great strength.

As they walked towards their destination Doherty and

Lewis noticed that it was a traditional Japanese house with a single level and small dimensions. A dim street light burned on the corner next to the house. The immediate area seemed to be deserted.

"So, what do you think we should do now? We certainly can't just knock and introduce ourselves," Doherty said with a grim smile.

"I think we should go through the front door. Smash it down, I mean," Lewis replied.

"But they may be armed."

"So am I," Lewis announced as he pulled out a small, snub-nosed revolver from the inside pocket of his jacket.

"Alright, but what if they are not there?" Doherty asked. "What if it's someone else?"

"We will just apologize and leave. We'll say 'sorry, wrong address.' I am sure that they will understand."

Doherty smiled grimly again. His stomach was beginning to churn in a familiar manner.

Lewis positioned himself several yards in front of the house, clutched his revolver in his right hand and ran straight for the door at high speed. His feet both left the ground at the same time and smashed into the door. Its flimsy wood splinted into many pieces as his body hurtled through it and into the room within. As he tumbled onto the floor his revolver fell out of his hand and disappeared into the pile of wooden debris. Coming in immediately after him was Doherty, his large left fist cocked and ready to act.

The four Osaka Gang members sprang to their feet from the floor where they had been sitting and eating. They were not in possession of their weapons. Farley and Morgan were nearby, gagged and tied to their chairs.

Lewis punched Tokugama in the stomach with a sickening thud. The Japanese collapsed onto the floor, clutching his stomach in breathless agony.

Captain Sendai was momentarily immobile with shock, but he finally recovered and tried to run from the room. Lewis tackled him and then smashed Sendai's face into a bloody pulp with several powerful blows.

Lewis turned to Tokugama and knocked him senseless with a single punch to the head. Blood poured out of Tokugama's nose and mouth.

In the meantime, Yasu and Meiju wrestled with Doherty on the floor. The Canadian had still not recovered from his wound in Korea, but he managed to hold his own against the two much smaller Japanese.

Meiju raised his hand to give Doherty a judo chop to his head, but at that moment Lewis intervened. The powerful American punched Meiju in the face, picked him up, lifted him up like a 130 pound weight, which Meiju was, and threw him against one of the thin walls. The Japanese created a large cavity in the flimsy partition and cried out in agony before passing out. Several of his teeth were left on the floor.

Doherty stood up and caught Yasu with a devastating left hook to the face. A second blow shattered Yasu's jaw and he fell to the floor in an unconscious heap.

Lewis and Doherty then moved to the two captives. They removed their gags and untied them from their chairs.

"Thank God!" Farley exclaimed as soon as Lewis removed his gag. "Where did you guys come from? How did you find us? Miles! Miles Lewis! It's great to see you again!"

"Never mind, Red," Doherty replied. "We will tell you later. Let's get the hell out of here while we can!"

Farley looked over anxiously at Morgan who now lay on the floor in an unconscious state. She had fallen asleep in her chair immediately prior to the violent entrance of the two rescuers and had fainted from shock when the ensuing fight took place.

"She is alright," Lewis said. "She is breathing normally."
He then reached down and picked up his revolver from the
wooden debris.

At that moment three Japanese policemen burst into the
room. They all carried pistols. "Sit on the floor, all of you!"
one of them ordered in English. "And give me that pistol," he
ordered Lewis.

"But these b'ys be criminals," Doherty said indignantly. He
pointed to the four crumpled, bloody and unconscious Japanese
on the floor.

"Sit quietly, please," the same policeman answered.

Within a few minutes three other Japanese police officers
arrived, and shortly after that, 10 heavily armed U.S. military policemen.

Baiu, after a lot of hesitation, had telephoned the U.S. military police to advise them about the departure of Doherty and
Lewis for 1965 Edo Street. A nearby Osaka Gang informant had
overheard Baiu's call and had informed the Japanese police.

Morgan awoke and put her arms around Farley. He held
her closely and reassured her. "We have been rescued," he said.
"These are my friends, Miles and Jim."

Tears ran down Morgan's cheeks. "I'm sorry," she said.
"Yes, I remember both of you. I watched your fight in Korea.
Thank you Miles and Jim."

"We will be responsible for the Japanese and will take them
into custody," the English-speaking Japanese policeman said.

An American military policeman carrying a Thompson submachine gun stepped forward. "No," he said firmly. "You will
not. At least one of these men appears to be war criminal and a
fugitive from justice. We are going to hold all of them."

"But they are our citizens!" the English-speaking Japanese
policeman protested.

"Not anymore," the large American MP said. "You can have

them back if and when we are through with them, and that may take a while. We hear that some of your people are insiders and have been helping this gang. Now bugger off quickly before we also decide to take all of you into our custody." He raised his weapon.

The Japanese policemen briefly conferred, looked angrily at the American MPs, and then drove off in their vehicles.

The four Canadians and Americans were loaded onto waiting American jeeps and taken to a building housing the U.S. Army Headquarters in Tokyo. The four Japanese Osaka Gang members were transported in a separate vehicle and interned in a nearby U.S. detention centre to await trial.

Shortly afterwards Farley, Morgan, Lewis and Doherty were paraded before a U.S. major and a Canadian army major. The American was short, red-faced and spoke in a high-pitched voice. The Canadian was tall, thin and had a deep voice.

"I'm Major Perkins," the American said, "and this is Major Watson from the Canadian Army. Please tell us what happened as best you can."

The two officers listened quietly as the four told their stories. Then they withdrew from the room for a conference. After about 10 minutes the officers returned.

"You are all to be commended," Major Perkins began, "for your courageous actions in dealing with the Osaka Gang. But at the same time, I regret to say, you have breached military regulations."

"But sir," Farley protested, "what regulations have we breached?"

"Lieutenant Morgan," Perkins replied sternly, "I am charging you with being out of uniform and with carrying on a liaison with a foreigner of non-commissioned rank. However, you are an officer and I will discuss this privately with you afterwards."

"And what did I do, sir?" Lewis asked indignantly.

"You are charged with carrying a weapon while on leave," the Major replied. The revolver that Lewis had carried sat on the table in front of the U.S. major. "You know, or should know, that all weapons must be left in Korea. Moreover, that weapon is not a standard issue."

Major Watson, the Canadian, then spoke. "It is my duty to remind you, Sergeant Farley, that you have breached regulations by having a liaison with an American officer."

"Why is that an offence? Where did you find that regulation, sir?" Farley knew that he was guilty of fraternizing with an officer, but he wanted details.

"I am charging you under Section 118, which is called 'Conduct to the Prejudice of Good Order and Military Discipline.' I'm sure that you are familiar with this code."

"Oh! That one! That's the one you use when you can't think of anything else! It's a catch-all that covers everything!" Farley exclaimed in an exasperated voice.

"You two majors are both full of shit!" Doherty suddenly shouted angrily. "You are stunned as me arse, b'y", by which he meant, in his suddenly resurrected Newfoundland dialect, that they were both extremely stupid. He could no longer control himself. "You guys in Japan are bunch of non-combat rear-echelon assholes! Why ain't you at the front in Korea doin' somethin' useful?"

The two officers both rose from behind their table. They stood shaking and speechless for several seconds.

"That's four out of four!" the Canadian major finally responded. "You, Private Doherty, are hereby charged with abusive and insulting behaviour towards commissioned officers of the United States and Canadian armies!"

"Private Doherty? That's fine with me. I never asked to be a corporal. Screw you, you asshole b'y! Take these stripes and shove them. I can't think of anyone I would rather abuse than you two silly bastards. Pardon my language, Lieutenant Morgan."

"Take them away!" the American major said to the military policemen standing in the room. "But leave Lieutenant Morgan here with me."

"What about the rest of our R and R leaves?" Lewis asked sarcastically.

"Your leave is finished, sergeant. "You are being sent back to your unit in Korea immediately."

Morgan put her arms around Farley. "I love you Peter. I will wait for you," she whispered. Then she looked towards Doherty and Lewis. "Thank you, Jim and Miles," she said. "I will always remember you and be grateful!"

Farley held her closely. "I love you too, Morgan," he quietly replied. "and I will wait for you forever."

"Alright, let's go!" one of the military policemen yelled. Everyone then left the room except the American major and Morgan.

"I'm sorry about all of this," the major said to Morgan. "You have been charged, but I am sure that I can fix things," he said with a smile. "Would you like to have dinner with me this evening?"

The invitation to dinner was a part of his plan and strategy. He had earlier convinced a weak Canadian major to charge the two Canadians and, at the same time, to charge the two Americans. He knew that the charges were weakly founded, but he wanted to remove Lieutenant Morgan from the company and influence of the others. She was a beautiful and desirable woman, he reasoned, and perhaps she would reward him with her favors.

"No, major, I do not want to have dinner with you this evening or any other evening. I respectfully request to be transported back to my unit in Korea immediately," Morgan angrily replied.

"You are making a mistake, lieutenant, but as you wish. Your charge stands and will be reported to your commanding officer."

Later that evening Farley, Lewis and Morgan were flown back to Korea. They were all on separate planes and did not see each other again.

Their cases were reviewed in the days that followed by their commanding officers. Farley, Morgan and Lewis all received mild reprimands.

Doherty's demotion to private remained in force for two weeks before he was re-instated to the rank of corporal. About a week later he was promoted to the rank of sergeant. He became the chief non-commissioned-officer and head of the Shimya R & R leave centre in Tokyo. He had a strong business mind, secured a secret liquor supply source from a Japanese contact, and made almost $5,000 by selling inexpensive, tax-free whiskey to American and British Commonwealth soldiers on leave in Japan. He deposited his money in the Bank of Japan, sent a considerable sum to his mother in Morgan's Cove, and mailed a cheque for $100, the money he owed, to his uncle in Ottawa.

Doherty began visiting Baiu, the exotically beautiful, half-Caucasian Japanese waitress, and they became very good friends. They fell deeply in love with each other and were married in two separate ceremonies. One was a traditional Shinto ceremony, and the other a western Christian wedding. Their marriage was not immediately recognized by Canadian military and civil authorities.

A month after his wedding to Baiu Doherty was transferred back to the Fusiliers in Korea. Five weeks later, shortly before he was scheduled to return to Canada, Doherty, with a $200 under-the-table payment for "services rendered" to an American load-master, had his dog Blackie transported on a Dakota supply aircraft to Tokyo. As previously arranged, Blackie was picked up by Baiu and taken to her home. Baiu, like Doherty, was a dog lover. Blackie continued to live with Baiu.

After he returned to Canada Doherty was given six weeks of leave. With the political help of Winston Crosby, his dynamic and aggressive Newfoundland Member of Parliament, Doherty was able to overcome Canadian bureaucracy and bring Baiu and Blackie to Canada. The Minister of Immigration, a close friend of Crosby's, by means of a special ministerial permit, allowed Biau and Blackie to come to Canada on an immediate basis.

After a lengthy and difficult trip across the Pacific and Canada, Biau and Blackie arrived in Morgan's Cove in Newfoundland. Martha Doherty was initially opposed to her son's marriage to "an unknown oriental, foreign woman," but she quickly learned to like and appreciate Baiu very much.

Following his leave, Doherty was assigned to the School of Infantry at Camp Borden Ontario. Biau and Blackie joined him and they all lived together in a house at the base permanent married quarters. In the years that followed, Biau, Blackie and, in due course, their two beautiful children would move with Doherty, during his successful military career, to various bases in Canada and abroad.

CHAPTER 28
CAPTAIN LEVINSON'S PRISONER

Intelligence Officer Captain Mike Levinson sat in an elevated bunker at the edge of the Kapyang highway adjacent to Hill 787. He held his .38 caliber pistol in his right hand and peered closely at the large numbers of people who were walking quickly southward down the highway. Sitting next to him with a mounted .303 Bren light machine gun was his batman, Private Roger Wilson. Several other Canadians from the Fusiliers Regiment sat in nearby trenches. They were all a part of an advance party that had been sent by Lieutenant-Colonel Jim Strange. They were waiting for the rest of the battalion to arrive. Their job was to lead the battalion's companies and other units to designated defensive positions on Hill 787.

Levinson was the Jewish Ukrainian Canadian, who, as interviewed by Strange at the senior officers' dinner meeting held during the voyage across the Pacific, had spent his childhood years, from ages five to 17 in Peking, where his father worked as an engineer for an American company. Although he attended an English language school in Peking, he had many Chinese friends, and went to a Saturday school and evening schools that taught Mandarin, the principal Chinese language used and understood, in the early 1950's, by about three-quarters of a billion people. He became very fluent in spoken Mandarin. He was also able to read this complex written language with considerable understanding.

"Who are these people, sir?" Wilson asked Levinson. "They all look like gooks to me to me." The term "gooks" was commonly used by American, Australian, British and Canadian soldiers. It came from "megook", the Korean word for an American.

"Most of them appear to be South Koreans fleeing from the area of the 7th ROK Division", Levinson replied. "The 7th were attacked by the Chinese yesterday. Their 1st Capital Division are good and the Koreans are holding but they are under intense pressure. Once the Chinese break out they are going to head straight for Hill 787."

"Are they all Koreans? Are they all civilians?" Wilson asked.

"It is hard to tell," Levinson said. "Most of them appear to be refugees, but a few may be Chinese infiltrators. Some are likely South Korean soldiers who have bugged out. The Chinese have captured a lot of American uniforms and equipment, not only from the South Koreans, but from the Americans as well. It is easy for them to disguise themselves, and especially because the South Koreans are wearing American uniforms. The Chinese like to penetrate behind our lines so that they can disrupt our supplies and also inform their oncoming forces of our defensive locations."

"Sir, what is so important about Hill 787?" Wilson asked.

"It is the highest mountain in this area," Levinson answered. He spoke in a remote manner, almost as if he was answering his own question. "The main road to Seoul, the likely Chinese objective, runs past right this mountain. If we control this high feature we will be able to fire upon any Chinese moving along the road. They need Hill 787 very badly. I have also been told that this hill is a sacred place for Koreans. Many important people are buried here in various small cemeteries near the top. Apparently it has a strong religious and mysterious presence in Korean history."

At that moment Levinson spotted a relatively tall soldier walking quickly down the road next to his bunker. The soldier wore the helmet and clothing of the kind issued by the Americans to South Koreans, but he held an unusual weapon, a Russian burp gun that Levinson immediately recognized. It was a Soviet weapon used in WWII and in later years issued to the North Koreans.

Levinson became immediately suspicious. He jumped out of his bunker and confronted the soldier with his revolver. "Stop!" He shouted loudly in English.

The soldier suddenly became very agitated and tried to move his weapon down from his shoulder. Levinson pointed his revolver and fired a shot into the ground close to the soldier's feet. The soldier froze in terror.

Levinson looked into the soldier's face and immediately recognized him as an ethnic Chinese, and not a Korean. Levinson's batman, Wilson, and most other Canadians would not be able to make this distinction, but Levinson, with his many years of living in China, could immediately tell.

"Come with me," Levinson told the Chinese in the Mandarin language. The Chinese remained frozen with terror and did not move. "Come with me or I will shoot you," Levinson warned. The Chinese now realized that his life might be in danger. He put his hands up over his head and he followed Levinson to his bunker at the side of the road.

"Wilson," Levinson ordered his batman, "take this guy's burp gun and check to make sure he does not have any other weapons. Grenades especially." Wilson removed the burp gun from the Chinese and patted him all over to check for weapons. He found nothing.

"Keep your Bren on him while I ask him some questions," Levinson told Wilson. "I am going to find out if he knows any English," Levinson told himself.

"Stand well back, Wilson," Levinson said. "He is a spy. I am going to shoot him in the head".

Wilson recoiled in shock but the Chinese remained calm and showed no fear for his life.

"Relax, Wilson. I am not going to shoot him," Levinson said with a smile. "I just wanted to see if he understands English. Obviously, he does not. He would have become very fearful if he thought he was going to die."

"What is your name and what is the name of your unit?" Levinson demanded in Mandarin. The Chinese sat silent and pretended not to understand.

"I warn you," Levinson said. "You should realize that, as far as I am concerned, you are a spy, and according to the Geneva Convention and rules of war, you can be legitimately executed. That's what the Americans did when they found Germans posing as American soldiers at the Battle of the Bulge. They shot them. If you do not tell me who you are, and what you are doing, I will have you shot. However, if you speak truthfully, I will show mercy and accept you as a prisoner of war. I make you this promise as an officer in the Canadian Army."

"I am Soo Chow", the Chinese replied. "I am a member of the 79th army of the Chinese Peoples' Volunteers. I have been sent south to obtain information about the defensive positions of the British, Australian and Canadian battalions. I am also supposed to disrupt your communications facilities by cutting your telephone lines wherever possible."

"What is your rank?" Levinson asked.

"I am a lieutenant, but our army is very democratic and ranks are not important. We believe in equality. We lead by example rather than formal ranks."

"You are wearing South Korean clothing of the kind provided by the Americans but you were carrying a Russian submachine gun, a weapon we call a burp gun. That is strange. Didn't you know that your weapon would arouse suspicion?" Levinson inquired.

"Yes, it was foolish of me to carry a Russian weapon," Soo Chow replied. "I should have carried an American M1 or carbine. We have captured many of these weapons from the South Koreans. I just could not find one before I left."

"That's very interesting," Levinson said. "And how did you know that the Canadians, British and Australians are in this area?"

"You promised to save my life and treat me as an ordinary prisoner of war, is that correct?" Soo Chow asked.

"Yes, you have my promise," Levinson replied.

Soo Chow decided to ingratiate himself to Levinson. He wanted to stay alive and felt that he should make himself a valuable prisoner. He would provide as much information as possible.

"You have an informer in your midst," Soo Chow stated. "He is an officer of some kind in your army and a communist sympathizer. He passes on pieces of information to a Korean who pretends to be a houseboy, or servant to a Canadian unit, but who is in reality a North Korean communist. It is very easy for this Korean to move back and forth from one side to another. He dresses in the traditional white Korean clothing of farmers. The Canadian officer also sends messages by way of radio from time to time."

Levinson was startled by this revelation. "Holy shit!" he exclaimed in English. "And who is this agent?" he continued in Mandarin. "What is his name? What is his position? How do you know this?"

Soo Chow was now more relaxed and less afraid. "I honestly do not know anything more. We heard about this Canadian comrade during an informational briefing, but we never received any description of him. In fact, his presence became known only by accident. We were later told that the briefing officer should not have revealed this information to us. The existence of the Canadian officer was a highly confidential matter, and we were warned never to speak about this with anyone."

Levinson was convinced that the Chinese soldier was telling the truth. "Wilson", Levinson said to his batman, "tie up this guy's hands and feet. He is an important prisoner of war and we can't let him escape."

"Sparks!" Levinson yelled to the unit's radio operator. "I need to send an urgent message to Lieutenant-Colonel Strange. Raise him on the radio at B Echelon."

Levinson knew that the battalion's Commanding Officer was currently at B Echelon, about 10 miles behind his own position near the front line. Strange was there making final arrangements for the move to Hill 787. The military police, or "meatheads" as they were commonly known, ran a detention centre, or "piss can" not only for Chinese and North Korean prisoners, but also for Canadians who had violated orders or broken military laws. Soo Chow would initially be deposited there and eventually in a large prisoner of war camp located on Koje Island.

The operator began calling B Echelon but was not immediately successful. The many mountains in Korea often made radio communications difficult. However after several minutes Sparks smiled, looked at Levinson, and said: "I have Colonel

Strange on the line, sir!"

Strange was not in a good mood. "So what in hell do you want Levinson? I have a lot of fucking work to do and not much time to do it. This had better be important." Strange used "fucking" a lot whenever he was in a bad mood.

"Yes, sir," Levinson replied. "This is very important. It is also very confidential and I can't give you any details over this open radio channel. I have got to speak to you privately and urgently."

"Privately? Urgently? What in hell do you think I am? A father confessor? A rabbi? Are you in some kind of trouble?"

"No, sir, I am not in trouble. I just need about 10 minutes of your time. You will understand after I have spoken with you."

"Alright, Levinson. I'll give you 10 minutes. Get in your fucking jeep and drive here immediately. This had better be good. I am only going to be here for about another three or four hours. After that I am heading back to our battalion camp. We have to get ready to move to Hill 787. We don't know how long the South Koreans are going to be able to hold out, and we have to get to the top of 787 before the Chinese arrive."

"Yes, sir. I will leave right away. Thank you." Levinson handed the phone back to Sparks and turned to Wilson. "Get that Chinese soldier into the back of my jeep. Is he safely tied? We are driving to B Echelon. It's about 10 miles south of here."

"*Oh crap! We may have a security problem,*" Levinson told himself. "*The colonel has just finished telling me, over an open radio channel, that our unit is moving to the top of Hill 787. I would have cautioned him, but he did not give me a chance. He spoke without thinking. If the Chinese find out our battalion is there they are going to send their best units to take 787. Canadians have a powerful reputation from the first and second world wars. They are considered to be among the best soldiers in the world.*"

"I need a volunteer," Levinson said to the men in front of

him. His eyes immediately came into contact with Tony Fontano, the large and muscular Italian Canadian rifleman sitting in a nearby trench.

"Fontano," he announced, "you have just volunteered to help us bring this Chinese back to B Echelon. Keep your eyes on him and make sure he does not free himself."

"That's great, sir!" Fontano responded. "I am sick of eating these canned C rations every day. I think that they have a field kitchen and hot meals at B Echelon. Is that correct?"

"I think so," Levinson replied. "But don't count on it. Don't you think of anything else besides food?"

"Yes, sir, I often think of Michee, the beautiful Japanese girl that I met in Tokyo on R and R leave."

Levinson ignored Fontano's answer. "Move your asses. We don't have a lot of time."

Wilson and Fontano loaded the Chinese into the back seat of the jeep. Fontano climbed in beside him. Wilson took the driver's seat and Levinson sat beside him. They drove away in a cloud of dust down the dirt highway towards B Echelon.

Levinson's jeep stopped in front of a large bell tent at the battalion's B Echelon. A single guard with a Lee Enfield .303 rifle stood at the entrance.

"We are here to see the Colonel", Levinson announced. "Tell him we are here."

"Yes, sir. You must be Captain Levinson. He is expecting you." The guard went inside and re-emerged moments later. "Come in, sir," he said. "He is ready to see you."

Levinson, Wilson, Fontano and the Chinese soldier entered the tent. Levinson saluted. Strange was using a large ammunition box as a desk. He sat in a folding chair.

"What in hell is all of this about?" Strange barked in a gravel voice. "I did not invite this fucking Chinaman, or Korean, or whatever he is. What in hell is he doing here? You have better have a good answer".

"Sorry, sir, I do have a good answer. He is the Chinese who we captured at Hill 787. He has provided very important information that I want to share with you."

"So what is the information? Get on with it."

"This has got to be a private conversation, sir. May I ask Wilson and Fontano to leave?"

"Yes. Wait outside the tent, and don't get too close," Strange ordered the two privates. They promptly marched out leaving only the Chinese and Levinson with Strange.

"So who is this Chinaman? Why did you bring him here?" Strange asked impatiently. "I am, of course, pleased, if he can provide us with information."

"Soo Chow is a lieutenant with the 79th Chinese Army. I threatened him in Mandarin and he opened up. He told me that we have a traitor in our midst, an officer, or maybe even a senior N.C.O., who is passing on valuable information to the Chinese communist forces."

"What?" Strange exclaimed. "A traitor? One of my officers? Does he know who it is?" Strange felt an urge to reveal that he had already been advised of this possibility by the Canadian Chief of the Defence Staff several months earlier. He did not think that Levinson, his intelligence officer, was a suspect, but he decided to keep this information to himself at least for the time being.

"No, sir, he does not know. I'm sure he would tell me if he knew. He has already compromised himself. If his superiors ever found out about the fact that he revealed this information, he would be immediately shot."

"So how does our filthy bastard Canadian spy pass this information on to the Chinese?" Strange asked.

"Apparently he passes written messages on to a Korean houseboy. The houseboy wears white Korean clothing. All the houseboys do. He slips through our lines and hands these messages over to the Communists. It appears that he also sometimes sends messages by radio."

"Yeah, that could happen," Strange muttered. "We have radios that are often just laying around. Anyone could pick one up and send a message."

"As you know, sir, I've been to intelligence meetings at divisional headquarters on several occasions. The Americans have a special unit that monitors radio signals that are sent out from American units and other neighboring U.N. units as well. They listen to some of the messages that we send. They don't think that any information is leaking through our radio signals, at least not in English."

"What do you mean, not in English? What else is there?"

"Mandarin, or maybe Russian. But their language capability is limited. They have only one Mandarin speaking operator and he can only do so much. Incidentally, they recorded the recent Ukrainian messages between Kabaluk and Farley and did not know what language was being used until they asked and I told them. They have one Russian speaker who said the language sounded Slavic and similar to Russian, but that he did not understand it."

"Levinson, I am going to take you into my confidence. This whole thing is driving me crazy and I need your help. I was advised several months ago of the fact that we probably have a spy in our midst. I need to find this spy. You have given me a lot of valuable information and advice, and so I know that are not the spy. I hate to say this, but it's possible that one of my company commanders is the man we are looking for. Do you have any suggestions?"

"A major? That's shocking! Maybe we can set a trap of some kind."

"What kind of a trap?"

"I have been reading about the very successful so-called Red Orchestra espionage ring that operated on behalf of the Soviets and against the Germans in the last war. The brilliant leader, of course," he said with a laugh, "was Jewish. Traps were commonly used by both sides."

"And you are Jewish," Strange said with a smile. "What kind of a trap would work for us?"

"Suppose that we spread some false information. Let's say that the 1st Marine Division, a powerful and respected fighting force, is preparing to attack Chinese occupied Hill 529 in a few days. You can provide all of your company and platoon commanders with this false information and then secretly watch to see where, if anywhere, it goes. This is the kind of critical information that is very useful to the enemy and our spy will be very anxious to forward it."

"How will we find out how and where it goes?"

"We can plant hidden, camouflaged two man listening posts immediately in front of and directly behind our lines. Keep these posts occupied 24 hours a day, maybe with two shifts of 12 hours each. These men should be given secret instructions to watch for and intercept any Koreans, and houseboys in particular, and to search them for written messages. Tell your officers that these are simply listening posts to detect enemy movements. I don't think that any suspicions will be aroused. Listening posts are quite common."

"That sounds like a brilliant idea, Levinson!" Strange said excitedly. "I am familiar with the handwriting of all of my senior officers and I will be able to identify the author of a written message quite easily!"

"What will you do now, sir?"

"We need someone to provide leadership for this spy strategic plan. A senior NCO or junior officer. Do you have any suggestions?" Strange asked.

"What about Sergeant Farley? He came in first place at our recent NCO school. He is very intelligent, reads maps incredibly well, can operate a radio and knows how to direct mortar and artillery fire. He is exceptionally capable."

"Yes, I remember Farley. I agree. He fits the bill. I once fined him for a leave without absence, but that happened a long time ago and is another story. He has matured. Get a hold of him right away and explain the plan. In the meantime, make bloody well sure that you keep all of this to yourself and Farley."

"Is there anything else?"

"I am going to ask for further, more recent and detailed background checks on all of my officers and senior N.C.O.s. All that I know about them right now is that most of them served honourably in various infantry battalions in the war in Europe."

"They are all decorated veterans of the last war," Levinson observed.

"But that means fuck all. The Russians were also on our side and served honourably in the same war. Ottawa will not respond right away. Investigations take time. In the meantime we are going to quietly watch all of these guys to see if their behaviour betrays them. Levinson, I am going to need your help. You and I are the only ones who know about this, except, of course, the Chinese. Whatever you do, keep this whole thing to yourself and Farley. I trust you because you have brought this to my attention. "

"Thank you, sir. And what are you going to do with this Chinese infiltrator?"

"I want you to spend more time with him. I am going to keep him in our own piss can for a while. Eventually I will send him to the big POW camp on Koje Island. Drag him into conversations. Try to find out if he knows anything else."

"Yes, sir, I will."

Strange then called out for his batman-driver, jumped in

the front seat of his jeep and sped off in the direction of the 24th U.S. Division headquarters to which the Canadians were attached. He wrote quickly into a notebook that he was carrying. He needed to have a message ready so that it could be sent as quickly as possible. He cursed occasionally when the jeep bounced, but did not blame the driver. Speed was necessary. The Americans were located about another 20 miles south of the Canadian B Echelon and had communication facilities that were able to send messages to military stations in Washington, D.C. and elsewhere in North America.

Strange's jeep was stopped at the entrance to the Divisional Headquarters. "Yes, sir," a corporal, one of the armed guards asked, "How may I help you?"

"I am the Commanding Officer of the Fusiliers, the Canadian infantry battalion located north of here. I need to speak to your commanding general very urgently." Strange pulled out and showed his Canadian Army identity card.

"I can't promise anything, but I will try, sir," the sentry said. He went into the small guard house located at the side of the entrance gate and called someone on the telephone located inside. Several long minutes passed. Strange was becoming impatient, but he decided to sit quietly rather than provoke a confrontation with the guards. In the meantime, the sentry inside the guard house held the receiver next to his ear and waited for an answer. Finally it came.

"General Ramsdell will see you," the sentry announced. "If you let me ride with you I will take you to his headquarters tent."

"Jump in," Strange ordered, "and tell my driver where to go."

They drove slowly through a maze of large tents and stopped in front of one with a 24th Division flag mounted in front.

"This is it," said the corporal. Two guards with M1 rifles

stood at the door. "The General is expecting us," he told the guards and led Strange through the door of the tent. The General, a short, stout man with a shaved head and large mustache, sat at a small metal desk.

"Welcome. I am General George Ramsdell," he said while holding his right hand out at the same time. Strange saluted and Ramsdell returned the salute. They shook hands. "You can go now, corporal. Thanks."

"So what is it, Colonel Strange? I am very impressed by your Canadians. They are good soldiers. We know we can depend on you, which is more than I can say for some of the others that are here in Korea."

"What do you think of the South Koreans, General?" Strange asked. We currently have two South Korean divisions, the 7th and 1st Capital sitting in the front line in front of us. We wonder if they can hold before we get to the top of Hill 787."

"The North Koreans have a big advantage as soldiers," the General replied. "You know why? Communism is easy to understand even by uneducated peasants. The Korean communists are going to take from the rich and give the poor, which means most of them will benefit. As a result, the North Koreans become fanatical soldiers. They think that they have a lot to gain. Democracy and capitalism, on the other hand, are much more difficult to comprehend and defend. I don't even understand it myself!" he concluded with a laugh.

"That's an interesting explanation," Strange said. "Maybe we can meet and have a longer discussion sometime. Right now I need to send a very confidential message to my headquarters in Ottawa, Canada. It has to do with the security of our Battalion. I know that I can count on you and your communications people to keep this a deep secret. This information must not be divulged to anyone else, and certainly not to any other Canadians."

"I understand, Colonel. One of our operators works in Morse code and will be able to send your message to Washington. From there it can be directed to Ottawa. I will order my operator to keep this thing to himself. The information in your message will not go anywhere else."

"But is there a chance that this message will be intercepted by the Chinese or North Koreans?" Strange asked.

"No," the General replied. "We use carefully guarded telephone lines when we send messages to our headquarters in Japan or to the United States. And it is all sent in a secret code."

"Let's drink to our friendship!" Ramsdell said. He pulled out a bottle of Canadian whiskey and proceeded to pour two drinks without even asking Strange if he wanted one.

But Strange was happy to accept. "Here's to the American Army," he said while raising his glass.

"And here's to the Canadian Fusiliers!" the General responded.

They both swallowed their drinks in single gulps.

"Thank you, sir," Strange said. "Now please introduce me to your signaler. I have got to get this message away as soon as possible."

Strange was led away by the General to an adjoining tent. A signaler sergeant sat in front of a large communications facility. "Sergeant," said the General. "This Canadian colonel has an important and highly secret message that he needs to send to his headquarters in Ottawa, Canada. Send it to our headquarters in Washington and they will know how forward it. And keep this to yourself under all circumstances."

"Yes, sir," said the sergeant. "I understand".

Strange saluted the General. After the General was gone Strange produced his written message for the sergeant to transmit. The sergeant read through it and then began typing the following message in Morse code:

"TOP SECRET:

Message for the Chief of Staff and Intelligence Section, Canadian Army Headquarters, Ottawa, Canada via U.S. Army Headquarters, Washington:

This is further to my meeting with the Chief of the Defence staff last September in Ottawa. It has come to my attention that one of my officers or NCOs may indeed be a traitor and that he may be sending messages to the Chinese and North Korean forces that are opposing us in Korea. Initially it was believed that the spy held the rank of major, but the list of suspects has now been expanded. An earlier message suggested that this might be a diversionary tactic and that a spy might not actually exist. It appears that he does exist and that he is among us in Korea. A captured Chinese lieutenant has informed us that this officer, of unknown rank, has been passing information either by means of a sympathetic Korean courier, or perhaps by way of radio messages.

I am doing everything in my power to try to identify this traitor, but it is a very difficult task. In the meantime, I request your assistance. Please conduct a further investigation on the political and social backgrounds of my officers and senior NCOs to see if you can establish a pattern that suggests sympathy with communism. I assume that his affection for communism is his motive for acting in this treacherous way. Money may also be a factor. Needless to say, this matter is of considerable urgency and I await your response.

Respectfully Submitted, Lt. Col. James Strange,
MC, DSO, CO, 2nd Fusiliers."

After several minutes had passed the signals sergeant turned to Strange. "Okay, sir, it has been sent."

"Very good, sergeant. Thanks. But Washington and Ottawa are a long way away. Are you sure the message will get there?"

"Yes, sir. It will. It actually goes by relays. It does not go directly. But it is on its way and it will get there within a few hours."

CHAPTER 29
THE ARTILLERY OBSERVER

Lieutenant-Colonel James Strange prided himself on being able to mix freely with his men, but at the same time maintain a proper air of aloofness. The Canadian Army, unlike its U.S. counterpart, would not tolerate familiarity between officers and men. Distance, in keeping with British army tradition, was required in order to maintain discipline. Officers lived in separate quarters, had their own messes, expected to be saluted regularly, and insisted that "sir" be added to almost every statement made by "other ranks", including non-commissioned officers.

The day after meeting with Captain Levinson and his Chinese prisoner, Strange had led his Battalion of Fusiliers to the top of Hill 787, which had the highest elevation in the area. He had acquired a lot of defensive and offensive experience in the mountains of Italy during the Second World War, and he used this experience to personally lay out interlocking defences on the hill. *"If I was the Chinese commander attacking this hill,"* he asked himself, *"which approaches would I use?"*

Strange ordered his medium machine guns to be placed at the most obvious attack routes. Barbed wire was installed in front of all four rifle companies. Slit trenches were dug and camouflaged. The battalion's 81 mm. mortars were zeroed in on the areas immediately in front of each rifle company so that defensive fire would be immediately available.

The day after the Battalion was established and dug in on Hill 787 Strange met with his intelligence officer, Captain Levinson, for the purpose of setting up the previously discussed spy trap. They agreed that the 1st Marine Division false story should work, and that listening posts should be established as suggested by Levinson. Strange then briefly visited with each company and platoon commander on an individual basis and very casually told them the Marine story. He also asked his four rifle company commanders to provide him with "six exceptionally reliable and intelligent" men each for the purpose of establishing the listening posts that Levinson had recommended.

Levinson, on the previous day had met privately with Farley. He explained the plan in detail. "Sergeant Farley," he said, "you are going to be responsible for the proper implementation of this plan. The colonel and I are depending on you."

"I will do my best," Farley said. "Thanks for your confidence in me."

The next day Strange, Levinson and Farley met with the 24 men selected at Strange's battalion headquarters.

"I am giving you a very important task," Strange told them. "We are going to establish listening posts in front of each rifle company, as well as a couple behind our lines. You will be working in shifts of 12 hours each. These posts will be hidden, camouflaged, and be operating day and night. If you see any enemy movement then obviously you will radio back and let us know. All of you, I am sure, know Sergeant Farley. He is going to be in charge of this operation. Any questions so far?"

There were no questions and Strange continued. "In addition to enemy activity, we also want to monitor the movements of our Korean houseboys. I want all of you to keep this very confidential. Do not discuss this with anyone. You are all going to be staying at my headquarters, but if you happen to see any of your officers or anyone else say absolutely nothing."

Strange turned to Levinson. "Captain Levinson, I am going to ask you to explain why and how we are going to monitor the movements of our houseboys."

"Thank you, sir," Levinson said. "As all of you know, our houseboys are all volunteers. They arrive from God knows where and offer to work for us. Most of them are honest, but a few may be communist sympathizers or even spies. If you see any houseboys moving into no man's land, either during the day or at night, stop them, at gun point if necessary, and search them. Look, in particular, for any messages that they may be carrying. If you find a message of any kind, immediately escort the houseboy carrying it to us at headquarters."

The listening posts were established later that night. It was especially dark and the movements of those digging and camouflaging the posts were not visible. Digging was conducted as quietly as possible. Farley visited each location to be sure that all arrangements were in order and that everyone understood the task at hand. He recorded precise map coordinates for each post.

Strange spoke to each of his company commanders shortly afterwards. "Let the Chinamen come," he told his company commanders by telephone. "We are ready. Tell your men that under no circumstances will we retreat from our positions. We are here to stay for as long as is necessary. Incidentally, I have some good news. It has been confirmed that the 1st Marine Division is going to be attacking the Chinese on Hill 594 in a few days. That should remove a lot of pressure from us."

The day after the move to Hill 787 had been completed Strange decided to begin a series of visits to inspect the positions of his four rifle companies. He began with Dog Company, which was at the highest and most forward position.

Like most of his men, Strange wore the standard Canadian army battle dress uniform and a brown beret. He did not want to be too visible to the enemy. He arrived at Dog Company's location unannounced and moved casually and quietly from trench to trench. He always insisted that his men carry on as though he was not present, and so his frequent visits were unusually unobtrusive. His men became used to his presence. They remained relaxed, bantered back and forth and even made occasional light-hearted but respectful remarks to Strange.

Strange arrived at one of Dog Company's slit trenches where a young soldier manned a Bren light machine gun.

"How are things going?" Strange asked the soldier. "It's pretty quiet, I hear."

"That's right, sir. Nothing except the odd rat or large black snake."

"Better them than the Chinese. Where is your artillery observer?"

"He's usually in that trench under that tree," the soldier replied. He pointed to a large decapitated evergreen. "A big blond guy. I think he's there now."

"Thanks, soldier," Strange said. He then walked up to the trench and looked down into it. His eyes blinked and a startled expression crossed his face. "It can't be!" he exclaimed in a loud voice. "I must be dreaming."

Dozing at the bottom of the trench was a heavy-set blond haired Canadian sergeant with "Royal Canadian Mounted Artillery" shoulder flashes. Strange recognized him instantly. It was Henry "Buzz" Grabowski, known to Strange as the chief negotiator for the International Bus Drivers and Ticket Agents Union of America!

"God, I don't believe this!" Strange exclaimed. "What in hell is he doing here? Grabowski! Wake up! Is that you, Grabowski?"

The sergeant leaped up quickly and rubbed his eyes. "Yes, sir," he replied with a worried look on his face, "Grabowski here."

"Grabowski? How did you get here?"

"I'm sorry sir. I did not know that you were the commanding officer of the Fusiliers until after I enlisted in the army. I'm sorry about what happened in Vancouver. I guess I deserved that cold lemonade."

"Don't be sorry, sergeant. That seems like a long time ago. But how did you get here?"

"The same way as you did, I guess, sir. I joined up. The union fired me after my last session with you. I had no job and I decided I'd get into the army again. I did not know that you were in the Fusiliers. You didn't say anything in Vancouver. You just left."

"The artillery? How did you get into the artillery? I thought that you were in the infantry in the last war."

"I was. I originally intended to join the Fusiliers. In fact, I was a Fusilier for a few days. I asked to be transferred to the artillery after I heard that you were the commanding officer of the Fusiliers. No offence, sir. I hope that you understand. I just did not want to bother you again."

"Forget about the past, Grabowski," Strange said reassuringly. "Both of us have new jobs to do. Let's do them to the best of our abilities."

"Thank you, sir. I will, sir."

"I'll come for another visit one of these days, Grabowski," Strange concluded. 'In the meantime, carry on." He then turned and left.

After returning to his bunker at battalion headquarters at the highest point of Hill 787 Strange telephoned Major Larry Holmes, the commanding officer of the artillery battery to which Grabowski was attached. He had first met first Holmes in Italy during the Second World War.

"Larry," Strange began, "I have just finished visiting with Sergeant Grabowski, your forward observer. I met him in Vancouver last year when he worked for a union. How is Grabowski doing? Is he any good?"

"Yes, he is a very good forward artillery observer. I've got to give him credit. He calls in fire very quickly and accurately. He understands how a rifle company works. He is quite intelligent, I think. You are lucky to have him and so am I. He does, however, behave strangely sometimes."

"What do you mean?" Strange asked.

"I mean that Grabowski is different," Holmes replied. "He seems to have a lot of money. He plays poker and makes big bets some of my men tell me. Money seems to be no problem. He buys and sells black market whiskey, beer and fresh fruit. He's a loner. He wanders away by himself from time to time whenever he has any free time. But he is reliable and present when needed."

Strange's interest in Grabowski was now suddenly much more intense. "Where do you think he got or gets his money?" he asked.

"I asked him that once in a joking way. He told me that he got a large settlement from his union when he left. He had a contract, he said, and they had to pay him off when they let him go."

"Larry, I want you to do me a favour. Keep your eye on Grabowski. Don't say anything to him, of course. Just watch him closely. Let me know if you see anything unusual."

They exchanged greetings once again and then concluded their conversation.

Strange sat down and began thinking about Grabowski's suspicious circumstances. He took out a note pad and pen and began to jog down some questions to consider.

"Grabowski" he noted, *"was considered to be one of the best union negotiators in North America but he claims he was fired and given a big settlement in cash because he had a contract. That does not seem to make sense. He joined the army at a salary that was much less than he was getting. Why would he do that? He seems to have a lot of money and he spends it freely. According to Larry Holmes he is intelligent, and if so, how is he using this intelligence? Aren't forward artillery observers provided with a lot of information about the location of friendly units, and would this information not be valuable to the enemy? Grabowski has a radio and can use it in any way he wishes."*

His questions to himself continued. *"Is he really of Polish origin? Or is he actually a Russian or Ukrainian communist? Some Ukrainian Canadians belong to communist organizations. Can he speak Russian? Is it possible that Grabowski is the spy that the Chief of Staff warned about?"*

The following morning he climbed into his jeep and drove, once again, but this time alone, to the Divisional Headquarters that he had previously visited. The commanding general was absent but he was able to speak to a colonel who gave him permission to send another message to Ottawa. The message read as follows:

"Request security check on Sergeant Henry Grabowski, who is with the Royal Canadian Mounted Artillery in Korea at this time. This check is in relation to my meeting with the Chief of Staff last August. I strongly recommend that answers be obtained for the following questions: (1) Was Grabowski fired from the International Bus Drivers and Ticket Agents Union of America,

and if so, was he given a cash settlement as compensation for his contract, and if so, how much did he receive? (2) What is his ethnic origin and does he speak any Slavic languages, and in particular, Polish, Russian or Ukrainian? (3) Has he ever belonged to any communist organization or political party? This matter is of utmost urgency and I will anxiously await your response. Respectfully, Lt. Col. James Strange, Commanding Officer, Canadian Fusiliers."

Strange climbed into his jeep and returned to Hill 787 immediately afterwards. A Chinese attack was expected at any time and he wanted to be in his headquarters and ready.

CHAPTER 30
GENERAL PENG

During the time that Peter Farley and his comrades were making preparations for a defence of Hill 787 Chinese General Peng Dehuai was meeting with his senior officers. It was a sunny and warm spring day at Daesong, a village in North Korea a short distance from the front line. Chinese, North Korean and Russian military commanders were assembled. Present besides General Peng, the commander of all Chinese Peoples Volunteers in Korea, was Colonel Deng Xiaoping, the aide to Peng; Colonel Andriy Shykov, the Soviet liaison officer; and Colonel Kim Chosen, the North Korean liaison officer. Most conversations and reports were made in the Mandarin Chinese language. Cantonese and Korean were also used occasionally. The Soviet Union did not have any front line soldiers in the Korean War, but it did provide many rear echelon observers and advisors such as Colonel Shykov.

The winter of 1950-51 had been exceptionally frigid. Cold

winds from Siberia had swept the whole Korean peninsula, including the south. Early April had brought more moderate temperatures. The snow had melted and the rivers and streams overflowed. Trees began sprouting leaves and flowers bloomed on the sides of the mountains. Peng Dehuai had decided that the time has come for another Chinese offensive against the American, United Nations and South Korean "puppet" forces.

General Peng opened the meeting. Although he could speak Korean fairly well, he used Mandarin Chinese most of the time. Peng was almost six feet tall, which was well above the height of most Chinese. Like most senior Chinese military commanders, he was not formally well-educated. However, he did a lot of reading and tried to impress his listeners with his knowledge of Chinese culture and history. He liked to quote from Sun Tze's *The Art of War* when discussing military strategy, and Confucius whenever he felt in a philosophical mood.

"Comrades," Peng said, "I have exchanged messages with Chairman Mao and he has agreed that we should proceed with my recommendation for a new offensive against the Americans and their puppet allies. Spring has arrived and we will no longer have to suffer the many temperature related casualties that we had from November to March. I have been told that we have endured the coldest Korean winter in recent memory. Of course, I will not blame this weather on our Russian comrades! I am sure that they did not send their cold Siberian winds south on purpose!"

Colonel Chosen responded. "The North Korean Peoples Army is ready to participate. But as you know, we have suffered grievous losses in the past few months. At most, we can provide about six divisions with something like 10,000 men each. Most of our Russian T-34 tanks were destroyed by the American Air Force. However, we have captured a lot of American equipment from the South Korean puppet forces and also from the

Americans themselves. We have obtained something like 200 mortars with 81 mm. barrels, and many thousands of mortar shells to use in these mortars. We have also secured a large number of .50 caliber and .30 caliber American machine guns and related ammunition. We have liberated approximately 100 jeeps, as well as a large number of big trucks."

"I am pleased," said Peng, "that you are willing to join us in the attack. It is your country and we are here to help. We have very little air power, and a shortage of artillery pieces, but our manpower advantage is huge. Perhaps you can share some of your captured weaponry with us."

Chosen remained silent. He was not particularly enthusiastic about sharing any weapons. In any event, most of the captured weapons and vehicles had already been distributed to NKPA units, and he knew it would be very difficult to retrieve them. The Soviets, prior to the beginning of the war, had lavishly endowed their North Korean allies with military equipment and supplies, but most of this had been lost during the American and UN drive from the Pusan perimeter to the Yalu River bordering Manchuria.

Peng continued speaking. "We are receiving some inside information from Korean communist comrades. These 'insiders' have been integrated into the ranks of the foreign invaders. They act as servants, or 'houseboys', as the Americans, British and Canadians call them. We also have a sympathetic Canadian soldier planted within the Canadian forces who will be working on our behalf. The information that this Canadian provides will be especially useful. He should be able to tell us where the various units are located as well as their strengths and weaknesses. This knowledge is critical, especially when we are planning attacks. I am grateful to the Soviet government, and in particular to the Soviet Embassy in Canada. I understand that the Canadian soldier was recruited by an official in that Embassy."

Lieutenant Colonel Andrey Shykov, the sandy-haired, blue-eyed Soviet liaison officer cleared his throat and raised his right hand. "Comrade General, I am pleased that the Canadian we recruited will be providing valuable assistance. Please excuse my heavily accented Mandarin. I do not speak well, but I hope that you will understand me. My father was the Soviet ambassador to Peking prior to the Great Patriotic War, and I went to Chinese schools during my childhood. But we spoke Russian at home."

"Don't worry!" Peng re-assured him. "You speak clearly. I understand everything that you are saying. Your Mandarin is much better than my Russian. I lived in Moscow for a while, but unfortunately, not long enough to learn your beautiful language well."

"Thank you, Comrade General," Shykov responded. "You are very kind. My question has to do with your proposed military goals and strategy for this offensive. How do you plan to proceed?"

"Let me say, first of all", said Peng "that we shall be grateful for any help that you can provide. We know that you generously supplied our friends in the North Korean Peoples Army, and we could certainly appreciate similar support. Do you have any influence over your government or your military commanders? No need to answer this question right now, but please give it some thought. I shall respond to your question about strategy in only general terms at this time. Our first objective is to capture Seoul, the capital of the puppet South Korean regime. The so-called president of this illegal state is Syngman Rhee, who claims to be a democrat, but who is, in reality, a vicious despot."

"How did Rhee get to this position of power?" Colonel Chosen asked, even though he already knew the answer to his question.

"Rhee received a lot of his education in the United States, and he is a virtual vassal of that capitalist country. The South Koreans are totally dependent on the Americans for everything they have, and in particular all of their large quantities of military equipment and supplies. Without the Americans, South Korea would collapse overnight."

Colonel Kim was showing some signs of impatience. Korea, after all, was his country, but the Chinese and Russians seemed to be taking over the conduct of the war. "Our government," Chosen interjected "will certainly be pleased to get Seoul back. As you know, this is the largest city in Korea and also the centre of our ancient and honourable Korean culture and history. It will be the capital of our liberated country. But what happens after Seoul is re-taken? What is the next phase of your plan? Our government needs to be fully involved in this decision".

Peng seemed to ignore Chosen's question. "First of all comrades" he continued, "let me quickly review of where we are and how we got there. In 1945, at the end of the Great Patriotic War, as our Russian friends call it, Soviet forces occupied the northern part of Korea. The southern part below the 38th parallel was controlled by a vile regime sponsored by the Americans, and led by Syngman Rhee. Rhee is so Americanized, comrades, that he even puts his personal name in front of his family name! This is an insult to all Koreans!"

Peng paused for a moment and took a drink from the glass on the table next to him. He looked sternly at his audience to be sure that all were paying attention.

"The Americans," Peng continued, "initially showed little interest in Korea. Following a provocation at the border by the puppet South Koreans, Kim Il Sung, the president of North Korea, decided to move south to remove the illegitimate government of Rhee. The Americans then suddenly decided to intervene. They were almost driven into the sea at Pusan by the

North Korean Peoples Army, but General MacArthur launched a huge force at Inchon, next to Seoul. Our Korean allies were then pushed all the way to the border of China at the Yalu River. Mao Tse Tung, our glorious and all wise leader, after serious consultation with his advisors, decided to strike back."

Shykov raised his hand. "Why do you think that Comrade Mao decided to intervene?" he asked.

"Because China could not and would not allow the capitalist Americans to hold a strong foothold on the Korean peninsula," Peng replied. "Chinese forces drove the Americans and their puppet allies back across the 38th parallel. Seoul was recaptured, and then lost again as the result of an American offensive. That is where we are now. We are sitting at or near the 38th parallel, and it is our intention to push south, retake Seoul, and then drive the enemy southwards until they have been completely destroyed and removed from Korea."

Peng took another sip of water and then continued. "So what do we plan to do in this first phase of our attack? Let me say, first of all, that we intend to launch attacks across the whole front. Our objective is Seoul, but we need to keep the enemy off balance. Attacking them at all points of the front line will also prevent them from reinforcing the centre. I need to resurrect a painful reminder. As you know, the NKPA came very close to driving the Americans and their allies into the sea at Pusan. Only General MacArthur's invasion with massive forces at Inchon saved the Americans. We will not allow this to happen a second time."

"How are you going to prevent MacArthur from doing the same thing again?" Colonel Chosen interjected. A look of skepticism appeared on his face.

"We are going to strongly garrison Inchon and all other strategic coastal and inland places. Although we are lacking in aerial, armoured and artillery support, we will surge south in massive numbers. We will attack mostly at night and thereby render the American Air Force largely ineffective. The so-called UN forces will be driven into the sea at Pusan and that will end their evil adventure in Korea."

"And finally, comrades," Peng concluded after a brief pause, "let me quote from Sun Tzu's The Art of War." He held a well-worn book in his hand and read from its pages. "Regard your soldiers as your children, and they will follow you into the deepest valleys; look on them as your own beloved sons, and they will stand by you even unto death. If, however, you are indulgent, and unable to make your authority felt, kind-hearted but unable to enforce your commands; and incapable, more-over, or quelling disorder, then your soldiers will be likened to spoiled children; they are useless for any practical purpose."

CHAPTER 31
THE DEATH OF A CAT

The Chinese were taking longer to attack Hill 787 than expected. Their attack was probably delayed, the Commonwealth Division's commanding general advised Strange, because they had advanced very quickly and were short of ammunition and other supplies. An eventual attack, however, was a virtual certainty.

Soon after their arrival at the top of Hill 787, the Canadians were joined by a number of cats of various colours. The cats had learned, in previous encounters with Americans and Canadians especially, that these strange human creatures possessed large amounts of delicious meat and that they were willing to share it. To a large extent, these partly domesticated felines lived by killing and eating mice and rats, but ham and beef from the tinned C-ration cans was a welcome and delicious change. Although leery at first, a few of those with previous human upbringing became affectionate companions. Their presence tended to keep the rats and mice away, and also helped to relieve the boredom and tension of the Canadians as they waited for a probable Chinese attack.

Ham and lima beans, a common presence in U.S. C rations, was disliked by most Canadians, and they willingly shared it with Korean refugees, cats and dogs. The cats and dogs quickly consumed the ham, and occasionally, if very hungry, even ate some of the beans.

Lieutenant-Colonel Strange had a fondness for cats, but he was especially interested in these camp followers because they helped to keep the rodent population under control. "Feed the cats so that they will stay with us," he ordered his officers and men. "Happy cats will mean fewer mice and rats. Dogs are also useful, and if any show up, feed them and keep them. Dogs are good companions, and they may be able to detect enemy activity, and especially at night, when the Chinese like to attack."

Shortly after arriving at the top of Hill 787 a large black cat arrived at Peter Farley's slit trench. "Tom. I am going to call you Tom. You look hungry, Tom," Peter said with a smile. He opened a tin of British bully beef and presented it to the cat. Tom devoured the beef quickly and looked at Farley with friendly eyes. Then he jumped into the trench with Farley and began purring. Soon afterwards it became dark. Farley was not scheduled for guard duty on this particular night. He felt very tired and soon fell into a deep sleep. The cat lay by his side.

Early the next morning a shot rang out. Farley jumped out of his trench and ran in the direction of the loud noise. Shortly after passing through some low bushes he encountered Jim Higgins who had, two weeks previously, tried to steal and kill a young cow that belonged to a Korean girl. The renegade Fusilier had also been the leader of the gang of three who had stolen fruit from the officers' storage area during the Pacific Ocean voyage to Korea. Higgins sat on a rock and held a .303

Lee Enfield rifle.

"Higgins! What are you doing here?" Farley shouted. "I thought that you were in the piss can. Didn't the commanding officer give you 30 days after you tried to shoot that Korean girl's young cow?"

"Yeah, I just got out yesterday. Major Karpinski, the medical officer, examined me and said that I am sick. I heard Strange tell Karpinski that I am riff raff, and to get rid of me. I don't give a shit. I hate this place and everyone in this fucking Battalion."

"So why are you still here? Were you not also, about a month ago, charged with stealing someone's money and boots, and for trying to run away from the front line?"

"I don't know why I am still here. Someone fucked up. A truck was supposed to pick me up and take me to Kimpo Airport in Seoul, and then back to Canada, but it did not show up. I was forced to climb this fucking hill along with the rest of the Battalion. I could not stay in the valley all by myself because the Chinese are coming."

"What was that shot about? Did you fire your rifle?"

"Yeah, I fired it."

"Don't you know that the Colonel has ordered that no shots are to be fired unless they are directed at the Chinese or North Koreans?"

"Yeah, I know, sergeant, but I don't give a shit."

"What did you shoot at?"

"A large black cat. It's over there. I hate fucking cats," he said in a casual and unconcerned manner.

Farley walked over to the place where Higgins had pointed. A large black cat lay on the ground with a large, bloody hole in its head. It was Tom, the cat that he had befriended the previous evening. Farley was stunned. He became very angry, pulled out his .45 revolver and returned to the rock where Higgins remained seated.

"You son of a bitch, Higgins, I feel like putting a bullet into your ugly head," Farley shouted in anger. "You are under arrest. Drop your rifle and come with me."

"Fuck you, you bohunk sergeant. I don't have to listen to you," Higgins snarled and began walking away. "I am going back to Canada. I am no longer in this fucking unit."

Farley was furious. He ran up to Higgins, grabbed by his right arm, swung him around and hit him with full force in the mouth with the butt of his revolver. Higgins dropped his rifle and fell to his knees. "My teeth," he screamed. "You have smashed all of my teeth." He then spit out several onto the ground. Blood gushed from his mouth.

Farley commandeered two soldiers in a nearby trench and they were ordered to guard Higgins while he reported the incident to the orderly officer.

Later in the morning Higgins and Farley appeared before Lieutenant-Colonel Strange, who sat at a large steel ammunition box in his bunker. Higgins stood at attention and was flanked by two military policemen. A clerk sat in a nearby table and recorded the details of the military trial that was taking place.

"What is the charge?" Strange asked Farley. Farley stood to attention at the left front of Strange's desk.

"Private Higgins," Farley replied. "discharged his rifle even though no enemy was present and in violation of your orders, sir."

"Why did you shoot your rifle, Higgins?" Strange asked.

"I shot a cat," Higgins replied in a garbled voice. "But look at my face. Sergeant Farley hit me in face with his revolver. I lost most of my front teeth. He is the one who should be charged."

"Did you hit Higgins in the face, and if so, why?" Strange asked Farley.

"Higgins, sir, shot one of the cats that you ordered us to maintain and keep. He fired his rifle in contravention of your orders. I tried to arrest him and he resisted."

The killing of the cat angered Strange. "You have already caused us a lot of trouble, Higgins. You will now have to spend some time in our detention camp, or piss can, as it is commonly referred to."

"But sir, I am scheduled to return to Canada. I was supposed to return to Canada several days ago, but someone screwed up." His words were slurred because of his missing teeth and badly damaged mouth.

"You will return to Canada, Higgins, but only after you have served 90 days in the piss can. You are a despicable disgrace to the army. I am not authorized to give you more time in detention. If I could, I would give you a year or more. March him out of here," Strange ordered the military policemen.

"Fuck you, Colonel, fuck all of you!" Higgins screamed in a garbled voice as he was led away.

Farley saluted, made a sharp right about turn, marched out of the tent and walked back to his trench. He began experiencing severe grieving for Tom, even though he had only known the cat briefly. In the future, a hungry and affectionate Tom would frequently appear in Farley's troubled dreams.

CHAPTER 32
SURROUNDED ON HILL 787

Sergeant Peter Farley sat with his radio in a trench under a rocky ledge facing the Kapyang Valley. Besides his rifle he had a Bren light machine gun that he had unofficially acquired from Support Company's quartermaster for a bottle of scotch.

Farley's eyes focused on a black Mamushi Pit Viper which sat coiled up next to a large rock about 10 yards in front of him. Large numbers of these Korean venomous snakes had been displaced by the explosions of artillery and mortar shells in the area and were now moving haphazardly in all directions on the hill. Farley felt inclined to shoot the snake but decided that a shot would warn the Chinese infantry of his presence. His weapons remained silent. Soon afterwards the snake slithered away and disappeared. Farley felt relieved. He hated killing of animals of all kinds, including even poisonous snakes.

Farley was not alone on Hill 787. Riflemen sat in slit trenches on both sides of him. He called back to Metro Kabaluk who was located with the 81 mm. mortar platoon near Battalion Headquarters. Farley designated four specific target areas as "Fox One, Fox Two, Fox Three and Fox Four." A dozen ranging shots were fired by the mortars before Farley was satisfied that they would land in the required areas. A Chinese assault was expected very soon..

"That's good," Farley advised Kabaluk in Ukrainian. "All four foxes are zeroed in."

"Roger, Kapusta, why don't we call them 'red foxes'? Over."

"Red foxes?"

"Yeah, after that red-headed foxy lady at M.A.S.H! Over."

"Hooreewka!" Farley shouted into his microphone. "I don't know how you found out, but keep it to yourself, will you? I could get into more deep trouble. Over."

"I know how it feels. I get into deep shit a lot," Kabaluk replied.

"Another still?

"No. I quit. I buy some Japanese Asahi beer and good Canadian rye with the money you gave me to deliver the letter. I think I am going to take a job with the post office when I get back to Canada. You can't beat the pay and working conditions. Over."

Farley then walked to Battalion Headquarters, a short distance away. He met Lieutenant-Colonel Strange and Captain Levinson. They were getting impatient. They knew that all of the men at the recently established listening posts would have to be quickly withdrawn in the event of a Chinese attack. If that happened, no houseboy would be apprehended and the spy would not be identified, at least not for the time being.

"Everything is under control," Farley reported. "I have visited all of the listening posts and they are all ready."

"Very good, Sergeant," Strange said.

The sun was beginning to sink behind the western mountains.

Strange was getting sleepy and his eyes had closed when Farley suddenly shouted at him excitedly.

"Sir, a message has come in from listening post #3. It's from Martens and Williams."

"What does the message say?"

"They have a houseboy in custody and have discovered a written message on him. The message, they say, says something about an attack by the U.S. Marines. Our trap has worked! Our problem is solved! They are on the way back. All we have to do now is interview the houseboy. I'm sure that we can get him to talk and identify the spy, the Canadian he has been working for!"

"You damn right, Sergeant. He will talk. I will make damn sure of that!" Strange said in a loud and emphatic voice.

About 15 minutes later the figures of Martens and Williams appeared from some bushes a short distance away. They were carrying .303 rifles with fixed bayonets. Walking in front of them was a short Korean dressed in the traditional white clothing of his country's farmers. His hands were tied behind his back. Both of the Canadians held their rifles in ready positions. The Korean turned to look at his captors but they threatened him with their bayonets. He quickly faced the front and kept walking.

A loud rifle shot suddenly rang out. Strange, Levinson and Farley were startled. They ran into a nearby sandbag shelter with their weapons drawn.

Martens and Williams fell to the ground and instinctively took up defensive positions.

The Korean in front of Martens and Williams stopped walking. He turned back again towards his captors with an anguished look on his face, and then fell onto the ground with a dull thud. Blood poured out his back and chest. He had been shot by an unknown sniper.

"Bring him in!" Strange shouted. "Maybe he is still alive!"

Martens and Williams heard the voice of their Commanding Officer and they knew they had to obey. Martens threw the limp Korean over his shoulder and ran quickly to the shelter where Strange, Levinson and Farley were crouched. Williams carried Martens' rifle as well as his own and followed closely behind.

Martens laid the Korean gently onto the ground inside the shelter. The Korean was still alive. He looked plaintively at his captors but said nothing.

"I know him," Williams said. "We call him Little Kim. There is another houseboy who we call Big Kim. Little Kim does not seem to belong to any particular platoon but he usually hangs around Baker Company. He wears U.S. fatigues but sometimes switches to white Korean clothes, like now. He often brings us hot meals from our field kitchen. Everybody likes him. His English is pretty good."

A short time later Little Kim groaned. His eyes closed, he let out a deep sigh, and then lay still.

"He's gone! Where is the message he carried?" Strange asked. He had a look of dismay on his face.

Martens reached into his pocket and produced a rumpled piece of paper. He handed it to Strange.

Strange straightened the paper and began reading. "Shit!" he said. "This message is about the Marines, as we expected, but it is printed in capital letters! There is no handwriting, and there is something that looks like Chinese at the bottom!" He handed the paper to Levinson. "What do you make this?" he asked.

Levinson looked at the paper. "The message at the bottom is in Mandarin," he said. "It is a translation of the printed message above. Both messages warn about an impending attack of the 1st Marine Division. The sender, I presume, printed the English version so it would be easier to read. The Chinese often have trouble reading our atrocious handwriting."

"It looks like Little Kim was shot by one of our own people!" Strange said angrily. "It can't be the enemy. They are not here yet. Somebody wanted him dead so that he would not be able to talk."

At that moment loud whistling noises filled the air and a series of explosions shook the ground. Chinese artillery and mortar shells began raining down in large numbers on the Fusiliers rifle companies and Battalion Headquarters.

"Martens and Williams," Strange said calmly. "You stay here. We may need some extra protection if the Chinese break through." He then turned and faced his Intelligence Officer. "Captain Levinson, take control of the men from the listening posts. They should be back here shortly. Post them around battalion headquarters for all around defence. Farley, go back to your forward mortar position. The shit is ready to hit the fan."

As the enemy artillery and mortar barrage continued Farley and the other Fusiliers in the front line positions waited anxiously for the expected arrival of the Chinese infantry. The sun had sunk in the west but a bright full moon illuminated the landscape.

"Hooreewka," Farley shouted into his microphone. "Kapusta here. Get ready on Fox One. We have visitors. They are maybe 50 yards from our wire and coming fast. There must be at least a couple of hundred. It looks bad. Over."

"Roger, Kapusta," Kabaluk replied calmly from his position with the 81 mm. mortars near battalion headquarters. "Ready on Fox One."

As the Chinese approached the barbed wire they broke out into trot and began shouting. A loud and piercing bugle call came somewhere from within their ranks.

"Rapid fire on Fox One!" Farley shouted into his microphone and shortly afterwards mortar shells began landing among the Chinese with crunching and flashing explosions. The Canadian medium machine gun located close to Farley opened up at the same time, its barrel spewing 600 rounds a minute in a wide arc across the barbed wire. The Chinese began falling in large numbers but a few reached the barbed wire and began cutting it.

"Kapusta" Kabaluk called. "How is your support? Is the mortar fire landing correctly? Over."

"Yeah," Farley responded, "but its kind of thin. We need a lot more."

"It will have to do for now. All the companies are calling for mortar fire. The Chinese are even coming in from behind us. The six .50 caliber machine guns mounted on our Mortar Platoon half tracks have just wiped out a bunch of Chinese coming towards battalion headquarters. The Colonel says that our battalion is surrounded. Over."

At that moment a group of five Chinese soldiers began advancing towards Farley. They wore quilted jackets and cloth caps and carried burp guns. Farley fired several rounds from his Bren gun and three of the Chinese immediately fell to the ground. The other two spotted Farley and fired bursts from their burp guns in his direction.

Farley felt a sharp spasm of pain in his right shoulder. He looked down and saw blood running down from his arm, through his shirt and onto his pants. He sank to his knees and felt as though he was going to pass out.

A mortar shell fell and exploded with a thunderous blast at the edge of Farley's trench. Fortunately, he was sitting at the bottom and was not hit by any of the shrapnel. But blood began to trickle out of both ears. There was a loud ringing in his ears and he was temporarily deaf.

In the meantime the two men on the nearby medium machine spotted the Chinese in front of Farley's position. They fired a long burst and the two remaining Chinese fell.

Farley sat on the ground inside his bunker and called Kabaluk. "Hooreewka, how do you hear me? I'm in trouble. Over."

"Hooreewka here. What kind of trouble?"

"I've been hit in the shoulder. Blood is coming out of my ears. I can hardly hear. My ears are ringing. I've covered the wound with a bandage from my first aid kit, but some blood is still coming out. I'm feeling weak. Can you send a medic?"

"Hang in there. I'll try. We have lots of wounded so I don't know how long it will be. Sorry. I'll do the best I can. Over and out."

The Chinese attack had been stopped, at least for the time being. Everything was suddenly very quiet except for the moaning of several Chinese soldiers who were wounded and entangled in the barbed wire in front of the Canadian position.

After about 30 minutes a medical corps corporal arrived at Farley's bunker. He dressed Farley's wound and the bleeding stopped. "There are two bullet holes in your shoulder. You have lost some blood but you are going to be okay," he told Farley. He then injected a shot of morphine into Farley's left arm. "This is to kill the pain," he explained. "A U.S. helicopter ambulance will be here early in morning to pick you up and take you back to the M.A.S.H. about 30 miles south of here."

"That's great!" Farley exclaimed. "I hope it's the right M.A.S.H.! I have a friend who works at a M.A.S.H. Thanks, corporal!"

The corporal left and Farley soon fell into a deep sleep as a result of the morphine. He dreamed about Morgan. He was holding her tenderly and she was gently sobbing. "Don't worry Morgan, I love you," he said. "Will you marry me?"

CHAPTER 33
THE EXECUTION

As Farley slept fitfully in his bunker the Chinese renewed their attack against Battalion Headquarters by means of a very heavy artillery and mortar barrage.

Strange had been visiting his rifle companies and had just returned to his Headquarters area when the barrage began. Shells were landing in large quantities. He needed to get into his bunker as quickly as possible.

As he reached the main entrance he noticed that it had been demolished by a hit from an artillery or mortar shell. He moved around to the left of the mound like structure until he came to a ventilation shaft camouflaged with branches. He needed to get to the radio in his headquarters so that he could communicate with his company commanders as well as the Brigade Commander. He tore away the branches and slithered down into the darkness below.

It was very noisy, even inside the bunker. The ground shook

as shells landed and exploded. He noticed that a dim Coleman lamp shone at the end of the bunker. Someone was sitting at the headquarters radio set and talking excitedly. Strange could only see his back. The unknown radio operator was speaking in an oriental sounding language. A .303 sniper rifle was laying on the floor beside him.

Strange drew his .38 revolver from his holster and moved towards the mysterious operator. "Who are you and what are you doing?" he asked in a loud voice.

The radio operator turned quickly and faced Strange. He looked terrified and did not reply.

"Henderson! Major Henry Henderson!" Strange exclaimed. "What are you doing here? You are the commanding officer of Baker Company and should be with your men."

"I came to see you, sir," Henderson stammered. "You were away and I came in here after they started shelling. Why are you pointing your revolver at me?"

Strange did not answer. "Why were you sending a message and to whom? What language were you using? You once told me that you could not speak Chinese, but your radio conversation sounded very Chinese to me. Or, was it Korean?"

Henderson did not answer.

"What are you doing with that sniper rifle? Officers do not carry sniper rifles," Strange continued. "Did you use it to silence Little Kim, the houseboy and your helper? I know damn well you did. You are the reason that we lost many of our men in our recent patrol. You told the Chinese about their whereabouts and they were decimated. You are a bloody traitor. I also happen to know, Henderson, that you received a large sum of money from the Soviet Embassy in Ottawa."

"You can't prove any of these things," Henderson finally responded. "All of your evidence is very circumstantial. I will deny everything. I will be acquitted if you decide to court martial me. It will be embarrassing to the government, to the Fusiliers and to you. Why don't you just send me back to Canada. Get Karpinski to certify that I am sick."

"Henderson, you are absolutely right," Strange conceded. His voice was suddenly calm and collected. "A court martial probably won't solve anything. Even if you are convicted you will probably only serve as short period of time before some bleeding heart judge or parole board lets you go. Moreover, I certainly don't want to drag the good name of the Fusiliers through the filthy shit you have created. Yes, it could be long, messy and inconclusive."

"So, sir, what are you going to do?" Henderson asked. His voice sounded hopeful.

"I am going to execute you. You have committed a grievous crime against your country. You are a traitor and a spy. This is going to be an execution on a field of battle. Our Chief of the Defence Staff told me, last August, that it might be the right thing to do."

"Execute? No, sir, please, sir. You can't!" Henderson said in a shaking voice. "I'm sorry for my disloyalty. I'll confess everything!" His face turned pale. "For the sake of my wife and three children, please don't!" he pleaded. He remained seated.

"Why didn't you think of your wife and three children when met with a Soviet agent and betrayed your country? The Chinese were provided, by you, a lot of information about our strength and about our precise location."

Henderson pulled out a photo from his pocket. "Here are my kids," he said. "Let me live for their sake. They are not responsible for the things I have done." He handed Strange the photo.

Strange hesitated and then reluctantly took and looked at the photo. His revolver remained pointed at Henderson's chest.

"Yes, you have beautiful children," he said quietly. He began to question his decision to execute Henderson. "Maybe I should charge you and let you go to trial. If I kill you I will be your judge, jury and executioner. Will I be able to live with this for the rest of my life?"

"My kids love me and I love them. They will miss me. Please let me live," Henderson pleaded.

"Henderson!" Strange suddenly shouted. There is a snake under your chair! It's a poisonous Mamushi Pit Viper! Don't move! We have been warned about these Korean snakes!" It was a black snake with white markings and it was coiled and ready to strike.

Henderson was terrified of snakes and he had been all of his life. He was once bitten by a rattlesnake while working at an oil facility near Medicine Hat in Alberta.

Henderson jumped up from his chair and his sudden movement aroused the snake. It bit deeply into Henderson's right ankle. Henderson let out a loud scream. "Sir," he told Strange, "I need medical help. I am very allergic to snake venom. Call Karpinski!"

Strange aimed his .38 at the snake's head and fired. The snake quivered violently and continued to do so even after its life was over.

"Medical help? It may be too late. The poison from a Mamushi will probably kill you," Strange quietly replied. "The venom is strong. But I am going to carry out this execution by myself. I can't take a chance. The venom may not kill you." He pointed his .38 revolver at Henderson's chest and fired two quick shots.

"You bastard," Henderson whispered hoarsely as he slowly sank to the ground. "Yeah, I did all of those things and I am glad. Long live the revolution! "Then he rolled over on his back and died.

CHAPTER 34
CAPTIVITY

When the sun rose on the day following the first Chinese attack the Canadians saw that large numbers of Chinese bodies were laying all around their positions, with many hanging on the barbed wire and a few even among their trenches. They were all dressed in their traditional padded jackets and cloth caps. Burp guns and rifles were scattered next to their blood-soaked bodies. Most carried bags of seeds, their meager front line food supplies, slung over their shoulders. Some of the seed bags had been penetrated by shrapnel and bullets and seeds were scattered next to some bodies. Large black ravens feasted on the seeds and paid no attention to the living and dead soldiers in their midst.

A young Chinese soldier was found alive on the barbed wire. He looked to be about 17 years old but was probably older. One of his legs had been punctured by a rifle bullet. He had managed to stop the bleeding but was entangled in the barbed wire and could not escape. He was freed from the wire by two Canadian medics and carried on a stretcher to the Regimental Aid Post at Battalion Headquarters. He was covered with a blanket and placed on the ground with a group of wounded Canadians who were waiting to be evacuated. He was being saved, not only for humanitarian reasons, but because he was a potentially valuable source of information.

Peter Farley lay among the wounded. He had been given a blood transfusion and more morphine. He was in a deep sleep. He happily dreamed that he had already arrived at the M.A.S.H. and that Morgan was dressing his wound. "I love you Morgan! Will you marry me?" he kept saying. She smiled but did not respond. The morphine was having at least a temporary beneficial effect. He was no longer experiencing bad dreams.

Later that morning two helicopters appeared in the distance. They were small, flimsy looking aircraft, with coffin-like pods installed on both sides to carry away wounded soldiers. As they approached the Canadian positions machine guns began chattering and rifles began cracking, although from a considerable distance. It was apparent that the Chinese surrounding the Canadian positions were trying to shoot the helicopters out of the sky.

The helicopters landed and four of the most seriously wounded soldiers were loaded into their pods. As they clattered away in a southerly direction Chinese machine guns and rifles opened up again. They returned an hour later, loaded up four more wounded men and disappeared. They made a total of three more round trips before it was finally Farley's turn to be evacuated.

Farley was lifted and placed into the left pod of one of the helicopters and the young wounded Chinese soldier into its right pod. The helicopter rose straight up about 50 feet and then roared southwards towards the main United Nations front lines.

However, as the helicopter swooped over the Kapyang Valley its engine was suddenly struck by a burst of Chinese machine gun fire. The Chinese had been firing at the helicopters continuously, but they had previously missed because of their long distances from their targets. Now they had finally succeeded.

The American pilot maneuvered his craft desperately, trying to prevent an uncontrolled crash. He succeeded to some extent, but the helicopter dropped rapidly, slid into a large rock and burst into flames. The pilot was instantly killed.

Farley broke out of his pod and began to run away. He looked back briefly and saw the Chinese soldier trying to free himself from his badly damaged pod. He raced back into the intense heat, pulled the Chinese out of the wreckage, threw him over his unwounded shoulder, and raced away from the flames. Farley was still weak, but the Chinese was small and felt no heavier than a sack of potatoes. He managed to cover about 20 yards before the helicopter exploded and blew him and the Chinese onto the ground in two semi-conscious heaps. Several small of pieces of metal from the helicopter had penetrated the bodies of Farley and the Chinese and they were bleeding in several places. The wounds were shallow and superficial but appeared to be serious.

A group of Chinese soldiers came running up to the place where Farley and the wounded Chinese had fallen.

"It's a Canadian and one of ours!" a tall Chinese soldier with a rifle exclaimed.

"The Canadian looks badly wounded. He is bleeding a lot. Shall we finish him off?" another one asked.

"Yes," a nearby sergeant replied. "We have no medical facilities to look after him. He will probably die fairly soon. There is no point in allowing him to suffer."

The tall Chinese soldier raised his rifle and pointed it at Farley's head.

"Stop!" Farley's wounded Chinese companion shouted. "You can't shoot him! He saved my life!"

The tall soldier lowered his rifle slightly. He turned towards the sergeant with a look of uncertainly on his face. "What shall I do?" he asked.

The sergeant looked down at the wounded Chinese on the ground. "Comrade, I know how you feel," he said quietly, "but this Canadian seems to be badly wounded. He may be better off dead than alive."

"Please don't shoot him!" the wounded Chinese pleaded. "He may die, but at least we will not be responsible for his death. Let some greater power decide his fate."

The Chinese was a Christian, but he kept his religious beliefs to himself. The communist party of China, like that of the Soviet Union, was atheistic and opposed to religions of all kinds.

"All right, comrade," the sergeant said. "We will not take his destiny into our hands. Put both of them on stretchers and take them back to our medical aid post at headquarters."

Before leaving the crash scene the Chinese stripped the clothing from the dead American pilot. He had been thrown clear by the explosion of his helicopter and his body had not been burned. The Chinese also took his revolver and watch. His body was left next to the burnt out helicopter. Three hungry, large vultures waited patiently on the branch of a nearby tree whose leaves had been stripped of leaves by artillery fire.

In the meantime, Lieutenant Laura Morgan had been working with the M.A.S.H. surgeons in her unit for 14 continuous hours. She was exhausted but she did not want to leave. Many of the wounded arrivals were Canadians from the Fusiliers and her heart ached in anxious anticipation as each of the helicopters unloaded their blood-stained and bandaged cargoes.

"Is he still alive?" Morgan wondered. *"Has he been wounded?*

Will he come in on the next helicopter?"

The last helicopter arrived and Peter Farley was not on it.

"Are there any more Canadians to bring out?" she asked the pilot.

"That's it for now," the pilot replied. "The Chinese seem to have broken off contact. The Canadians have been relieved by the 25th Regimental Combat Team. They aren't surrounded anymore."

"Oh, that's good," she said.

"Yeah," the pilot continued. "But we lost Watson. His helicopter crashed and burned in the Kapyang Valley."

"Oh! I'm sorry!" she said softly. "Was anyone with him?"

"A wounded Chinese and a red-headed Canadian sergeant. They all went up in a ball of flames."

"Oh, God, not him!" she screamed. She turned and ran into one of the nearby tents. Tears were streaking down her cheeks.

"Hell!" the pilot exclaimed to another pilot standing nearby. "Why didn't someone tell me that she know Watson? Then again, come to think of it, how could she? Watson just got here yesterday."

A few hours earlier the Chinese soldiers at the site of the helicopter crash in the Kapyang Valley placed Farley and the wounded Chinese soldier on stretchers. They were carried northwards by unwounded British captives. After they had gone about three miles they were joined by other stretcher bearers who carried two badly wounded Australians, three British soldiers and several Chinese. Soon afterwards both of the Australians died. Their bodies were unceremoniously dumped in a nearby ditch.

Farley was taken to the Headquarters of the 27th Chinese Division. He was placed in a guarded hut on a pile of straw, where he lay in a semi-conscious state for two days. He received no medical attention of any kind, but with the aid of his previous treatment his wounds began to slowly heal on their own. Farley was young, strong and healthy, and he was determined to survive his ordeal.

On the third day he awoke early in the morning. His guards fed him some kimchi, the Korean food staple consisting primarily of fermented cabbage. He had not eaten since leaving Hill 787 and he wolfed down the spicy fare quickly. His guards watched with amusement, from time to time, commenting upon his strange red hair, slender nose, green eyes, and tallness. Other Chinese soldiers in the area also came to look at him. He began to feel like an animal in a zoo.

General Pai Chung-hsi, the commanding officer of the 27th C.C.F division and his senior officers were initially unaware of the presence of the Canadian prisoner. They were preoccupied with the details of their assault and subsequent withdrawal during the first two days of Farley's captivity and did not find out about him and the other prisoners until after three days had passed.

Late in the afternoon of the third day of his captivity Farley was brought before the General and his adjutant. Fu-shun, the English-speaking radio operator was also present to translate and help the General in his interrogation of Farley.

Farley was placed on a bench in front of the General, who sat at a small wooden table. The adjutant and Fu-shun sat beside him. Two guards armed with burp guns stood by the door.

"What is your name?" the General asked. Fu-shun translated.

"Peter Farley."

"I see by the stripes on your uniform that you are a sergeant. Where are you from?"

"Canada."

"What is the name of your unit?"

"The Canadian army."

"Don't be impertinent, young man. You must cooperate.

Otherwise, we may have to deal with you very harshly. In any case, we already know that you are from the Canadian Fusiliers."

Farley did not reply. He was starting to feel very weak and giddy. His mind began to wander over the dramatic events of the past few days. For some reason everything that was happening to him seemed to be strangely amusing. A wide smile came across his face.

"Have you eaten anything?" the General asked. "If you cooperate perhaps I can arrange to provide you with a delicious meal. We have some captured American food in our possession."

"Yes, I have eaten," Farley said with a slightly hysterical laugh. "I ate a lot of kapusta this morning."

"Comrade General," Fu-shun said excitedly, "he's just uttered the code word that has been used on some of the Canadian radio transmissions. Colonel Andrushko told my lieutenant that this word is of Slavic origin, with Russian, Polish or Ukrainian as possibilities. This man is using the same word!"

The General's eyes flashed with anticipation. "Summon Colonel Andrushko!" he ordered his adjutant. "Tell him to come immediately on a matter of great importance."

Within a few minutes Colonel Andrei Andrushko, the Soviet liaison officer to the 27th C.C.F. division, arrived. "Yes, comrade General," he said with a yawn. He had been sleeping. "How can I help you?" He wore a blouse-like shirt with epaulets showing his rank, breeches and well-polished brown boots. A revolver was strapped to his right hip. He was of medium stature. Dark red hair was visible from the sides of his peaked cap.

"You may be able to assist us with this prisoner," the General said. "He is a Canadian from the Fusiliers battalion. We were interrogating him when he suddenly used the word 'kapusta'. He said that he had eaten some kapusta. You will remember that as one of code words used by the Canadians on some of their radio transmissions."

"Of course," Andrushko said. He was now fully awake and showed interest. "That's the Slavic word for cabbage." He looked at Farley curiously but did not speak to him.

"What is his name? Did he tell you?" Andrushko asked Fu-shun.

"Farley. He said his name is Peter Farley, comrade colonel."

Andrushko walked over to Farley. "Kapusta?" he asked.

Farley did not reply.

"Where did you learn to speak the Russian language ? Are you a Russian? What are you doing in the Canadian army? Aren't you ashamed of yourself?" Andrushko rapidly asked in Russian, his voice booming out in a cajoling manner. He was suddenly intensely interested in the young man before him. Farley's red hair added to his interest. Whenever he saw men or women with hair of a similar colour to his own, he felt an immediate attraction to them, in the same way that he did when he noticed those who were left-handed like him.

Farley looked into Andrushko's bright brown eyes. Andrushko's words sounded vaguely familiar, but he could not quite understand their meaning. "I think he is saying something in Russian, which is similar to Ukrainian," he thought. "He must think I'm a Russian."

"I don't understand," Farley said to Fu-shun. "What is he saying?"

Fu-shun smiled but did not reply.

"Farley," Andrushko continued, "your name is Farley? You are long way from home. What are you doing in this country?"

Farley suddenly understood and was startled. The Soviet officer was now speaking in Ukrainian, although in a dialect that was considerably different from his own. Farley opened his mouth to reply, and then closed it again and remained silent.

"Don't be afraid," Andrushko continued in Ukrainian. "I'm one of your people. I'm a Ukrainian. I will not allow them to harm you."

Farley stared at the floor.

"Your name is Farley, right?"

"That's right!" Farley blurted out in Ukrainian. A look of anguish came over his face. He realized that he had betrayed himself. "Now he knows," he thought. "He knows that I speak and understand Ukrainian."

"That's much better," Andrushko said gently. "Don't be afraid to speak with me. I've never been to Canada but my family is from Galicia, in western Ukraine. My grandfather moved to Moscow, but our family continued to speak Ukrainian in our home. Two of my grandfather's brothers went to Manitoba in the late 1890's, where they took up farming. My grandfather used to receive letters from them, but eventually lost touch."

"That's interesting."

"Are your parents farmers?"

"Yes, my father is a farmer. He has a small farm and also works on the railway."

"Why did you come to Korea?"

"I don't know. I wanted adventure. I wanted to help the Korean people. I wanted to see the world."

"Don't you know that this is an evil war, and that the Americans are using you as cannon fodder? Canada seems to be not a real country. It's just a colony of the United States. The Americans will eventually take over all of Canada. That is what they keep saying. They want to control all of North America. Our foolish czarist government sold Alaska to the Americans in the last century. "

"We may look like Americans and speak like Americans, but we are Canadians. Canada decided to enter the Korean War on its own. We will always be Canadians. In any case, my priest says that communism is evil and that it should be resisted in

Korea and everywhere else."

"What does your priest know?" Andrushko asked angrily. "The priests are a part of the capitalist bourgeoisie. The church is wealthy. Priests have never done anything to help the workers and peasants."

"Maybe that's what some Ukrainians in Russia think. Canada is different. Most Ukrainians in Canada are not communists. We live a good life and are not interested in changing the system."

"If that's true, then our people in Canada are misinformed."

"Perhaps," Farley said confidently, "but that's the way of the world." His photographic memory suddenly projected one of the lectures that Father Boleschuk frequently gave at the Ukrainian summer school in Sweet Grass.

"We are taught certain things as children," Farley continued, "including religious beliefs, social attitudes and philosophies of life. Although we are both Ukrainian, we obviously grew up in much different circumstances. I am a Catholic, while you are probably an atheist. I believe that people should be able to express themselves economically and politically in a free society, but you likely think a highly-structured, authoritarian system is preferable. These are the beliefs and attitudes that we learned as children. They are engrained into our systems."

Farley was using his photographic memory to plagiarize Boleschuk's words, but he was pleased with himself and did not feel guilty, even though he was very aware of the fact that he was not a strong, practicing Catholic. He believed in God but rarely went to church and lived life according to his own values.

"Your thinking is erroneous, but you are obviously an intelligent person," Anrushko said with apparent sincerity. "Are you well-educated?"

"I attended a university for two years."

"Why did you leave?"

"I ran out of money."

"Aha! You ran out of money! In the Soviet Union you would not need money to go to university!"

"There are places in Canada where money is not needed, where everyone is equal, where benefits are the same, and where all have access to free education, including university studies if they have the desire and aptitude."

"What are these places?"

"They are called penitentiaries."

"Now you are becoming very impertinent, young man," Andrushko said with a trace of annoyance. At the same time, he could not resist a smile.

Andrushko then turned to the General. "This man," he said in his fluent Mandarin, "is an exploited Canadian of Ukrainian peasant stock. He is a simple, common soldier, and does not appear to have any information that is of any value to us."

"What about kapusta?" the General asked suspiciously. "Why did he use that word in my presence? Isn't he one of the radio operators that were sending messages in Ukrainian on the night that our troops were caught in that devastating mortar barrage?"

Andrushko turned to Farley again. "Were you a member of the Canadian patrol that went out in early July?" he asked. "You know the one I mean. You lost a number of your soldiers. You directed mortar fire against a concentration of our forces. Many Chinese soldiers lost their lives as a result of your mortar barrage. A large number of Korean women and children died at the same time because they were located in the same area."

Farley did not reply, but the information about the death of Korean women and children caused him grief and anguish. He felt deeply responsible and guilty. He also remembered, very painfully, that horses had also died during this barrage.

"Fu-shun, our English interpreter and radio operator said

that a lot of Ukrainian seemed to have been spoken on the night of this particular patrol. Unfortunately, I happened to be away at the time, or I would have heard you."

"Why does it matter?" Farley asked.

"It matters because someone directed a very accurate barrage on the troops of our division. Many were killed or wounded. Our attack was delayed for several days. "

"That's war, I guess," Farley said with a painful look on his face. "The best laid schemes of mice and men aft gang aglay: often go wrong, that is."

"Who said that?"

"A Scottish poet called Robert Burns. We studied him in high school."

"Did you study Pushkin? He's a better poet, I'm sure."

Farley did not respond. He looked at Andrushko, wondering if he would be betrayed and turned over to the unpredictable, volatile Chinese.

"As you say," Farley finally replied. "I am one of your people. We are members of the same race. I've carried out my duties as a good soldier, and not because of a personal malice towards you or your Chinese allies. Many Canadians have also died in Korea, including some of Ukrainian origin. If you had been born a Canadian, I think that you would have acted in the same way."

Andrushko turned to the General again. "What I said previously still holds," he said. "This man is a common soldier. There are many Ukrainians in the Fusiliers. Undoubtedly two of them were radio operators during the Canadian mortar attack, but we have no way of knowing or proving that this man was one of them. I strongly recommend that you treat him like any other prisoner of war."

"I don't agree!" the General said angrily. "I don't understand your language, but I think that you are trying to protect him because he is one of your own people. Frankly, colonel, I am getting tired of your arrogance and interference. I am in charge of this division, and not some pale-faced foreigner from Europe!" He looked towards the guards in the room. "Take the Canadian away and dispose of him," he ordered. "He is criminally responsible for the deaths of many of our comrades!"

"My dear comrade General," Andrushko said calmly. "Remember that I have been assigned to your division by virtue of orders from your Central Military Committee as well as my Soviet command. You depend heavily on supplies and support from the Soviet Union. If you execute this Canadian in this unjust and arbitrary manner I will report the circumstances to your superiors as well as my own. I will also report other questionable activities, such as the illegal business transactions that you have carried on in the past. Your career will be in great peril."

"On what grounds are you protecting this man?" the General asked with some hesitation. "I am sorry for my unkind words. They were spoken in a moment of anger. But you must give me a good reason for sparing him." The General had, in fact, on three occasions, illegally sold some military equipment and kept the proceeds.

"You must spare him," Andrushko said quietly, "because he is simply a soldier doing his duty in the same way that we are doing our duty. Besides, he seems to have communist tendencies. He believes in equality and economic justice. You should be able to educate him quite easily in one of your camps."

"Why don't you take him?" the General asked. "I have heard that many American and other prisoners of war have been transported to Siberia. I believe that Comrade Stalin wants to rehabilitate them."

"That may happen eventually, but for the time being he should be sent to one of your camps," Andrushko said.

"All right, comrade colonel, I accept your assessment. Personally, I still have some serious doubts about him. That red hair disturbs me. He looks like a creature that is associated with a devil, except that I don't believe in devils." He turned and spoke to the guards. "Take him away," he ordered. "He is to be moved north and interned in the normal manner."

Andrushko was both amused and annoyed by the General's comment about red hair. It appeared that the General had forgotten that Andrushko's hair was also red. But Andrushko decided to say nothing. He did not want to arouse the General again.

"Good luck, colonel" Farley said as the guards led him away, "and God bless you!" Although he did not understand the conversation between the two officers, he sensed that Andrushko had managed to have him spared.

"Thank you, sergeant," Andrushko replied with a smile. "I hope that he will bless me. I haven't spoken to God since I was a small child."

After Andrushko had left the General turned to his adjutant. "Lin Baio," he said, "I want this Canadian sent to Haeju, the internment camp run by the Koreans rather than one of our own. The camp commandant at Haeju is English-speaking and specializes in getting his inmates to admit that the Americans are using germ warfare and committing other war crimes. I have spared the Canadian, but after he gets to Haeju he may find that life there is not worth living!"

About a week after the U.S. ambulance helicopter crashed with Peter Farley on board, his father Orest Farley in Sweet Grass, Manitoba received a letter of condolence from *"General Headquarters, United Nations Command, Office of the Commander-in-Chief."* The letter read as follows:

"Dear Mr. Farley: The presumed death of your son, Sergeant Peter Farley, has been a great shock. While no one can fully share

the sorrow which the loss of a loved one brings, he will surely be missed by his comrades, too. We earnestly hope that you will find some comfort in the knowledge of the understanding sympathy of those who knew him and who shared service with him in this command. There should also be some measure of consolation in knowing that he met his fate manfully in the service of his country. I have faith that his devotion to duty, in defense of all that we and the free people of the world hold most dear, has helped us on the long, hard road by which alone we may expect some day to reach a just, honorable and enduring peace. May God grant we continue to follow that road whatever be the sacrifices entailed. With sincere sympathy, I am, respectfully, M.B. Ridgeway, General, United States Army."

CHAPTER 35
HAEJU

On the day following Farley's capture by the Chinese a Regimental Combat Team of the United States Army broke through the Chinese encirclement and relieved the exhausted Fusiliers. But it was too late for Farley. He was now a prisoner of war.

Farley and the other prisoners being held by the 27th C.C.F. Division were divided into two groups, with one group to go to a Chinese camp and the second group to a North Korean camp. Farley was placed with the group bound for the North Korean camp. He was fed raw potatoes and cabbage leaves from time to time and was lodged at nights in Korean houses, shattered buildings or simply out in the open. Finally, after seven days of marching, he and his fellow prisoners reached Haeju, an abandoned village that had been converted into a prisoner of war camp by the North Koreans. It was here that Farley was destined to spend the next part of his life.

The village of Haeju was located in North Korean territory about five miles from the Yellow Sea and 50 miles above the 38th parallel of latitude. Its civilian population deserted it in December, 1950, and never returned. In February of 1951 the North Koreans converted its cluster of relatively intact thatched cottages into a temporary internment facility for United Nations prisoners, but as the months went by it gradually acquired the status of a permanent P.O.W. camp.

The North Korean Army took very few prisoners during the early months of the Korean War. Thousands of South Korean soldiers and hundreds of American soldiers were simply shot after they were captured. In some instances, American bodies were found with their wrists tied behind their backs and bullet holes in their heads. However, following the Chinese entry into the war in November, 1950, U.N. prisoners were treated more humanely, even though the People's Republic of China did not officially subscribe to the principles of the U.N. with respect to the treatment of prisoners. The Chinese were more compassionate than their North Korean allies and they prevailed upon the Koreans to act accordingly.

The day after he arrived in Haeju Farley was brought before North Korean Major Kyong Park, the English-speaking camp commandant. Park was born in Hawaii to a Korean father and Japanese mother in 1923 and lived in Hawaii with his parents until they returned to Seoul in 1937. He was fluent in Englisb, Korean, and to some extent, Japanese, the language of Korea's occupying power from 1910 to 1945. He hated all Americans with a deep intensity. His Caucasian classmates in Hawaii sometimes called him a "dirty little Jap." A communist sympathizer, he joined the North Korean Army in 1946 and rapidly rose to the rank of major. He was, in psychiatric terms, as Farley later noted, a malignant narcissist, a sadist who and took pleasure in torturing his inmates.

"Why did you come to Korea?" the Major asked Farley.

"I'm a Canadian soldier. My government sent me."

"But you are not a conscript, like most of the Americans. In fact, you are a criminal mercenary, are you not?"

"All of Canada's soldiers are volunteers. We don't believe in conscription. Isn't your army the same?"

"Sergeant, I'm told that you were captured after you were in a helicopter crash. Keep in mind that your people probably think that you are dead. Do you understand? You must cooperate with us or suffer serious consequences. If we dispose of you no one will ask any questions. You are already dead as far as the rest of the world is concerned."

Farley stared straight ahead and did not reply.

"Do you know anything about the use of germ warfare?" the Major asked sternly.

"No. I don't know what you are talking about."

"Yes you do, sergeant. I would like you to make a statement to that effect. Tell your people, in writing, that the American and Canadian intervention is a criminal act against the Korean nation, and that this crime is even more dastardly because of the use of germs by the forces of the United States. If you help us in this way, your life will become much more bearable."

"Dastardly?" Farley asked with a smile. "I have not heard that word for a long time. It's used mainly in British novels. Canadians rarely use it. Canada is my country."

"Canada is not a country. It is an American slave state. Are you prepared to make a statement or not?"

"No. I honestly don't know anything about germ warfare."

"All right, then you must pay for your stupidity!" the Major said with threatening finality. "Take him away," he said in Korean.

Farley was marched into a nearby cottage and locked into a very small cubicle. It was windowless, with only a small opening in the ceiling, above which a guard sat with a burp gun. Farley's shirt was removed and drops of water were allowed to fall from an overhead cistern onto his head and back for several hours at a time. Whenever Farley protested and tried to move the guard shouted and pointed his burp gun at him in a menacing manner.

The torture was painfully effective, but it left no marks except on his mind. Farley had suffered from claustrophobia since early childhood, and his confinement in the tiny cell brought him to the edge of hysteria. After the third day of the water torture he began to experience hallucinations. He believed that he was being swept over a large and violent waterfall, and then that he was swimming helplessly in a wide and powerful river, and finally that he was being attacked by a horde of gigantic mosquitoes who penetrated deeply and painfully into his back.

The Major interviewed Farley very aggressively every day for two weeks, with each session taking place after the water treatments. He then decided to leave Farley alone. "This man is exceptionally stubborn," he told his adjutant, "and besides, his mind seems to be on the verge of collapse. We are wasting our time on him. Put him back with the rest of the prisoners."

Soon afterwards was taken out of isolation and placed into one of the cottages where three other prisoners were lodged.

One of the prisoners in Farley's new quarters was Private Max Taylor, a U.S. 81 mm. mortar man who had been captured by the Chinese in December, 1950. He was a short, dark New Yorker with a well-developed sense of humour. His lengthy imprisonment and an ability to absorb language easily had enabled him to learn a considerable amount of Korean.

A second inmate of the cottage was an Australian warrant officer called Malcolm Hughes. He had been wounded and captured by the Chinese during their offensive of April, 1951. He was a jovial man with dark hair and a blondish beard. His right hand was missing. It had been badly damaged by shrapnel and then removed by a Chinese army surgeon shortly after his capture. "It's a good thing that I am left-handed," was one of his favourite expressions.

The third occupant of the cottage was Roger Bailey, a handsome Englishman whose mind had apparently deteriorated under the stress of battle and captivity. Although he spoke sensibly for a part of the time, Bailey often seemed to live in an imaginary world of his own. He thought that he owned a motorcycle and a cat. A long, crooked stick served as his motorcycle, and the invisible cat was only present whenever he meowed on its behalf. He had a habit of frequently roaring around the camp on his stick, and always gave some of his food to his imagery cat. He insisted on being called "Major Bailey", but no one believed that he was an officer, including his captors, who decided to house him with other ranks rather than officers.

"Welcome to Haeju, sergeant," Taylor said as he extended his right hand.

"Thanks," Farley replied. "But where is Haeju?"

"We don't know for sure," Hughes replied as he offered his left hand. "I think it is very close to the eastern coast of North Korea. We are not far from the water. We can hear naval guns from time to timer. They sound different, and not like land-based artillery."

"How do you even know the name of the place?" Farley asked.

"Max has been here since last December," Hughes replied, "and he's learned a lot of Korean by talking to the guards. Most of the guards are reasonable and friendly, but Major Park is a miserable and vicious asshole. I think he is hated even by his own men."

While this conversation was going on Roger Bailey sat quietly in a corner. He said nothing at first, but looked curiously at the newly arrived prisoner of war. Finally he got up and extended his hand. "I'm Major Bailey," he said warmly. "I'm pleased to meet you. I'm the officer in command here. However, you will find me to be a decent chap, I'm sure."

"Yes, sir," Farley said. "But I thought officers are usually kept in separate quarters. Why are you here with us?"

Bailey did not answer Farley's question. "Did you bring any milk?" Bailey asked. "My cat would like some milk."

"Milk?"

"Yes, milk. My cat would like some."

"Sorry," Farley said with a baffled look. He tried to be congenial. "I have not had any milk for a long time. I also have a cat. He is called Billie. He is an important member of our family. We love him. He lives at my home in Canada, and I have not seen him for many months. I miss him, as well as my dog and horse."

"I also love cats and I have always had one. Well, then, excuse me," Bailey said. "It's time for me to inspect the camp. Make yourself at home, but keep everything neat and tidy. I won't stand for slovenly behaviour."

Bailey then placed a long stick between his legs and headed for the door. "Vroom! Vroom!" he roared as he directed his imaginary motorcycle out the door.

"That guy's crazy!" Farley exclaimed after Bailey was gone.

"You are right," Hughes said. "We try not to laugh, but sometimes we just can't help it. Don't pay any attention to what he says, but try to humour him if you can."

"How did he get that way?" Farley asked.

"Bailey was tortured for several weeks because Major Park believed, for some reason, that Bailey was personally involved in germ warfare," Taylor answered. "After his release from the torture chamber he started living in a fantasy world. He suddenly had a cat and a motorcycle. He is sensible some of the time, but he has told so many wild stories that we can't believe anything he says."

"Let me change the subject," Farley said. "Have you ever thought about escaping?"

"Yes," Hughes replied. "We have a plan. There is no barbed wire around this camp. They don't think that anyone will try to escape. We are easily identified white men in an oriental world. There are about 200 other prisoners in this camp, including a few Turks, but mostly Americans, Brits and Australians. That's probably why they posted the English-speaking Major Park to this camp. They wanted Park to get the prisoners to admit to germ warfare for propaganda purposes."

"Has Park been successful? Has anyone admitted to germ warfare? I have never heard anything about warfare of this kind," Farley interjected.

"I don't think that he has been very successful," Hughes continued. "None of us know anything about so-called germ warfare. We are friendly with the other prisoners but we have not mentioned our escape plans to them. We are afraid that Park will find out if too many are involved. It may sound selfish, but two or three have a better chance of getting away than if the whole camp goes. Our plan is to slip out at night, head east to the coast, steal a small Korean fishing boat, and then head south until we get well below the 38th parallel."

"Weapons? Will you not need weapons of some kind?" Farley asked.

"Yes," Taylor replied. "I liberated a British Bren light machine gun and a box of .303 ammunition from the camp's weapons storage area about a week ago. I also got a box of primed British hand grenades. The Koreans store all of the weapons that they confiscate from their prisoners in this hut. These weapons are usually distributed to their regular army units on a regular basis, but I managed to grab the Bren, ammunition and grenades while it was still in storage."

"How did you manage to do that? Isn't the hut locked at all

times?" Farley asked.

"The hut has a heavy wooden door and is usually secured with a large padlock. I noticed, one day, that the padlock was on the door but that it was not closed. I guess that one of the guards forgot to close it. I went back that evening, when it was pitch black. The lock was still open. The place was a clutter and probably not subject to any kind of accurate inventory. I removed the things I wanted, closed the lock, and hid the weapons under our cottage. I am sure that they did not miss anything because we were not questioned or searched the next day."

"What about food?" Farley continued. "You won't get far on an empty stomach."

Taylor smiled. "We have been taking and storing Major Bailey's cat food," he said sheepishly.

"Cat food?"

"Yeah," Taylor replied. "He puts out raw potatoes for his imaginary cat. We have been hiding them away, as well as our own, in preparation for our escape. Potatoes are ideal for this purpose. They last a long time and do not spoil easily."

"I'd like to go with you," Farley announced.

"Are you sure? Hughes asked. "It will be very dangerous."

"Yes, I'm very sure. I don't want to end up like Major Bailey. If they give me that water treatment again I will certainly go off the deep end."

"Okay, you are in," Hughes said and Taylor nodded his agreement.

Three nights later a very heavy fog descended on Haeju, with visibility being limited to about 10 feet.

"The time is right," Hughes said to Farley and Taylor. "The fog makes it ideal. It's now or never."

"The machine gun is in working order and I am taking it," Taylor said. "I am giving each of you four grenades. Be careful. They are primed and ready to go. I also have a white peasant's outfit and Korean conical hat that I am planning to wear. I am short and dark and that helps. If they see me at a distance they will ignore me if they think I am a Korean farmer."

"But what about Bailey?" Farley asked. "We can't trust him. He could give the whole thing away."

"I'll look after him," Hughes responded confidently. "We will leave in about 30 minutes. It should be dark by then. Get your grenades, potatoes and water bottles ready. Remember that the plan is to head east until you get to the junction of the two roads about a half a mile from here. We have been there and to the coast many times on work parties. We will go by way of seniority in the camp. Max will go first, and I will follow about five minutes later. Wait in the deep ditch beside the junction. Max and I know how to get to the water."

"Why such long intervals?" Farley asked. "Wouldn't it be better if we all go together?"

"We have discussed this in the past," Taylor answered. "Actually, first may be worst. I'll be a decoy. If they are on to us you will hear some shouting or shooting. If that happens stay put and get rid of your grenades, potatoes and water bottles."

"All right," Farley agreed. "That makes sense."

At that moment Bailey suddenly appeared in the door of the cottage. "Gentlemen," he boomed, "what is going on here?"

"Nothing, sir, nothing at all," Hughes answered.

"What are you doing with all those potatoes?" Bailey asked.

"We are going on a picnic," Hughes replied.

"Oh, good! May I come?"

"Certainly," Hughes said. "but Major Park was just here. He wants you to inspect the camp."

"At this hour?"

"That's what he said," Hughes answered.

"Well, if I must, I must," Bailey said with a sigh. "But wait until I get back. I want to go with you. I have not been on a picnic for many years!"

"Take your time, Major," Taylor suggested .

"Vroom! Vroom!" Bailey yelled as he went out the door mounted on his stick.

Taylor then pulled a sack out from under his bunk and dressed quickly into the Korean clothing it contained. "Ahn yung hah sim ni kah!" he exclaimed, meaning "how are you?" in Korean. "It fits," he said with a smile. "I am small and the same size as most Koreans. We had better start right away. Bailey usually takes about a half an hour to do his inspection. Count slowly to 300 and then follow me one at time. Good luck!" He saluted and disappeared out the door into the darkness and fog.

Hughes and Farley sat quietly on the floor each clutching small, hand made cloth bags full of grenades, potatoes and water bottles.

Hughes stared at the wall and counted under his breathe. After what seemed like a very long time he sprang up and headed for the door. "300!" he exclaimed. "Start counting, Peter! I'll see you in a while!"

Farley was now alone in the cottage. He counted slowly under his breathe, but his mind wandered. *"What am I doing in this place?"* he asked himself. *"Am I any more sane than Bailey? I wonder what Morgan is doing? Does she know I am still alive? Will I ever see her again?"* Then he suddenly realized that he had lost track of his count. Was he still in the one hundreds, or in the two hundreds?

Then he heard a noise at the door. It was Bailey with his stick.

"Sergeant," Bailey said. "You are under arrest!"

Farley sprang to his feet. "Why, Major, what for?"

"For betraying me. Where are the other two rascals?"

"I don't know. Maybe they went for a walk."

"What you mean, Sergeant, is that they have gone on their picnic without me."

"Take it easy, Major. I'll go and find them. Let me out!"

"No, stay where you are," Bailey ordered.

Farley grabbed his bag of grenades and potatoes and water bottle and rushed towards the door. Bailey raised his heavy stick and as Farley went by hit him over the head. Farley sank to his knees, clutched at his head and then sprawled unconscious onto the floor. His grenades and potatoes broke out of their flimsy bag and rolled in all directions.

"Aha!" Bailey screamed. "You have been stealing my cat's food, which makes matters even worse. "Major Park! Major Park! We have an insurrection on our hands!"

Two Korean guards came running into the cottage, their burp guns cocked and ready to fire. They shouted excitedly and backed Bailey against one of the walls.

Shortly afterwards Major Park entered. "What is going on?" he asked Bailey. "Where are the other two, the American and the Australian?"

"They have gone on a picnic," Bailey replied. "They went without me."

"The Canadian, American and the Australian are probably trying to escape!" Park said in Korean to the guards. "Sound the alarm!" Then he ran towards the door, slipped on one of Farley's potatoes, went flying out the door and cursed with anger and pain as he fell off the steps and onto the ground, where his right arm broke with a sickening crack. "Get them!" he screamed in Korean. "Get them and kill them!"

The guards lifted Park from the side of the steps and carried him towards his quarters where he could be treated for his broken arm. Park screamed in agony as they took him away.

In the meantime, Bailey sank into a state of confusion. He mounted his imaginary motorcycle, summoned his imaginary cat, and began running around the camp. "It's an escape!" he shouted. "It's an escape!"

An escape? Many of the prisoners decided to take up the apparent opportunity. They dressed quickly, noted that the thick fog provided an excellent cover, and began leaving the camp in all directions. They had no food, no weapons and no plan, but they had a strong desire to leave in spite of the dangers involved in an escape.

Farley woke up shortly afterwards and saw that he was now alone in the hut. His potatoes and grenades were still scattered across the floor and he gathered them into his cloth bag and staggered out the door. He was dizzy but eager to leave. He headed through the fog in the previously planned direction.

By this time Taylor, dressed in his Korean disguise, had reached the ditch where the escapees' rendezvous was to take place. He put his Bren machine gun on the ground and waited. He was joined shortly afterwards by Hughes. Suddenly a group of Korean guards appeared through the fog immediately in front of them. They saw Taylor, but in their eyes he was just another peasant and they ignored him. They did not see his Bren. Hughes threw all of his grenades in their direction and he was then cut down by a burp gun.

Taylor picked his Bren and fired a long burst. Several guards were instantly killed or wounded. He then ran from the ditch and headed for the seashore where the Korean fishing boats were located.

The burst of machine gun fire and sudden deaths of some of their comrades caused the posse of Korean guards to stop in their tracks. The burst of gunfire was unexpected and the thick fog made a further advance appear to be very hazardous. Was the enemy present in great numbers? Were they South Koreans? The guards did not know. This allowed Taylor to reach the seashore without any further resistance. He climbed into a small boat, picked up an oar, and paddled away from the shore and in a southerly direction. For the time being at least, he was free.

Farley heard the machine gun fire just as he reached his destination, the ditch previously designated by Hughes and Taylor. As he crouched in one of the crevasses at the side of the ditch, he heard the shouts of a group of Korean guards as they approached. As they gathered in a group at one end of the ditch, Farley threw his grenades in rapid succession into their midst. Loud explosions and screams followed.

Farley jumped out of the ditch and ran in the direction of the seashore. As he approached though the fog he was suddenly confronted by three Korean guards. He tried to run but one of the guards clubbed him on his head with his burp gun. Farley once again sank to a state of unconsciousness. He was thrown onto a truck and hauled back to the camp.

Early the next morning all of the camp's prisoners were lined up in an open area in front of their cottages. Major Park stood in front of them, his right arm encased in a thick white bandage and cast.

As Park called the roll a Soviet made truck rolled up. Four guards then threw the bullet-ridden, lifeless bodies of Hughes and a dozen other prisoners onto the ground.

Taylor was noticeably absent. The contingent of Korean guards was also sharply reduced in numbers. Many had died during their encounter with the machine gun and grenades of the escapees the previous evening.

Park continued the roll call as though no interruption had taken place.

"Everyone is present," Park finally announced, "including those who tried to escape. Taylor is temporarily absent, but we will find him."

A chorus of loud boos and hisses came back by way of response.

"There will be no more potatoes for two weeks!" Park said

angrily. "I hope that all of you like cabbage."

Farley was badly bruised and his head ached but he stood upright in the front row of the prisoners. "I love kapusta!" he yelled sarcastically.

"Oh! There you are, Sergeant Farley. I had almost forgotten about you. I can see that you need the water treatment again." He walked over and slapped Farley violently across the face. "Take him away and begin the treatments immediately," he said in Korean to the two guards standing with Farley. Farley was led away to begin his ordeal all over again.

CHAPTER 36
FARLEY'S ESCAPE FROM HAEJU

Major Kyong Park, the Haeju prisoner of war commandant, was a sadist. He hated all Americans. Canadians, in his mind, were also Americans. Canada was not a real country. Canada was nothing more than a colony of the United States.

Park considered executing Farley after the aborted escape attempt. Park was seriously humiliated even though the escape had failed, and his painful broken arm made him very angry. After some consideration, he decided to spare Farley's life. Rather than kill Farley, he would punish him severely. He ordered the water treatment in a very small cell for several hours each day for an indefinite period of time. Farley was, in keeping with Park's orders, also taken out of his small cell and beaten by the guards on a regular basis. His face and body was covered with massive bruises. Park expected that Farley would eventually die, but he wanted to keep him alive and in pain for as long as possible.

The day after he was locked into his water treatment cell, Farley's mind began to break. He had been claustrophobic since early childhood, and his severe confinement, along with the water torture, beatings and deaths of his fellow prisoners resulted in a mental breakdown. He had been knocked unconscious at Edo Street and now, with similar violent force, by the butt of a burp gun. He was suffering, unknowingly, from the effects of a concussion. He had nightmares and dreamed about the Chinese soldiers, Korean civilians and horses that had died in his presence, and to some extent, as a result of his actions. He felt guilty and sank into a deep depression. He lapsed into a semi-conscious state in which his dreams became so vivid and detailed that they seemed to be actual events in the real world. His mind was deeply disturbed and reality was difficult to comprehend.

Only one prisoner had escaped from Haeju during the attempt, and that was Max Taylor, the American who had dressed himself in Korean peasant clothing. After reaching the seashore and taking a small fisherman's boat, he had rowed southward along the shore for four days before finally reaching a South Korean coastal village where a battalion of U.S. Marines was located. After being advised about the Haeju prison camp, the Americans took aerial photographs of the area. A decision was made to act quickly to free the prisoners rather than subject them to the capricious whims of their North Korean captors.

Early one morning in early July a company from the battalion of U.S. Marines landed on the coast immediately east of Haiju, the cluster of Korean houses located about five miles west of the coast. The Marines quickly surrounded the camp and forced Major Park and his North Korean guards to surrender.

Major Park was locked into one of prisoner's huts pending transfer to a United Nations prisoner of war compound. He did not last long. Within a few minutes of his captivity a group of former prisoners broke into his place of confinement.

"I am prisoner of war," Park pleaded. He held his hands high in the air. At that moment he was clubbed in the stomach with a wooden plank by a British soldier.

"Take that, you filthy bastard," the soldier shouted. "You are not a prisoner. You're a fucking demented beast!"

Park fell to the floor screaming and holding his stomach in agony. He was booted in the head by several other prisoners. Others clubbed him with wooden poles and steel bars. Blood poured out of his mouth. He rolled over one final time and died.

The liberated prisoners were loaded onto landing barges and transported to the American ship waiting offshore. Farley, along with several other prisoners in serious medical circumstances were flown to an American Stars and Stripes Military Hospital in Tokyo.

Farley had lost a lot of weight and had very high periodic malarial fevers. The attending American military physician produced the following report:

"Sergeant Farley has a severe psychological disorder apparently as a result of major traumatic experiences that he has had in Korea. He was awarded the Canadian Military Medal in Korea which indicates that he is a courageous soldier. At the present time he has symptoms of depression and extreme irritability. He feels guilty because many of his comrades have died and he has survived. He has flashbacks, recurrent nightmares, and overreacts to sudden noises. He is sometimes confused and seems to live in an unreal world.

He has advised that he was knocked unconscious on two occasions while in Japan and Korea, and it is quite possible that he has had one or perhaps two concussions.

On several occasions, he has revealed that he has a severe case of claustrophobia. Being incarcerated for several weeks in a very small cell by his Korean captors probably provoked and exacerbated this phobia from an earlier childhood experience. Included among this patient's symptoms are an accelerated heart beat, nausea, fainting, shaking, sweating and a fear of actual harm. His condition and required treatment will need to be more accurately assessed.

It appears that his hearing has been damaged. He has stated that blood came out of both ears after a mortar blast on one occasion. He often does not respond to questions unless they are posed at a high volume.

He has been infected with malaria and is being treated with chloroquine. Because depression and anxiety are sometimes associated with the long term use of this medication, special vigilance should be taken in this case."

One day a letter arrived and was presented to Peter while he was laying in bed in the hospital in Tokyo. The Seattle, Washington address on the back of the envelope said that it was from Jean Haines.

"*Dear Peter,*" the brief letter said. "*I am writing to tell you about our daughter Julie. You will be pleased to know that she has bright red hair, blue eyes, and a beautiful face. I am sure that she will, like you, also have freckles one day. I love her very much and I still love you. Please write and come to see us. I think of you often. Love, Jean.*"

After reading the letter he sank into a state of confusion. He remembered Jean and still had a strong attachment to her. A daughter? His daughter Julie? What should he do? He also loved Sonia and, to a much greater extent, Laura Morgan. He felt torn and confused.

For the next several weeks his mind was immersed in a dreamlike state in which he projected the events of his future life, and in which the principal characters were the three loves of his life. Would he marry and live with Sonia, with Jean, or with Morgan? Or would he spend the rest of his life alone? He still remembered his love for his mathematics teacher Michelle Brown, but she had disappeared from his life a long time ago and would probably not return. The Americans had stolen her.

After what appeared to be a long time in the hospital, Farley believed that he was being sent home to Sweet Grass. In a realistic dream his father Orest and Sonia Kereliuk met him at the railway station and they all cried with joy. The Town Council held a reception in the Ukrainian Hall and it seemed that the whole town and district came. Many of them asked about the Military Medal that he wore. His father was very proud of him. Billie, Fido and Charlie received him with great joy and treated him as though he had never been away.

Sonia suddenly became very beautiful and attractive in his eyes. Her teaching experience made her more sure of herself. Her intelligence was now much more in evidence. She was more assertive and sometimes seemed cool and distant. She occasionally implied that she might be interested in Johnnie Michaluk, who recently played several more games with the Toronto Maple Leafs. Her coolness and detachment made her more exciting to him. He noticed, once again, that she had a exceptionally pretty face and a perfect body. Peter loved beautiful and intelligent women and Sonia was certainly one of them.

Peter and Sonia were married, in one of Farley's dreams, in the Ukrainian Catholic Church in Sweet Grass by Father Boleschuk. Jim Doherty, Peter's comrade in Korea, acted as his best man. Miles Lewis, the African American from Detroit, sent a wedding gift but did not attend.

The dreaming continued. He was interviewed for entry as a student into the School of Medicine at the University of Manitoba. He worried because in the years prior to WWII Canadian medical schools all had secret, unpublished ethnic quotas for women, Jews, Ukrainians, Poles, Italians and other "foreigners." This practice largely disappeared after World War II because it was no longer enforceable. Foreigners changed their names, lost their accents and were often no longer easily physically identifiable. Ukrainians and others of European origin often looked like the English. Following Farley's interview he was accepted into medicine because of his excellent academic background, his skill as a hockey player, and the impressive impression that he gave to the Faculty of Medicine selection committee. They did not know that he was a Ukrainian.

Farley returned to the University of Manitoba. He became a star forward with the University's Buffalo hockey team. Veterans' Affairs paid for his tuition and gave him a generous living allowance. The Toronto Maple Leafs asked him to come for a try out. He appreciated but declined the professional hockey offer. He continued enthusiastically with his medical studies. The dream ended on a happy note.

CHAPTER 37
COMING HOME FROM KOREA

The Royal Canadian Air Force North Star aircraft sat close to the main terminal at Haneda airport in Tokyo. Its noisy four engines had been shut down by its pilots earlier that morning. Several ambulances were parked nearby. Their occupants, Canadian soldiers, many in casts, bandages and on wheelchairs were being escorted by Canadian nurses and loaded onto the North Star. Some soldiers walked with crutches. Others were laying on stretchers and were being carried by attendants. Most were recovering from wounds, but a few, like Sergeant Peter Farley, were being hospitalized because of severe cases of malaria and other maladies.

One of the wounded soldiers being carried on a stretcher, his head swathed in bandages, propped himself up on his right elbow and looked deliriously in all directions. "Where am I? Where in hell are we going?" he shouted.

"Relax, soldier," a nurse walking next to his stretcher said.

"You are going home to Canada." The soldier did not respond. He stared at the nurse briefly, went back to his prone position and closed his eyes.

These veterans of combat in the Korean War had recently arrived from the American Stars and Stripes Military Hospital in Tokyo. They were scheduled to be flown on the North Star, with a brief re-fueling stop in Alaska, to McChord U.S. Air Force base near Takoma, Washington, and from McChord on another Canadian North Star, to the Flanders Military Hospital in Vancouver.

The North Star was equipped with hospital facilities, including cots for patients with serious injuries. Rows of seats were provided for others.

Sergeant Peter Farley, classified as a malaria patient, strapped himself into his seat on the North Star. His malarial fever was in remission, but it could flare up at any time. His temperature, two days earlier had reached a perilous 109 F. degrees. He had almost died. He experienced hallucinations, confusion and convulsions. Rubbing alcohol, a temperature reducing remedy of that era, had been smeared on his naked body and as a result his temperature had declined to a safer level of 102 F. degrees.

As the four engines on the North Star roared to life in preparation for takeoff, Farley closed his eyes and soon afterwards fell into a deep sleep. Two nurses sat beside Farley on the North Star. One was Lieutenant Janet Smythe, a Canadian nursing sister. The other was Lieutenant Jeong-hui Song, a young Korean nurse who was on an exchange program designed to introduce South Koreans to Canadian nursing procedures and to improve their knowledge of the English language.

Smythe was Song's mentor and the two were assigned to take care of the nursing needs of Peter Farley, as well as other military patients, while he was at Flanders Military Hospital in Vancouver. The pair had flown with a contingent of other nurses on the same North Star from McChord to Tokyo. They would now, along with the wounded and ill soldiers under their care, return to McChord and after that to Vancouver.

On the way home on the Canadian North Star Farley was dealing with not only with a serious case of malaria. He also had a serious mental disorder but this had been diagnosed on only a tentative basis by his American physicians in Tokyo. The nurses on the North Star were initially unaware of his mental instability. Because of the stigma, he did not openly reveal to his Canadian nurses, doctors or anyone else that he had bouts of depression, hallucinations, nightmares and flashbacks, caused mainly as a result of his prison experience, but also because of the other horrors he had witnessed in Korea. At times he could not clearly perceive reality. At other times he lived in the real world and understood the problems he faced. His mental disorder was like his malaria inasmuch as it appeared and then disappeared without any kind of logical reason or sequence. On some days he thought and behaved normally, and on other days he did not.

As the North Star winged itself eastward across the Pacific Farley experienced another nightmare. He dreamed that he was once again in a Korean communist prison camp. He was naked in a confined, claustrophobic space and being attacked and bitten by a swarm of giant mosquitoes. He was being beaten with spiked leather belts.

"Stop you sadistic bastards!" he screamed. "I don't know anything about germ warfare! I am a Canadian and not an American!" He suddenly realized that he was dreaming. He woke up and looked suspiciously in all directions.

"Why were you screaming? Did you have a bad dream?" he was asked by Lieutenant Smythe. He stared blankly and did not respond. He closed his eyes and pretended to sleep again. He remained mostly silent for the rest of his journey.

They arrived at Flanders Military Hospital, after stops in Alaska and McChord, in Vancouver three days later. Farley was hospitalized, but only for malaria. The American medical report from Tokyo had not arrived. His Canadian physicians were not immediately aware of his psychotic symptoms. His unusual behaviour was attributed to his bouts of high malarial fever.

One morning, shortly after his arrival at Flanders Hospital, and during a period of remission from his malarial and mental difficulties, he sat on a couch in the main hallway with Lieutenant Jeong-hui Song, the Korean apprentice nurse assigned to his care. He was able, on an interim basis, to think clearly and realistically. He recalled that there were other more important women in his life, and one in particular, but he could not, in spite of strong feelings of guilt engendered by his disloyalty, stop himself from trying to arrange a liaison with Song.

"Jean," he said, using the anglicized name he had given her. Jeong-hui was too hard to pronounce. "You are a lovely woman. Forgive me for saying so. I am very attracted to you. I did not realize Korean women could be so beautiful. The ones I saw in Korea were refugees and dressed mostly in rags. I hope you are single. It doesn't matter. Can we have dinner together after I get out of this place?"

Song was indeed a beautiful woman with classical Korean physical characteristics. Her radiant black hair was kept in a western style pony tail. She had dark, bright, slightly rounded oriental eyes, a perfect complexion and a slim figure. At 5 feet, 5 inches, she was taller than most Korean women.

Like most women, Song was strongly attracted to Farley, but she was extremely shy and lowered her head after his unexpected dinner invitation. She needed to consult with Janet Smythe, her mentor, but Smythe was away on a course for two days. *"Was it dinner or something else he wants?"* she asked herself.

She was still trying to decide how to respond when a black and white dog suddenly entered the front door of the Hospital. It wagged its tail and came running over to Farley. It had a collar and a short leash hanging from its neck.

"This can't be!" Farley said very excitedly. "This is my dog. It is Pacek, the same black and white dog that saved me from certain death when I was five years old!" He got down on his knees and hugged the friendly dog. Tears came to his eyes.

"Where you live? You had five years old?" Jeong-hui asked with some astonishment in her broken, heavily-accented English. She was not aware of Farley's mental instability. "That was 15 years in past? This not same dog."

"My father worked as a section labourer on the CN Railway in Manitoba," Farley explained. "We lived in a converted boxcar near the tracks with bushes everywhere. There were no people living anywhere near us. One day I wandered into the bushes and my dog Pacek, as always, followed me."

"So how dog save you?" she asked sympathetically.

Farley continued hugging the dog and tears continued to roll down his cheeks. "My father and grandmother," he continued, "searched and yelled desperately as soon as they saw that I was missing. I tried to answer but they could not hear my weak, five year old voice. Then they heard Pacek barking. My father ran in the direction of the barking. He found Pacek and me in some bushes more than a mile away from home. Pacek was my best friend and he saved my life."

Farley paused and patted the dog's head. "Then Pacek disappeared," he continued. "I don't know why he went away or where he went, but I always hoped that he would come back one day. I cried for many days when he left. I loved Pacek. And now Pacek is back! My prayers have finally been answered!"

At that moment a short, chubby hospital security guard in a dark blue uniform and peaked hat suddenly arrived. He grabbed the dog by its leash and began dragging it to the front door. The dog resisted and the guard kicked it.

Farley was enraged. "You fucking son of a bitch!" he screamed in a loud voice. He delivered several blows to the guard's head. The guard dropped the leash, gurgled and fell to the floor in an unconscious heap.

Two burly military policemen were standing a short distance away and they ran towards the scene of the conflict. Farley was on his knees and hugging the dog when they arrived. "You are under arrest," both said almost simultaneously. One tried to pull the dog away. Farley stood up, and fueled by a strong surge of adrenalin, delivered several blows to their heads. Both were bleeding profusely from their noses and mouths before they were able to subdue and handcuff Farley, but not until a third military policeman arrived to assist them.

CHAPTER 38
THE PSYCHIATRIST

Following his violent outbursts with the hospital security guard and military police Farley was sedated and confined to a room in an isolated ward. He was then charged with assault and referred for a psychiatric assessment. A psychiatrist arrived in Farley's room on the following day.

"Sergeant Farley?" the gray-haired, distinguished-looking man with horn-rimmed glasses and white laboratory coat asked as he entered the hospital room. He carried a notebook and pen and had a stethoscope hanging from his neck.

The tall, somewhat emaciated young man with handsome features, freckles, green eyes and light red hair rose from a chair and looked suspiciously at the intruder. He wore an unbuttoned khaki Canadian army battle dress tunic of WWII vintage. A single red, white and blue Military Medal ribbon was attached above the left pocket.

"Yes, I'm Sergeant Farley," Farley responded. "And who are

you? Where is my dog? Where is Pacek?"

"I'm Dr. Henry Stanhope. Don't worry. The dog is being looked after. I'm here to help you with your problems. I need to take some notes while we are talking. Please excuse me when you see me writing."

Stanhope glanced at the medical summary on the sheet that he was holding. He noted, in particular, that Farley was 6 feet, 3 inches tall and that he had weighed 200 pounds at the time of enrollment in August, 1950. His current weight was 160 pounds. Why had Farley lost 40 pounds? Stanhope was concerned.

Before he could question Farley about his substantial loss of weight while in Korea Farley interrupted him. "Why are you here?" Farley asked. "To see me about my problems? What problems? Is it because I punched out an abusive guard? He deserved it and I am not sorry. Are you an army psychiatrist?" His voice betrayed anger and annoyance. "I want to see my dog."

"Sit down again, please, Sergeant," Stanhope said. "Your dog is in good care." He pulled up another chair and sat facing Farley. "Yes, I'm a psychiatrist, but I'm not in the army. I'm on a contract with the Department of Veterans Affairs and Defence Headquarters in Ottawa. Don't worry. I am very familiar with the army. I served as a medical officer during World War II and took my psychiatric training after I returned home in 1945."

"What makes you think I need help, sir? It is true that I'm exhausted and troubled in some ways as a result of my experiences in the Korean War, but I consider myself to be perfectly sane. I have some serious doubts about psychiatry. Psychiatrists do a lot of theorizing, but they do not have much scientific evidence for their theories. They do a lot of guessing."

"And how did you come to this conclusion?"

"I took pre-medical courses at the University of Manitoba for two years before I joined the army to go to the Korean War."

"I don't think that pre-medical students study much psychiatry during the first two years," Stanhope said in a surprised voice as he wrote in his notebook.

"That's true," Farley replied. He was feeling unusually expansive, and decided that he wanted to talk with Stanhope, a medical specialist with whom he could share and test his ideas and concerns.

"But," Farley continued, "I have read a large number of books on psychiatry and psychology. I have a photographic memory and all of this information has remained in my mind. The medical library at the University of Manitoba has an excellent selection. One day, when I graduate from medicine, I will probably specialize in psychiatry."

"I am a psychiatrist and I am flattered by your strong interest in my profession. What has generated this interest?"

"My father suffered from schizophrenia and was confined to a mental hospital for a period of time. I have read several books on the subject because I was concerned that I might have inherited a predisposition to this mental illness. I am certain that I don't have schizophrenia. I do not suffer from delusions and I do not hear unreal voices. I do not act bizarrely. I am familiar with the symptoms and I don't have them."

Farley then stopped speaking and looked at the floor. He suddenly realized that he had revealed information that he had been keeping strictly to himself. The sedation medication he had been given was having a relaxing impact on him. He felt at ease and relieved and decided to continue.

Dr. Stanhope, at this point in the conversation, concluded that it would be best if he went along with Farley's comments, even though he was annoyed, as a physician, with what he considered to be expressions of limited medical knowledge. He also began to assess Farley's symptoms.

"Predisposition is a valid concept," Stanhope said with

assurance. "We believe that many mental conditions are linked to problems with genes, but that mental illness only occurs when a psychological trauma of some kind takes place. In other words, even if you are genetically susceptible does not mean that you will inevitably suffer from a mental illness. Other factors, such as extreme stress, need to be present."

"I remember reading about the daughter of a Jewish holocaust survivor," Farley interjected. "Apparently the daughter felt melancholia and guilt for being alive. She suffered from depression and anxiety even though she had been born in Canada and had never personally experienced the horrors of the Nazi death camps in Europe. This is an added immediate hereditary dimension that needs to be explored."

Stanhope was impressed by Farley's observation. He had never encountered anything of this kind in his psychiatric studies or practice. "That's very interesting", he said. "About 20% of Canadians will experience a mental illness of some kind. If we look far enough, all of us will find problem genes of some kind."

"The worst thing about mental illness, sir, is the stigma," Farley continued. "When my father was confined to a mental hospital because of schizophrenia, there was a deathly silence. People, including even my closest friends, did not ask about his illness or express any kind of sympathy. They said nothing. Although I was confident of my own good mental health, I worried about the genetics. Did I carry genes that might emerge in my children, if indeed I ever had children? Should I avoid marriage? Should I decide not to bring children into the world because of my suspect genes?"

"I understand," Stanhope said sympathetically. "Deathly silence, as you call it, is an unfortunate frequent response to mental illness. But what about your experience in the army? Have you felt any stigma in relation to your current troubles?"

Stanhope, whose oldest son was suffering from bouts of severe depression, was subconsciously following the same tradition of silence. He said nothing about his son.

"Yes, there is a huge stigma," Farley replied. I did not personally experience any because no one knew about my problem when I was in Korea or after I came back to Canada. I vaguely remember having a discussion with an American medical officer at the hospital in Tokyo, but I kept most of it to myself. Soldiers who suffer from shell shock or combat stress, or whatever it is called, are often considered to be cowards or malingerers by other soldiers and their officers."

"Isn't that something that only happened in previous wars?" Stanhope asked.

"Previous wars?" Farley replied. "I remember reading that 25 Canadian soldiers in World War I were shot by Canadian firing squads because they were so-called deserters from the front line. The British executed about 300 of their own people for the same reason. We don't shoot people with war neurosis any more. We just label them as cowardly scum and send them home in disgrace."

"Marriage takes place and children are born, often without genetic considerations of any kind," Stanhope observed, "even though most parents have suspect genes, as you call them. My father and his brother died of heart attacks, probably as the result of bad genes, when they were still in their early 70's. This knowledge did not prevent me from marrying and having two children. I decided to take a chance. All parents take chances. An element of luck is involved when we procreate." He was willing to talk about the heart problems of his father and uncle, but not about the depression problems of his son.

"Heart attacks," Farley said emphatically, "are not subject to shame and stigma as in the case of schizophrenia. When my father began acting bizarrely someone reported him and two

Royal Canadian Mounted policemen in uniform came to take him away. I was 10 years old and I was terrified. They took him to a mental hospital. Fortunately, he improved after a few months and came home again."

Farley paused briefly and then continued. "Many, I think, have a hard time dealing with mental disease because some mentally ill people are violent and dangerous."

"Yes," Stanhope replied, "but only a small percentage of the mentally ill are violent towards others. They are more inclined to hurt themselves. The vast majority of murderers are not mentally ill."

"But most people do not understand these numbers. They are afraid of the mentally ill. The genetic problem is still there," Farley said quietly.

"I understand," Stanhope responded. "But life is a crapshoot, as they say in the army. We can never be sure of the results. And besides, even if you happen to have the genetic weakness you have mentioned, you should not write yourself off. You probably have more positive characteristics than negative ones. I am sure that you are highly intelligent and creative. Perhaps you will one day, if you go into medicine, find a cure for cancer or depression, or some other serious human malady."

"Extreme stress needs to be present to develop mental illness?" Farley asked. "Yes, I experienced extreme stress in Korea, but I don't think that you or anyone else can do very much about it. I do not wish to sound disrespectful, sir, but are you a disciple of Sigmund Freud? Am I supposed to lie down while you interview me?" Farley spoke with trace of humour and annoyance in his voice. "Hasn't Freud been discredited?"

"It is not necessary for you to lie down," Stanhope replied with a slight smile. "Some of Freud's theories have been discredited, but he still has a major influence on modern psychiatry. He said, for instance, that sexual desire is the primary motivational energy in life, and that theory has been at least partly challenged by some prominent and influential psychiatrists."

"But I agree with that theory. I have read most of Freud's work. I have a photographic memory. I remember everything. In his *Three Essays* he wrote about the importance of interpersonal relationships. He makes sense. Sexual desire has been a powerful force in my life. It began during my first year in school at the age of six, when I developed a strong sexual attraction for a gorgeous young teacher with the face of an angel and prominent breasts. I felt a strange excitement and urge to touch her, even though I knew nothing about sexual behaviour at that age. It continued and developed in the years that followed. I fell in love several times in elementary and high school. I fall in love very easily."

"That is normal," Stanhope interjected. "I think that all boys go through an experience of this kind, although in varying degrees. Perhaps you are at the upper end of the scale."

"Whenever I met pretty girls or women," Farley continued. "I was always strongly sexually aroused. When I was 16 I slept with a beautiful woman who was 27 years old. I loved her intensely but she moved to the United States. I felt guilty because I found it difficult to be loyal to whatever woman was the most important in my life at any particular time. I suppressed feelings of guilt and disloyalty until after my encounters had finished. I concluded that I used repression as a defence mechanism. I wonder if I have a sexual addiction of some kind."

"That's interesting," Dr. Stanhope said with a smile. "Sexual desire, even without strong personal relationships, is normal in my opinion. Freud also had a theory about what he called the defence mechanism of repression. This theory was enhanced during the period of the First World War by a British psychiatrist, W.H. Rivers, who said that the worst symptoms of shell shock, or war neurosis, as he called it, was the attempt by the sufferers to try to banish from their minds memories of the terrible events that they had experienced and witnessed. "

"I wonder," Farley replied, "why I have been affected so much by my experiences in Korea, but that many of my comrades have been relatively unmoved. They see death and destruction but it does not seem to matter much to them."

"I believe," Stanhope said emphatically, "that some people are born with a strong tendency towards sensitivity. Death and destruction, as you call it, affects them much more than most other people. If they possess this characteristic of hyper-sensitivity, soldiers may develop war neurosis, or battle fatigue as it has been called. It appears that you have this trait. You must try to overcome your bad memories about Korea."

"But I can't."

"You must try. I have to leave to for another appointment. I will be back at 0900 hours tomorrow to discuss your experience in Korea. I am pleased. We have had a good discussion." Stanhope stood up and left the room.

Farley did not respond. His mind was clear and realistic. His memory was intact. His malaria was in remission. Speaking with Dr. Stanhope had been very helpful.

His thoughts went back to the four most important women in his life, all of whom he loved intensely. Michele, Sonia, Jean and Morgan he clearly recalled. Where were they now? Did they know that he was in Flanders and recovering from war neurosis caused by his internment as a prisoner of war? Did they know that he was recovering from a severe, life-threatening case of malaria? Did they care?

At that moment Lieutenant Jeong-hui Song, his Korean nurse, entered his room. "Medication for you I have!" she said enthusiastically with a bright smile.

"You are my medication, Jean!" he responded in a deep voice. "I love you more each time I see you." His eyes surveyed her beautiful face, slim, enticing figure and exotic, bright oriental eyes. The four most important women in his life suddenly disappeared from his thoughts. "When are we having dinner together?" he eagerly asked. "I invited you the other day but you did not answer."

"I ask Lieutenant Smythe about our dinner. She say you sergeant and I lieutenant. No dinner should take place. I have commission rank. No fraternization allowed. But I like you so much. When you leave hospital I see you somewhere, sometime. No tell anyone. This be our secret."

"You make me very happy, Jean. Thinking of you will help me to get better. Do you have a civilian dress? We can't be seen in uniform together."

"I have beautiful dress. You will love it."

CHAPTER 39
FARLEY'S KOREAN EXPERIENCE

Dr. Stanhope, as he had promised, returned to Farley's room again at 0900 hours on the following day.

"Talk to me about Korea," Stanhope began. I am here to help. You have nothing to lose. Everything you relate will be kept confidential. Please tell me about the events that caused you the most stress in Korea. There were many, I'm sure, but go to one or two that affected you the most." Stanhope raised his pen and wrote another brief note.

"Alright. Here is one I cannot forget. It was early February and the temperature was about minus 30 degrees. Very cold winds always blow in from Siberia to Korea in the winter. We were fired on by snipers from a small village and we responded by shelling the village with hundreds of rounds from our 81 mm. mortars. After the shelling, as we moved through the village, I heard children crying from the inside of a badly damaged house. I looked inside and found a young woman with her head almost blown off and the entrails of her stomach spilled onto the dirt floor. Two small children, a boy of three or four, and a girl a bit older, were slightly wounded and bleeding from shrapnel and were crying hysterically at her side."

Farley suddenly stopped speaking. Tears came to his eyes. "I am sorry," he continued. "All of this is very difficult for me. An orange cat and a small black dog sat cowering next to the dead woman. I opened a tin of beef and offered it to the children. They refused to eat and continued to cry hysterically. I divided the beef into two portions and gave them to the cat and dog, who devoured it quickly. I opened more beef and fed the animals again. I placed several cans of rations, all I had left, on the floor beside the children. I wanted to help more, but we were ordered to move."

"I can see why this would be a very traumatic experience for you," Dr. Stanhope said sympathetically. "Then what happened?"

"A medical orderly arrived at the house and told me that he would look after the children. I have never forgotten them. The dead woman, children, cat and dog often appear in my dreams. They are all hungry and ask me for food. Sometimes the woman opens her eyes and screams. I worry because I seem to have more sympathy for the cat and dog than the woman."

"You should not worry," Stanhope said. "When did your strong love of animals begin? Has it always been there?" he asked.

"I am, and have been since early childhood, an extreme animal lover, and especially of cats. I also love dogs and horses. Maybe it's because domesticated animals are more vulnerable than people. Cats, dogs and horses depend on people and often demonstrate an intense love for the people they know. Their characteristics are almost human."

"I understand," Stanhope said sympathetically. "There is

nothing unusual about your love of animals. I have two dogs and a cat and I love them dearly. "

In actual fact, Stanhope did not like cats. A cat lived in his household only because his son, who suffered from depression, had asked for one. But as a physician he was able to understand that some people have a strong, possibly genetically generated love of cats, dogs and other animals.

"On another occasion," Farley continued, "I directed a large amount of mortar fire into a group of Chinese soldiers who were massed in a valley. It was a terrible slaughter. I don't know how many died, but it may have been hundreds."

"But that was your job. Didn't you also do this on other occasions?"

"Yes, but this was different. The Chinese had a number of pack horses in their midst, and some of these horses were injured or died in the mortar barrage I ordered. I don't know why, but the deaths and suffering of the horses bothered me much more than the deaths of the Chinese. Maybe that was because the Chinese were preparing to kill me and my comrades, but that the horses were innocent animals who did not deserve to suffer from wounds or to die. I remembered my horse Charlie at home in Canada and wondered if he missed me. Yes, I am a very intense animal lover."

"Many people are animal lovers. That is why we have humane societies," Stanhope pointed out.

"I also learned," Farley continued, "after I became a prisoner of war, that the mortar barrage that I ordered killed a number of Korean refugees, mostly women and children, who were camped near the Chinese. I have never forgiven myself. At times I feel like a murderer."

"You were a prisoner of war? Tell me about that. Were you treated properly? Were you subjected to torture or mistreatment of any kind?" As he spoke, Stanhope quickly scribbled another note.

"Yes, I was tortured. I was kicked and punched frequently. I was locked into a very small cubicle and subjected to what was called the water treatment. Drops of water dropped onto my head from above for many hours at a time. But the worst thing was the confinement in the very small space. I have suffered from claustrophobia since I was a small child, and this created a condition of hysteria. The other prisoners and I lived mostly on a diet of cabbages, potatoes and a bit of rice. I lost a lot of weight."

"Yes, your medical record tells me that you lost 40 pounds in Korea. "You say that you had claustrophobia as a child. Please tell me more."

"We lived in a converted boxcar on a small farm near the tracks of the CN Railway close to the town of Sweet Grass, Manitoba, where my father, a Ukrainian, worked as a section labourer. In keeping with the farm practice of his ancestors in Ukraine, he dug a deep pit where he kept milk, butter, meat and other perishable foods. It was very cool at the bottom, and especially because he dumped ice into it. The CN cut large chunks of ice from a nearby river and stored it in sawdust during summers in a tall ice storage building. My father had access to it. The man who was responsible for the ice building was a friend of my father, and he allowed my father to take ice."

"That's interesting. But how did you experience claustrophobia?" Dr. Stanhope asked.

"I was about five years old at the time. My father used to lower me on a rope to the bottom of this pit so that I could retrieve the food that was located there. I was terrified because I thought that the dirt walls would collapse on top of me, but I said nothing to my father. I was worried that he that he would be angry with me and call me a coward. He was a stern disciplinarian, and at 6 feet, 6 inches, a very large man. I was sometimes afraid of him even though he never hit me or threatened me in any way."

"Are there any other symptoms that you can describe? You previously told me that you are exhausted and troubled in some ways."

"I sometimes feel very angry. I have never hit or hurt anyone, except on one occasion when I smashed my revolver into the face of a scumbag in our battalion. Actually, he was lucky, because I almost shot him. My occasional outbursts of rage frighten me. I find it difficult to tolerate what I consider to be inappropriate or stupid behaviour on the part of others. I feel a strong need to punish them violently and physically. Fortunately I am usually able to contain this urge. The hospital guard was an exception. He deserved what he got."

"I often feel rejected by a lot of Canadians," Farley continued, "most of whom have never experienced war, and some of whom consider soldiers to be virtual criminals. Letters to the editors and newspapers, and even speeches in our Parliament, mostly by communist sympathizers, often voice opposition to our involvement in Korea. One day the people of Korea will express gratitude for our sacrifices and Canadians will understand, but that will not happen for many years, and probably at a time when I am old and no longer care. And besides, I sometimes feel that I am not even a Canadian."

"Not a Canadian? How is that?" Stanhope asked. "Farley sounds like an English surname."

"Yes, it sounds English. The people of Sweet Grass and elsewhere call me a Ukrainian even though my mother was English and Scottish. My family, for many generations, has recorded and discussed our history, and I am aware of the fact that I also have Irish, Polish, German, French, aboriginal Cree Indian and Jewish ancestors. Is my red hair Irish or Jewish? I don't know. One of my grandfathers was Jewish, very tall and red-headed.

Or maybe my hair is Ukrainian because some Ukrainians also have red hair. Red Vikings invaded Ukraine a thousand years ago. Heredity fascinates me!"

"You were born in Canada and you are certainly a Canadian," Dr. Stanhope said.

"Yes, but when I joined the army they asked me to identify my nationality on a questionnaire. I told them I was a Canadian, but they said that was unacceptable. A drill sergeant in Calgary once became angry with me and called me a bohunk. I have also been called a bohunk by drunks in beer parlours. The army classifies me as a Ukrainian because my father is a Ukrainian. Canadians, apparently, are defined as those whose parents are English, or Scottish, or maybe Irish, and whose families have been in Canada for several generations."

"I have flashbacks and nightmares," he continued after a slight pause. "I experience the same traumatic events over and over again. I also suffer from periods of depression. Helplessness is a good way to describe it. What is the meaning of my life and that of others? Does it really matter if we behave honourably or badly? We will all die sooner or later. I experience deep gloom."

"Do you hear unreal voices?" Stanhope asked. "Do you ever have any strong beliefs that are not substantiated by evidence? In other words, do you suffer from delusions?"

Farley did not answer the question. Farley knew that Stanhope was asking questions about schizophrenic symptoms. Farley had heard voices but he always knew that they were not real. Even in the depths of his nightmares, because of his strong intellect and knowledge about mental illness, he was eventually able to focus on reality.

"Why did the Chinese, Koreans and horses have to die in such horrible circumstances?" Farley continued. "Will God forgive me for my complicity? I feel very guilty. I see no hope for the future. When in the depths of depression, I sometimes wish that I would die then and there, rather than later and in some other place. All of these flashbacks, bad dreams and negative feelings occur even though I have done a lot of research and understand the reason for them. I feel trapped and unable to escape. I also have periodic outbreaks of high fever because of the malaria that I developed".

Farley suddenly realized that he had revealed much more about himself than he had initially intended. He stopped speaking and lowered his eyes.

"Malaria? Did you take anything for it?" Dr. Stanhope asked.

Farley remained silent for more than a minute. He looked despondent and confused.

"Chloroquine," he finally responded. "That's what they gave me at the American field hospital, a so-called M.A.S.H. It helped for a while but I still get high fevers once in a while. Our battalion medical officer, Major Karpinski, told me that chloroquine sometimes causes depression and anxiety. As a result, I stopped taking it."

Stanhope remained silent for a minute as he wrote into his notebook.

"I notice that you are wearing the Military Medal on your tunic," Stanhope said following the minute of silence. "That tells me that you performed bravely on the field of battle. Can you tell me something about this award?"

"It was given to me after I went on a dangerous patrol and directed mortar fire on the large group of Chinese that I mentioned previously. That's ironic, I know. I was given an award for an event that has haunted me ever since it happened."

"You should be proud of your achievement. You performed admirably even though you were under great stress."

"I was actually recommended for a Distinguished Conduct Medal, which, as you know, is higher than a Military Medal and second only to the Victoria Cross."

"So why didn't you get a DCM?"

"The recommendation of my battalion commander, a Canadian Lieutenant-Colonel, had to be approved by the commanding officer of our British commonwealth division, who was a British major-general. He turned the recommendation down. I later heard that he did not think much of colonial Canadians. He gave out awards freely, but only to soldiers in the British units. On one occasion he gave a Victoria Cross, the highest award, to a British Lieutenant-Colonel whose bad defensive strategy led to the destruction of his battalion. He got his medal because he behaved heroically while a prisoner of war."

"That's unfortunate. I am sure that his decision about your award was disappointing. Did the British make you angry?"

"Yes, some British officers made me very angry, but not ordinary British soldiers. We got along well with them. We also liked the Australians and New Zealanders. We were especially close to the Americans. We talk like Americans and act like Americans. Some British officers were arrogant and pretentious, and especially if they came from the so-called upper classes. I have read that many received commissions because of their family connections, rather than as the result of ability and intelligence."

"I have one final question," Stanhope said. "Even though you have lost a lot of weight you exhibited an extraordinary amount of strength when you knocked out the hospital attendant and punched the faces of the two large and powerful military policemen who came to arrest you. Both policemen sustained facial injuries. Where did you find the strength to deliver such violent blows?"

"I did not mean to seriously injure anyone and I am sorry," Farley replied quietly. "I read about this extraordinary unleashing of strength in a medical journal at the University of Manitoba. Under acute stress a body's sympathetic nervous system pumps adrenalin into the blood stream. Apparently my body is especially prone to this kind of reaction. I become very, very strong. I respond whenever animals or humans are being hurt or in peril."

"So this has also happened in the past?" Stanhope asked.

"Yes. More than once. When I was 15 years old I saw a farmer hitting his horse with a steel bar. I punched the farmer several times until he was unconscious. I was summoned to court, scolded but then excused because the judge, apparently an animal lover like me, concluded that my action against the farmer was justified. The farmer was investigated for other incidents of animal cruelty. The farmer was severely fined and was prohibited by the court from owning animals."

"Excuse me for a moment," Stanhope said as he glanced at the brief notes that he had written. He read silently: "Medical student with some basic psychiatric knowledge; schizophrenic father; promiscuity; strong carnal desire and guilty feelings for disloyalty to women he loves; claustrophobia and related abuse as a prisoner of war; uncertain about his Canadian identity; relapsing malaria; classical symptoms of war neurosis, with anger, rejection, depression, flashbacks and nightmares; extremely sensitive to human and especially animal suffering; appears to gain extraordinary adrenalin fueled strength during periods of stress, and especially insofar as animals are concerned."

"I have to leave you now, Sergeant Farley," Stanhope said. "I have another appointment. But I think that we have made progress. I believe that I now have a good understanding of your difficulties. I think that I will be able to have the charges against you quashed because of your medical circumstances. I will be back again before too long."

Farley did not respond. He turned his back to Stanhope and stared out of the window. "I suddenly have a severe headache and I think that I am developing a fever," he said in a low and inaudible voice. He was speaking to himself and not to his visitor. "I need to rest. I am very tired." He felt very alone, as if Stanhope had never arrived and as if they had never spoken. He wanted to sleep but was afraid that the flashbacks and nightmares would return.

An avid reader, he remembered that Albert Schweitzer had once said that "two means of refuge from life's miseries are music and cats." Farley agreed, but he knew that beautiful women also provided relief.

On the following afternoon Jeong-hui Song visited Farley in his room. He was very excited by her presence. She was as beautiful as usual. He jumped up from his bed and held her in a warm embrace for a long minute. His mind and body suddenly felt normal.

"You still want dinner by me?" she asked with some hesitation.

"Yes, I would love to have dinner with you!" he exclaimed.

"This be a secret with us," she continued. "Janet Smythe away again for some days. I all alone. Join me at front door at 8:00 this evening. I be there. We will get taxi. We will have dinner at the Colonial Room in Hotel Vancouver. We be great friends."

They travelled that evening together by taxi to the Hotel Vancouver in keeping with the arrangements made by Jeong-hui. Farley insisted on paying for the taxi and dinner.

They discussed their lives in Korea. She was born and lived in Seoul, and had trained to be a nurse in a university in that city. Several members of her family had died in the war. Her parents still lived there.

"I love Canada," she said. "One day I stay here. I also love you. You make me feel so good! How I can say this to you?"

"I love you too, Jean. But I should tell you that there are

other women in my life."

"Other women? They be for another time. This be my time. I always will remember my dinner with you."

Following the dinner they took a taxi back to the Flanders Military Hospital. She was surprised but secretly relieved that he had not tried to bring their friendship to a more intimate level. She was a virgin and was unsure of how she would respond if he initiated a sexual encounter. She was a Baptist Christian and had some serious reservations about pre-marital sex.

Farley's mind was now on the verge of a full recovery and he suddenly realized that Morgan was the woman that he needed in his life. He was sexually and emotionally attracted to Jeong-hui but a sense of strong loyalty to Morgan prevented him from carrying out any kind of intimacy with the beautiful Korean nurse.

Before entering the front door of Flanders they held each other in a warm embrace.

He kissed her gently on her lips. "Good night, Jean," he said. "Thank you for being my friend and for helping me to be healthy again."

"I remember you forever. You be my favourite Canadian," she said with a sigh. "Forever and forever."

CHAPTER 40
THE REST OF HIS LIFE: PART I

Farley's frequent conversations and his memorable dinner with Jeong-hui helped him to experience periodic episodes of normality. His body and mind gradually improved, but his first few weeks at Flanders were often hazy, erratic and difficult. He sometimes lived in a dream world. He was attended to on a regular basis by Dr. Henry Stanhope, the psychiatrist employed by the Army and Veterans Affairs, and these psychotherapy sessions were highly effective.

Three elderly ladies from the Imperial Order of the Daughters of the Empire came to see him shortly after he arrived in Vancouver. They brought him chocolates, cookies and magazines. "You are a true hero of the Empire!" they said.

He was polite and thanked them for the gifts and visit but he did not know what Empire they were talking about.

Two American officers, with Canadian official military approval after a lengthy bureaucratic delay, visited Farley a week after his arrival in Vancouver. They presented him with a U.S. Silver Star for the bravery that he had demonstrated when he had wiped out the nest of 10 Chinese in Marine territory near the Han River in Korea several months earlier. He accepted the award quietly but did not remember the event and did not know why he was being honoured.

His two brothers in Vancouver, Nick and Harry, tried to visit him on the day he arrived in Vancouver, but he rejected them. "I don't have any brothers," he told the hospital staff.

A woman in Hawaii phoned him on his second day at Flanders but he refused to speak to her. She said that she was Laura Morgan, an American nurse, and that they had been in Tokyo together, but he did not remember her. "I want to be left alone," he said. The hospital respected his wishes and he remained in isolation from that point on.

In his mind he returned to Sweet Grass. His father Orest, Billie, Fido and Charlie greeted him warmly and with great happiness. He dreamed, in vivid detail, that a welcome home party was held in the Ukrainian Hall, but that not very many people came.

He paid a visit to the local Royal Canadian Legion hall. Two members of the Legion, both of whom had served as army clerks in Canada during WWII, told Peter that he had been in a police action and not a real war. "The Korean conflict", they said, "was not a great crusade against an evil empire, or even a war to end all wars. It was a minor military incident that would soon be forgotten."

He became very angry and called the veterans "zombies", the term used to identify soldiers who had stayed in Canada during the war and who had never fired a shot in anger. He surged into a violent rage and punched both zombies repeatedly until they became unconscious. The Legion expelled him and told him never to return. He left the Legion and became a member of the

Army, Navy and Air Force veterans organization.

His greatest disappointment was in not being able to see Sonia Kereliuk again. She had married Johnny Michaluk and had moved to Toronto where he temporarily played for the Toronto Maple Leafs. His father Orest told Peter that Johnny had been sent to the minor leagues. Although Peter was secretly pleased with Johnny's reduced status on one hand, he was also ashamed of his jealousy. He always considered himself to be a better hockey player than Johnny, and had often, like many Canadian young men, dreamed that he would one day play in the big league. A career in NHL hockey, during his teen years, was even more appealing to Farley than one in the professions such as medicine, law or education.

On other occasions he clearly remembered that the women in his life, Michelle Brown, Sonia Kereliuk, Jean Haines, Laura Morgan and Jeong-hui Song were all beautiful, highly lovable and intelligent human beings. He remembered the Snow White lyrics, "mirror, mirror, on the wall, who is the fairest of them all?" Jean Haines, he decided, was the fairest and most physically perfect. Sonia, Michelle and Jeong-hui came a close second. But it was Laura Morgan that he loved the most. Why had Morgan disappeared from his life? Where had she gone?

"Sonia should have waited for me," he thought. But he was not sure that he still wanted her. He remembered that Sonia did not love cats, dogs and horses, and that this would probably have been a major handicap in their marriage. It was not his fault, he reasoned, that she should now have to live in Cleveland, or Providence, or some other minor league God-forsaken place.

CHAPTER 41
THE REST OF HIS LIFE: PART II

Sergeant Peter Farley spent six months in the Flanders Hospital in Vancouver. Under the care of Dr. Henry Stanhope and dedicated nurses, his mind returned to normality and reality. He no longer had flashbacks or nightmares.

Dr. Henry Stanhope, whose oldest son had recently committed suicide as the result of severe depression, developed a very strong empathy for Farley. Stanhope decided to devote many personal, unpaid hours in order to treat Farley. The amount of psychiatric time allotted to Farley by the government was very limited and inadequate. Psychotherapy was needed, and Stanhope had a master's degree in psychology as well as post-graduate specialization in psychiatry. Farley regained his mental health mainly because of Stanhope's dedication.

After his release from the hospital and discharge from the army, he stayed at home in Sweet Grass for a month and then enrolled in the University of Manitoba's School of Medicine.

Following his graduation he began working as a family physician in Happy Valley, a small Manitoba town.

In spite of several attempts to contact Laura Morgan during his years as a medical student, he was not successful. She had become, following his recovery to good mental health at Flanders Hospital, the focus of his life. He still fondly remembered Michelle Brown, Sonia Kereliuk, Jean Haines, and Jeonghui, but only as footnotes in his life. His previously uncontrolled urge to be intimate with more than one woman was now gone.

He believed that Morgan had received his letters because they were never returned as undeliverable. Letters mailed to members of her family in Minneapolis went unanswered. If she had a telephone number, it was unlisted and not available.

Shortly after he began working as a physician, he traveled to Minneapolis to try to find her. The names and addresses that Morgan had given to him in Japan had been retained in his wallet. His contacts with members of her family drew either curiously vague responses or none at all.

"She isn't here," her sister Martha answered.

"I think that she is living somewhere in California, or maybe in Hawaii," her cousin Henry replied.

Her brother's wife Anita said that "my husband is on a business trip and I have not seen Laura for ages. I think she still in the army somewhere."

Her mother was not home. She was on a trip, Farley was told. Laura's father had died several years earlier.

It was almost as though Morgan had disappeared from the face of the Earth, never to be seen again.

The first year after his discharge from Flanders Military Hospital was the hardest, with his insides aching constantly with longing to see her again. From time to time he heard *Laura* being played on radio stations, and on these occasions overwhelming nostalgia and a searing sense of loss surged through him.

There were also other frequent reminders. Sometimes, at a distance, he would see the flash of a young woman's red hair somewhere in a crowd. Was it Morgan? At these times he felt an urge to run forward, to look into her eyes, and to hope that she would somehow appear again with her infectious smile, freckles, bright blue eyes and mischievous voice.

Why had this woman meant so much to him? After all, he had only seen her on a few brief occasions, and often under the most trying of circumstances. They had spent time together in a M.A.S.H. tent, in a muddy Korean rice paddy, at a Japanese hotel for one ecstatic and memorable night, and for hectic and perilous days as captives in Tokyo. Was that all? Wasn't there anything more? In his darkest moments he contemplated his fate with anger and bitter resentment. Why had God punished him?

There were poignant stimuli: red dresses; oriental faces; American women in uniform; rubbing alcohol; flowery perfume; nurses; and the songs of the early 1950's. For the first few years, until he was permanently cured, his high malarial fevers returned from time to time, along with the associated delirium and euphoria. During these periods he felt her presence in vivid detail, with every feature of her personality, voice and body etched into his mind with such intensity that he almost believed that she was actually with him.

Then there was his "standard Korean War dream". It occurred frequently, and was always exactly the same. He was on a ship, going back to fight another war in Korea. The smell of rotting human flesh permeated his nostrils. As he watched helplessly, large numbers of screaming Chinese soldiers with burp guns advanced towards him. Where was his rifle? Where was his .45 pistol? His hand grenades? They were all missing. He had stupidly forgotten them at home.

"Peter! Peter!" Morgan's voice kept calling from a distance until he woke up shivering. And yet, strangely enough, these dreams could not be classified as frightening or painful as in the past. Indeed, he looked forward to them with a kind of pleasurable fatalism, for they reminded him of the most exciting period of his life. The former disturbing dreams that had generated during the time of the Korean War were now an unpleasant but distant memory.

On the eve of the 10th anniversary of the armistice that ended the Korean War, Farley decided that he would return to the "land of the morning calm." The South Korean government had sent out invitations to selected Canadian war veterans to mark the anniversary, and he resolved that he would return to the places where he had spent the most significant period of his life. He wondered if, by some small chance, Morgan had also been invited, and he decided to write to her one more time.

"*Dear Morgan,*" he wrote. "*I have not heard from you since we were last together in Tokyo. I have often thought of you over the years, and I've wondered about the course of your life. Did you stay in nursing? Did you marry and have children? Why didn't you ever answer my letters or return my calls? I am sure that there are good reasons for your silence, even though they are beyond my understanding. I'm planning to go back to Korea on July 15th. The South Korean government is sponsoring an official re-visit to mark the 10th anniversary of the end of the Korean War. Why don't you come? It would be wonderful to see you again, even if only for a few days. I hope and pray that you will respond*".

He folded the letter into a plain envelope and wrote another addressed to the Department of Defence, Washington, D.C. The second letter read: "*Ladies and Gentlemen: The enclosed envelope contains a letter written to Laura Morgan, who was a nurse and a lieutenant with the U.S. Army Medical Corps in the*

Korean War. She served with the 12th M.A.S.H. She was born in 1929 in a small town in Minnesota and raised in Minneapolis. Miss Morgan was a very good friend of mine in Korea, but I lost track of her after the war. If you have a record of her where-abouts, please forward my letter to her. Alternatively, if she has been released from the Army, perhaps you can forward my letter to your Department of Veterans' Affairs. I shall be very grateful for your assistance. Sincerely, Dr. P. Farley, P.O. Box 29, Happy Valley, Manitoba, Canada.

July arrived but he did not hear from Morgan. He was disappointed but not surprised. *"Maybe she is no longer alive,"* he thought. He did not know anything about her circumstances and had no way of finding out.

In July Farley flew to Vancouver and then to Seoul, Korea. In spite of some initial political instability, South Korea had progressed rapidly in the years after the war. The Korean people proved to be very intelligent. They worked hard and began to produce modern buildings, well-stocked shops, first class restaurants and efficient industries. South Korea would eventually enjoy one of the highest standards of living in Asia and become a major world democracy and economic power.

On the third day of his visit buses took the returning veterans to Pusan, the southeastern coastal city where he had landed during the war. A military ceremony took place at the United Nations Cemetery, where a lot of his friends lay buried. He stood among the many rows of graves marked by wooden crosses. In later years these crosses would be replaced with granite monuments by a grateful South Korean Government.

As he walked further into the Canadian section of the cemetery he suddenly came to a group of names that were very familiar to him. They marked the resting places of those who had not survived the patrol across the Han River. He stood at the graves of Big Indian, Little Indian, and others. He remembered that he had some Cree Indian blood in his veins. He was suddenly overcome with emotion and began to shake. "I could easily have died and be laying here," he muttered to himself. "Only a handful of us returned from that patrol."

"Peter!" a voice suddenly called out from behind him. "It's me, Laura!" It was Morgan. Tears poured down her cheeks.

"Morgan?" Peter exclaimed. "I can't believe it!" They rushed into each others arms and remained silent for more than a minute.

"How did you get here? How did you find me?" Farley finally asked. They sat together on a nearby bench and held hands.

"I received your letter but it took me a long time to decide to come. It was too late to contact you so I came on my own. The re-visit to Korea, I learned, was for Canadian veterans only, but the Korean authorities were very helpful."

"They have always expressed gratitude for our help in the Korean War," he said.

"After I arrived in Seoul," she continued, "they told me that you had left for Pusan and that I was welcome to join you as an official member of the delegation. They said that I was being included because I was also an honoured veteran. They even transported me to Pusan on one of their buses. They were very gracious, understanding and helpful."

He suddenly noticed the beautiful diamond ring that encircled her left hand ring finger. "Morgan!" he exclaimed. "You are still wearing the ring we purchased in Tokyo! That makes me very happy. It tells me that you have not forgotten your promise to marry me."

"I have not forgotten, Peter. You have always been in my thoughts. And that reminds me. Whatever happened to the money that you deposited in the Bank of Japan?"

"It is still there. I forgot all about this money during the time I was a prisoner of war. I did not remember it until several months after my recovery at Flanders Hospital in Vancouver. Veterans Affairs paid for a large part of my medical education. My brothers in Vancouver insisted helping me financially. I left the money sitting in Japan. I secretly hoped that you would claim it, and that by doing so, you would reveal your whereabouts."

"That is your money, Peter. I left it in Tokyo because I believed that you would eventually claim it. It has probably, because of interest, more than doubled in value."

"I am going to buy you a much larger diamond ring with this money! You look wonderful, Morgan. In fact, you've changed hardly at all. We have missed 10 good years. What might have been, I mean."

"You look good too, Peter. You have not changed either. I have always regretted that things did not work out."

"Why didn't they work out?" Farley asked. "Why didn't you call me after I returned from Korea? Why didn't you answer my letters?"

"I have a confession," Morgan said quietly. "I am very sorry, Peter. Do you remember, when we were in Tokyo, that you told me about your father's schizophrenia? You said that you were worried that any children that you brought into the world might inherit this mental disease. You wondered if you should avoid marriage."

"Yes, I remember," Peter replied. "I wanted to be honest with you and to make you aware of my genetic concerns."

"At first I did not care," Morgan continued. "I was deeply in love with you and nothing else mattered. After returning from R & R in Tokyo I continued working at the 12th M.A.S.H. I was told that you had been killed in a helicopter crash and I went into a period of severe grieving."

"I was in a helicopter crash but I survived. That's when I became a prisoner of war."

"Several months later I had a conversation with a wounded

Canadian officer. I mentioned your name, and he told me that you had been a prisoner of war and that you had been sent to a military hospital in Vancouver to recover. I was deliriously happy. You were still alive!"

"So why didn't you call me at the hospital? I was there for six months?"

"I did call," she replied quietly. Tears ran down her cheeks as she spoke. "I found out that you were staying at the Flanders Military Hospital in Vancouver. I telephoned and spoke to one of your nurses, Janet Smythe."

"Yes! I remember her! She helped me to recover."

"She asked you to come to the phone to speak with me but you refused. She told me that you denied knowing anyone called Morgan. She said that you also refused to acknowledge that you had two brothers living in Vancouver, both of whom had tried to visit you. She revealed that you were mentally incapacitated, with nightmares, flashbacks, and depression."

"I'm very sorry, Morgan. I don't remember any phone calls from you or anyone else."

"I was very worried about your mental condition. I did not know that you had been tortured as a prisoner of war, and that your mental incapacity had been caused by this torture. I decided, with a great deal of reluctance, to take you out of my life. After all, you did not even seem to know of my existence."

"I don't blame you. I understand completely."

"I tried very hard, but I could not get you out of my mind. Even if you were mentally ill, and even if this illness was caused by errant genes, I still wanted to see you and be with you."

"Did you try to contact me?"

"Yes, after about six months I decided to try to find out if you had returned to Sweet Grass. I spoke to an operator who told me that you had been a prisoner of war, that you had suffered from a mental breakdown as a result of torture, and that you had just returned from Flanders Hospital in Vancouver. She said that she knew you and your family."

"Sweet Grass is a small town. Everyone knows everyone else," he said with a smile.

"The operator gave me your phone number. I called, asked for Peter Farley and a woman answered. I am Peter Farley's wife. He is away for a few days she said. I was absolutely devastated. Why didn't you tell me that you were married?"

"I wasn't married!" he exclaimed loudly in a trembling voice. "Morgan, the operator must have mistakenly connected you to the wrong Peter Farley. You must have been speaking with Rosalie, my cousin's wife!"

"You mean that your cousin's name is also Peter Farley?"

"Yes".

"I'm sorry, Peter. How could this have happened? Why didn't you tell that you had a cousin called Peter Farley?"

"We had more important things to talk about, like how we were going to get out of that horrible place on Edo Street."

"At least we have survived, and we are still here!" she said with a sigh of satisfaction. "We really were two ships passing in the night".

"Tennyson. You still remember!"

"Yes, I've always remembered the things you said to me. It is like yesterday."

A warm breeze began blowing in from the Yellow Sea. In the distant mountains they could see the scrubby pines, the steeped rice paddies, and all around them the graves of the young men they had served with a decade ago. They embraced again for several minutes and remained silent.

In the distance a trumpeter played the Last Post. A Korean military band followed with O Canada, and in acknowledgement of Morgan's presence, with the Star Spangled Banner.

"We have lost 10 years," Farley said, "but we still have the rest of your lives".

"Does that mean that you never married, and that you are free?" Laura playfully asked. A bright smile crossed her face. The tears were gone.

"I am unmarried and free," he replied with a laugh.

"So am I," she immediately responded. "And by the way, Minneapolis is always looking for good Canadian doctors. Are you willing to become an American?"

"I will do anything to make you happy," he cheerfully announced. "But maybe you would be happier as a Canadian. Are you willing to become a Canadian?"

"Yes, I am more than willing to become a Canadian. But maybe it does not matter. Maybe Canada will one day be a part of the United States. Are we not really the same country and the same people?"

EPILOGUE

Animals, circumstances, events and people in alphabetical order:

ABOUT THE COLD WAR IN 1950: In the years after the ending of World War II Peter Farley's world was one of political unrest, cultural stagnation, military confrontation, and foreboding pessimism. Leo Szillard, a distinguished nuclear physicist, predicted that all life would be extinguished within 15 years by the hydrogen bombs of the United States and the Soviet Union, even though a Soviet bomb had not yet been perfected.

In the United States primarily, but in Canada and Western Europe as well, the Soviet Union was viewed as an evil empire intent upon destroying all vestiges of human freedom, dignity and initiative. A group of U.S. politicians, led by Senator Joseph McCarthy, worked feverishly and unrelentingly on the notion that all non-Soviet communist and even socialist parties were networks of spies rather than legitimate political organizations.

The anti-Communist forces were aided by the powerful Roman Catholic Church. In 1950 the Church formally denounced Communism in all its varieties, as well as other anti-religious heresies such as existentialism, idealism, and pragmatism. The Church's position helped to divide the world into two hostile camps, with the United States, Canada and the rest of the western world on one side, and the Soviet Union and its satellites on the other side.

The 14 million people of the "Dominion of Canada", during the period 1945 to 1950, were subject to the same external forces and fears. Canada, in fact, became the centre of international attention in 1946 when a Royal Commission, investigating the revelations of Igor Gouzenko, an ethnic Ukrainian working in the Soviet Embassy in Ottawa, confirmed that secret information had been given to the Soviets by some Canadian officials.

When the Korean War broke out on June 25, 1950, the Canadian government, after some hesitation, decided to support the United States and the United Nations. Three Canadian destroyers were sent to Korean waters to serve under the U.N. Planes from the R.C.A.F. transported supplies from Canada to Korea. A "Special Force" infantry brigade of about 5,000 men was formed. Defence appropriations were more than doubled, and a 40 percent increase in Canada's armed forces was authorized by Parliament. By the time the Korean War ended in July, 1953, about 26,000 Canadians had served in Korea.

ABOUT THE CULTURE OF NORTH AMERICA IN 1950: North American popular culture in 1950 consisted mainly of a continuation of the styles and trends in music, dress and attitudes that had prevailed since the end of the Second World War in 1945. Jazz still dominated the dance scene, along with waltzes, fox trots, and Latin American steps such as the tango and rumba. Couples danced very closely together except when they "boogied". Rock music was in its earliest stages. The song that was played the most on radios in 1950 was *Goodnight Irene*. Other musical hits of 1950 were: *The Third Man Theme;*

Harbour Lights; There's No Tomorrow; Mona Lisa; and *Laura.*
North America in 1950 was a man's world, in which double-
standards not only prevailed, but were generally accepted
without question. Men boasted openly about their sexual
conquests, but "good girls" were usually virgins when they
married. Unmarried females were "old maids". Young ladies of
the middle and lower classes generally attended universities or
took low-paying, clerical jobs, not because they had any aspirations for permanent careers, but rather to establish locales for
finding appropriate husbands..

Although conditions in the post-war years had improved
considerably from the Depression of the 1930's, unemployment
was still a problem. Veterans from the war returned to Canada
in large numbers after 1945 and began looking for jobs. Some
veterans entered the universities and trained to be professionals
of various kinds. But many of those who had grown up in the
1920's and 1930's, even if academically talented, were without
complete high school educations and were unacceptable to the
universities. The Canadian Special Force recruited in 1950
included many skilled and intelligent individuals, but most had
never completed high school.

The world in 1950 was full of great uncertainty, fear and
tension as created by the conformation of the two super powers,
the United States and the Soviet Union. The hopes, aspirations
and optimism of 1945 following the defeat of the barbarous Nazi
and Japanese empires had been shattered by the realities of the
"Cold War." Ordinary people in both of the ideological camps
continued to lead their lives as best they could, but realized
that everything on the planet could be destroyed in the sudden
flashes of a nuclear holocaust. These fears were reinforced on
Sunday, June 25, 1950 when Soviet-supported North Korean
troops crossed the 38th parallel and invaded the U.S.-backed
Republic of Korea.

ANDRUSHKO, ANDREI, COLONEL: Returned to Soviet Army Headquarters in Moscow to a staff position after the Korean War ended in July, 1953. He became a member of a secret Ukrainian nationalist organization. Ukrainian nationalism was considered to be a subversive and illegal activity in the Soviet Union. His Ukrainian affiliation was discovered by the NKVD secret police. He was subjected to a brief military trial, drummed out of the army and sentenced to 20 years in a gulag in Siberia. He presumably died in captivity because his family never heard from him again.

BAILEY, ROGER: Bailey, a warrant officer in the British Hampshire Light Infantry was captured by the Chinese in November, 1950, and after confinement in a temporary Chinese P.O.W holding facility, was transferred to the North Korean Haeju camp. He was tortured and at some point during his captivity he experienced a serious mental breakdown. He lived a largely imaginary life with a cat and a motorcycle that did not exist. He met Peter Farley at Haeju. His rescue by the U.S. Marines created additional confusion in his mind, but he went along to freedom quietly. He was returned to Britain shortly afterwards and spend several years in a mental institution before suffering a heart attack and dying at the age of 70.

The British Department of Veterans Affairs refused to give Bailey a disability pension because they decided that his mental illness was the result of a pre-existing hereditary condition, and not caused by his war experiences. Max Taylor, the American who lived with Bailey in Haeju, learned about Bailey's dire circumstances and sent him money from New York on a regular basis. Taylor wrote to the British government and to several British newspapers to complain of Bailey's treatment, but to no avail.

BILLIE, FIDO AND CHARLIE: Billie the cat, Fido the dog and Charlie the horse, by their sad expressions and subdued behaviour, showed that they missed Peter intensely during the time he was in Korea and in the hospital in Vancouver. But Orest, Peter's father, was attentive. Orest put out food and water for them each day, and he always took time to spend with them.

After Peter returned from the hospital in Vancouver he lived on his father's farm briefly before entering the Faculty of Medicine at the University of Manitoba. His animal friends still remembered and loved him in spite of his lengthy absence. Orest loved animals as much as Peter. After graduating as a medical doctor, Peter brought Billie, Fido and Charlie with him to his new residences and places of employment. Billie lived to the age of 17, Fido to the age of 15, and Charlie to the age of 22. Peter cried, when no one was watching, when they died.

BOLESCHUK, JOHN: A post World War II immigrant to Canada, Boleschuk served as the well-liked and respected parish Ukrainian Catholic priest in Sweet Grass from 1948 until 1957. He was appointed as a bishop in 1957 and was transferred to Edmonton in the same year. He met an intelligent and attractive woman in Edmonton, a Ukrainian immigrant like him, and briefly considered marriage with her. Although Ukrainian Catholic priests, unlike Roman Catholic priests, were allowed to marry, he experienced some opposition from church superiors and decided not to marry. He studied English diligently, took evening courses at the University of Alberta and graduated with a B.A. in 1967. He was appointed to serve in the office of the Cardinal Vicar in Rome in 1968. He died in Rome in 1978 and was buried in a Catholic cemetery in that city.

BROWN, MICHELLE: Taught mathematics at Sweet Grass High School for the months of September and October of 1947.

She was an exceptionally beautiful, intelligent and eccentric 27 year old woman who played classical music in her classes and during her love-making, and who was sexually and emotionally attracted to 16 year old Peter Farley. His attraction to her was equally strong and they consummated their relationship with a memorable sexual encounter on the last weekend in October, 1947. Shortly afterwards she resigned her position as a teacher at Sweet Grass High School and left to begin medical studies at a university in the United States. Michelle and Peter both had a strong love for each other, but the fear of revealing their illicit affair kept them apart. She wrote to him shortly after her departure, but her words were cautious and measured because of the threat of being convicted of having a sexual relationship with a minor and a subsequent term in a penitentiary.

Peter spent two years in pre-medical studies at the University of Manitoba, and she traveled to Winnipeg to join him on five occasions. She would have joined him more often but it was difficult for her to leave her medical studies. She was impregnated after their fifth encounter in Winnipeg and took a year's leave of absence from her university. Her mother, a wealthy widow, looked after the baby, a beautiful auburn haired girl, during the years that Michelle continued with her studies. She graduated with a medical degree, and after an interview, joined a medical firm in Miami, Florida. The interviewing physicians were impressed, not only by her academic marks, but by her spectacular physical assets and sparking personality. Several months later she married a medical doctor who practiced in the same firm. She divorced him a year later.

She wrote, with considerable sadness and regrets, to tell Farley of her new circumstances. She did not see him until 20 years later, when he attended a medical convention in Miami. It was on this emotional occasion that he met Janet, his daughter, for the first time. She tried to entice Farley into another sexual encounter during his visit, but he gracefully declined. His loyalty to Morgan was now very strong. Michelle and Peter continued to correspond in the years that followed.

DEHUAI, DENG, GENERAL: Appointed by Mao Tse Zedung to the command of all Chinese armies in Korea in November, 1950, he continued to serve in this capacity until the war ended with a truce in July, 1953. Although a war hero who was highly respected by his troops, Deng was arrested during the bloody, irrational and violent Chinese Cultural Revolution in 1967 because of his alleged "anti-party thinking and activities." Many other soldiers and civilians were also arrested even though most of them were completely innocent of the charges against them. Millions died. Deng was stripped of his rank and removed from the army. He died in 1968 while under house arrest. In 1971 he was posthumously restored to his rank and was named a hero of the communist revolution in China. He was also revered in communist North Korea.

DEMOCRATIC PEOPLE'S REPUBLIC OF KOREA: NORTH KOREA: After the Korean War ended in July, 1953, Kim Il-sung became its dictator, and following his death, its "Eternal President." His son Kim Jong-il, then took power as the "Supreme Leader." North Korea became and remained, in effect, a Stalinist dictatorship with a cult of personality around the Kim family. The country maintained one of the world's largest armies. North Korea's human rights record was one of the worst in the world. Millions died of starvation and its per capital income eventually was only about 5 % of the per capital income of South Korea.

DOHERTY, JIM: Doherty married Biau, the beautiful half-Caucasian Japanese woman that he initially met at the bar in

Tokyo during his Edo Street adventure. Biau and their dog Blackie joined Doherty in Canada after his return from service in Korea and Japan. Although he was exceptionally intelligent and very impressed by Peter Farley's account of his university experiences, Doherty decided against furthering his education. Veterans Affairs declined to support his application for a university education, in spite of his very high IQ, because he had not finished his high school standing. Moreover, his widowed mother and brothers and sisters needed his financial support. He also now had a family of his own to look after.

He decided to remain in the army and make it his career. He served in Germany, Cyprus, Egypt, Camp Borden in Ontario, Currie Barracks in Calgary, and at Rivers and Shilo in Manitoba, where he qualified as a paratrooper. He wrote to Farley frequently, attended Farley's wedding, and visited with Farley and his family often over the years. He also attended the wedding of African American Miles Lewis in Detroit.

He and Biau had two sons. Peter Doherty, the oldest, was very talented academically and eventually became a physics professor at Memorial University in St. John's, Newfoundland. His second son, who learned to speak Japanese fluently from his mother, owned and operated a very successful Japanese restaurant in Toronto. Doherty retired as a 1st Class Warrant Officer. He built a new home on the site of his childhood home at Morgan's Cove and happily lived there with Biau and their dogs.

FARLEY FAMILY HISTORY: The Ukrainian grandparents of Peter Farley came to Manitoba in 1897 and settled on 160 acres of land in the Zhitomir district of Manitoba. Anthony, the grandfather, was a large man with flaming red hair and sparkling blue eyes. He possessed a great deal of intellectual potential but this potential was never fully developed because he only attended school for three years in Galicia, the Ukrainian populated province of the Austro-Hungarian Empire from whence he came. Peter Farley's grandmother Maria was a tall, hazel eyed and dark haired woman whose family had arrived from Germany two generations earlier, and who had subsequently intermarried with Ukrainians. Maria, like her husband Anthony also had limited formal schooling, but a high level of latent intelligence.

The Farley family began life in Ukraine in the 1750's when two red-headed Irish brothers, Sean and Seamus O'Farrell came to Galicia, Ukraine, to build a flour mill. They married Ukrainian women, changed their name to Farrelly, which eventually evolved into Farley. Anthony Farley, whose ancestor was Seamus O'Farrell, arrived five generations later and by this time the Farley's Irish blood was greatly diluted. The family, however, remembered their Irish connections and orally, as well as in writing, passed on their family history from generation to generation. Remembering their history was a family tradition.

Peter Farley's grandfather Anthony was the son of Natalia, an unmarried young woman in Senewa, a village located in the southeastern part of Ukrainian Galicia. She was a beautiful, green eyed blonde from a poor Ukrainian family. One day, when she was 18 years old, Benjamin Metzler, a 6 foot, 6 inch, wealthy, handsome red-headed Jewish business man noticed Natalia when she was selling potatoes at a farmers' market. He had a reputation as a womanizer, an easy role because women found him to be exceptionally attractive. He offered her a position as a maid in his large mansion, where his wife, four children and two servants lived. Natalia's parents could not afford to keep her. They raised no objections and Natalia readily accepted Metzler's offer of employment. Natalia became pregnant soon afterwards. When the pregnancy became visible Sarah, Benjamin's wife, immediately suspected that her husband had impregnated Natalia, and she angrily ordered Natalia out of the Metzler residence.

Natalia was forced to return to the home of her parents, and that is where her red-headed son Anthony was born. Benjamin Metzler did not openly admit to being the father of Natalia's son, but he felt a strong sense of responsibility to Natalia and Anthony. He felt especially attached to Anthony because of the child's red hair. For the next 15 years, until the day he suddenly died, Benjamin secretly passed on money to Natalia for the maintenance of their son.

Anthony became a tall, 6 foot, 5 inch, intelligent, strong and ambitious young man. He traveled to Germany to work on farms for several summers. He saved his money and married Maria Mazur, the daughter of a wealthy Polish family soon after 21st birthday. His father-in-law provided a substantial dowry and the newly-weds used this money and Anthony's savings to go to Manitoba in the spring of 1897.

Peter Farley, the grandson of Anthony Farley and third son of Orest and Irene Farley, was born in the town of Sweet Grass, Manitoba, in 1931. Irene Robertson, Peter's mother, was born in Saskatchewan and was primarily of English, Scottish and Icelandic ancestry. She also had, as photos showed, a beautiful Metis, French Cree Indian grandmother. Irene's parents were strongly opposed to having a "foreign son-in-law", but she loved Orest Farley and married him in a Ukrainian style wedding that her parents did not attend. They had three sons, Harry, Nick and Peter. Peter was the youngest.

The Farley family, although nominally and legally Ukrainian, was actually a blend of several European nationalities. A small stream of aboriginal blood also ran in their veins.

FARLEY, OREST: Orest, the father of Sergeant Peter O. Farley, continued to live on his small farm at Sweet Grass after the Korean War ended and after his son Peter had returned to Canada. He was deeply distressed by Peter's illness, but managed to keep his own mind under control, primarily because he felt that he needed to give Peter, as well as Billie, Fido and Charlie, Peter's beloved animals, his attention and support.

When he reached the age of 80 he began having physical health problems and his sons in Vancouver, Nick and Harry, persuaded him, in spite of considerable reluctance on his part, to come to Vancouver to live. His schizophrenia never returned. In later years, after he had finished his medical training, his son Peter concluded that his father had suffered from schizophrenia at least to some extent because of his extreme sensitivity. Peter also concluded he was also extremely sensitive by nature, and that his own mental problems had at least partly developed as a result. Extreme sensitivity was apparently a characteristic shared the father and son. Orest lived in Vancouver quite happily until he died very suddenly of a massive heart attack at the age of 95.

FARLEY, PETER DMETRO: Sergeant Farley's cousin and namesake, Peter Dmetro Farley became a very successful farmer and businessman. Peter Dmetro's brother, the oldest male in the family was scheduled to inherit the Farley family farm, but he died over Germany in 1944 while serving as a pilot with the Royal Canadian Air Force. Peter Dmetro was the second oldest son, and so, according to Ukrainian tradition, he inherited the farm.

After his marriage to Rosalie Prokopchuk, Peter Dmetro continued to develop and expand his acreage in the Sweet Grass district. He had a shrewd business sense and bought up neighboring small farms whenever they became available. He began with 160 acres, a typical early acreage in Manitoba, and eventually owned 1,280 acres, or the equivalent of two sections of land. He was a prosperous and progressive farmer, and also ran a very successful seed business. Peter and his wife had two children, a boy and a girl. Their son Tom liked farming and decided to stay, as his father's partner, with a view of eventually taking over the farm. Their daughter Mary graduated from Brandon College with B.A. and B. Ed. degrees and then became a teacher and eventually a school principal in Winnipeg.

FARLEY, PETER OREST, SERGEANT: Following their emotional meeting in the United Nations cemetery in Pusan, Korea on the 10th anniversary of the end of the Korean War Peter Farley and Laura Morgan were married in an Episcopalian Church in Hawaii, where Morgan was stationed. She resigned her commission in the United States Army a month later. Peter then took post-graduate work in psychiatry at the University of Toronto. Morgan worked as a nurse in the nearby University Hospital. Billie and Fido lived with them during these years. Upon their move to Toronto, they had to leave Charlie on the farm in Sweet Grass. Charlie was affectionately looked after by Peter's father Orest, and his cousin Peter also visited often to be sure that Orest was managing satisfactorily. Charlie rejoined them in later years.

After graduating as a psychiatrist, Peter worked in a mental hospital in Minneapolis, Minnesota for three years. A beautiful dark-haired daughter was born to them during their stay in Minneapolis. He then joined a medical clinic in Vancouver, British Columbia. Two more children followed: a red-headed son and a blonde daughter. He became a very close friend of Dr. Henry Stanhope, the psychiatrist who had restored his mental health. He published several books on psychiatry, taught courses at the University of British Columbia, and became wealthy on the basis of real estate and other investments. His brothers Nick and Harry built Peter and Morgan a beautiful mansion on

English Bay, and they also maintained a house and acreage in the Fraser Valley where they kept horses, dogs and cats, including Charlie until the time of his death. Billie and Fido had died by this time. Morgan worked as a nurse at Flanders Military Hospital until the time of her early retirement at the age of 50. She was then involved as an unpaid volunteer in several charitable and cultural organizations in Vancouver. They traveled frequently for nostalgic visits to Sweet Grass and Minneapolis.

Peter's daughter Julie Haines, the result of his sexual encounter with Jean Haines in Seattle, came to visit them every summer for two weeks while she was still going to school. Jean also accompanied Julie on several occasions. Peter explained his relationship to Jean and Julie to his other children and to Morgan in a thoughtful and straightforward manner, and they all seemed to understand.

Farley went on a medical convention to Florida in 1970. He saw Michelle Brown for the first time in two decades. Michele's beautiful daughter Janet joined them at a dinner, but no mention was made of the fact that Farley was her father. Michelle tried to lure him into another sexual encounter, but he politely declined her offer. It was a strong emotional experience for all of them. Peter returned home and continued to correspond with Michelle in the years that followed. His professional work continued and he was eventually classified as one of Canada's most outstanding psychiatrists.

GRABOWSKI, HENRY "BUZZ", SERGEANT: Grabowski was promoted to the rank of sergeant and served as a forward observer for the Canadian Mounted Artillery in Korea for almost a full year. While in his final week in Korea prior to being rotated back to Canada he was severely wounded by a sniper bullet in the right shoulder and was sent to a U.S. military hospital in Japan. He was then transferred to Flanders

Military Hospital in Vancouver where he remained for two months. Peter Farley was there at the same time but they did not know each other and did not speak to each other. He was visited by Maggie Marek, his longtime companion, on a daily basis until he recovered from his wounds and was discharged from the hospital, as well as the army, three months later. His right arm never fully recovered from the bullet wound and Veterans Affairs awarded him a small disability pension for the rest of his life.

He married Maggie in St. Mary's Polish Catholic Church in Chicago shortly after his discharge and they moved to Chicago after he received and accepted a job offer from the International Hod Carriers and Common Laborers of America, whose head-quarters were located in that city. Buzz and Maggie had three beautiful children. He became a citizen of the United States, but also retained his Canadian citizenship. Maggie also became a dual citizen and they often traveled to Canada for visits to their families and friends.

HAINES, JEAN: Jean Haines loved Peter Farley and was deeply disappointed by his decision not to return to her. She hoped that the birth of their red-headed daughter Julie would attract him, but to no avail. She understood his reluctance to join with her because she knew that her background as a former "call girl" would forever taint her in his eyes. She completed a Bachelor of Nursing degree at the University of Seattle. She then worked as a very competent surgical assistant at the Seattle General Hospital. She lived briefly with two male partners but did not did not marry and Julie remained as her only child.

HAINES, JULIE: Julie learned, at an early age, about the cir-cumstances of her mother's liaison with Peter Farley and her subsequent birth. She longed to have him as her permanent father, someone that she could see on a daily basis, but she soon came to understand that this would never happen. She appreciated the fact that he was making regular financial contributions to her upbringing as well as the generous allowances that he sent to spend as she pleased. She first saw her father when she visited with him at the age of 10. She noticed that he had the same basic facial features as well as the same red hair, light skin and freckles as her. The two weeks that she spent with her father each summer were glorious, memorable adventures that she longed for during the winter months when she attended school in Seattle.

She eventually graduated with a Bachelor of Social Work degree from the University of Seattle and married a lawyer in that city. She had two sons, including one with red hair. Peter Farley visited Julie and her family on a regular basis in the years that followed. Julie's children turned out to be Peter Farley's first grandchildren because his other two children did not marry and have children until several years later.

HARVEY, RICHARD, M.C., LIEUTENANT: Although Richard Harvey had died when his jeep was destroyed by a buried bomb in Korea in 1951, he was not forgotten by his home town in British Columbia. The local branch of the Royal Canadian Legion established a scholarship in his name. His photo and Military Cross were displayed in the Legion Hall, as well as an account of the heroic deeds that he had performed in Korea. Harvey's name was also carved into the stone of the war monument located at the town hall. At total of 20 soldiers from the district had died in World War I, and a further 13 in World War. II. He was one of three district soldiers who had died in Korea, and all of their names were also recorded on the district monument.

HIGGINS, JIM: Higgins, the leader of the small group of Fusiliers who had stolen fruit on the ship going to Korea; and who later took and tried to kill a young cow belonging to a Korean girl, whose mother he had earlier raped; and who, in a final act of cruelty, shot Blackie, the cat adopted by Farley, was returned to Canada and dishonourably discharged from the army after serving 90 days of detention in a military detention barracks in Korea. He managed to smuggle three .45 caliber U.S. revolvers into Canada in his kitbag. His two companions, John Busby and Albert Perkins were also returned to Canada and dishonourably discharged from the army. Shortly after their return this trio of ex-convicts, armed with the three revolvers provided by Higgins, tried to rob a bank in Toronto. All three were killed in a shoot-out with police.

KABALUK, METRO, PRIVATE: Kabaluk left the army in 1953 and returned to Alberta where he worked as a welder in the oil industry in Alberta for several years. He then bought a hotel and Ukrainian restaurant in Swift Current, Saskatchewan, even though he knew very little about the hotel and food business. His elderly parents were pleased because innkeepers in Ukraine had a high social status. He had strong and intelligent business instincts and hired Ukrainian housewives to prepare perogies, holopchi and other Ukrainian foods cheaply in their homes for his restaurant. He constructed an alcohol still deep the woods of a rural property he owned, and proceeded to make large amounts of "hoorewka", a powerful homemade Ukrainian whiskey similar to the kind he had produced in Korea. He sold his whiskey only to middle men or to well-known friends and acquaintances rather than directly to casual clients, and thereby avoided being caught by the police. He also mixed some of his whiskey with the regular commercial, government approved brands that sat on the shelves of the bar in his hotel, and this significantly lowered his liquor costs. Customers sometimes commented about the unusual taste and power of the whiskey in Kabaluk's bar, but most did not notice or care.

He met and married Jessie, a beautiful Blackfoot aboriginal girl and they had eight children together. Five of their children obtained university degrees. Three became teachers and two became lawyers. The other three became plumbers, and after a loan from their father, developed a very successful plumbing business together. Their oldest son Joseph, a very successful lawyer who worked for several Indian bands, was elected and served as the president of the Canadian National Metis Federation for many years.

KERELIUK, SONIA: Sonia Kereliuk was deeply in love with Peter O. Farley and went into a deep depression after she learned that he would not be coming back to Sweet Grass to marry her. She was, to a lesser extent, also attracted to Johnny Michaluk and eventually, after she realized that Peter was a lost cause, agreed to marry Johnny. He played for the Toronto Maple Leafs on an occasional basis for the first few years of his NHL career, and then in the American Hockey League for various teams for the next 10 years. They moved back to Sweet Grass after Johnny's hockey career ended. He began working for the Canadian National Railway as a fireman, and after several years became a frequently absent but well-paid locomotive engineer.

Sonia worked as a competent and popular elementary school teacher in Sweet Grass. She had two miscarriages and after her second tragic event, with Johnny's full support and approval, decided to adopt a child. They received a beautiful little girl from an adoption agency and she soon became an important part of their lives. Sonia frequently thought of Peter and often dreamed about him, but she realized that her life must go on without him.

LEVINSON, MIKE, CAPTAIN: After the Korean War ended Mike Levinson left the regular army and attended Harvard University in the U.S. where he obtained M.A. and Ph.D degrees in Economics. He was a brilliant student and won a gold medal for standing at the top of his Ph.D. class. He returned to Canada, began teaching at McGill University, and eventually attained a full professor's position in that institution. He married Sarah Cohen, the daughter of a wealthy Montreal businessman. Mike and Sarah had two children, both of whom graduated from McGill as medical doctors. Mike became an officer in the Canadian Army Reserve force and eventually attained the rank of colonel. He published five books.

LEWIS, MILES, SERGEANT, U.S. ARMY: Miles Lewis was promoted to the rank of sergeant while serving in Korea. He won a Silver Star for his courage in combat and was rotated back to the United States after serving a full year in Korea. He left the army and attended the University of Chicago where he obtained B.A. and M.A. degrees. While attending the University he met and married Jessie Jefferson, an attractive and intelligent fellow African American student. They both were employed as social workers in Chicago for many years after their graduation. They had one daughter, who also graduated from the University of Chicago and who became a journalist for the Chicago Tribune. Miles and Jessie attended the wedding of Peter Farley and Laura Morgan in Hawaii, and in later years, the wedding of Jim Doherty and Biau in St. John's, Newfoundland. Peter Farley and Jim Doherty were both present at the wedding of Miles and Jessie, and they all kept in touch by means of Christmas cards, letters and occasional visits over the years.

PACEK: The black and white dog that came running to Farley while he was sitting in the main hallway of the Flanders Military Hospital belonged to an elderly couple who lived in a condominium about a block away. His real name was Archie. He had often been to Flanders because his owners took him to visit with the wounded and sick veterans staying at the facility. He was a therapy dog that was trained to provide comfort to patients. On this particular occasion, Archie had run away from a nearby park where his owners were sitting. He proceeded directly to Flanders, a place of familiarity, and into the hallway where he met Farley. Archie was returned to his owners and they, on several occasions, brought him to see Farley. Although he was disappointed when he learned that this dog was not the one he knew in his childhood, Farley appreciated Archie's company. The dog's presence greatly helped Farley to recover.

REPUBLIC OF KOREA: SOUTH KOREA: After the Korean War South Korea developed into a prosperous democracy and a major world economic power. The people and government of South Korea were very grateful to the United States, Canada, Britain, Australia, New Zealand, South Africa, Belgium, Colombia, Ethiopia, France, Greece, Luxembourg, the Netherlands, the Philippines, Thailand and Turkey, all of whom sent combat forces, as well as Denmark, India, Norway and Sweden who provided medical units. As an expression of gratitude, the South Korean government invited, at its own expense, an annual quota of United Nations Korean War veterans to return to Korea for re-visits. Peter Farley and Laura Morgan were two of the veterans who came back to Korea on this basis.

RYKOV, NICHOLAS: FIRST SECRETARY, SOVIET EMBASSY, OTTAWA: After the defection of Ilya Zinoviev Nicholas Rykov and most other staff members at the Soviet Embassy in Ottawa were swiftly returned to Moscow. Rykov feared for his life because he thought that Zinoviev would publicly reveal Rykov's information about the presence of a spy in the ranks of the Fusiliers, and that he, Rykov, would be blamed for telling Zinoviev about the spy. Zinoviev did, in fact, tell the RCMP about the spy, but this information was never made public. As a result Rykov was saved from discovery and punishment by the NKVD, the Soviet Secret Police. After spending several months in Moscow, Rykov was posted to the Soviet Embassy in London, England. He loved the life of the British people, and seriously considered defecting, but decided against it because his parents, wife and children were still in Moscow and would suffer serious consequences if he defected.

SONG, Jeong-hui: Her professional and social life revolved around Peter Farley during his stay at Flanders Military Hospital. She developed a strong emotional attachment and affection for Farley and wanted to share her life with his. He was also strongly attracted to her, but after his mind returned to a healthy condition he began to search for Morgan, the woman he deeply loved.

After Farley regained his health he left Flanders and returned to his father's home in Sweet Grass. Soon afterwards Jeong-hui met a handsome Korean Canadian heart surgeon. They experienced a romance for a year and were then married in a combined Korean and Christian ceremony at the Korean National Baptist Church in Burnaby, British Columbia. Farley attended and insisted on incorporating a Ukrainian element into their wedding. He hired a three piece Ukrainian band and organized a reception line where envelopes of money were presented to the newly-weds. He maintained his friendship with Jeong-hui and her husband in the years that followed.

STRANGE, JAMES, LIEUTENANT COLONEL: Lieutenant-Colonel Strange confidentially reported the circumstances of his execution of Major Henderson to the Canadian Brigadier, the commander of Canadian Forces in Korea after the battle for Hill 787 had concluded. Major Henderson, he told the Brigadier, was caught passing information on to the enemy, and he was therefore a traitor and a deserter. Henderson's execution in the field was justified Strange declared, and the Brigadier agreed. The execution of traitors and deserters was a common and accepted practice in the British forces, and Canada's army followed this tradition. This information was passed to the Chief of the Defence staff in Ottawa, who also gave his approval for Strange's action. However, the incident was kept as a secret among the three officers. The Chief of Staff thought about advising the Minister of Defence, but decided that it was unnecessary. Strange, after serving a full year in Korea, returned to Canada and was eventually promoted to the rank of a Brigadier General. He retired from the Canadian Army after serving with distinction for 35 years.

TAYLOR, MAX: After his escape from Haeju prisoner of war camp Max Taylor spent three months in a military hospital in Japan. He was awarded with an American Silver Star for his brave escape. He was released from the United States Army the following year. He returned to his home in New York City and started a retail clothing business. In the years that followed he very successfully expanded his business. He eventually owned a total of 20 stores in New York City, Boston and Washington. He became very wealthy and a generous philanthropist. He sent money on a regular basis to his former fellow prison inmate,

Roger Bailey, who was neglected by the British Veterans Affairs bureaucracy and ensconced in a mental hospital in London, England. Taylor married an immigrant Korean woman and they had three attractive and talented children.

ZINOVIEV, ILYA, ASSISTANT PRESS SECRETARY, SOVIET EMBASSY: After defecting to Canadian authorities, Zinoviev was given a false name and corresponding identification papers as well as a generous re-location allowance. He was moved to Windsor, Ontario where a job as an automobile assembly worker with General Motors was surreptitiously arranged for him. He lived and worked in Windsor for the rest of his life, which ended at the age of 75. His wife Maria and two children, who had remained in Moscow during his posting to Ottawa, were subjected to severe harassment and punishment by Soviet authorities. Maria was sentenced to 10 years in a Siberian gulag after being falsely accused of "anti-Soviet activities." Their children were placed in an orphanage and assigned to low standing trade schools rather than university entrance institutions in spite of the fact that they were very intelligent and academically oriented.

Zinoviev had escaped, but his wife and children paid the price. Human rights did not exist in the Soviet empire. The Soviet, Chinese and North Korean communist dictatorships were monstrous political entities where millions of people like Maria and her children were trapped in lives of misery. The Korean War of 1950-53 was the first phase of the war that became the Cold War.

Michael Czuboka on leave in Tokyo, summer, 1951.

MORE ABOUT THE AUTHOR:

The son of Ukrainian immigrants and also with some Polish ancestry in his background, Michael "Mike" Czuboka was born in Brandon and grew up in Rivers, Manitoba. He served as a private with the 2nd Battalion, Princess Patricia's Canadian Light Infantry in Korea. He was present at the Battle of Kapyong in April, 1951 where 2 PPCLI was surrounded by the Chinese communist army, and for which 2 PPCLI was awarded the U.S. Presidential Unit Citation for "extraordinary heroism." After returning from Korea he became a military paratrooper and airplane pilot. He was awarded a trophy for being the "outstanding officer candidate" at a Canadian Army

C.O.T.C. training course at Camp Borden. He qualified as a 2nd lieutenant and eventually reached the rank of a reserve captain. He served in Germany with N.A.T.O. forces in the summer of 1957. He is a former Commanding Officer of 249 Beausejour Air Cadet Squadron.

His father, a CN Railway section labourer, was unjustly interred during WW1, along with about 6,000 other Ukrainian immigrants in Canadian internment camps, because the Ukrainians, as former residents of the Austrian Empire, were considered to be enemies of the British Empire.

His late brother Walter served as a Flying Officer with the R.C.A.F. and completed 52 missions over the Atlantic Ocean and Europe during WWII. His brother Bill was with the Canadian Army for 35 years and is a retired captain living in Ottawa.

After leaving the Canadian Army he obtained B.A. and B. Ed. degrees from Brandon College, which is now Brandon University, as well as an athletic trophy for being the most outstanding sportsman at Brandon College. He then received M.A. and M.Ed. degrees from the University of Manitoba. He pursued a career, at various intervals, as a high school and university history teacher, the Principal of Neelin High School in Brandon, a superintendent of schools, and as a teacher of administration courses at the University of Manitoba. He is a past president of the Manitoba Association of School Superintendents. His students at the U. of M. described him as an outstanding teacher in their formal, written evaluations.

He has published five books: *An Examination of Tenure; Why It's Hard to Fire Johnny's Teacher; Juba; They Stopped at a Good Place;* and *Ukrainian Canadian, Eh?*, which became a best-seller.

He is married to Helena, has three children, two grandchildren, and two cats all of whom he loves.

His grandnephew Mike Czuboka, the grandson of Walter

Czuboka, stands at 6 feet, 3 inches, which is the same as the main protagonist in *Manifest Destiny*, and 6 inches more than the author. His granddaughter Laura is red-headed. He admires physically attractive, tall red-heads with characteristics of empathy, intelligence and high morality like those of Peter Farley in *Manifest Destiny*.